# SIERA

# LONDON

## CHASING AVA

A BACHELOR OF SHELL COVE NOVEL

# Dear Reader

The Bachelors of Shell Cove series grew out of my love for my hometown of Jacksonville, Florida, the nursing profession and my twenty-two years of service in the United States Navy. The city of Shell Cove, the setting for this novel, is a fictional portrayal of Florida's beautiful northeast coast. In tribute to nurses in uniform and out, the heroine of CHASING AVA transitions from a civilian career to commissioned officer status in the US Navy Nurse Corps.

In CHASING AVA you'll meet the Walters and Masters families and the colorful staff of Shell Cove Medical Center. I hope you enjoy Logan and Ava's story, as well as the other romances in the Bachelors of Shell Cove series. I love to hear from readers. You can contact me at my website, www.sieralondon.com, and chat with me on Facebook.

All the best in life,

Siera

# Dedication

*To my phenomenal husband ~ whose loving support and patience through the years made this writing journey possible.*

To the amazing ladies in my life - my mom, Lenora, Veronica, and Natasha, thank you for believing in me before one word was on the paper.

To the most awesome critique partners and beta readers a neurotic writer can have -Tammy, Soni, Cherlyn, and Devri, this book would still be filed in my computer without your invaluable input.

To my fabulous mentors, Mary Wine, Elizabeth Johns, Tamra Lassiter, and L. Francis, I cannot thank you enough for helping me chase my dream.

*Now faith is being sure of what we hope for and certain of what we do not see.*

*-Hebrews 11:1*

# CHAPTER ONE

Ava stood in the elegantly adorned grand foyer outside of the Coastal Towers ballroom, her feet firmly rooted to the plush carpeted floor. For the third time, she reached to adjust the non-existent watch usually on her wrist. A statue had more fluid movement compared to her at the moment. A random assembly of colleagues milled about outside the ballroom. Some made eye contact with Ava, offered greetings, and moved along without a second glance. She should have stayed at home tonight.

To her left, she had a picture perfect view of the city's namesake, Shell Cove, and the larger Queens Bay in the distance. A scattering of waterfront mansions with private docks and moored yachts dotted the waterscape. Nestled on the east coast of the Atlantic Ocean, thirty miles south of the Georgia border, Shell Cove was an eclectic mix of historic waterfront communities, an urban luxury city center to the west, and seven pearly sand beaches covering twenty miles of coastline. The temperate Florida weather coupled with year-round golf, a wealth of cultural attractions and the subtle affluence of the region made Shell Cove a haven for a diverse group of residents. In her peripheral vision, she could see the frown on her best friend's face.

"Ava Elaine Walters, you can't back out now. You are two size seven stilettos away from the party," Lina chided.

Lina James, her best friend since elementary school, gave being an extrovert a new meaning. They both were registered nurses at Shell Cove Medical Center, or SCMC for short. The clinicians at SCMC were the leaders in medical research in the Northern Florida area, and Ava was proud to be a part of the team. Though she and Lina shared the same profession, the two of them couldn't be more different. Lina was cocoa to Ava's butterscotch complexion. Ava's petite frame lacked the fluid poetry of Lina's full curves. Lina had the type of figure that teenaged boys cut out of magazines and hid under their mattresses. Ava lived her life backstage while Lina chose to be in the center spotlight.

Tonight, she'd allowed Lina to talk her into a group social event. Ava had sworn off non-clinical social interactions six years ago. If she hadn't made a personal connection before the spring semester of her sophomore year, then there was a "no admittance sign" firmly tacked on her forehead. From that moment forward she trusted a friend like Lina who'd proven herself to be faithful and true to her word. She did not let anyone new into her inner circle.

Pop tunes wafted through the lobby with every evening gown clad young woman entering the ballroom. A reliable indication, the SCMC fundraiser gala had hit its full swing.

"It was a mistake to come. I'm horrible at social interaction. Thanks to you and Jace, I left the house on a Saturday night. That's celebration enough for me." Tonight would be classified as another foolish decision in a long list of errors.

"It's a Christmas miracle and you'd be better at interacting if you tried it more often." Lina rolled her eyes heavenward, a hint of laughter reflected on her face.

"Don't worry about driving me back home. Go join Jace inside. The valet can hail me a cab."

"I'm not worried because we are going to sashay through these doors together." Lina pointed to the twin ornate brass handles on the twenty-foot high doors.

Ava ground her teeth in frustration. Nothing grated on her nerves more than friends and family telling her what to do. The worst part, they genuinely believed she needed direction. The fault lay with her. How had she sunk to making those closest to her feel responsible for her life? It was official. She had baby-bird syndrome. She was dependent and too weak to leave the nest. She should have been a nurse in the United States Navy along with Janna, her college roommate, but fear had kept her tethered to the familiarity of home. *Pathetic.*

"We both know what's waiting for you at home." Lina placed her hands on her hips, careful not to crease the fabric.

Ever the diva, Ava thought. Hands on her hips meant Lina was ready to drive her point home.

"How could 'we' know that when I'm not at home?" Ava smiled at her snappy come back.

Her response earned her a 'you've got to be kidding me' look. Taking her arm, Lina led her to the coved seating area away from the ballroom doors.

"I know all about your grandmother's Holy Ghost hook-ups. Let me activate my super powers and predict your future. This, my reclusive friend, is a retelling of the voicemail you received before we picked you up tonight."

Lina paused before raising her elbows and stacking her forearms in an *I Dream of Jeannie* imitation. Of the two of them, Lina was hands down the grand diva of dramatic gestures.

"Granny Lou has invited another borderline social security recipient to Sunday dinner."

Ava gave no outward appearance of hearing the statement. Lina continued on.

"She's hopeful that you'll show a remote interest in the male species before Jesus calls her back to Heaven." At that, her best friend offered an *I know I'm right* expression.

Ava had more than a remote interest in one particular man. He was probably on the other side of those ballroom doors. She chose to ignore said interest.

Did the entire populace know that her grandmother had taken on the mission of finding Ava an eligible man to marry?

Unfortunately for Ava, her grandmother's social circle consisted of the senior citizens club and the church auxiliary. Louise Stanton, affectionately known as Granny Lou, was well-intentioned, but also a meddlesome matchmaker packaged into five foot two inches of sparky banter and sequined Velcro comfort shoes.

Ava rolled her eyes heavenward, taking in a deep breath. A telltale sign that Lina's assessment of the situation was accurate. Ava loved her family, but she didn't do relationships.

The silence stretched between the two women. Ava squirmed with the subtlety of a car seat restrained toddler under her friend's scrutiny.

"Your silent routine doesn't work with me Ava. Which wife-seeking, God-fearing deacon has she invited to Sunday dinner?"

Never one to let her off the hook, Lina's face held an expectant gaze. It was in times like this that Ava regretted having a psychiatric nurse as a best friend. Ava gave a resigned sigh then offered the name of her would be suitor. "Deacon Hill."

Ava knew the exact moment Lina recalled the porky gentleman. Wide eyes stared back at Ava as Lina's mouth opened and closed several times before she hid her smile with a carefully placed palm over her red velvet colored mouth. Lina would risk her friend's ire by laughing, but never would she suffer an accidental smudge to her perfectly painted lips.

"He's the one with the three adult children and five grandkids living in the house?" A vestige of humor at Ava's expense shone in her eyes.

"That's the one." Ava curled her fingers against her temples forcing a breath through her pursed lips. A high definition image of the aged, wide girthed man danced a gig across her mental LCD screen and she cringed.

"Save tomorrow's worries for tomorrow. Tonight is about us having fun. This isn't a matchmaking attempt by Granny Lou Incorporated. Come on Ava, please." Lina flashed her a million-dollar smile.

Ava was unmoved. Lina was the queen of improvisation, so her friend switched tactics.

Lina's pout heaped on another layer of ever-present guilt, but Ava couldn't give her family or friend what they wanted. They wanted her to be open, welcome a date with a nice man, and be social. But being social led to meeting new people. Meeting new people led to making connections. Connecting to new people, especially men, made you vulnerable. She didn't want to be vulnerable. Not ever again.

"Stop making me feel bad."

"So let me get this straight." Lina stepped closer, their shoulders touching. "At the tender age of twenty-six, you prefer to be alone on a Saturday night with thoughts of a dreadful Sunday dinner looming rather than walk into a party with me?"

As the reality of Lina's words settled between them, Ava felt the sadness reflected in Lina's gaze. "You'll be with Jace," Ava stated matter-of-factly. "I'll spend the night watching the two of you doing the Humpty dance."

"Ewe, I am so not into watchers," Lina said, crinkling her nose.

Her best friend always kept the mood light. "You know what I mean. Besides, I think I forgot my ticket." Diverting her eyes heavenward Ava offered a silent *forgive me Lord*, but desperate times required desperate measures.

"Excuse deferred. It's your work anniversary. The SCMC Foundation covered your ticket price. Now apologize to the Lord for lying," Lina countered with a snap of her fingers. "The ticket is a formality. Your name is on the attendee list."

Ava quickly scanned her mental Rolodex for any plausible excuse that would get her back to the safety of her home.

"You can meet some new people tonight. There are other nurses here. Those are our peeps, waiting behind these doors."

More people entered the foyer, bubbly voices talking one over the other, eager to join the festivities. The rhythmic music beat drew them into the ballroom. It had the opposite effect on her.

Ava raised a brow in doubt. She wasn't likely to meet a single person tonight. She knew it and so did Lina.

"Stop worrying about everything. It's a party packed to capacity with gray suit wearing administrators, a few pocket protector wearing clinical researchers and a truckload of fashion deficit doctors." Lina fashioned a mock pocket protector in the middle of her leather bustier, then mimicked stuffing it with pens.

Ava released a snort of laughter at her friend's antics.

"Nothing is going to happen. Do this as a gift to me."

A gift. She had little reserve left in her emotional tank to offer anyone. Ava needed to gift herself a box of hope. One big enough to drown out the self-doubt and the emptiness that plagued most aspects of her life.

Some days the emptiness weighed so heavy on her chest that emotional collapse seemed better than to greet another day of nothingness. The loneliness abated with work. Tending her garden helped, but the emptiness was a stealth army slowly advancing through her existence. It threatened to decimate the fragile threads of a new beginning she desperately clung to.

Relationships and connections were out of the question, but the truth couldn't be denied. She was lonely. Tonight was a beacon cast in a sea of endless nights. She was all dressed up with somewhere to go. Heck, she was here lingering in the foyer, on the outside catching glimpses of life through the cracks.

She had reason to celebrate. Her Navy nurse commissioning application was complete except for the employer endorsement. The unsuspecting, navy blue file folder containing her future had been hand delivered to Kathryn Quest, the pediatric nurse manager, on Friday morning. Perhaps, one night of fun to capstone the budding joy she felt at starting this quest would fuel her emotional tank. Only two people knew what she had done. Lina wasn't one of them. She needed to take this first step on her own. Without the deterrence she knew would come from those closest to her.

Ava proffered her elbow in acceptance. This was an evening dedicated to goodwill, and she had her best friend to share it with. She worked side by side with several of the attendees. Her safe zones were home and work, everything would be fine. Lina interlocked their elbows, gently guiding Ava to the ballroom doors.

"Okay, I'll take the plunge."

# CHAPTER TWO

Logan Masters mentally kicked his own gluteus maximus for wasting his time at another SCMC Foundation fundraiser. A noble cause, but the haughty chatter he could do without. The foundation existed for the sole purpose of raising funds to support the medical center's research and innovations division. He had a special interest in the foundation's activities. Foundation donors were the largest contributors to his pediatric wound care project. Not to mention, he wanted the vacant seat on the board of directors.

From the twenty-sixth floor of the Coastal Tower, the floor to ceiling windows offered a panoramic view of the dense, muted green forestry surrounding Queens Bay expanse to the east and the city lights of Shell Cove to the west. Hardwood flooring gleamed in the fading light of the setting sun. The warm ballroom was overripe with a citrus scent that clashed with the whiskey he'd been sipping for the last thirty minutes. This was a lively bunch compared to last year's gala especially when confronted by the soon-to-be retired chief surgeon jerking on the dance floor with the rhythm of a river trout flopping on a yacht deck.

"You're supposed to mingle Logan. The foundation doesn't select board members who scowl and display the social graces of a pit bull. Besides, who's better to highlight the contribution of your research to the increase in foundation donor activity? You're a local celebrity," his brother said.

Distracted by the sights on the dance floor, he hadn't noticed Darwin's stealthy approach to the bar. Leave it to the youngest member of the Masters clan to point out Logan's failure of duty. Usually, their mother sent the family loyalty reminders. Darwin had served in the Navy as a Surface Warfare Officer until four months ago, so he understood duty and strategy better than most. He had been the chief engineer on the Navy's newest assault ship. When an engine room fire left one of his sailors permanently disfigured, Darwin resigned his commission and returned home to Shell Cove. Though cleared of any negligence or wrongdoing, he refused to talk about the incident. Logan hadn't pushed for details. The past was best left alone.

"Walk away little brother."

"You cut me deep with the 'little' reference."

There was nothing little about the men in the Masters' family. They both topped six feet with an additional two inches bestowed to Logan purely for taunting moments. Darwin was blond haired and blue eyed, a mirror image of their mother. Logan's hair was a combination of blond with a red brick undertone, a remnant of his father's Irish ancestry.

Darwin took a swig from the long neck bottle before speaking. "How did you arrive with Rebecca Lynn Holbrook on your arm?" Darwin sat the bottle on the mahogany polished bar, looked him in the eye, and waited.

"You can thank our darling mother for that surprise. She told Rebecca last week I would be her date for the evening."

"She prefers Rebecca Lynn," Darwin added, "and you never mentioned it."

Logan narrowed his eyes at Darwin's accusatory tone. "That's because I was informed two hours ago."

"Would you have refused if given prior notice?"

The twitch Darwin tried to control in his jaw let Logan know his question was anything but casual banter. Their mother, Maribelle Masters was a force of nature when it came to her clan or cause. Securing the foundation board member position was more than just a personal goal for Logan. It was a family agenda. In the Masters clan, everyone had a responsibility in maintaining and/or elevating the family's elite social status.

Logan's skill and talent as a surgeon was important but powerful alliances were critical. Rebecca was the only daughter of Samuel Holbrook, the Chairman of the Shell Cove Medical Foundation. Partnering with her was a necessary sacrifice to cement his board selection. The Masters family name was a game changer, and enough to make him a first round draft pick with the influencers in Shell Cove. With Rebecca by his side, as his mother pointed out at every opportunity, he was guaranteed a long career in the major leagues.

"I would have preferred to meet her here, but I can play my role when the cameras are flashing. Why all the questions?"

Darwin studied him. Dissecting his response for what?

Logan admired her business tenacity, but that was where his interest in Rebecca Lynn Holbrook came to a dead end. What they had was a partnership, not a relationship. He knew it and so did she.

"Trying to figure out where your head is at, that's all big brother." Darwin gave him a reassuring grin, but it didn't reach his eyes.

"My position has not changed if that's what you're getting at. Rebecca is nice enough, but she's not my type of woman."

"She's a beautiful, successful woman last time I looked."

Logan picked up on Darwin's protective tone. "Rebecca is all those things and more. She also does not want me." Logan had no use for love. One female related catastrophe had excised that overrated emotion. However, mutual attraction and compatibility was a must. "To be honest, the woman does not even need me. She wants a man that's climbing the corporate ladder."

"Hate to break it to you Logan, but you just described yourself."

Logan had no desire to discuss his non-relationship with his brother. He focused on the wait staff as they lit a candle at each table centerpiece. With the dance floor at capacity, they seized the opportunity to remove used plates and emptied champagne flutes. Darwin's exaggerated throat clearing interrupted his silent study of the ballroom and its inhabitants.

"You were saying?" The half empty beer bottle Darwin held clanged against the polished brass bar railing.

"She wants the title, not the man holding the title. She's good at playing the doting date in public, but I am only a tool to her, a means to a pre-determined end. Like I said, she's not my type." Logan turned his attention to the crowded ballroom scanning the room for their topic of conversation.

Rebecca, a short distance away, worked the room as usual. A form fitting, beaded, black gown tastefully hugged her curves before flaring at the knee. Tendrils of her blonde hair were swept up in an elegant chignon. She looked like royalty.

Seeing Maribelle at Rebecca's side was a visible testament to the Masters-Holbrook alliance. It was a flawless execution in a show of power strategy. Allowing both women to stagger their questions, they gleaned insider information from each board member simultaneously. The families believed he and Rebecca would be the next power couple in Shell Cove. Admittedly,

Rebecca was an expert at giving the impression that there was more between them, but marriage, absolutely not.

He turned his attention back to Darwin, who was focused on something behind Logan, his gaze intent over his right shoulder, blue eyes narrowed.

"What are you looking at?" The feel of thin arms circling Logan's waist had him stiffening. "Logan honey, I saw you looking for me."

Rebecca's sugared southern drawl wafted across his ear. Her toned, statuesque frame pressed into his back. He stopped himself from pulling away remembering the bulbs were flashing. Lights, camera, and action.

"I need to deliver a case file to my assistant before morning. We can pick it up from my place and maybe share a nightcap, before I go to the office."

A healthcare law attorney for SCMC, Rebecca was naturally competitive and always had an angle. Whatever game she was playing, Logan didn't have a piece on the board. His joystick powered off. Being alone with a woman of Rebecca's ilk left a man vulnerable to shotgun weddings, paternity testing or both.

"No late nights for me. Dad and I have a seven forty-five tee time with Graham."

Graham Hamilton III was Logan's lifelong friend. An obstetrician/gynecologist at the SCMC beach location, they were both graduates of the Johns Hopkins University School of Medicine. Graham's father, Hamilton II, was a powerful business mogul that you wanted in your corner on any issue. Logan did not make the distinction of which Graham he referenced knowing Rebecca would always acquiesce to business regardless of the lineage.

Logan pried Rebecca's steel reinforced fingers from his midsection all the while skimming the room for photographers. He caught a glimpse of a petite, honey colored beauty across the room. Everything in the room faded to gray for Logan when she came into full view. Ava Walters, the nurse from the pediatric unit, was here. His thoughts scattered at first. He did a double take to make sure his eyes hadn't deceived him. After Ava completed her shift, the woman literally vanished, only to reappear the next workday. Until tonight, he had never laid eyes on her outside of the medical center.

From his vantage point, he could see the midnight blue halter dress she wore ended at shapely calves, accentuating her form to perfection. It occurred to him that the sexy, four-inch sandals made her the ideal height for him to plant kisses on her neck. Her hair was gorgeous. A loose mass of chocolate curls and waves flowing down her back. He realized this was the first time he'd seen it unbound.

The only thing missing was her smile. Ava's smile rivaled the Florida sun. He wanted to be the earth to her sun. Feel her heat on his skin. For over six months, she maintained a distance between them. Keeping just out of his orbit.

"Logan."

Rebecca's refined drawl drew his attention. In response to his previous dismissal, she moved to stand in front of him.

"We are supposed to be seen together, honey. You've spent most of the evening holding up the bar."

He would never be used to Rebecca's compulsion to live her life according to her father's pre-planned script. They had posed for photographs upon arrival at the fundraiser. His red carpet appearance was done.

"I distinctly remember you being at my side when a parade of flashing cameras met us at the door," he said, offering a sardonic smile.

Darwin had not moved away. He stood watching their interaction, a scowl on his face. While Rebecca contemplated his words, he turned his attention back to Ava. She was across the dance floor with the SCMC

Operations Officer.

Randall Lester was approximately six feet tall, with a spit-shined bald head, dark brown skin and a goatee mustache. The man was big everywhere. Maybe they came to the party as a couple.

Logan consciously unclenched his teeth at the sight of Ava with another man. The response surprised him. He had only witnessed her with male colleagues in a professional setting. He realized the graphic display of her intimate contact with Randall disturbed him.

His thoughts lingered on her more than he cared to admit. Forcing himself, he released the visual hold on her face as sensual images of them together invaded his mind. Of him burying his face in those chocolate curls, drinking in her scent. His body pulsed in response to Ava occupying his fantasies.

Ava was an intelligent and highly competent nurse. With her easygoing demeanor under pressure, the nursing and physician staff often commended her. He respected her opinion and more importantly, he trusted her clinical judgment. Currently, she was one of the nurses trained to care for the more complex patients enrolled in his research study.

He wanted to get to know her better, but the few times he thought appropriate to ask for a date, she'd extricated herself before he could broach the subject. He had begun to wonder if she had contrived those "emergencies" to avoid close contact with him. Tonight, there were no distractions to foil him from talking with her.

The night had just begun, the last remnant of daylight now hidden behind the moon and Ava was here. He could not have planned an infinitely better night.

# CHAPTER THREE

She was trapped. Ava scanned the ballroom, arms crossed over her chest as Randall Lester lifted his shifty gaze from her breasts to meet her eyes. Since entering the ballroom, she'd danced with fifteen high-heel donned staff nurses and Spencer, the sole male pediatric nurse on her unit. Surprised at seeing her, the group welcomed her to their loosely formed soul train line. Pleased with her decision to stay at the gala, much needed energy surged through her veins, ramping higher with each twirl on the dance floor. Seven disco hits and one Electric Slide later, beads of perspiration covered her forehead. Needing to rehydrate, she broke ranks to grab a mini bottle of water from the open bar before taking a standing position near the floor-to-ceiling glass windows.

Then Randall found her…alone. The euphoric feeling at being out of the house extinguished with the swiftness of a glass container dousing a candle flame. His herculean frame crowded her personal space. He was too close. He had effectively formed a coffin with his body and sealed her inside.

Swallowing several times, Ava told herself to breathe.

"I can admire the view can't I, Ava?"

He flashed a crooked grin as he conducted a slow perusal of her body. A mixture of smoke and hard liquor made his breath acrid and hot. She averted her face dodging the next foul breath when he spoke. *Think of an exit plan.*

"I enjoyed watching you on the dance floor, little doll. Seeing you here tonight is the highlight of my evening. Your confirmation was absent on the final guest list on Friday." He quirked a brow in question.

Knowing that he had looked for her confirmation sent a sickening tremor through her gut.

"You have beautiful penmanship. That was the first thing I noticed on your employment application all those months ago. Your career goals piqued my interest in you even more. You really poured your passion into the response. I've been monitoring your progress. As a friend, I am more than willing to lend my support to your efforts after a reasonable amount of time under my tutelage."

His tutelage, no doubt, included late nights in horizontal studies. Menace wafted from him, a repeat of their previous encounter. From their initial meeting, her sixth sense had screamed to stay clear of him. He'd watched her that first day at the personnel office. When their eyes met, her natural inclination was to smile in greeting. The predatory glint in his eyes stalled the smile from taking shape on her lips. Rumors about Randall's inappropriate attentions were noteworthy among the nurses on the unit.

The offer of support did little to veil the threat of sabotage. His words hung in the air, a verbal guillotine looming over her dreams. Thoughts of escape flooded her mind. She tightened the hold on her body, pressing her nails into her shoulders. She squeezed herself tighter, staving off the shiver that snaked down her spine. The jeweled straps of her stilettos bit into her ankles, the muscles in her calves contracting in sequence as she shifted from one foot to the other.

"I own a private tower suite. You and I can talk about helping each other."

Ava pressed her back into the wall as pure villainy consumed his possum-like features. She shook her head, rejecting every word he uttered.

"I'm not going anywhere with you. Please leave me alone," she said, shrinking against the unyielding wall at her back. Though delivered in a whisper she was hopeful that *nothing is ever going to happen between you and me* was conveyed. She sounded pitiful to her own ears. A coward. There was a time when she was confident and didn't hesitate to speak her mind. Six years ago she would have confronted this schoolyard bully masquerading as an executive; that was before she'd learned to be afraid.

A wide, toothy animalistic grin spread across his bearded face. There was a hint of something sinister behind that grin. He stepped closer narrowing the distance between their bodies. The synthetic stench of his cologne permeated the thin layer of air that served as her last safety barrier.

"I appreciate when a woman says please. And you will say please or that professional endorsement you need may never materialize."

Her pulse raced, her heart pounded against her rib cage as the breath seized in her lungs. Her eyes shot to his face, wide and frozen.

"Surprised? I've done my research RN Walters. This partnership will be beneficial to both of us. You'll learn to like what I have planned for you."

His facial expression communicated the savagery behind his innocuous words. The 'you'll like it' phrase must be highlighted in the depraved male handbook. The same words Marcus would say before he'd hurt her.

*This is your fault* her internal voice accused. She applied a mental brake to the self-berating rant. This was not the time for a mental breakdown.

Faced with limited options, she would not be a sheep led to slaughter. Lina's laughing face mocked her from the dance floor. She and Jace danced to a popular tune, while she was suspended in a living nightmare, looking on.

"Get away from me." The scar on her lower lip started to burn. The sensation reminded her to modulate her tone. Men get angry when women raise their voices. She trapped the now thin ridge of scar tissue between her teeth hoping to halt the sensation. The burn increased to the point of pain, she applied more pressure.

The tree trunks that doubled as Randall's arms were planted on either side of her body caging her in place. He must have been a mountain of muscle in the distant past. The firm muscles had long since vacated his physique yet the bulk had remained. He could pluck her out of her shoes and swallow her whole before the partygoers realized she was gone.

"Make me."

Physically, she was helpless against his brute strength. "No one is coming to save you," he taunted. Who would rescue her? These people didn't know her, not really. She was a nobody compared to Randall. The man was responsible for all staff hires at SCMC. He had power. Power he had no qualms about abusing.

Movement in her periphery had her turning her head to the right. She could hear the blood pulsing through her veins as a hard knot tightened in her stomach.

*Oh God, his hand moved. He's going to touch me.*

The old fears surged with renewed power, threatening to overtake her. Her mouth opened but not a hint of sound escaped. The impending touch had her rapid heartbeat revving to an erratic pace that strangled her next breath.

*Get away from him.*

Her body had the response of a plastic doll, lifeless and unresponsive. She was incapable, yet again, of heeding her own call to action. She closed her eyes trying to calm her breathing. She willed herself to think beyond the panic.

*Dear God, please don't let this happen to me. Not again. I can't fall apart in front of these people.* She wanted to sob.

What choice did she have? She could hear the revelry in the ballroom; see the smiling faces of people she knew. People who didn't realize they were blind witnesses to her emotional unraveling. She froze their jovial faces in her mind, then disconnected. A barely audible "help me" passed her lips as she allowed her eyes to drift shut.

Something was wrong. Ava's body language was incongruent with the woman Logan had come to know. She wasn't smiling. She always wore a smile. Logan registered her creased brow, the arms crossed protectively over her chest, the nails digging into her skin, as if she were purposefully trying to make herself smaller. The frantic eye movements gave the appearance of a frightened animal. The expression on her face had his jaw clenching.

Meanwhile, Randall's massive body cocooned Ava's smaller frame against the wall. Randall's reputation as a talented businessman with questionable tactics preceded him. Had Ava come to the party with him? No. Relief flooded his system easing some of the tension. Ava was not involved with anyone. He would have known. Hospital gossip spreads faster than a fungal infection.

A surge of jealousy entangled with anger ran through him. He suppressed it and any contemplation regarding the emotions he felt when he looked at Ava. Women and emotions were a lethal combination. Even now, his heart increased a few beats.

She appeared to be searching every inch of the dimly lit ballroom. Her teeth were hard pressed into her lower lip. He could see she wanted to be anywhere other than where she was. Randall would have to be a blind man if he could not see the tautness in her body. His fists tightened in response to her distress. Something was wrong with Ava, and Randall was the reason.

Every protective instinct he had rushed to the surface. Rebecca stood between him and Darwin. His family worked the key players in the room campaigning on his behalf. The cameras were rolling. He made a split second decision.

"Darwin take Rebecca home." Without waiting for a response he brushed past them, taking long, powerful strides in Ava's direction.

The closer he got to Ava the more rigid his body became. Half way into his approach, her eyes fell closed, but her lips moved. He thought it odd, but continued to maneuver through the crowd in her direction. What if his assessment of the situation was wrong? No better way to find out than to insert himself into the equation. He studied his opponent on approach. Randall had him by thirty pounds of flab. The man was a huge block of soft Florida pinewood. Was he considering physical defense against another man because of a woman? Not any woman. Ava.

In his gut the truth rang out. He'd flatten Randall without hesitation.

"Ava." Her eyes sprang open at the sound of her name. Randall's gaze turned in Logan's direction. One look at her expressive face and he knew he was right to intervene.

Logan extended his arm, hand open, palm side up. He didn't touch her. It would be her choice to accept or reject his offer. "I've been waiting for you. We have a date on the dance floor, remember?" The life raft was in the water. Would she climb aboard?

# CHAPTER FOUR

Ava knew the owner of that coarse, sexy baritone. The sharp, deep tone was a double shot of espresso to her pulse rate. Ava looked up and locked gazes with Dr. Logan Masters. Her mouth felt dry, her stomach dipped. Clear signs that she was in close proximity to him.

What was he talking about? She would never agree to dance with him. Short of diving under a bed, she did everything professionally acceptable to minimize contact with Logan; to control the sizzle over her skin whenever she looked into his eyes. The increasing pulse rate she experienced had everything to do with being in Logan Masters' presence. Precisely why she avoided sharing his air space. But tonight, his presence equaled shelter from the storm. The grip of fear slowly gave way to an infusion of common sense. He'd offered an "escape the pervert" card. He'd orchestrated a rescue for her.

Moving closer to her side, his heat pushed away the chill lapping at her skin. The black on black suit showcased his broad shoulders better than the lab coat he usually wore at work. He was a series of sharp, clean angles. His sculpted sinewy build was covered in hand dipped bronze skin. The chiseled angle of his jaw, complete with a full mouth and a well-defined bottom lip perfect for kissing, had her burying her head in a chart every time he spoke. His arrow straight nose that flared slightly at the nostrils was framed by piercing green eyes that never failed to steal her breath when they were aimed at her. If only Ava's problem with him was limited to simple physical attraction.

She prized the entire sun warrior package. His mind, the powerful build of his body, the man himself. The thick, close cropped blonde locks cut with precision at the nape, was a stark contrast against the black collar and his tanned skin. She drank him in. Her throat wasn't parched anymore. The sight of him had her mouth watering. He looked more handsome, more powerful, more decadent, more…everything.

How did he know she needed him? *Where did you come from*, her eyes questioned. What did it matter? His presence was the distraction she needed to deliver herself from the clutches of Randall. She mentally grabbed hold of the verbal rope he threw, tied a knot and hung on. Normally, his presence would trigger a hasty retreat. For the first time, she didn't want him to keep his distance. This was the night for surprises.

"Yes," she stammered, "I apologize for not returning to you sooner. The city lights are so beautiful underneath the stars. The lovely view distracted me. I know better than to linger when I have someone waiting for me. Thank you for coming over. I might have been stuck here all night." She swung her eyes in Randall's direction in rapid sequence hoping Logan would pull her to safety. *Please get rid of him* she pleaded with her eyes.

"I should have returned before you had to search the ballroom for me." *From stammering to rambling, stop Ava. The Three Stooges could understand the situation.*

Logan was no fool. A calculating look crossed his face, followed by a narrowed hard glare aimed at her captor. A sigh of relief fell from her lips. He understood the precarious position Randall had created by pinning her against the wall with his beefy body.

"The view is breathtaking," Logan agreed with his stormy green eyes fixed on her again.

He extended his well-manicured hand, encouraging her to release the death grip on her shoulder.

There was no hesitation as she grabbed hold of his hand, holding tight.

Randall got the message and dropped his arm away from the wall. A firm, yet gentle grip closed around her much smaller one as Logan pulled her into his side. It appeared that was the only option to free her, as Randall's substantial sized wing-tipped shoes remained anchored to the hardwood flooring.

"Have a nice night, Randall." He looked Randall squarely in the eye.

The message was clear. Randall's presence was unwanted.

There was definitely some silent communication happening between Logan and Randall. Both men appeared tense and war ready. Whatever was going on between the two men as they stood facing off, Logan was the clear winner. Ava could tell the minute Randall decided he was no longer the alpha male in the scenario. He took a slow step back, eyes surveying Logan then her. The corners of his mouth rose into a wide, faux smile that didn't reach his eyes.

"See you soon, Ava." Randall's voice was steely and flat.

Ava didn't focus on Randall as he walked away. She felt like a gazelle that had outmaneuvered the cheetah. A brief smile crossed her face, looking down to where Logan was holding her hand.

The pad of his thumb made slow sweeps across her knuckles. It felt nice.

"Are you alright?"

His voice was hypnotic, a warm wind tunnel cocooning her body. His presence was tangible against her skin. "I will be. Thank you for what you did." The words were breathy to her ears. Relief coated each syllable. She was so grateful she could cry.

"You are very welcome. I could see you needed rescuing from across the room."

She glanced across the room taking in the throngs of merriment on the dance floor.

"I was at the bar with my brother and a family friend." He turned in the direction of the bar. "I noticed you."

She regarded him with open curiosity. He had noticed her through the crowd. How interesting.

"It's hard to believe you spotted me and came over when you did."

"You recognized my extraction technique and didn't give me the deer in the headlights look. Your comeback lines were perfect."

He smiled down at her. *Stomach dip number two.*

"You think on your feet. And I like the image of you returning to me."

She swallowed, disconcerted at his compliment. In the far corners of her brain the "Logan alert" button was flashing exit now. She'd never allowed herself to be in his presence for a prolonged period of time. His eyes were more emerald than green, with rich bands of burnt amber. His smile was warm and calming. Everything about him was eye catching, vivid, and high definition. *Walk away. You don't do relationships. Stop thinking about how good he looks.*

"I am glad you have an emergency extraction protocol. He was making me…" she paused. "He was making me uncomfortable again." She swallowed the fear that hovered at the border of her thoughts. "You saved me. A victory for team pediatrics." She tried to lighten the mood that had transitioned to something somber.

"We will have to decide on the spoils of our victory."

She tried to laugh, but the reality that she needed a savior to get rid of a human parasite sent a shiver down her spine. What would have happened if Logan hadn't intervened? The shiver morphed into all out trembling, the movements obvious and uncontrollable. *Not now.* Angling her body away from his direct view, trying to hide the tremors racking her body. Too late.

A spark of awareness flashed in his green orbs. "Ava?"

He stepped into her field of view, looking her in the eyes. Concern and something more feral marred his handsome face. For some poorly understood reason she gripped him tighter to steady herself.

"What did he do to you?" His voice was low and menacing. His expression had transitioned from calm to thunderous.

"He cornered me. I didn't do anything to get away." She couldn't stop trembling. *Keep it together, until you get home.*

"Don't say anymore. You are upset and he will answer to me." He spun in the direction Randall had gone.

Realizing Logan's intent to confront Randall, she shook off the bad headspace she'd crashed landed into. How weak was she that someone else had to fight her battles?

She placed her hand on his forearm. She could feel the muscles in his forearm flex and release. She tightened her grip. "Logan, please. Don't go after him."

His steps halted. She could feel the tension in his muscles.

"I'm okay. He scared me." Actually she'd been terrified. She pressed and released his forearm in comfort for both their sakes.

His gaze suddenly dropped to her hand resting on his arm. Had she done something wrong? He raised his head, their gazes locked. The golden ring circling his verdant eyes glowed with heat reminding her of slow burning coal in an open flame. She kept her hand steady on his muscled forearm though her insides turned to liquid.

He covered her now idle fingers with his large hand, curling the digits protectively around hers. "You used my name." A look of surprise, then something more primal framed his face.

"Yes, I did." She touched her hair with her free hand to quell the surge of nervous flutter in her gut.

He moved closer to her. "You always refer to me by title. You don't use titles for the other doctors, but you do with me."

She touched her hair once more before he secured both her hands in his. "I know." *She had slipped up.* There was no escaping this one.

A drop dead, too gorgeous to live smile covered his full mouth. Ava's heart rate increased by another ten beats.

"You're deliberately formal with me because you feel it too."

It was a statement. His chest appeared to expand by another four inches. This was dangerous territory for Ava. She parted her lips, then spoke the words she should the second she was free of Randall.

"I think I should call it a night." She dropped her head forward, not wanting to see his response to her statement.

"I disagree. You came to have a good time. Let me help you with that."

Not looking up, she briefly closed her eyes willing her foolish heart not to consider the option.

Curiosity killed the cat, but Ava was certain the downward spiral started with temptation. The gaiety of the evening had been a needed change from her drab routine. It was a wondrous feeling to step outside of her guarded reality and experience the life of a normal twenty-six-year-old woman. A woman that didn't suffer with elements of post-traumatic stress disorder.

"Call me Logan." His right index finger came to rest under her chin. He slowly lifted her lowered head until their eyes met. "No more Dr. Masters."

He seemed as if he wanted to say more on the subject, but thought better of it. She felt a light tug on her hand.

"Come on, I want my dance."

That low, deep voice coupled with those full lips curved upward in a melt for me smile that had her heart fluttering. His steady gaze and firm, yet gentle hand holding told her he was resolute in getting what he wanted.

This was her one night to have fun. Taking a dose of Logan's determination, Ava decided she wouldn't surrender this moment because of Randall. Male predators had taken too much from her. She would dance with a man whose mere presence penetrated the numbing haze that was her life.

"Okay," she replied in what sounded like a sure voice. With that one simple word, the night's energy once again pulsed through her veins. The sense of liberation swallowed the earlier darkness. For the first time since Randall's retreat, she could feel the vibrations of the music moving through her body. It felt good. Better yet, it felt great. "We can do whatever you want."

*Where the heck had that come from?* Being near Logan brought out bravado that had abandoned her long ago. A genuine smile spread across her face for the second time. She was okay. She inhaled a deep, shuddered breath releasing the final remnants of Randall from her mind. She was safe. Logan must have sensed the direction of her thoughts.

"He won't get near you," he said with a set jaw.

The words held such authority she had no choice but to accept them as truth. She nodded her head in acceptance.

"One more thing."

She looked up at him expectantly. The way he slowly studied her made her smile slip briefly.

"Don't say anything you don't mean Ava. I will hold you to it."

Though delivered in a playful banter there was no mistaking the ring of truth in his voice.

She gave a shaky laugh because she didn't know what else to do. "Don't hold me to a million-dollar marker or anything close to it. Remember, I'm a nurse, not a pediatric surgeon."

He was still studying her when she noticed her hand rested protectively in his. She started to pull back and his grip tightened.

"Stay."

The sensuality in his tone took her by surprise. Her body quickened at the soft play of his fingers along her knuckles. Being near him left her exposed and reactive to her need.

"Excuse me?" Inhaling a deep breath to clear her rattled brain only heightened the response. Now she was busy cataloging every trace element of his scent. She had never behaved this way with a man.

"It's my responsibility to keep you safe. To do that, I need you close."

The way he said *close* had her gaze roaming from his lips down his biceps to their joined hands, then back up to meet his crooked smile. Was she that obvious? *Yes.* She needed to put all the raging hormone pills back in the bottle before she danced with him.

"Okay Logan, come and get me when they play a fast song. I'll be at that table." He couldn't know which table she referred to without her pointing it out. She tugged her arm backwards trying to extricate her hand. His grip tightened.

"I have you now, why would I let you go?"

At her quick, indrawn breath, he chuckled. It was an excellent question to which she had no reply. An "um" escaped her lips before she could seal them. *Say something bold and sophisticated.* She looked up at him, and that was a mistake. The carnality in his expression undid her. The desire she saw on his face was the opposite of calming. It had her insides flipping, tumbling, and sinking.

"This is a nice song. Come with me."

He moved toward the dance area, with her falling instep behind him. The late Luther Vandross crooned *So Amazing to be Loved* in the background.

Focused on what she would say to Logan during the dance, Ava didn't notice the slight incline leading to the dance floor until it was too late. The toe of her shoe met with the incline edge and stayed put while the rest of her body maintained its forward momentum. Her right forearm flew to her face in preparation for a crush landing that never came. Hard hands circled her waist before she felt hard muscle against her body.

"I've got you."

A brief glance up into those gorgeous green eyes and Ava had to agree. He had her. She took a moment to compose herself, inhaling a deep breath before moving a step back.

"Thank you," she managed to push out in a shaky voice. "Hopefully, you won't have to rescue me a third time in one night."

A wicked grin spread across his face and her heart did a back flip in her chest.

"The hero always gets the girl."

The breath in Ava's lungs froze at the statement. He wasn't asking a question because he knew. A tug at the hand he still held had her in motion as he navigated the dance floor. Avoiding the partygoers with all four limbs moving simultaneously and the soul train line enthusiasts, they joined the other couples at the margins of the floor. Some were young, maybe earlier twenties or so, some older, but all looked content to be in the arms of the one holding them.

He positioned her with the grace of a man accustomed to handling delicate things and then pulled her into his embrace. The warmth of his arms encircled her when he fused their bodies from chest to hip. She felt an arc of energy at the contact and relished the strength in his touch. Tonight she would lower her shields allowing herself to savor the pleasure of his confident hold on her body. The fluid motion of his body was a song within itself. Logan was a large man, but he covered the dance floor with masculine elegance. Effortlessly he led her through each step.

His name was nice. *Logan, Logan, Logan* was the refrain that kept running through her mind. The feel of his body was comforting and solid. She couldn't stop herself from sampling his scent. With care she pressed her nose into his left pectoral muscle. She took a deep, slow breath savoring his male aroma as it crashed into her senses triggering an endorphin high. To feel his body as she breathed in his masculinity was magnificent. His fresh, cedar wood scent slowly engulfed her. Heat crept up her inner thighs as her breasts tingled, and swelled. Her nipples came to attention with the swiftness of soldiers on duty. *Oh no, that's not all the endorphins have turned on. He's going to think I'm a slut.* Heat infused her face, and she refused to look at him. Maybe he hadn't noticed.

His feet stopped moving. *He noticed.* She stiffened in his arms. Lifting her head a fraction, she gave a cautious glance in their immediate vicinity, hoping no one else saw them. She felt like her nipples were neon red lights flashing *look at me I'm erect.* A few staff members she recognized chose that moment to make eye contact.

"Ava."

Her heart rate spiked at the husky change in his voice.

"It's been a rough night for you. I want to keep you safe…from everything."

The way he spoke made her think he had included himself.

"I need you to stay in control, or there will be no undoing what will happen between us tonight. Do you understand?"

He thought she was wanton. Being a gentleman, he was chastising her without judgment in his tone. He was kind to have asked her to dance and look how she repaid his courtesy. She was hopeless. Lead weights anchored her feet in place. How could she have let this happen? There was a reason she kept away from him. *Oh, God this is awful.* The baritone of his voice obliterated her run away negative self-talk.

"You are an ocean away."

He pulled her into his heat. His hip pressed into her lower abdomen. The warmth of his breath tickled the side of her neck.

"Come back to me Ava."

One command dispelled the trance her mind had created. Instantaneous autopilot was a skill she had perfected through the years. Only those closest to her could identify when she disconnected from the surrounding world. He had noticed.

"What did you say, Dr. Masters?" She wiggled within his embrace trying to put distance between them. Maybe she could salvage his impression of her. An additional inch of separation would go a long way in re-establishing her equilibrium. He seemed to sense her intention.

"Stay right where you are."

She felt his cheek nuzzle the top of her head. It felt so good to be touched by him. "I like the way you feel in my arms."

*I do too.* His hands moved from the soft flesh of her arms. With the skill of an experienced masseuse he caressed up and down the bare skin of her back, conducting a tactile study of her anatomy. She felt the soft brush of his lips against the shell of her ear.

"My name is Logan." The warm caress of his breath sent an electric current down her spine. "I want you to say my name."

If he only knew. She felt his hands descend to her waist and squeeze.

His nose brushed along her neck. She bit the inside of her cheek trapping the throaty moan threatening to escape. The sensual rhythm of his hands kneading and molding her skin created a slow burn of heat and moisture in her core. She reveled in the foreign experience that was all her own. For the first time in years, she felt desirable. Could one man erase the damage left by another? She didn't know, but she would pretend he could tonight. She placed her head on Logan's muscled chest, closed her eyes in contentment and followed his lead.

Lina's voice at her side and the subsequent tap on the shoulder was a giant stop button on the live video streaming through her head. A scalded cat would have been more graceful compared to Ava's theatrics as she sprang away from Logan. Forced to relinquish her hold on his broad shoulders she pivoted in Lina's direction.

"Logan, you're looking handsome tonight."

Of course, Lina would flirt with him. She flirted with everybody.

"A compliment from the lovely Lina James? I am honored."

Ava's lips thinned at his response. She didn't appreciate the playful ease of their exchange. Impatient with her friend's interruption, Ava cleared her throat. The conversation stopped and Lina glanced in her direction.

"What?" Lina questioned with the smile of innocence on her lips.

"Never mind," Ava scoffed. She couldn't be jealous. It was just one dance. And Lina was harmless, but it bothered her to see how effortlessly the two of them could dialogue. She had never been comfortable talking with

Logan.

"Would you excuse Ava for a moment." Lina gave her a gentle push at the elbow.

"Of course, I'll be here waiting, Ava."

Oh goodness, that husky tone of his worked its mojo on her, again. Her legs wouldn't move. She was standing in the exact same spot when Lina grabbed her hand and walked her over to the edge of the dance floor.

"Aren't you full of surprises tonight Miss Ava," Lina joked. "How did you end up on a body bumping exploration with Logan?" That question ended the mojo effect.

"I was not exploring." Ava waved away Lina's comment. Denial is the best defense when guilty as charged.

"I saw you discovering all the hills and valleys of his anatomy from across the room. How did you go from wallflower to star power in sixty minutes?"

Ava shook her head in dismay. She recounted the incident with Randall. "I'm not sure how I got there." She threw up her hands beckoning some understanding of everything that had happened tonight. "That creepy Randall Lester trapped me and I had a borderline freak out. I was begging for an exit route when Logan appeared at my side for our dance."

"Oh no." Lina said, eyebrows drawn together, with a hand at her throat. "Don't tell me Randall has you on his radar. I've heard he's a sneaky one. I'm glad Logan went all *Return of the Jedi* on him before I had to take a can opener to Randall's dangling parts."

Ava winced at the visual. Then Lina paused a beat, rubbing her forehead.

"I'm confused. When did Logan ask you to dance? You were swallowed by the soul train line and I couldn't see you."

"That's the thing, he made up the whole dance promise to get me away from Randall."

"So he spotted you, black woman in a dark dress, in a dimly lit ball room full of people?"

"Yes."

Lina raised both hands, tucked her chin length hair behind both ears, before pointing to her ears.

"Did I hear you say he concocted a pre-arranged dance story to get you away from Randall only to keep you by his side?"

"I know it sounds crazy, but that is how it happened."

Lina was beaming from ear to ear. "By the way, you didn't deny the body bumping. I know I said I wasn't into watching, but the hand expedition thing was juicy." Lina offered her a triple blink followed by a double wide-eyed expression.

Heat warmed Ava's cheeks. "You're embarrassing me."

"Okay I'll stop, but that doesn't explain how you ended up stroking your hands all over hard, hunky, and handsome."

Her face had to be scarlet. She pivoted to see Logan waiting six feet away where she had left him.

"Are you serious Lina? Did it look like I was feeling him up?"

"No, it did not look like you were feeling him up." She paused for effect. "To me, you were hand cruising each other, making a wish for a hotel suite." Lina bounced on the balls of her feet.

Ava glanced in his direction hoping Logan hadn't noticed her friend's theatrics.

"Stop looking over my shoulder Ava Elaine. Logan's my friend, and he knows I joke around."

"No more kidding from you. This is not funny."

"Fine. I interrupted your dance for a reason. Jace and I are driving to the cove for a nightcap. He wants to discuss something important with me," Lina whispered.

Ava could not miss the excitement in Lina's voice.

"Finally, after six months of dating he's going to commit. Ava, this is it! Do I still look good? Never mind. I know I do."

Lina was practically glowing. Ava was reluctant to ask the next question. Lina was one of her dearest friends and she didn't want to see her hurt again. Lina wore her heart on the front of a bumper car.

"Are you sure that's what he wants to talk about? It could be something else. Don't set yourself up for disappointment."

"Stop it. Not all men are bad." Lina smiled at her through watery eyes.

"Be happy for me. Cease already with your doomsday scenarios and enjoy life. I am."

Lina twirled on her heels in delight. "My man is taking me to my favorite romantic rendezvous to talk about the next level in our relationship."

Ava forced a smile. Jace wasn't a bad guy, but that didn't mean he was a good guy for Lina.

He was a clinical psychologist on staff at SCMC. He and Lina had worked closely together on the process improvement committee before they started dating. Lina was on every committee and action team ever created. There wasn't an event she couldn't get you into. He was about three inches shorter than Lina, maybe five six or seven, with dark hair, pale skin and blue eyes. The few times he'd accompanied Lina to Sunday dinner he looked uncomfortable. Lina would pull him into the conversation and that only made matters worse.

"I know Jace," Lina said in a clipped tone. "He's distracted tonight. He keeps touching me to reassure himself. He does that when he's contemplating a major decision."

Ava watched a flash of hesitation cross Lina's well-constructed mask.

"I know this is so wrong in the best friend realm, but do you think one of the other girls can take you home?"

Ava threw up her hands in exasperation. She spun face-to-face with Lina placing Logan at her back. "Are you punking me? You're the one that guilted me into coming to this party." Ava's hands came to rest on her hips as she glared at Lina.

"I'll take you home."

The close proximity of Logan's voice had her stepping back to collide with his muscled chest. Accustomed to his touch, she softened when his right arm closed around her middle. She looked up to discover his intense green eyes focused on her face. Oxygen slowed its transit through her lungs. Heat infused where their bodies touched and her skin started to tingle.

"No," she said on a whisper. When had he closed the distance between them? How much of their conversation had he heard? He had been silent after Lina interrupted their dance. His quiet stealth lulled her to slip into a simple interchange with Lina and not notice him listening in the background.

"Ava, before you reject my offer do you see anyone you would ask for a ride home?"

Her protest could be over any number of things at this point; her traitorous body's response to his attention, the offered ride home, or the possibility that he'd heard some of their conversation.

Had he overheard the hand cruising, body bumping, Ava the Explorer comparisons? First the neon headlights on the dance floor, now this was embarrassment number two for the evening.

Lina stared at her with a Cheshire cat grin. Ava's eyes scanned the darkened ballroom, praying to glimpse a familiar face. Her gaze landed on Randall standing at the bar, watching her with a menacing scowl on his face.

Her palms grew clammy and cold at the sight of him. She swallowed several times, forcing the unease back down her throat. There was no one within visual range that she felt comfortable asking for a ride home.

"No, I don't see anyone that I can get a ride home with."

Riding on a city bus with Logan was a temptation, sharing a car ride was detrimental to her emotional safety. She didn't have a good reason to decline his offer.

"Let me take you home, sweetheart." Both women spun to face Logan. Ava knew she looked none to pretty with her eyes bugging out of her head and mouth wide open. Lina in contrast, was talking faster than an auctioneer.

"Logan, give me a second with Ava." Lina grabbed her hand then maneuvered them away from Logan's apparently bionic hearing.

Lina whispered conspiratorially. "He likes you. In the five years I've worked with Logan, I've never seen him hover around any woman until tonight. It's okay for him to drive you home. He was raised a rich kid. But he went to school in Baltimore, so he has some swagger, if you know what I mean. You know I wouldn't entrust my best friend to any Tom, Dick or doctor. Think of it as an early Christmas present."

"It's October," Ava said crossing her arms over her chest.

"A birthday gift then."

"My birthday was in July." At Lina's continued bargaining, Ava added a vigorous head shake *no* to the crossed arms.

"How about a pre-Columbus day sales event?"

Ava furrowed a brow at Lina's hopeful expression. She couldn't allow Lina's enthusiasm to overshadow her displeasure at the turn of events. Spending additional time with Logan qualified as a big-ticket item purchase. She couldn't afford the cost that any personal association with Logan would surely bring.

"Sale items are marked up before they are marked down twenty percent, but I'll give you two points for originality," Ava responded matter of factly.

"Dang Ava, I'm trying to help. It's one ride home. This night could be a little treasure made just for you."

*That's what she was afraid of. This night had a short half-life.*

"You never have to ride with him again after tonight."

Ava released a low groan at her best friend's ill-disguised innuendo. She felt her internal resolve crumbling. Maybe if she told Lina about the raw sensations running rampant through her body at this very moment she would be more helpful.

"Lina," Ava leaned in close to ensure he didn't hear her next statement. "He makes me feel weird things."

"What does that mean?" The other woman looked at her with open confusion.

"You know, all topsy-turvy, small boat, big ocean kind of stuff."

"That description confirms my suspicions. You've been working with children too long, and why is your skin all dewy and flushed?"

Ava rolled her eyes heavenward. "I need you focused."

"I am focused, Ava Elaine. Small boat my foot, you're all 'flame on' for Logan Masters."

"I think I should …." Ava stopped mid-sentence because Lina was staring at her like she was from another planet.

"You're attracted to a man. You like Logan," the other woman squealed. "The last time this happened it was illegal for me to drink." She looked ready to scream the good news from the rooftops.

"Lina, stop talking and help me."

At Ava's stern retort, Lina's expression sobered.

"Not to worry. Stand back and watch your best friend handle this."

A wave of sadness washed over Ava. This was what she wanted. To be alone and safeguarded, so why did she feel like she'd just lost something valuable? Lina stood in front of her, observing the internal struggle reflected on her face. Ava offered a hint of a smile.

"Thank you, thank you. When you give him my excuse, talk loud enough so I can hear. I want to keep the story consistent."

Lina was more subdued than the minutes before. The last thing Ava wanted was to ruin Lina's night. The sooner Ava returned home the better.

"No problem, I'll help you," Lina replied, before she turned away taking the ten steps to reach Logan.

Ava pasted on what she thought was a *'I had a wonderful time, but I can't let you drive me home'* expression, and waited for Lina to deliver the supporting dialogue.

"Thank you for volunteering to take Ava home. I hope this does not interfere with your plans for the evening."

"Not at all, Ava has my undivided attention."

Ava's mouth dropped open. Lina was supposed to get her away from Logan, not put them in a car together. Her best friend would get a prescription grade laxative added to her food the next time she came over for dinner.

"You have nothing to worry about, I'll take care of Ava."

His words seemed to be steeped in double meaning, but she could've misinterpreted them with all the ringing in her ears. Stupefied, Ava watched as Logan approached, a wide smile on his face. She could almost see the smoke rising from Lina's metallic gold heels as she sashayed in the opposite direction. Never looking back as she walked into Jace's waiting embrace. Logan touched the limp arm at her side and her skin tingled under his fingers.

"Let's finish our dance, sweetheart."

This was going to cost her, big time.

The soft scents of honey and vanilla that were unique to Ava intensified as they swayed to the sensual melody filling the ballroom. With Lina's hasty departure, the tension returned to Ava's limbs. Thinking it best to reassure her that she was safe with him, Logan commandeered a well-lit table at the edge of the dance floor.

He pulled out a chair for her allowing his hand to linger at the small of her back as she lowered all those graceful curves into the white covered chair. The subdued lighting and candlelit table accentuated the glitter in her eyes. Without saying a word, he relocated two of the four chairs to the adjacent table, took his seat beside her, then pulled her high back chair flush with his. He didn't want to examine why he needed her close.

His thigh brushed against hers. His intent was to move away until he heard the hint of a sigh escape her berry-glossed lips. Her body spoke to him on a primal level whether she realized it or not. Every part of him, mind, body, and soul was calibrated to this woman's frequency. There was no way he could ignore the sensual vibe she emitted.

She was too quiet for his taste. Faint crescent shaped tension lines framed her mouth. Was it being in his presence that caused this reaction? After years of talking with patients prior to surgery he recognized anxiety. Maybe they both could benefit from a drink or two.

"What is your drink of choice? Wine or a cocktail?"

"I'll have a ginger ale with lime, thanks."

He raised a brow in question. "Are you wanting to keep your wits about you?" He studied her with a piercing gaze. Was she concerned he would take advantage of her?

"I never acquired the taste for alcohol Dr. Masters. If I did drink, I would not be partaking tonight."

Back to the formal title. Her defense system would rival that of the naval base in the neighboring state.

"That's good to know and stop using my title as a monkey wrench." Her lips formed an "oh" but she didn't speak. "Don't try to deny it. I'm your ride home and you are trying to run me off."

"I haven't forgotten."

The little minx hadn't corrected him on trying to get rid of him. She was not as mild mannered as she seemed. She could match wits with him. He relished the idea of driving her home. Time he would use to win her over.

"Good." He was not an inexperienced teenager to be waved off. "You should know I have the aim of a heat seeking missile when it comes to getting what I want." He knew his smile was pure wickedness and seeing the color deepen in her cheeks was a good sign to him.

"Well you are definitely packing enough heat for the both of us."

*She's teasing me. Don't poke the bear, sweetheart.* Logan smiled. The tension had left her features. He had succeeded on one front.

"One more question. Is it safe to assume nothing that has been said or done was under the influence of alcohol, cough syrups, or decongestants?"

"You're correct. I am in full control of my faculties."

"I am pleased to hear you say that." He didn't want to scare her, but he wasn't a man that danced around his intent. "I like you Ava," he said, widening his devilish smile. "I'm glad I came tonight."

The last thing he saw before he turned in the direction of the bar were wide stretched eyes from the woman that would be his. Understanding obvious in her intelligent eyes. Ava wasn't getting away from him.

Logan seemed to go out of his way to touch her. His touch was doing funny things to Ava's insides. Her body was broadcasting its own signals and she couldn't control them. Her stomach kept plummeting to her feet, a thin sheen of perspiration gathered between her breasts, and her nipples refused to return to a neutral position. They were pressed so hard against her dress there were permanent indentations in the thin fabric.

Ava couldn't sit still. Her senses were on high alert. The pure energy flowing through her body was unnerving. She was in a fight or flight state; she needed to separate herself from Logan. And fast. He wanted her to call him Logan. She couldn't do that. Every time she said his name her body warmed another degree. The man was pure sensuality wrapped in flesh.

"Are you hot or cold?"

She startled at the sound of Logan's voice and a wave of her essence soaked her panties. His head dipped close to her ear, warm breath wafted across her neck down the cleavage of her dress.

"I see evidence of both." He placed her drink on the table, his arm extending over her shoulder.

These panties were lousy. Was she supposed to feel all this moisture? Her own sexual heat was fueling her arousal and clouding her brain. "I'm sorry, could you repeat your question?"

"Are you hot or cold?"

Sexual overtones hung on every syllable. He had to know what he was doing to her.

"I'm fine." Her voice shook. Goose bumps erupted across her arms and it had everything to do with the man feasting on her with his eyes. Her single intimate encounter was sorely lacking in comparison to the steady increase in circulating sex hormones. She wanted to do the *naughty nurse* with the man pressing his muscled thigh against her leg.

He removed his jacket, laying the weighted material over both her shoulders.

"You can take it off whenever you want."

Take it off? Not in the next twenty-four hours. The jacket had to be laced with nurse catnip. His scent had her enthralled. It was driving her insane with need. She almost groaned in satisfaction as fine threads of sensual energy tingled all over her body. This must be how women felt when they woke up naked with a sexy stranger in their bed after a night on the town. She felt drunk with sensation. Was she panting? Possibly, but her brain was shrouded in a sexual fog. Images of her tearing off that expensive suit gazing on his naked glory flooded her mind.

It had to be the combination of his presence, the jacket, and his scent. His personal brand of aphrodisiac had her body spiraling out of control, pulling her deeper into unfamiliar territory. Ava pushed away from the table and stood, almost toppling her chair with the swift rise.

Logan stepped back giving her additional room to move. And breathe. Fresh air, minus the Logan factor would be nice.

"Is everything all right, Ava?"

"Yes, of course. If you will excuse me." She sounded breathless to her own ears.

He moved in front of her before she could take another step. "Where are you going?"

"To the ladies room." She moved to shrug out of his jacket.

"Keep it. I wouldn't want you to get chilled again."

A fierce blush crossed her cheeks. She wouldn't look down, knowing she was still high beaming.

He stepped aside without another word.

A stream of well-dressed ladies, standing in an orderly fashion greeted her as she entered the corridor to the ladies room. Why was the line to enter the ladies room always three times longer than the men's? Ava retraced her steps before detouring to the guest elevators. The lower floors had to be less crowded. After two failed attempts on the floor immediately below the ballroom, she took the elevator to the lobby knowing a restroom had to be available for use without a security key.

Reapplying her berry gloss, she barely recognized her reflection in the mirror. Her color was high, a fine sheen of perspiration glistened on every inch of visible skin despite the cool night. She was in a heightened state of sexual arousal fueled by mutual desire. And Logan would add more gasoline to the fire the instant she returned to his side.

Ava pressed the up arrow and waited. The quiet of the lobby ushered in a moment of clarity. When the elevator arrived she didn't step inside. She strolled past the open elevator doors refusing to look at the mirrored walls. *I am a grown woman. I can make my own choices. No promises were made.* While determination bolstered her temporary confidence she entered the revolving door and pushed her way to sanity.

She stepped out into the cool October night. The bright lights of the tower entrance illuminated her immaturity.

The valet immediately stepped up to her. As an afterthought she remembered that Logan's jacket draped her shoulders. Checking the pockets, no keys, no wallet, and no cell phone. Good.

"Taxi please." She could return his jacket on Monday with a guilt free conscience. She wasn't leaving him stranded.

# CHAPTER FIVE

The dashboard clock read ten forty-three when Logan killed the engine in the driveway of Ava's 1940's style single story bungalow. The solar lamps outlining the stone walkway allowed him to see the manicured yellow and orange pansy gardens landscaped in the front yard. White azalea bushes were trimmed short along the front of the house and fern plants filled hanging baskets on the full-length porch. A tropical teak table and two coordinating chairs were to the right of the door. It felt warm and inviting. Logan delivered two thuds to the densely paneled door with the authority of a SWAT team leader. Panic raced through him at the thought of Ava not answering. Had Randall intercepted her en route to the ladies' room? He infused more power into the blows landing on the door. *Be here Ava.*

When soft yellow light illuminated the covered porch the needle on his internal pressure gauge started the downward arc to safety.

A feminine, "Who is it?" came from the other side of the closed door.

"It's me. Open the door." He meant to sound more controlled than the equivalent of a male bark.

A moment of hesitation passed before he heard the distinct slide release of a chain lock. Ava's sweetheart shaped face came into view. Relief replaced the tension that had held him captive, the bunched muscles in his back slowly unfurled.

"What in God's name are you doing at home?" No background noise came from inside the house, only the soft sounds of night creatures. She'd left him to sit in a quiet house?

The shock of his being at her door glinted in her eyes, before it gave way to something more cautionary.

"Leave God out of this. And how did you know where I live?"

"Where you live, are you serious? You said you were going to the bathroom. I called Lina when you didn't return," he said, through clenched teeth. "I couldn't find Randall. I thought … never mind what I thought. Why did you leave without me?"

"I'm sorry, Dr. Masters."

She took a step back allowing him a clear view of her and the small living area. The room was an open rectangle with a white stone wood-burning fireplace on the right wall. An overstuffed couch with rolled arms and block feet was separated from the hearth by a burnished metal table with an oak base.

"I never meant for you to worry."

Her voice pulled him back to the natural feminine beauty on display before him. From the bottom to the top, he assessed the woman that had him running to her doorstep. He spied well-toned legs and the soft yellow boy shorts covering her curved hips through her half open robe. Petite bare feet peeked from behind the door. Her springy locks were still loose around her shoulders. His hands tingled at the thought of running his fingers through the thick tresses. *Delicious, that is what she is.*

"You're forgiven." Now came the blockbuster question. "Why did you leave me?"

"I never thought you'd come looking for me." She angled her head towards his Lexus sedan to make a point. "But, it wasn't a good idea for you to drive me home."

"Clever woman. Help me understand this. You're apologizing for causing me to worry, but not for leaving me." An unrepentant flicker danced in her eyes. She was gorgeous in her defiance.

"Why didn't you come back to me?" He didn't know why her response was important, but somehow he knew it was. She seemed to study him as if determining the best way to answer his question. He didn't want some contrived response to soothe his bruised ego. He needed honesty from her.

"The truth, Ava."

"I was coming back to you, but on my way up to the ballroom, I thought it best that we leave things the way they were…collegial."

What happened on the dance floor was more than a collegial response. Logan could tell she was choosing her words carefully now.

He smiled at her premeditated "ditch the doctor" retelling. She was trying to put space between them. She had felt the pull as strong as he did. He smiled then. "You are a clever one."

"That's the second time you've called me clever. How old are you?"

The question took him by surprise. Ava was a master at deflecting the attention away from questions she didn't want to answer. His age? He did not see that one coming. It took him a moment longer to respond.

At his silence she filled the void. "I'm sorry. It's rude of me to ask. You don't have to answer."

There couldn't be more than ten years between them. He wasn't too old for her. "I am thirty-four. Is my being older than you a problem?"

"Why would your age be an issue?"

Deflecting again. "Answer my question."

"No. Your age is your age. Do you want to know how old I am?"

"Sweetheart, you have to work on your game face. You are trying to avoid answering the question. I am not going to let you. You are over twenty-one and I like you, so I don't care about your exact number. So, let's simplify this for both our sakes. Ava do you have a problem being involved with me because of our age difference?"

"Wait, we're involved?"

He grinned at her question. "From the moment you placed your hand in mine."

Ava had left the fundraiser an hour ago. Party clothes discarded and dressed for bed, her mind and body hummed with sexual energy. She was too charged to sleep. How was she going to face Logan on Monday after running out on him? Before she could formulate a sane explanation for Logan, the banging at her front door had her leaping off the bed, yelping with fright. The hand at her chest did little to slow her rapid heart rate. She grabbed a mid-thigh length robe from the foot of the bed. The flutter in her stomach told her it was Logan. Being in close proximity to Logan always triggered a physical response. This warranted boundary management, avoidance mastery, and minimal contact protocol on a daily basis at work. Tonight he had launched a covert invasion. The breach had caused irreparable damage to the perimeter wall guarding her heart. Her front door rattled within the frame for the second time. He had followed her home and her silly heart leapt in her chest.

*Might as well get this over with, since he's not going away.*

She reached for the porch light switch, then cracked the front door enough to see a handsome, but stone faced Logan.

He stood bathed in the soft light the two porch sconces afforded, tie gone, tuxedo shirt open, and a small "v" of short golden red hair visible from the open collar. Pure sex poured into a suit. She could almost taste his heat tantalizing her oral receptors.

*Definitely mouthwatering.*

His cedar wood scent came to her on the crisp night breeze. Inhaling she hoped to gather enough of it to subdue the sizzle that had hijacked her body from the moment she heard his voice this evening.

Her heart fluttered. Her pulse raced. Ava had to cross her legs as heat and dampness spread through her center for the second time tonight. Part two of this evening would take place on her doorstep. Evidently her fleeing the party was not a deterrent for Logan. Embarrassment blossomed in her cheeks at her lack of self-control.

"Are you going to invite me inside?"

Why did she have to be attracted to this gorgeous man she worked with every day? Now, he was using words of possession-come with me, safe with me, stay with me, and involved with me. It was all too much for her reclusive brain to handle. Even now a smoldering of desire laced his conversation. He wanted her.

*Logan wants me.*

She replayed the unfamiliar mantra a few times in her head. The thought of a man in her life was terrifying. But the thought of Logan didn't raise the panic flag to full mast. The revelation that it didn't shoot her emotional barometer to the danger zone had an erotic effect on her. Heaven help her, there was a place inside her that craved his attention.

"That's not going to happen." She wanted to keep him. Her naughty nurse had awakened with an appetite. And Logan was the only entree on the menu.

"I can respect that."

He peered over her shoulder taking in the small, cozy chic, living area. The pale yellow oversized couch with tufted twin chairs was her first purchase after getting the keys. They didn't clash with her blue and white nautical theme. Would he view her decorating style as unique or a collection of colorful junk? Before she could contemplate why his opinion was important another question was fired in her direction.

"Who lives here with you?"

Folds of fine Egyptian cotton formed around the front of his shirt as well defined pectorals flexed and bunched. *What lovely muscle anatomy.*

"No one, it's my house. I've owned it for two years."

"It's a nice house. I like what I can see of your landscaping. It has character, similar to a pediatric nurse I know."

There was that smile again, undoing her barely maintained calm. He fixed those mesmerizing emerald orbs on her and she knew the next thing out of his mouth would be a doozy.

"You said you wouldn't let me inside, but do you want to?" He had a laser beam focus on her face.

*Yes,* echoed in her ears, but there was no way she would say it aloud. She felt his heat, her desire, and the air that moved from his body to hers. Everything was tangible where he was concerned.

Then she became aware of the warmth and weight of his palm cradling her cheek. Of their own volition, her eyes sank closed as she nestled into his hand increasing the contact. To be touched was bone melting. His thumb made slow, languid strokes across her cheek. She liked his touch as much as he seemed to like touching her. Never had she experienced such gentleness and care from a man. Some small part of her savored the thought, the response to his touch. It pleased her to know she could respond to a man's touch without the fear overpowering her. But at the same time, it was too much to experience the sexual needs she'd buried after she'd gotten free of Marcus.

"Let me take you to dinner tomorrow." His voice was closer now.

His statement brought her crashing back to reality. Instinctively she moved away from him. Cautious eyes focused on the man before her. She used her tongue to graze over the scar on her lower lip. No one would notice the imperfection now. She swept the thin ridge with her tongue, a permanent reminder of what happens when a man doesn't get what he wants. He watched her. Those beautiful eyes were studious, looking for a weakness in her defenses. This would end in disaster if she allowed it to progress.

"It's sexy when you play with your lip."

Pain registered in her entire body, her hand tightened on the door to keep her standing, each breath a scalpel across her lungs.

"Ava? What's happening?" He reached for her.

She extended her hand preventing him from making contact. "Don't touch me."

Why couldn't she heal? Move on with her life? Instead, she was suspended in this emotionally stunted existence. She wanted Logan, but the need to feel safe was more compelling. Until Logan walked in her life, she had ignored all men. She had no desire to relive the pain she knew would come. She had a choice, trust another man or guard her heart. She had trusted a man once and he had nearly destroyed her.

*No more pain.*

"No, I can't go to dinner with you. I spend Sundays with my family.

Besides, it's not a good idea."

"Ava, just think about …"

"I don't want to think about anything between you and me. I appreciate your help with Randall. I am sorry for the ride stuff. I can give you gas money."

"Keep your money," he said through gritted teeth. "I'm moving too fast for you. I can see that, let's take it slower."

Listening to him would only encourage his pursuit.

"Your speed of acceleration is a moot point because we are not on the same course. Have a good night Dr. Masters."

With that, she took a step back, closed the door and turned off the porch light. She didn't do relationships.

Logan had been dismissed. What had gone wrong? The more he replayed the evening's events, his gut twisted. Something was definitely askew with Ava's response to the incident with Randall. Why hadn't she just told the man to get away from her? Or walked away. He didn't understand, but the fear he saw in her eyes was real. No way could she fake the physical reaction he witnessed. She looked as if she would collapse from acute pain at any moment.

The woman he had enjoyed all evening had vanished. Ava had dismissed him. He should be relieved that Ava had pushed him away. His focus should be on securing grant funding and the board position, but his body thrummed with desire for Ava. The hands free phone link signaled an incoming call. Recognizing the number, he considered allowing it to go to voicemail. He connected the call.

"What were you thinking?" No greeting, straight to business, that was his mother.

"Hello Mother. How was your evening?" He was not in the business of explaining his actions.

"My evening was fine until you sent Rebecca home and disappeared. How are you going to cement this deal if you refuse to spend any time with her?"

"I have the situation with Rebecca under control." He could count on Darwin to soothe the waves on his behalf. His brother could charm any woman into submission.

"You didn't network with one board member tonight."

That was not true. Randall Lester was on the foundation's board of directors. Randall made him think of Ava.

He still wanted the little minx even though she had rejected his invitation. He smiled to himself as the car came to a stop under the covered drive of his remodeled colonial revival style home. The moss-draped oak canopies lining the brick paved streets were a stark contrast to Ava's middle class neighborhood. The architecture of his home complemented the Queen Anne styled mansions on his cul-de-sac. He'd purchased the house five years earlier. The main house had five bedrooms with four and a half baths spread over thirty-five hundred square feet. The detached two-car garage with a second floor apartment sealed the deal for him. The covered drive worked until hurricane season arrived, then having a garage was better than a backyard swimming pool.

Ava may have thwarted him tonight, but not before he saw the temptation to take him up on his offer brightening her coffee colored eyes.

"It's late, Mother. We can have this conversation during brunch tomorrow." Sundays were reserved for golf with his father and Darwin. It wasn't unusual for Graham, his best friend, or Gideon, another doctor at the hospital, to join them. His mother did not enjoy golfing and would join them for brunch afterwards.

"Logan." He knew that tone, the pull on the leash. "You are close to obtaining everything you ever wanted. Don't allow yourself to be distracted. The family is counting on you."

"Goodnight, Mother." The call connect button dimmed when he killed the engine. Family loyalty, an ever present weight kept him behind the steering wheel. He accepted his responsibility to his family, but he would have Ava.

This time it would be different. He would keep his emotional safeguards in place. No crazy love scenarios, he would stay in control of their interactions. Relationships could be built on mutual attraction and he had that with Ava. Recalling her warm vanilla and honey scent made his body stir with lust. He didn't care that she wasn't in a position to advance his career. He didn't care that she lived on Main Street while he was born on Wall Street. Forget the social boundaries their relationship would most definitely slam into.

Ava was his.

Ava awoke feeling everything, but rested. Her night with Logan infiltrated her dreams. With him, she was a younger version of herself, before her foolish actions with Marcus. Knowing that the woman she had once been still lived inside of her should have been comforting. But it wasn't. Logan had the uncanny ability to penetrate her defenses. And stupid as it was, she didn't want to fight his allure. What if she was destined to repeat the same mistakes?

She forced herself to prioritize the days "to do list." With her parents expecting her for dinner, she would go for a run before church. Nothing compared to a five-mile trek through nature to clear the mind. Kicking the bedcovers to the foot of the bed, Ava grabbed the cordless phone from the bedside table before she thought better of it, and pushed speed dial. She should talk with Lina before the morning was in full swing. The phone rang several times before she answered.

"Hey girlie, what took you so long to answer the phone? It must have been a wild night with Jace."

"That's one way to describe my night," Lina said flatly.

Ava heard the other woman yawn, seconds later the sound of running water filled the receiver. Lina didn't offer any details about her night. That was strange. Lina was a play-by-play storyteller.

"You told Logan where I lived?"

"I did. I thought Randall Lester the Nurse Molester had gotten you. Logan was going all Incredible Hulk over the phone and I didn't know what else to do. Please tell me you didn't run out on Logan."

Ava confessed everything that happened up to Logan arriving at her door. Without the water distorting the sound. She could hear Lina shaking her head at her antics.

"Logan is one of the good ones. I trust … I think he's okay." Lina's voice sounded strange, teary.

"I don't know anything about him." Though she did have lots of questions. Putting the phone on speaker mode Ava started her morning routine. She pulled socks and running gear from the middle drawer, selected a pair of bright orange running shoes, before heading into the adjoining bathroom.

"Ava, answer me this question. You spent the better part of last night with the man. Did you ask him any questions?"

"Yes," Ava remarked with smug satisfaction. "I know he's thirty-four years old."

"I'll play along. What else did you ask him, Miss Twenty Questions?"

"That was the only question I asked. I didn't want to seem too interested."

"What are you afraid of?" Lina's voice was gentle now, no longer teary, but she still didn't sound right. "Everyone in the ballroom could see you two were digging each other."

"I don't know. Do you really think he's into me?"

Ava was terrified of choosing the wrong man. Of being consumed by another person, till she no longer mattered. Her heart rate increased at the possibility of it happening again.

"Of course I do. You know I do not joke about male attention."

That was true. Lina could be counted on for a laugh, but not when it came to relationships. When Lina started dating Jace, she was so full of hope that he would be the one.

"Why would Logan be interested in me? Why would anyone? He doesn't know anything about me." Which was probably for the best. She knew she had his professional respect. It was stupid to put her reputation on the line.

"You are a generous, beautiful, intelligent woman. Why not you? He should be kissing your tired nurse's feet in my opinion."

Ava burst out laughing. "Anyone that touches my feet after a twelve-hour shift is a saint. What about the race thing?"

"What about it? You aren't ignorant enough to allow skin color to dictate your decisions," Lina said, in a venomous tone. "The color of your wrapper doesn't matter to Logan. I saw how he looked at you, how he held you in his arms. He sees how amazing you are, not your skin color."

Ava's self-confidence soared at Lina's words. But she didn't miss that Jace had somehow screwed up last night. There was no ignoring Lina's foul mood.

"Lina?" She proceeded with caution, not wanting to cause her friend any more pain. And talking about Jace was obviously painful. Usually, Lina was the first to tell Ava about her dates with him. "What happened with Jace last night?"

"Jace is a human turd. He's lucky the beachcombers didn't find him doing the turd float this morning. I don't want to talk about yesteryear. Something else happened with Logan or you would have called last night when he showed up at your door."

Lina knew her well. "He asked me on a date," Ava said, shyly.

"And your answer was?"

"I said no, but in my defense everything happened so fast last night. First Randall, then Logan materializing out of the dark."

"Ava! It's been six years. Stop punishing yourself and Cricket."

Thank goodness the phone wasn't at her ear or Lina would've heard her yelp. Cricket was Lina's pet name for a clitoris. According to Lina, if a man knew what he was doing in the bedroom, the Cricket would let you know. Ignoring Lina's comment, she continued on with her story.

"He said he likes me. Wants to know me better. He used the word *involved*. I came to the party as a third wheel and I'm *involved* by midnight. It's crazy, right?" Crazy events should be labeled what they are, a temporary deviation from the normal state of being. Morning light burns away the folly of darkness.

"Slow down. Take a breath. It doesn't have to be crazy. Logan is a man that tells you what he's thinking. Do you know how lucky you are? You don't have to play these games like the rest of us." Her friend sounded disheartened.

"Oh, Lina, I am sorry. What am I doing, talking non-stop about Logan?"

"You're thinking like a woman with her brains scrambled by a man. It's about time." Lina released a soft giggle.

The statement dropped a dose of reality at Ava's feet.

"Lina, what if...?"

"Don't say the words. Give yourself a chance. You are not the same person you were in college and Logan is definitely not the same type of man."

"You sound sure about me."

"I am. You're stronger than you realize. You can have whatever you want."

Ava wanted to believe her friend. Glancing at the phone's digital clock, she needed to end this call now to get in the miles before the ten o'clock church service.

"I'm about to go for a run, do you want me to come over later?"

"Don't bother your brain cells with my drama. I have to work the mid-morning shift today. Run an extra mile for me. According to Jace, my butt is too big."

"That's not true," Ava yelled. "You have a figure celebrities would pay for."

"I know. Jace was being a jerk, as usual. He wasn't right for me, but there's a man out there who is. My heart's desire."

Lina, always the romantic.

"You can have your heart's desire too, Ava."

"Thanks for saying that. I'll call later tonight." She needed to believe she could have her heart's desire because life had taught her otherwise.

# CHAPTER SIX

Ava should have considered it a rare honor to escort a group of SCMC financial donors through the pediatric unit. A twenty-bed state of the art medical and surgical hybrid unit framed by contemporary glass walls, trimmed in high gloss wood and accented with polished chrome. The physical building was as impressive as the patient care and clinical research occurring under its roof. The group was comprised of seven diamond-clad ladies, ranging in age from mid-fifties to early sixties, coiffed and couture to perfection. One gentleman, maybe in his early fifties accompanied the group. He was lean with an athletic build, a dark complexion, military haircut, and intelligent eyes. So why did she have the distinct feeling of being beaten like a drum? Kathryn had asked her to showcase how foundation research grants and the medical innovations division worked together to develop the best practices in pediatric inpatient care.

"You are very knowledgeable about the pediatric research at the facility."

That was from a short woman with pale skin and bright blue eyes near the back of the group. Ava offered a smile at the compliment as she led the group past a medical storage area.

"It's her job."

The brisk retort was directed at no one in particular. The comment came from the woman who walked in front and slightly away from the group. The gold-buttoned nautical theme jacket with matching knit skirt made her look like a military commander to a squadron of Barbie dolls.

"Thank you," Ava replied. "I serve as the primary nurse to several of the patients enrolled in the pediatric wound care project." A project that Logan led and she believed in. She was privy to the lifesaving treatment regimens developed from his research. Trying not to think about Logan, Ava focused on all the lives and limbs that had been spared because of the wound care project. That was enough to renew her determination to make a lasting impression on the donors.

The medical center depended on the annual infusion of grant monies and she wanted to do her part to help. She sutured her smile in place and continued with the tour.

"Take us to the patient care pods I've heard so much about."

It was Commando Barbie again. The woman had to know all the renovations were included on the tour. Ava didn't need to be told what to do on the job. This was her domain. Care pods were a cluster of patient rooms oriented in a clover design. The nursing team was housed in the center of the clover with the ability to visually assess every patient at a glance if necessary.

The donors beamed at the upgraded room designs, a tangible representation of foundation dollars at work. New paint and equipment was much easier to conceptualize than medical research.

The final stop was the healing garden addition. An enclosed terrace complete with automated babbling brooks, natural sunlight and padded benches nestled under palm trees.

It was her favorite part of the unit. Cabin fever could be hard on children that required a prolonged hospital stay. The garden was a touch of normalcy.

"I hope the nurses aren't hiding out in here." Barbie, the battle-axe was at it again. "What policies are in place to ensure this remains a haven for patients rather than the nurses?"

With clenched teeth, Ava reminded herself that the funding and Logan's research were priority, not her pride.

"The professionalism of the nursing and medical staff at SCMC is above reproach. Our priority is the care of the patient, not the hospital based amenities." Ava was proud of her response. She met the woman eye to eye, not backing down.

"If there are no more questions, this concludes the tour. Thank you again for taking time out of your schedules to visit us today." That was the closing pitch with a cherry on top.

"Nurse."

Ava turned back to look at the Barbie, lips pinched in frustration. *The devil wears St. Johns.*

"Bring me a bottled water. I get so parched after these walks through the service wards."

*No this woman did not say service wards. What was this, World War II?*

"I'll have to remember to hydrate before we visit the clinics tomorrow," she said for the entourage.

The woman seemed bent on relegating Ava to a position of servitude.

According to the unit manager these were annual visits, so why hadn't she brought a personal stock of Perrier water to quench the thirst of the beast? Not only was her attitude grating on Ava's nerves, the woman's perfume had the stench of hair dye. Ava dug deep in her bag of love for all God's creatures and pulled out the last of her patience with this woman. With her smile cemented in place she turned to speak.

"The drinks available on the unit are for patient consumption only. There is a drinking fountain and vending machines in the hall as you exit the floor." Blonde, flat-ironed tresses partially obscured the woman's face, but not enough to hide her scowl.

"A public watering hole. I think not."

Ava offered her most professional persona, as she led the group to the fire safe exit doors. Thankful that the tour was over, Ava turned on her heel in the direction of the staff lounge. She needed a moment to unwind before she checked on each patient.

The charge nurse signaled to her from the nurse's station. "Ava. Room 2B is requesting you?" The weariness she felt after escorting the donors was immediately replaced by concern.

Ava made a beeline to her patient's room fearing the sixteen-year old had taken a turn for the worse. Monique Faulkner had been admitted to the unit from the SCMC emergency department three days before with fever, worsening arm pain, and drainage from her surgery site. The girl had suffered a vicious attack by a then boyfriend, resulting in a three-point break to her right forearm. Metal plates and screws had been surgically implanted to stabilize each bone segment.

"Ava! Where have you been, girlfriend?"

Monique's thick braids where twisted in an intricate knot on top of her head. Her cherubic face wore a smile, and her eyes danced in merriment. Ava returned a smile in kind as she moved closer.

"Monique, I was worried. Why did you ask for me?"

"I'm bored. I need someone to talk to. I'm sorry if I took you away from another patient."

Monique lowered her head but not before Ava recognized her shame. Time with Monique was a treat, especially after Commando Barbie. "It's okay. I got pulled for escort duty this morning, but I have time to talk."

"With the President or something?"

"No, no one that esteemed. But, they are important people to this hospital."

"That's cool. Ah …"

Monique didn't hesitate. She was vocal when it came to something she wanted. "What's up Monique? You can talk with me about anything."

"Are you sure? Because it's probably not right or selfish or something, but … I was wondering."

"Yes, go on." Ava moved closer to the bed. She took Monique's uninjured arm giving it a gentle squeeze of encouragement.

"When you're on duty can you be my nurse?" Monique imitated mock air quotations.

"Has something happened?"

"No, no. Everybody is great, but you and me, we kind of have a mini bond thing happening."

Ava hesitated a moment, not because she didn't want to, but out of respect for the charge nurse she needed to discuss the staffing mix with the supervisor before giving an answer.

"It's okay if you don't want to, I just thought …"

"Of course I want to do a mini bond kind of thing with you. Let me talk with the nurse in charge to work out the staffing. We have to divide the more complex patients amongst the nurses."

The smile radiating on Monique's face warmed Ava's heart.

The sound of the room door opening drew their attention.

"Just the two ladies I wanted to see."

The stomach dip told her it was Logan before she could focus on his face. She had been avoiding him since the fundraiser.

"Dr. Masters, Ava has agreed to be my nurse. Isn't that great? Now I have my favorite doctor and nurse together."

The look that Logan gave her seared her insides and she gripped the bedrail to steady herself.

"This is great news, Monique. We both have the pleasure of forging a lasting relationship with Ava."

She knew Logan wasn't referring to a professional relationship.

"Ava and I will talk about the plan of care for you after I finish your exam."

"Ah, Dr. Masters I feel fine."

"I'm glad to hear that since I am responsible for your care, but no short cuts allowed. I have requested your medical records from the hospital that performed your surgery, just in case we have to remove the hardware from your arm. We will give the antibiotic more time to kill the infection, but I want to be prepared if more needs to be done."

Monique did not look happy at the mention of another surgery.

"I'll step out to give you both some privacy." Ava gave what she hoped was a reassuring smile, squeezed Monique's hand once before she released it, and then moved to exit the room.

She felt his familiar hand close around her wrist as she brushed by.

"Wait for me outside, Ava."

Logan's expression told her there would be no escaping him today.

Logan's thoughts strayed to Ava more with each passing day. That night with Ava was groundhog's day on a repeating loop in his brain. Why had she rejected him?

She was attracted to him. He'd witnessed how responsive she was to his touch. He felt her very physical reaction when she pressed against him during the dance. She had leaned into his touch at her front door.

Today he was getting a date with her.

He didn't have to go in search of her as he expected. She was closing Monique's intake chart when he stopped in front of her. He let her see the determination in his eyes. Without a word, he took her elbow leading her to a more remote service corridor away from prying eyes.

"Why did you refuse to go out to dinner with me?"

In Ava fashion, she sidestepped his question, posing one of her own. "Dr. Masters, I'll do my best to support you in caring for Monique. She is a special young lady. Do you have a question regarding the patient?"

She'd emphasized the word patient. He took a page from her playbook with a reverse distraction of his own. "It's because I'm white. Are you refusing my invitations because of my color?"

"No. Are you wearing crazy pants?"

"Crazy pants?" He repeated in an uncertain tone. "What in hell are crazy pants?"

"Don't swear. It means it's a ridiculous question. I'm not a racist. You should be ashamed for suggesting such a thing," Ava responded in a loud whisper. A flash of annoyance covered her face.

Finally, a straight answer. No way was he letting up on the pressure. This woman was meant to be his.

"You've been deliberately avoiding me. It's not my age or race. What's holding you back?" He took both her hands in his. "Don't give me another excuse."

"I can't date you. Furthermore, we shouldn't be talking about this at work."

He smiled at her choice of words. "You've been thinking about dating me, yet you refuse my invitation. Fine, we can talk about us over dinner tonight."

"I'm not having dinner with you."

"Why not? There is nothing wrong with me."

"Other than being arrogant, bossy, and having a potty mouth," she responded matter-of-factly.

"Like I said, there's nothing wrong with me. I know you are attracted to me. Do you have something against a man with a job?"

"I prefer men with jobs. However, it would be poor judgment on my part to date a doctor I work with every day. I love my job Dr. Masters; we have a good working relationship. I can't handle any complications in my life."

"I am not a complication to be managed with the other sick patients. There's more between us than a working relationship. You have to be the only woman I know for whom my being a doctor is a liability." He took a deep steadying breath before he spoke. "I want to get to know you better. Let me feed you since we both know you're not too keen on car rides." They both laughed and he moved in close, taking her hands, determined to wear down her resistance.

He squeezed them lightly, willing her to accept him.

"You have to eat. All I'm asking is for you to share the table with me." He glimpsed the smile she fought to contain. Mischief danced in her eyes. The smile along with the glint in her eyes spoke to the cogwheel turning out an idea to slip out on him again.

"Ava," he chastised. "This dinner is for two. No sidekick, chaperone, or feeding the needy soup kitchen dates allowed."

On a gasp, her smile faltered. That was it. She was trying to get out of dinner.

"Say yes to dinner. Just you and me." He closed the space between them. "Bury any ideas of double dates, community events, visiting animal shelters or any other crazy venue you could dream up to avoid being alone with me." He flashed his best all American smile going for the touchdown. "Please sweetheart, give the doctor you work with a chance?"

"Logan, you don't want to do this with me. I am an emotional tornado trying to avoid dry land."

"I am your resident storm chaser reporting for duty," he said, with a fixed look. She thought herself an emotional tornado. *Forewarned, is forearmed.* He'd take the risk.

"I'll share one meal with you."

"Pick the date. I'll pick the time." He'd play for keeps the next time he had her alone.

"I'll go to lunch with you. Outdoors." That was good. Ava was proud of herself. Nothing with dim lighting and quiet intimacy, besides she loved being outdoors.

"Lunch?" Logan questioned.

She would fight the attraction every step of the way.

"Do you have to be in the house before the street lights come on?"

"Lunch Dr. Masters. Take it or leave it. Your choice."

"We've had this discussion before, but since you've been scarce of late I will remind you to use my name. And lunch opposed to dinner makes no difference."

Maybe not to him, but with her jelly spine, drop dead sexy pediatricians, and moonlit skies were a cocktail best avoided.

"When is your next day off?"

"I'm off this weekend. Saturday is best for my schedule."

His smile greeted her as she released the hold on his hands. During their conversation his grip had slackened, yet she had kept her hands nestled in his.

"Be ready at ten o'clock. Dress comfortably."

"Okay, Dr. Masters."

"Don't call me Dr. Masters on our first date. Doctor is my title. My name is Logan. I want you to say my name Ava."

"I won't call you Dr. Masters on our only date, Logan." If the day went as she planned she would eat a platter sized salad in silence, drink a gallon of water, make two trips to the bathroom and be back home in ninety minutes flat. No need to say anyone's name.

Saying his name aloud made her stomach dip. And this conversation about dates, dinners, and alone time with him made the sensation more tumultuous. At this rate, she'd be seasick standing in the hallway.

"The sound of my name on your soft lips is sexy."

That was Logan with his wind tunnel effect again. She liked the sound of his name, too. *Logan, Logan, Logan. Stop it. Focus on the man standing before you.* He smiled bright and her heart skipped a beat.

"I've told you before don't say things you don't mean."

She had every intention of following through with the one date limit. Her foolish heart was considering other options.

"I don't." Not normally, but a woman had to protect her heart. A heart that seemed determined to sample the forbidden fruit that was Logan.

He stepped to her side and she instinctively took a step back.

"I think you do Ava because I remember everything about our dance.

The feel of your body under my hand is a physical image seared in my mind." His lips ever so briefly touched her cheek. "I could sculpt your body from clay with these hands," he whispered close to her ear.

Her breath hitched. Then he cradled her face in both his hands and her breathing increased as her skin warmed. Closing her eyes, she willed her body to knock it off.

"Your body responds to my touch."

Her mind reeled at his statement. He dropped his hold on her, stepping back. Thank goodness.

"Have a nice morning, sweetheart. Be ready for me on Saturday."

*Be ready for him.* Would she ever be ready for Logan? Ava's heart raced. He knew she was attracted to him. It was too much to think about during working hours. On the way home, later that evening, when she was alone in bed, then she'd think about Logan.

*Oh birds and turds, Logan is my heart's desire. Dang it, she should have never gone to that gala.* She concentrated on keeping her body upright. Letting her head drift back until it came to rest against the wall, she rubbed a palm over her heart. The thought of being close to him had her breath coming in a short, choppy rhythm. "It's only lunch Ava."

Lunch was safe, but would she be?

# CHAPTER SEVEN

Logan took a minute to put his libido back in the box when Ava opened the door. She looked flawless and edible in a vintage, pin-up girl, sea foam green and pink sun dress that cinched at her waist, and draped seductively over her petite hips before stopping at her knees. Her hair was a shiny mass of curls framing her face as it cascaded down her back. Her fingernails were cut short and buffed to a shine. She was such a nurse. Nurses rarely wore nail color for fear of transferring bacteria to a patient, but pedicures were a different story. It didn't surprise him to see crimson colored toes. An image of her legs wrapped around his waist flashed through his mind.

"You look beautiful." He brushed his lips across her cheek while his hand palmed the back of her head. She softened in his grasp and he smiled. She was definitely affected by his touch.

"Are you going to let me come in?" he whispered the words across her ear.

"No! I mean that's not necessary because I'm ready. Let me grab my purse and your jacket off the table."

*Not ready yet.* At the mention of his jacket, he smiled at the lunch plans he'd made. Forewarned is forearmed. His unwavering belief in those three words had served him well.

"You can keep the jacket. You will have something of mine to keep you warm." He couldn't see her face from the open door, but her back went ramrod straight.

"Where are we going for lunch?"

Deflecting to another topic. Did she think he would forget the attraction they shared?

"It's one of my favorite places. This place has a lot of variety."

"What's the name of the restaurant? I am kind of a food connoisseur."

"I can't remember the exact name, but I think it will meet with your standards."

"What street is it on, I have probably eaten there before. I was born and raised in Shell Cove."

With only a Lucite pink purse in her hand, Logan guided her out the door closing it behind them without answering her question. His jacket was still in the house maybe he would join it by the end of the evening.

"Ava, I have plans for us. That's all you're going to get out of me, and that the restaurant is not in Shell Cove."

Logan had them on I-95 headed south in ten minutes.

Two hours later he pulled into a parking spot at the Disney World theme park. He killed the engine, pulled the keys from the ignition and disengaged the door locks. Telling Ava the restaurant was beyond Shell Cove kept her quiet for the first sixty minutes into their trip.

"Logan?"

He turned to face her. Prepared to meet her ire with pure masculine determination.

"Yes, Ava?"

"We are in Orlando, Florida. You brought me to Walt Disney World for lunch?"

"Walt Disney's Epcot Center to be exact. We can visit the International Pavilion for lunch."

Ava stared at him, shocked and disbelieving.

"This can't be happening." She felt a surge of awed irritation that she was more than an hour away from home in a car with a crazy person.

"Disney, Logan? Why not New York City or Los Angeles?"

"What? I happen to enjoy theme parks. Don't tell me you're anti-mouse," he grinned.

She snorted. Dozens of families exited minivans and SUVs, making a swerving conga line to the trolleys that would whisk them to the Magic Kingdom. She was experiencing somewhat of a magic carpet ride herself. There went her vision of a ninety-minute lunch and no complications. He had outmaneuvered her.

He chuckled at her response to Mickey Mouse. "We arrived in time for lunch."

Ava took in a slow, deep breath and released it. She repeated the process three times. She frowned. The experts didn't know beans from buttons. She didn't feel any calmer. She took in another big deep breath. This time she held it.

"Breathe easy Ava, it's going to be all right. Listen to me closely sweetheart. It took you more than a week to say yes to a date with me. Did you honestly think I would settle for one or two hours of your time?" He looked at her quizzically.

"I don't know what I thought." She'd hoped to wrestle her attraction to him back into a pill bottle.

"Really? You avoided me for a week. An unusual response when you aren't sure of a man's interest?" His tone was one of knowing laughter.

"Okay, Dr. Phil." Forming a coherent conversation proved challenging with her trying to devise a plan to get the desire back in the tamper proof container. She had to protect her foolish heart or she'd find herself falling for him.

"Logan, not Phil, and you underestimate my interest in you. I want you in every possible way and you'll discover I'm not easily deterred."

His expression said this was a journey for which he was well prepared. *What the heck did 'in every way' entail?*

"I know you want me, just as much as I want you. Now, let's go get you fed."

He reached over the center console to stroke her cheek. Oh, his touch was an instant buzz and loads of dizzying side effects. Shaking her head, she pulled away.

"What I want is to ride the roller coasters. Lunch can wait." Denial was a woman's prerogative. She released the door lock and stepped outside without sparing him a glance.

The lines to enter the theme park resembled a human ant colony. Ava looked down at her shoes and grimaced. A sensible pair of nursing shoes was what she needed.

"Come with me."

Logan took her hand, navigating them past small children with bungee-corded wrists, double strollers filled with sunscreen painted toddlers, and organized tour groups with matching shirts.

"Where are we going?" Ava asked looking up at him. She needed her sunglasses. The Florida sun was unforgiving, but she really wanted the shield between her and Logan. He had the uncanny ability to read her expressions.

"No lines for premium members."

He flashed that devastatingly handsome smile. And there was the corresponding sizzling in her veins. Kid-friendly theme park she reminded herself. No errant nipples allowed.

"You aren't secretly married with a wife and kids, right?" With his all American looks and chiseled features, he could have been a cast member of Mickey's Club House.

"Long line of golfers in the family. We play at Disney's Oak Trail Golf Course several times per year. Golf and free parking are parts of the package."

The next thing Ava saw was the gleaming, sphere of Future World filling three hundred and sixty degrees of her field of vision.

"You ready to leave Spaceship Earth?"

That was Logan referring to the adventures of the park, but she'd lost her anchor to this world on that dance floor with him.

"Doctor turned astronaut?"

"I can be anything you need."

Stomach dip number one. She did her best to appear unaffected by his presence. She nodded in his direction before facing forward. Waiting. Not wanting to acknowledge how much his words excited her.

Logan started their trek through the well-orchestrated, vivid color villages of Oktoberfest to Mission Space.

"Okay. The lady wants thrill rides. Let's do this."

She knew the roller coaster rides available in the park. But, her wayward eyes took in his muscled body and he was the only ride she wanted.

As the day progressed, Logan's touch became more familiar. Handholding at first, then his well-defined, muscled arm around her shoulders. Now the weight of his arm circling her waist had her pulse outrunning the Disney monorail. The rightness of them together wasn't lost on her. Stomach dip number two.

The sun was setting and the lunch hour had come and gone. She enjoyed being with Logan, but an audible tummy growl reminded her that they had failed to eat lunch. On her lunch date, that had extended into dinner. A man who got what he wanted. She should be upset, but truth be told, it was the best time she'd ever had.

The smell of jumbo smoked turkey legs and greasy fried dough sailed through the air. Ava smiled because she was getting one of each.

"Why the huge grin?"

"The thought of biting into one of those colossal turkey legs and then stuffing my mouth with the biggest funnel cake I can find."

She saw Logan zero in on her lips, flames alight in his eyes.

"You're not listening."

"I heard you, but I'm stuck on the biting and stuffing part."

She blushed until her face felt fire engine red.

"Sweetheart, I'm making you blush. Such a pretty blush, too. Tell me more things you want to eat, it's fueling my fantasies."

"I don't want to eat anything else," she said, shyly. He looked disappointed at her obvious cop out.

For some reason, she didn't ever want to disappoint him. She offered a compromise. "I want to drink a half gallon of the fresh squeezed lemonade from the cart in front of us."

"I'll make you a deal. You have a seat on the only empty bench in sight." He pointed to a bench partially hidden by a pretzel cart. "I'll go and make all your food fantasies come true."

"You don't have to wait on me Logan. I'll walk with you."

"No. You will do as I said."

"Fine. You, cave man, bring food. I, cave woman, will prepare our table." Secretly she was relieved Logan wanted to get their food.

Ava wished she had worn sneakers. Her sandals were modern day torture devices. Hot coals would have felt more comfortable. She tried not to limp, but that was near impossible with the heat of eight hours on asphalt trapped between her foot and the leather uppers.

Logan returned with their food. She was ravenous. The pain in her feet slipped to second place on her priority list when the fragrance of food reached her nose. Every morsel he put in front of her she devoured with gusto.

"You have a healthy appetite Ava Walters."

"Are you calling me a piglet?"

"There's my funny woman again. I'm glad you're not one of those women who don't eat on a date."

"Wow, you're easy to please. I'll be sure to eat all my food the next time we're out." She realized her mistake immediately. She looked up hoping Logan had missed the implication of her words. The smile on his face told her he had not.

"I look forward to the next time. You pick the place." He came to his feet, extending one hand down to her. "Come on, the Grand Illusions Light show starts in thirty minutes, let's find a better view."

He grabbed the hand she offered pulling her to her feet. They walked a short distance until they found a small spot on a grassy hill.

The fireworks were spectacular. She was glad they stayed to watch the show. It was time to leave the theme park and head home. She was giddy from the unexpected wonder of the day. The craving she had for Logan had grown exponentially as the hours slipped away.

"Ava?"

"Yes, Logan." She felt her body leaving the ground. "Hey, what are you doing?" she giggled. His left arm held her knees and his right arm cradled her back.

"You're smart, you tell me."

Her left arm, hip, and thigh made contact with hot, stone-hard muscles as Logan pulled her into his body. She pulled her arm free to wrap around his neck. She should've gone ramrod stiff in his arms, but the naughty nurse was in control and she rested her head on his chest.

"This is inappropriate." Her fingers were making slow circles on his chest. "Put me down," she said, in a dreamy voice. "I can walk."

"Let me carry you. I saw you limping. I'll put you down when we reach the car." She started to wiggle in his arms.

"Ava stop squirming or I will toss you over my shoulder for all the Mouseketeers to see."

"You wouldn't."

"It would give me great pleasure to have your sweet little apple bottom close to my mouth. I have some ideas about us creating a magic kingdom all to ourselves."

Her feminine center heated at his words. She took in his calm expression. He was serious about what he wanted to do to her. She gulped at the realization.

"Okay, I'll be still."

"That's what I thought I heard you say the first time."

Logan carried her through the theme park to one of the dozen exit gates. Some people openly stared at them as they fell in step with the exiting crowd.

At the unwanted attention, discomfort skirted up her spine. Attracting people's attention was something she had avoided most of her adult life.

"You can put me down. My feet feel better."

He ignored her statement, crossing the half-mile parking lot at a leisurely pace.

"I like carrying you."

"You're kind, but I have to be getting heavy." He looked affronted. Realizing she had committed an ego infraction she rubbed her cheek along his chest in apology.

The feel of him squeezing her tighter to him reassured her all was well.

"I can carry you across a dozen parking lots. Besides, in my arms is where I want you."

Minutes later they reached his car. He placed a quick kiss on her lips.

"Now I will put you down."

He placed her on her feet next to the Lexus's passenger door, reaching into the pocket of his khaki Dockers for his car keys. He unlocked the door then turned to capture her fingers in his warm grip.

"Kiss me, Ava."

That sexy baritone combined with the request, had her wetting her lips in anticipation. He wasn't taking, he was asking. She could refuse, but truth was she wanted to kiss him.

She hesitated a brief moment before she rose up on her toes and tentatively kissed his lips. When she would've backed away, he grabbed her around the waist lifting her up to his eye level. Her back was rested against the doorframe. His hold was firm, but not unyielding. Seductive.

"Again," he gently directed her.

This time she didn't hesitate. She captured his head in her hands and savored the feel of his lips on hers. His mouth was warm, invitingly wet, and she was lost. Lost in the sweet taste of mutual satisfaction. She'd tasted and wanted more. Their tongues dueled for dominance, then he drove his tongue into her mouth with the skill that only an experienced lover could master and subdued her hunger to his will. The moan she released echoed through her as he captured it with the warm heat of his mouth.

Logan abruptly ended the kiss. "Get in the car Ava."

She tried to gain access to his mouth, but he pulled back. She looked at him, seeing a hunger that mirrored hers. The confusion she felt must have shown on her face.

"Don't look at me with wanting in your eyes. I had to stop sweetheart. There's a part of me that is significantly larger since you placed those hot lips on mine. Are you ready for me to get lost in you for hours because that's what will happen if we continue? I'm willing to give the Mouseketeers something to talk about if you are."

She vigorously shook her head side to side.

"No, I'll pass on that scenario." She touched her forehead to his, rubbing her hands over his shoulders, grappling to restrain the desire raging in her.

He laughed, placing a quick peck on her cheek before lowering her to the ground. Helping her into the car, he reached across, buckled her seatbelt, closed the door, then rounded the car and slid in behind the wheel.

"Are you ready to go home?"

"I guess. Yeah, I am," she responded with more certainty than she felt.

They rode in companionable silence for the first half hour. She must have dozed off because she awoke to discover her hand resting on Logan's thigh. High on his thigh. She felt the defined muscles underneath her fingers. They itched to touch his bare flesh. She gave a tentative stroke to the warm flesh underneath her palm. At the feel of his muscle contracting she let her gaze rise to meet his. The electricity flashing in his emerald depths caused goose bumps to bead her skin. She fought the undeniable urge to move closer. To surrender to the beaconing desire radiating from him. To give into the pleasure his eyes promised. He rested his hand over hers, delivering a slow, circular caress to the back of her hand.

"Don't stop, Ava. Nothing about today can be undone. And trust me, nothing can get any harder than it already is."

She could not agree more.

It was approaching midnight when they pulled into Ava's azalea lined driveway.

Logan exited the driver's door and rounded the car. He couldn't resist pressing his lips to hers as he helped her out of the car.

"Thank you for a lovely day Logan. I had a good time with you."

The evening's magic had dissipated as the highway miles led them back to North Florida and awkwardness laced her words.

He could see the dismissal coming the closer they drew to home. He hadn't stopped her when she slowly pulled her hand from his thigh to rest in her lap.

Tonight would not end the same as their first night together. Before he could ruin the day by saying the wrong thing and she could react, he laid claim to her mouth. Pushing past her lips deep into her mouth. Initially he was alone in his quest, and then he felt her tongue tentatively stroke his. Ava's honeyed taste filled his mouth, fueling his need for her. He sucked and nipped at her lips. As he pulled her body closer, he pushed deeper, palming her head, holding her lips captive. She circled his waist. Her hands pressed into his back. He felt her fingers as they tensed and relaxed along the length of his spine. Like she was testing his solidity. Her lithe form filled the "v" between his legs and he coaxed her to continue the oral erotic dance till they both were near mad. Breaking their kiss, he studied her. Except for soft breathy panting her demeanor was calm, but he felt her rising heat against his skin.

"That was my attempt to stop your dismissal." He could see the truth of his statement reflected in her eyes. "Now that I have your attention and you are not focused on insignificant things outside of us, I think you are the most beautiful woman I have ever laid eyes on and I am going to taste every inch of your mouth."

She looked dumbstruck.

"You're joking, right? If that was the warm up kiss, I'm going to require cardiac resuscitation after the real thing."

"I'm well trained. I can bring you back to life."

"I believe you can."

She looked at him with expectant eyes. He could feel the heat of her body pressed into his. Her fingers curled into the fabric of his shirt as if she were securing her grip before a wild ride. But he wasn't ready to give into her seductive pull yet. He needed her to acknowledge that something real was happening between them.

"I'm waiting for you to say "yes," Ava." He knew passion and desire radiated from his piercing gaze. He wanted more than a kiss. He was sure he saw the same need, the same emotion, mirrored in her eyes.

Desire flashed across her soft features.

"I will take care of whatever you need."

"Yes," she said on a breathy whisper.

His right arm closed around her waist as the fingers of his left slowly ascended up her neck to close around her nape. He angled her head with his powerful hand as his mouth descended on hers.

He'd kept his craving for Ava on a short chain all day. He'd wanted to demand, to conquer, to take her, but he didn't. His body instinctively knew what she needed. To keep her, he would have to earn her trust, a subtle seduction of give and take. He loosened his hold on her giving her free rein to take what she wanted. Her kiss was far more dangerous than anything he had experienced.

There was care in her touch, a sense of awe, as her hands performed a provocative dance on his body. Her kiss ignited the fire in his veins. He deepened the kiss, stroking every corner of her mouth, savoring the taste of her. "You taste too good to be true." Stopping only to take a breath, their gazes met.

What he saw seared his soul. He knew she desired him, but to see pure hunger reflected in her eyes floored him. His next kiss branded her, staking his claim on this woman, his woman. She was a perfect vision. Her eyes sparkled after their kiss. Her response to him was untamed and primal, though she tried to hold back. He would slowly melt her apprehension. She was his.

"More Ava, give me more." She opened her mouth to him and he left no recess untouched. His hand abandoned her tresses, caressing the curve of her shoulder, the swell of her breast. The feel of her taut buds under his fingers shot fire straight down his abdomen and spread through his groin. Logan's body was tight with sexual tension. He wanted to bury himself in her.

Soft sounds of satisfaction flowed from her lips and he captured every one with his mouth.

A blast of pure lust raged out of control. He was losing control from her kiss. He shook with need. This woman evoked sensations he didn't realize he was capable of experiencing.

Walking away from Ava tonight would be the most difficult thing he would ever have to do. But she needed this time to accept their relationship. It was his responsibility to give her what she needed. That thought made leaving bearable. He would do anything for her, including sleep alone tonight.

Ava's heart thumped with the power of electric paddles against her chest. She drank in his taste and his caress. This wasn't kissing. This was his version of oral lovemaking. When he slowly sucked her tongue deeper into his mouth, she moaned, and pulled him closer. Thank goodness she didn't still live with her parents. Her mom would have turned on the porch light as soon as the car pulled in the driveway.

He spoke into her mouth, "Do you want me to come inside tonight?" His breathing was labored and deep.

She groaned inwardly, not allowing herself to speak for fear she would say yes.

She had to put a stop to this before she started ripping his clothes off to reach the magnificent body she could feel through his shirt. Just then, she felt the evidence of his arousal press into her stomach. Shock edged her words, "Oh my Todd, you really do want me." *A lot.* That last part she kept to herself. He was aroused because of her. She had done *that* to him.

Logan immediately jerked from his oral exploration of her neck. His hands stilled on the soft flesh of her upper arms.

"Whose name did you call me?" he growled.

She was slow to respond, still reeling from their kiss and the feel of his erection against her belly.

"I didn't call you anyone else's name."

"I haven't lost my hearing."

His hold on her transferred to her shoulders as if he were bracing himself for a blow. "Who is Todd, Ava?"

His sexy, green eyes flashed with anger, then she understood what he was thinking.

"You misunderstand." It was her turn to soothe him. She softly rubbed the tension from his arms.

"I know I heard another man's name on your lips after I had my tongue down your throat."

He looked unhappy and she was sorry she'd opened her mouth. "I'm not explaining myself well. I don't casually say the Lord's name. Instead of saying, oh my God, I say, 'oh my Todd'. I could never mistake you for someone else."

The vibrations in his chest transferred to her where he held her arms. He could not contain his laughter.

"You are a rare treasure, Ava Walters." The laughing had shifted to a wide smile. "What you're saying is, my kiss, my touch feels so good you want to call out to the heavenly Father. I can live with that."

He smiled down at her and all of her good sense leaped right out of her head. Whatever he asked next she was willing to give it.

"Give me another kiss, Ava. Let's add some new phrases to our vocabulary," he groaned.

"I don't know if my kisses ..." He pulled her closer, squelching her concern. Circling his neck with her arm, she pulled him down to meet her lips. Everything she wanted him to feel she poured into their kiss. She tried to wrap herself around him, pulling him closer with each tug of his lips. Her breasts rubbed against his chest and she pressed deeper into him. This was the most erotic experience of her life. A strong arm at her waist pulled her up into his body. She wanted to fuse into his body, blur the lines between him and her. He groaned, then took control of the duel between their mouths. His kiss was soft, hard, giving, taking … and soul stirring.

He ground his hardness into her stomach, stoking the fire burning in her core.

"You do this to me Ava, no one else. I want to give you everything you need. You want me too."

It was a statement neither of them could deny. The physical proof that she could excite a man like him pulsed against her belly adding to her yearning for Logan.

She did want him, but could she allow herself to have him? Sample a larger portion of his sensual temptation.

Of its own volition, her tongue tasted the skin at his neck. She slowly licked across his pulse, nipping him lightly with her teeth. His hands tightened on her waist.

He pulled back to look at her face. "Did you just taste me?"

She had upset him already. She took a step back embarrassed by her actions. "I'm sorry." She dropped her head. A fine tremor started in her hands and was becoming more obvious as her anxiety rose. She needed to get control of herself.

"Don't apologize. I appreciate a woman who shows passion for her man. You want me and I want you too. Nothing happened that warrants an apology."

He was right. She wanted him with an urgency that overwhelmed her. He reached for her, lowering his lips to meet her mouth. Ava pressed her lips together, effectively stopping his next kiss. Ava swallowed hard. It was time to end the night. "Logan, we should not talk about intimate, I meant to say personal …" She stopped abruptly. "You should go home."

"Okay, I'll go," he said evenly, looking down at her.

"Okay?" That was easier than Ava had anticipated.

He shrugged at her stunned expression.

"I'll go because you are not ready for anything else. I'll see you tomorrow."

"All right. No wait, I can't see you tomorrow. I have plans."

Logan stood stone still. "Who do you have plans with tomorrow?" His tone coupled with the stiffened stance took Ava by surprise.

"My family is coming over for dinner."

There was a prolonged pause between them. She didn't extend him an invitation knowing he would not ask. He was too arrogant to ask for almost anything. A crease formed between his brows at her silence. Yes, she had deep throat kissed him a few times, and would do it again, but she was not inviting him to dinner.

He remained quiet, his verdant eyes seeming to study her, then his posture relaxed.

"What time will you finish dinner? I'll come by later in the evening."

She released a breath she didn't know she was holding.

"They are usually gone by six thirty."

She had stumbled into a foreign land. Years of listening to her instincts were hopeless against his magnetic pull.

"Ava," he spoke with caution. "There's something between us and I'm not walking away without discovering what it is. I want us together. Today was good. Let's see where this leads. That is, if it's okay with you?"

"I like being with you, too. I'll try, Logan," she said, doubt in her voice.

"Don't look so forlorn, sweetheart. I'm a man, not an alien."

Except what was happening between them was foreign to her. The feelings his presence awoke were alien.

"Stop worrying about the job and other people. I'll see you after six o'clock tomorrow."

He kissed her forehead, her lips, and then he was gone.

She knew a restful sleep would be elusive tonight. Logan bombarded her dreams. He was touching her everywhere and it wasn't enough. In her dreams, she unleashed her hunger on him, triumph in her feminine power, bathing him in seduction.

Ava awoke the next morning, panting, drenched in sweat with moisture pooled in between her legs. She was in real trouble.

# CHAPTER EIGHT

It was Ava's Sunday to host the Walters' family dinner. The new Minister of Music preferred the dance club remix to every hymn. The Blessed Life Baptist Church Senior Adult choir had sung four selections in forty-five minutes. More parishioners were filling the pews thanks to the choir's improved sound quality, so the Pastor overlooked the time encroachment. At the benediction, Ava pushed through the Sunday morning worshippers exiting the small red brick church in a full on sprint.

No corner of the historic church and the surrounding collection of administrative buildings were untouched by the sun's rays. Beads of perspiration dotted her nose before she arrived at her Jeep. She didn't have time to spare.

Ava had just placed the sliced pork loin on the dinner table when her parent's red sedan passed her front room window. Aron's SUV was next. She was about to return to the kitchen for the ice bucket when an all too familiar station wagon came to a stop in at her mailbox. *Oh no, not today.*

The dining table was the largest piece of furniture in Ava's living area. The small two-bedroom, one and a half bath bungalow had a combination living/dining room area. Every seat at the table was occupied save for one.

"Ava, this meal is better than the last."

*Don't smirk at your elders.* This was her punishment for daring to put a Baptist choir on a time limit.

"Thank you Deacon Hill. It was kind of you to drive Granny Lou over this afternoon." Aron, her younger brother by eighteen months looked across the dinner table with a glimmer of amusement in his eyes. Granny Lou needed to cease and desist with these matchmaking attempts.

"No trouble, my dear. I'm a man who appreciates good food in the company of a beautiful lady." It was obvious he loved inviting himself to other people's houses. This was the third time in two months he had commandeered a meal by conveniently driving Granny Lou to Sunday dinner. He was a pleasant, yet persistent man. She wanted to scream, but she remained attentive to the conversation.

Ava pressed and released the flesh of her left forearm as her eyes threatened to drift yet again, to the ill-fitting Afro wig perched haphazardly on his baldhead.

"Another piece of cake before you leave, Deacon?" Ava rose from her chair moving into the kitchen.

"No. My dear girl, I've had my fill this afternoon."

He reared back in the chair, bringing his hands to rest on his huge belly. Ava closed her eyes in a failed attempt to destroy the mental image of the pregnant abdomen accompanying the man at her table.

"I'm glad you enjoyed the pork tenderloin. You should join Granny Lou for a home cooked meal at my parent's house. She and my mother cook a larger variety of food on their Sundays."

He seemed to consider the option before he spoke. "That's nice to know, but your momma lives another twenty minutes from here. I prefer coming to your house."

This conversation wasn't going in the right direction. The right direction meant him staying away from her family dinners. Maybe a different approach was the answer.

"My job schedule limits my availability to spend quality time with *my* family," she placed the emphasis on the *my* in hopes he would catch on. "This will probably be my last season hosting a Sunday dinner for a while."

"I'm sorry to hear that because what you provide keeps my body running with the precision of a well-oiled machine. Too much of the wrong food clogs up my gears for days."

No, he did not go there.

She could hear Aron's laughter above the Deacon's comment. Aron and his wife Zari were newlyweds. He laughed a lot these days, even at his sister's expense. The couple had met at the drug store where Aron worked as a pharmacist. Zari was a second grade school teacher at Shell Cove Primary. They made being in a relationship look easy. Ava liked Zari. She was happy for her brother. If only her experience with the opposite sex was as carefree.

"Don't laugh Brother Aron. You never know when you'll need a burst of power. You need the engine clear of debris for the best fuel efficiency," the deacon chastised.

"Is that right?" Aron queried, egging the man on.

She'd make him pay for that.

"Yes, indeed. I've lost sixty pounds in the past two years. The doctor told me my high blood pressure, high cholesterol, and diabetes will continue to improve if I lose another hundred pounds."

Ava blew out a breath. How had the conversation descended in the Deacon's bowel patterns?

"Losing sixty pounds is a wonderful accomplishment Deacon. Thank you for the compliment. The meal was prepared with herbs and vegetables from my garden. Mom and I canned a lot of the vegetables from the summer harvest."

"Well now, Granny Lou put your cooking on my radar, but I didn't know you could work the land. I know my grandkids would love to have you helping them mow the lawn and clean out the flower beds."

"Ah, gardening is different from lawn maintenance. Besides, Mom and I help each other with the gardens."

"I recognize the difference, but you've got natural ability, Ava my girl. You've been gifted with wonderful hands."

Ava noticed her sister-in-law's eyes tearing at the corners as they darted upward, then left and right in rapid succession. Zari's body trembled with pent up laughter. Aron was struggling more than his new wife. His recurrent throat clearing was a poor cover for the peals of laughter.

Deacon Hill seemed to grasp his poor choice of words after taking in her father's disapproving gaze.

"Hmm, I didn't finish my thought. What I meant to say is you have wonderful hands in the kitchen. You should cook a few meals for my children. They would welcome a home cooked meal from such a beautiful lady. My third wife spent most of her waking hours in the kitchen trying to keep the kids fed."

*No he isn't trying to turn me into a meals-in-heels for his grown kids.*

"That is a kind offer Deacon, but I am more adept at preparing meals for smaller settings. Perhaps you and all the children could join Granny Lou at my parent's house for a mini feast."

*Clue number four, please exit via the front door.*

"I'm sure the kids would love all the attention."

*Please take the hint. I am not interested.*

The doorbell chimed at six thirty-one. The bottom dropped out of her stomach.

*Please, please let it be Jehovah's Witnesses or those people selling weekly subscriptions of the newspaper. Not Logan.*

Everyone would be gone by now, if it weren't for the deacon. She didn't want to explain anything to her family about her budding relationship with Logan.

Aron was at the door before she could concoct an explanation for Logan being at her house.

"Ava," Aron called in a singsong voice, "you have a visitor."

Everyone turned to see Logan standing in the living room with a tropical fruit platter in one hand. His smile was fixed on Ava. She moved with robotic motion toward him. At the sight of him, her heart leapt with anticipation, while panic churned in her stomach.

"Hello sweetheart."

Logan bent and kissed her cheek. All the clinging of glasses, plates and utensils came to a halt in the background. Ava was temporarily comatose. No he didn't call her sweetheart and kiss her in front of her family, but he had.

"Now wait a minute, that's my Ava girl."

She heard her brother's, oh snap, but she couldn't move.

"I feel a burst of power coming on. We need to move outside so I have room to maneuver."

She recognized the Deacon's voice through the mental fog. Glancing right, Deacon Hill struggled to push his chair away from the table. His belly trapped under the table edge. Granny Lou's hand at his shoulder stayed him from rising to his feet.

*Please, don't let the Deacon to Father Time confront Logan at my dinner table.*

After witnessing Logan handle Randall, she knew Deacon Hill should remain seated.

Her mother's southern lilt drifted over the deacon's commotion "Not a visitor I see. Ava, don't be rude. Introduce this young man to your family."

Ava still hadn't found her voice. Logan stepped in to appease everyone's curiosity. "Mrs. Walters I presume, I'm Logan Masters."

Logan took her mother's proffered hand, delivering a business handshake with a charismatic smile. He was good.

"Ava and I work together."

"How nice of you to drop by. You're one of the nurses at Ava's job."

Her statement camouflaged the question in everyone's mind. Logan was good, but Ariss Walters was better. A collective, very audible, sigh rose from the table. Ava was sure the gay male nurse stereotype was the reason for the reaction. A reprieve.

"Actually, I'm one of the pediatric surgeons on staff."

Reprieve aborted. Gee thanks, Logan.

Her father's eyes narrowed at Logan's comment. He studied Logan from head to toe. Again he repeated the sequence. *Target identified* she thought. She knew what would come next, missile locked and loaded. Her father's base filled the room, "Why are you at my daughter's house?"

"Ava and I are seeing each other," Logan said in a firm and determined tone. He made eye contact with every person in the room before settling his gaze on Ava. Challenge hardened his stare.

"Well now, my grand baby is finally interested in something other than the Navy."

Granny Lou's shrilled *well now* had a siren quality on the room occupants. Every person in the room looked at her grandmother.

"Lord, I didn't see this one coming. You are a lot lighter than I expected, young man. The pastor's always saying we should be specific in our prayer requests." Granny directed her statement at Logan.

"Please don't say anything else, Granny Lou."

Ava wanted to bury her head in the backyard garden. Of course, Logan unleashed his charismatic smile on her grandmother.

"Yes ma'am, I may not be what you were expecting, but I will be sticking around."

The man had no shame. It had to be wrong to charm a woman's grandmother.

Ava turned to her mother, pleading with her eyes for help.

In two minutes, Logan had done exactly what she did not want to do, *let anyone know they were together.*

"Guess who's coming to dinner," her brother said.

Ava shot him a glare. Now was not the time for comedic commentary.

But his comment snapped Ava out of her vocal paralysis. "Logan let me take the tray. Thank you for the fruit. They are my favorites."

"You're welcome. There's a bed of quinoa under the fruit."

"I love it." Sitting the platter on the table, Ava gave Logan her attention. "Let me introduce you to everybody."

Logan grabbed her hand, holding it loosely in his grip. The action momentarily stilled the words in her throat. She lowered her eyes to their conjoined hands. Looking at him, reassurance glowed in his emerald depths. This was a huge step for her. He acknowledged that truth.

He instinctively knew what she needed. And he had met that need by offering himself and not just words. She was a grown woman with more unrequited needs than fulfillment in her life. Logan wanted her. And she wanted him. Admitting her desire for him bolstered her confidence.

Logan gave a barely perceptible nod. She took a deep breath of "big girls aren't afraid to introduce their boyfriends" into her lungs.

"These are my parents, Andrew and Ariss Walters."

Starting at the seats closest to the sitting area she worked her way around the eight-seater square oak table.

"It's nice to meet you Mr. and Mrs. Walters. I look forward to spending more time with both of you."

The table fell quieter than a judge's chamber. The shocked expression on her mother's face quickly gave way to a soft smile. Her father hadn't moved a muscle.

"See that you do, Logan," her mother continued, "Drew and I are both retired and would love the company."

Ava's father had retired from the postal service earlier that year. Her mother was so excited that they both were vibrant and healthy enough to enjoy retirement together. Her mother had retired from teaching after thirty years last summer.

"Isn't that right, Drew?"

Not a word came from her father's lip.

"Wouldn't it be nice to have Logan and the kids over for dinner when we return from our trip, Drew?"

Her father offered a grunt in response. Ava guessed Logan was the only man responsive to hearing his name. She decided to cut her losses and moved on to the next seated couple.

"My much younger brother Aron, greeted you at the door." Aron was slow to extend his hand in greeting. "And next to him is my favorite sister-in-law Zari."

Zari gave Logan a warm welcome, but not before she nudged Aron in the ribs with her elbow.

"I'm her only sister-in-law and it's a pleasure Logan."

"Thank you Zari, the pleasure is mine." Logan focused on a seated Aron.

"Aron, I noticed your Red Skins jersey, you a big fan?"

Leave it to Logan to identify the one thing Aron couldn't resist talking about.

"I bleed burgundy and gold, you?"

Logan looked affronted.

"Baltimore Ravens through and through. I graduated from Johns Hopkins."

"I look forward to the coming months. May the best team win," Aron replied.

"I'll buy your first Ravens jersey when they do."

"Oh, you got jokes? We will see who makes the playoffs this year."

Team sports bridged many a divide.

"Ah … this is my grandmother, Mrs. Louise Stanton. She answers to Granny Lou most days. Deacon Hill has been a friend of Granny Lou's for over thirty years."

Deacon Hill bristled in his seat at Ava's explanation of his role at the table.

"My older sister, Shaylah is a PhD student at Howard University in Washington, D.C."

"It's a pleasure to meet you all. Please don't let me disturb your meal. I can help Ava in the kitchen."

Ava recognized Logan's ploy to get her alone. He hadn't fooled her family either by the looks on their faces. Knowing Logan the way she did, he had every intention of giving her mouth what it had been craving all afternoon.

"Young man, Ava doesn't need any help in the kitchen, she's got experience with pots, pans, and a hot stove. You come sit yourself right next to me. Move down Deacon, we're about to get this interview started." Granny Lou clapped her hands in obvious excitement.

"No Granny." Ava was terrified for Logan. Zari gripped Aron's shoulder as if warding off a bad dream. Granny Lou made an FBI interrogation resemble Jeopardy. The level of probing Logan was about to undergo at the hands of the Walters' family matriarch was equivalent to exploratory surgery minus the anesthesia.

"Mom," Ava whined, "help us out please."

"There's an interview process?"

Logan laughed, but this was no laughing matter. He was about to be cracked open, the peanut under the boot heel. Logan was the unsuspecting peanut.

"Mom, do something," Ava pleaded for a lifeline.

"Granny Lou, let Logan sit down and enjoy dessert with us, before you bring out the electroshock therapy."

Logan's deep laughter echoed in the room. "For Ava, I can handle anything you throw my way."

She was beginning to believe he would.

Logan pulled out the vacant seat next to where she sat. Ava promptly cut a slice of cake, placing

it in front of him. If she kept his mouth full he couldn't answer any questions.

Her father peered across the table at Logan. "You ever been married?"

*Oh my Todd.* Her father had asked that question.

"Drew, that's a terrible question to ask." Her mom looked mortified. "No, I've never been married." There was a strain to Logan's voice.

"Ava is a grown woman. She doesn't need her parents to ask those types of questions."

Thank you, Mom.

"But since we're getting acquainted with one another. How old are you, Logan?"

Oh no.

"I'm discovering age is important to all of the Walters family. I'm thirty-four."

Some unspoken communication passed between her parents, but she recognized the message. *What happened to her in college would always haunt them.* That's what they saw when they looked at her.

"Whoa, Ava," Aron said, "you picking up guys that need to buy long-term care insurance?"

Ava shot him an icy glare.

"Aron Walters, you are sleeping on the couch if you crack one more joke at Ava's expense. I think it's fine if she wants to date an older man."

Thank you favorite sister-in-law.

"Well, I'm older than this interloper. And I've known Ava girl longer."

Oh my Todd, she had forgotten that the Deacon Hill was ready to duel on the front lawn.

"Ava's only twenty-six. That's a pretty big age gap."

She could hear the worry in her mother's voice.

"I care about Ava and we are already together. The age difference is not a factor in our relationship."

Logan reached for her hand, and squeezed. There was no mistaking the stress on each syllable. He sought her out for reassurance. This was a first.

Holding his hand tighter, she smiled up at him. It was nice to have someone depend on her. He deemed her worthy. Not a broken woman in need of a champion, shielded from life.

Two hours later Ava's family was at the front door headed for their respective cars. Granny Lou rested a weathered, fleshy palm on Ava's cheek. "Try grandbaby."

There was a sadness underlying her smile.

"What do you want me to try Granny Lou?"

"Being who you are."

Ava didn't know what to say.

"I love you Ava and remember what I said."

Granny Lou placed a kiss on her cheek. Then her gold sequined sneakers were carrying her down the few stairs across the walkway.

Being herself and speaking her mind hadn't worked in her favor. Would this time be different?

The measure of control she used to close the door spoke volumes to the trouble cresting on the tide. Ava closed the front door softly. Her attention on the man left in the room.

Propping a hip on the arm of the oversized couch, Logan watched Ava through the living room window. It was obvious she loved her family and they were concerned about her. Especially now that he had entered the picture. Interesting.

"Logan."

He couldn't help the smile that spread across his face at having her to himself. She wasn't screaming his name. He would take that as a point in his favor.

"You knew my family was still here. You should've left when you saw the cars in the driveway. How could you do that to me? I wasn't ready to tell them about us."

He hadn't done anything wrong in his opinion, but years of bedside training webinars kicked in at her unnatural calm tone. *Tread carefully.*

"Check your phone." He pointed to the two-toned wood console against the living area wall. "I called and texted you before I left home. The wait till cover of night and I'll sneak you in the house scenario will never happen."

She briefly glanced away from him in the direction of exhibit A. He could see her cellphone screen was illuminated denoting she had a message.

"You wouldn't deem my presence an intrusion if you had extended an invitation."

"You presumptuous man."

Her voice was taut with unnecessary restraint and she was biting her lip again. He took her hands and gently pulled, closing the distance between them.

"I am when it pertains to you," he said, in a low voice. "I apologize for telling your family about us before you had the opportunity." Suspicion peppered his thoughts. Why didn't she want them to know about him? Ava wasn't Brooke. A cheating fiancée and lying friends were his past. With Ava he could have a semblance of happiness. She wouldn't purposely deceive him.

"I haven't told anyone about *us*," she motioned with air quotes, "Us didn't exist until twenty-four hours ago."

"A lot can happen in a day." He couldn't keep his hands off her. He wanted her closer. Settling her between his spread legs, he placed his hands on her shoulders, delivering long, smooth strokes to her arms. "Not to upset you, but I am not sorry that they know about us. I will not be a secret, Ava." *Never again.*

She sighed, "That's not what I'm asking. Not really. It's just they might get the impression you'll be around for a while."

Where was she going with this? He'd told her and her family he wasn't going anywhere.

"I will be. Get used to it," he said, in a slow matter of fact tone. "You can meet my family when you are ready. I was ready."

"I don't know Logan. We are just getting to know each other."

Last night she knew she wanted him.

"What is it you don't know?" This was not what he had planned to talk about during their time together. When he'd arrived he was confident about them, but the encroaching uncertainty had him tense. He needed to know she was with him, that she wanted him to be a part of her life. No doubts, no boundaries. Being with Ava threatened to plunge his controlled, well-orchestrated life into chaos.

The words escaped Ava, how to explain the trepidation she felt about them being together. The demons she struggled against were complex, but her words were simple.

"I don't think I'm ready for you." She saw the green of his eyes expand, enough depth in them to carry her deep into an abyss.

"You lied to me? What's happened since last night? Or can't I trust you to tell me the truth."

"Logan." She kept her voice subdued. "Stop now before we both say something we'll regret later." The sudden rise in tension had the scar on her lip burning. "Please, let's sit down and talk." He didn't budge. Looking at his face she saw frustration, but there was something else there. Not sure what she was seeing, she reached for his face. He stilled her hands in midair.

"You said you would try. That you would give our relationship a chance."

"I know what I said. It wasn't a lie. This isn't how I envisioned my family finding out about us." Disillusioned, she pulled her hands free of his. She didn't know how to do this. What did she know about a normal relationship?

"It's done now. There's nothing to stress over at this point. Besides, I think they like me."

"Are you kidding me? News flash, watch your tone with a black woman's family. My daddy was about to rip you a new one."

"I know, but he didn't. They like me. What's the story with 'A' names in your family?"

"My oldest sister Shaylah is the adventurous one in the bunch. I think my parents were too tired to be creative by the time Aron and I were born. You ask a lot of questions. I just realized it applies to more than when we are at work."

"Caught unaware is more damaging than you can ever image."

"Why is that?" A dark shadow crossed his face and she thought he wouldn't respond.

"Asking questions is the quickest way to gather information. In the know is my chosen state of being. For example, Aron's your younger brother." She nodded her head in agreement. "How much younger?"

"Eighteen months. Although with his comedy routine you would think he was fifteen. He and Zari laugh about everything since they got married last June."

"See how that worked. When you ask questions you get answers. I am a researcher at heart. Information addiction is a signature trait and I don't do well with secrets. Forewarned is forearmed."

"Thanks for the heads up." Ava would be sure to monitor her comments. No way, did she want anyone researching her past. She didn't want anyone to know what happened six years ago.

"Do you think I'm too old for you?"

Logan was too persistent, too irresistible, too sexy, but not too old. Marcus had been a junior at Florida Agricultural & Mechanical University when she'd met him her freshman year. Only three years older than her eighteen years, but decades apart in life experience.

"Your seemingly bizarre question about my age kept me puzzled until today. Your mother seemed concerned because of our age difference."

Her mother was thinking about how easily Marcus had led her astray.

"Age is not a factor for me." Her family acted as a private security force, keeping her from stumbling into the land mines of life. After Marcus, she had needed their protection to function, but somehow it had continued. Now she felt more of a hostage and she didn't need to be rescued. They saw her as a victim, needing a family of advocates.

"I thought so, after meeting your would be suitor."

He was laughing at her.

"I know I can't count on you for senior citizen discounts. No more questions doctor."

"No more questions for tonight, but I want to know everything about you. I can tell you about the Masters family to balance the scorecard."

"Okay. But talk to me while I clean up from dinner." He seemed reluctant to release his hold, but he followed her as she moved to the dining table cluttered with dishes. Thank goodness there wasn't a lot of food left over. The last few slices of Zari's cake were gone. Deacon Hill had struck again.

"My parents, Robert and Maribelle, are from a small town in South

Carolina. They've been married for thirty-seven years."

"How often do you visit them?"

"My parents moved to Shell Cove years ago when my father was still practicing medicine."

They both grabbed an armful of dishes making several trips to the kitchen sink.

"They live at the Reserves on the Cove."

Ava stilled. The Reserves was an exclusive, estate home community complete with a private beach, yacht club and golf course. It was the wealthiest community between Northeast Florida and the southern Georgia border.

"Wow." Her voice sounded distant. "The Reserves is luxury living. It must be nice to live on the beach." Damp cloth in hand, head down, she wiped off the now empty dining table.

She and Logan were from two different worlds. Literally, there was a toll parkway that separated The Reserves from the city limits of Shell Cove. Logan was in the "rich people" stratosphere.

"I don't live on the beach. I live in Avondale."

She knew the area well. Avondale was a historic district along the banks of the Dasius River. The community brimmed with antique shops, boutiques, and gourmet coffee shops. It was home to the next generation of affluent Shell Cove residents that preferred the city life to suburbia. It was the inland rich peoples' neighborhood. As he told her of his family, she was careful to keep a distance between them.

"Come here, Ava."

Why did he want to hold her when it was even more apparent why they should be apart?

"Why?"

"I want to hold you close to me."

Logan was at her back now. His all too familiar scent intoxicatingly seductive. He pulled the cloth free of her hand and turned her to face him.

"That's enough talk. Your Granny Lou has the observation skills of a trained sniper. She wouldn't let me near you. I've been craving a taste of your lips all day. Give your man a proper kiss."

Obeying his command, she rose up on her toes, hungry for a taste of him.

"I didn't say you're my man." She grinned. He didn't. When she would have kissed him he turned away. He sank down on a dining room chair and pulled her across his lap. His left hand gently came to rest on her hip. She had disappointed him. *Hopeless.* Marcus's words echoed through her mind. The room felt cold now. His head sank along with her heart. She would never make Logan happy. He touched her face, softly stroking her cheek as he raised her chin.

"Look at me Ava."

Not wanting to see his disappointment, she resisted.

"Look at me," he repeated.

She was reluctant but followed his instruction.

"Tell me what I am in your life. I've been clear about my feelings for you. I know you are attracted to me. Are we together in building this relationship?"

The heat of her conscience burned like a spotlight. He had to see the pulse thumping at her neck.

The directness she had appreciated in Logan this afternoon with her family had lost its luster now that it was aimed at her. She fidgeted on his lap, afraid to voice her response.

"Don't toy with me. Give me your answer."

"We are from two different worlds Logan. You can enter and exit my world without notice. But … but the type of people you have access to probably don't associate with everyday people."

A small tic formed in his jaw.

"I assume you are referring to yourself. Meaning black people, working people, people with less money than me?" he questioned.

Not wanting to make things worse, she nodded her head.

"I save lives for a living. Not one is more valuable than the other. When I studied at Johns Hopkins, Graham and I spent hundreds of hours caring for people from all walks of life."

"Who's Graham?" She frowned.

"A friend. You'll meet him."

He sounded so sure. Ava remained quiet, letting the silence extend between them.

"My brother Darwin served in the United States Navy. Defending this country for people like you and me. And so did one of my best friends, Gideon Rice."

"Your brother was in the Navy? I would like to talk with him about his experience and I know Gideon. He's one of the adult psychiatrists at SCMC."

"That's the one. He and Darwin served together."

"Gideon was in the Navy?" She stared at him in surprise.

"The Marine Corps."

"That is so awesome that they both served in the military. It's been a dream of mine to serve in the Navy Nurse Corps. Janna Williamson, my roommate in college, is a Navy lieutenant serving in Okinawa, Japan." A dream that she hoped to make a reality.

"So now that I've proven myself worthy of your affection, tell me that you want this relationship. Can you tell me that you need me, the way I need you?"

He didn't look playful. Ava noted the tension lines around his mouth. He wanted an admission.

The question hit the intended target with the force of lightning, dividing want and need. Did she want Logan? Without a doubt she desired him. More than any other man she'd met. Did she need Logan? He saw her as a woman. Not a wounded bird, to be nursed back to health. Did she want to be with him? He gave her honesty and she could give no less.

"Yes."

He shook her gently demanding the rest.

"I want to be with you Logan."

"Prove it. You make the first move, come and get me."

Ava crossed her arms behind his neck and kissed him. The depth of her desire for him flowed freely through her, she didn't hold back, allowing him to share in the experience. His reciprocity stirred her sexual need to a boiling point. She rubbed her body across his chest, delighted when she felt her nipples harden. A burst of arousal started in her belly then spread with the voracity of a wildfire to her sex. Her nails pressed deep in his skin as throaty sounds spilled from her lips.

He groaned as he broke off the kiss.

"Touché, sweetheart." His eyes had darkened with need to a rich emerald.

"If we don't stop now neither one of us will be available for work tomorrow. I have an early morning case and a busy clinic schedule. I want us to do something special this week. Whatever you decide is fine with me."

"Kathryn has me working twelve hour shifts Monday through Thursday. I can cook dinner for us on Friday."

"Dinner on Friday works if it's at my place."

She paused, not sure she wanted to cross over into his domain.

"Ava, don't make this more difficult than it has to be. We are together. Come over to my place on Friday. I'll help you prepare dinner."

"I cook alone."

"Not anymore."

He captured her lips in another heated assault on her senses. He definitely was packing an igniter switch imprinted with her name on it. It was Ava that broke the kiss this time.

"Enough with the hot kisses, back to dinner plans for this week."

"There's nothing else to decide. You cook the food and I'll eat it. Relationships can be easy."

She stood then, backing out of his reach.

"Where are you going? There's still more kissing to be had before I leave."

"It's after nine o'clock and I have to clean the kitchen, before I starch and iron my scrubs for work in the morning."

"No wonder you are always wrinkle-free. You are worse than Darwin. Scrubs are supposed be wrinkled. Hence, the name scrubs."

She gestured with her head at the front door. "Go home, so you can be on time for your morning surgery."

"Maybe I'll help you clean the kitchen before I leave?" The sparkle in his eye said his type of help would result in her needing a clean-up.

"My grandmother spoke the truth; I don't need any help in the kitchen. I have a system to righting the house after Sunday dinners. The kitchen will be spotless in under forty minutes."

He stood to his feet, took her in his arms and kissed her breathless. Her knees were trembling when he finished.

"I'll see you on the unit after my case. Sleep well, sweetheart."

Since that first night with Logan, she didn't think she would ever sleep well alone, ever again.

Ava was preparing for bed when she heard the soft beeping of the bedside telephone. Abandoning the glass doors leading to the rear deck and garden, she rounded her queen-sided bed. She dove for the cordless receiver before the answering machine picked up the call.

"Logan?" She pulled deep, slowing breaths into her lungs.

"Baby girl it's Dad, and I'm glad to know you are home alone."

"Hey, Daddy what's up?" Ava collapsed onto the bed.

"Why are you out of breath?"

"I had to make a mad dash across my bedroom when the phone rang." Rolling over, she pressed her back into the cradle of the mattress with the phone at her ear.

"About Logan."

She sat up tall at the mention of Logan.

"What about him, Daddy?" This had never happened before. Andrew Walters didn't say much, but when he did everyone listened.

"Ava, there are several types of men in the world. The one I met at your house tonight knows what he wants. Do not play with this man. He's thinking forever. It's written all over him that he considers you to be his. He's possessive of you and don't think I didn't realize he was not invited to dinner. If you are not sure you want to be with this man, your brother and I will run him off, just say the word. Your momma and I will cancel our vacation if you need us to be here for you."

Her father had retired after thirty-eight years with the United States Postal Service. Her parents had spent the better part of two years planning for their RV drive through twenty-four states in twenty weeks.

"Daddy, I would never ask you to do that, but more importantly I don't need you and Mom to put your life on hold for me." Teetering on the precipice, she took the plunge. No taking the words back next week. "I really like him."

"I know baby girl. He appears to be a fine young man. If he makes you happy and you have chosen him," he put emphasis on his words, "then your mother and I welcome him with open arms."

"Thanks Daddy, I love you."

"I love you more, good night baby."

She'd made a decision. She had chosen Logan. Now she had to keep him from discovering all the ugliness of her past.

# CHAPTER NINE

Monday morning came faster than she expected after the high of "Ava has a man and the family knows it" faded. The pediatric unit was bustling with nurses, physicians, and technicians wheeling gurneys for the day's procedures. The carnival of the morning quickly gave way to organized chaos as the nursing staff assumed their duties and readied each patient for the day ahead. Food tray warmers littered the corridors creating a well-intentioned obstacle course. Her stomach growled in protest reminding her that her energy expenditure far exceeded the veggie omelet she'd consumed for breakfast. On cue, a familiar voice called to her from the supply room.

"Ava, you game for a hot lunch date to celebrate your application submission?"

Approaching the supply room, Ava raised one finger to her lips reminding Spencer Hayeswood this was their secret.

He mimicked turning a key, throwing it away and burying it with paw movements. Every woman needed a platonic male friend and Spencer fit the bill.

"I don't have time for a hot date, but if you're available we can go together." Ava was comfortable teasing with him. When she started on staff more than a year ago, somehow Spencer ended up on the inside of her perimeter defenses. She was grateful for his friendship.

Registered Nurse and female enthusiast, Spencer was fun to be with, always making her laugh with the grandiose version of every aspect of his life. He had an arsenal of "the woman of the month" stories.

"Spencer, Lina probably hasn't had lunch. Did you tell her to meet us in the cafe?"

"I called, but she's not working the psychiatric unit today."

He talked as he secured the supply room with his digital key code. Missing supplies were grounds for dismissal. Each nurse was assigned a key code to track those removed and returned supplies.

"The charge nurse said she called in sick yesterday and today." He placed the key card behind his name badge, and headed for the fire safe doors.

Wrinkling her brow, Ava thought back to the last time she'd talked with Lina. It had been more than a week. Her life with Logan overshadowed the fact that Lina had been scarce for days.

They left the unit, walking the three flights of stairs to the lobby cafe. Ava found a table behind a row of planters at the rear of the cafeteria. Spencer would find her after he grabbed food from the hot meal line.

This was the first moment she had been off her feet in six hours. Kathryn Quest, the charge nurse had assumed responsibility for Ava's team so she decided to make wise use of the time by fueling her body.

She allowed the mental shields to lower and the stress of the morning to flow out of her like the river to the sea. Visions of her body wrapped around Logan invaded her mind. She recalled the taste of him; the finest white chocolate with a hint of smooth liqueur. He had made a permanent imprint on her taste buds last night. Heat rose to her face causing a smile to grace her lips.

"I hope I put that smile on your face."

Dread churned in her gut as the owner of that voice registered in her mind. The hairs at her nape stood on end, her palms felt cool and damp. Looking up, Randall Lester stood over her. Dressed in a pinstriped, three-piece dark gray suit he looked harmless until you saw his flared nostrils and squinted glower.

"Finally I get you alone. You've been cavorting with a certain surgeon on staff. That's a poor decision for a nurse in your position. You wouldn't want to jeopardize his career or research funding."

Her eyes locked on Randall's bearded face a second before they widened in fear. He saw it before she could rein it in. The smile on his face brimmed with malice.

"I am not interested in what you're offering," she stammered. She quickly rose from her seat, almost colliding with the chairs behind her.

Ava scanned the cafe. Spencer was too far away to help.

"Not so fast, my pet. Your application packet was delivered to me this morning." He extended his hand to grab her wrist.

Preoccupied with getting away from him, she couldn't respond to the sinking feeling in her gut.

"Don't touch her."

A huge breath of relief left her lungs as that distinctive baritone sounded in her ear.

"Come here, Ava."

Mentally she reached for Logan before she took the first step. Ava spun on her heel, Logan stood, rage clear on his face, the muscles in his arms bulging underneath his lab coat. She did as he commanded coming to stand slightly behind him.

"Randall."

A tremor ran through Ava at the steel in Logan's voice.

"Stay away from Ava. Don't come near her again. Ever."

Anger rolled off Logan in pulsing waves. With a vicious snarl aimed at the other man, he said,

"Leave. Now."

Randall turned to leave, but not before he leveled a lethal stare at her. He wasn't done with her yet. His stare promised retribution.

Then a bizarre expression crossed Randall's face.

"I'll give your regards to Sam and Rebecca," he said to Logan.

Ava didn't understand the statement, but she felt Logan's grip tighten on her arm. Obviously, the message was significant to Logan.

Logan was dangerously close to losing his temper, and his bid for chief surgeon. What was Randall trying to do with Ava? Was he fixated on her, or was something else going on? He needed answers from her. But first, he had to calm down or he would find Randall and make him regret he ever knew a woman named Ava Walters.

Slowly, the hum of the cafeteria broke into his senses. The aroma of high fat beef and cooking oil drifted across his nose. Good, now that he was calm, he would get some answers from Ava about Randall's advances.

"Ava, is everything all right?"

Logan recognized the voice without looking over his shoulder. Spencer was the only male pediatric nurse Logan had ever met. The man approached at speed if the rattling food tray was any indication. Logan turned to see the man rushing towards them precariously balancing recycled cardboard food carriers and what appeared to be two fountain drinks and three bottles of water.

"No, but it will be," Logan responded to Spencer's question. Ava had been mute since the incident with Randall.

"Did something go wrong between you and the Operations Director?"

Spencer spoke to him, but his eyes were trained on Ava. When neither of them responded, Spencer looked from her face to settle a frown at him before glancing in the direction Randall had gone. No doubt he was trying to piece all the players and the visual into a workable diagnosis. Logan recognized the moment Spencer knew something bad had happened to Ava, and Randall was involved.

"Ava tell me what's going on?"

Spencer's voice had gone soothing. His tone was too informal from Logan's perspective. Another man comforting Ava. Encroaching on his territory. Had Ava been in a relationship with Spencer? Not liking the level of concern coming from the other man, Logan held Ava closer.

"You were with Randall at the party. I saw you two together."

Spencer thought to question his woman. Not in this lifetime.

Logan growled in response, "She was not with him."

Ava shook her head, as if clearing away a web. The shock of starring as the female lead in a workplace drama appeared to be wearing off. She was at least responding, though non-verbally.

"He won't leave me alone," she said with a slight shake her head.

"But, at the party, I saw … wait, has he been harassing you? I don't know what to say. I saw you with him, I assumed. Sorry, baby girl, I messed up."

Spencer placed the tray on a small rectangle table, taking a step toward

Ava with outstretched arms.

"Thanks Logan for getting that jerk away from her. I didn't realize he's been bothering her."

Logan stepped in front of Ava, blocking his path.

"There is no need to thank me. Ava is mine to protect."

Spencer's narrowed stare zoned in on him then Ava.

"Ava?"

Spencer's tone reeked of doubt. He wanted confirmation that Ava was his? Logan had staked his claim with her family. He'd stake his claim with her friend and anyone else that dare challenge that she was his.

Logan turned slightly moving Ava to his side. Cradling her face in both his hands, he placed a kiss on her forehead.

"Are you okay, sweetheart?"

Spencer's expression registered comprehension.

Logan watched as Ava scanned the nearby tables. The way she tensed, she must have recognized a nosy onlooker. She offered a slight nod in answer to his question as she removed his hands and lowered them to his side as inconspicuously as possible.

"I need to hear the words, Ava." He should have been the one practicing discretion, but it wasn't possible with two men wanting something from Ava. Granted Spencer's actions were noble compared to Randall's. No one would ever take another woman from him, Logan vowed.

"I'm okay because you saved me, again. I wish he would leave me alone," Ava said to Logan.

Spencer's mouth rounded into a big "O" before he turned away leaving the two of them standing in the cafe.

"Why did you leave for lunch without me?"

Logan stared at her, his eyes soft with concern. How did women navigate relationships? She could use some clues as to how to manage a boyfriend…a possessive boyfriend.

"You said your morning was booked solid with cases and the clinic. I didn't expect to see you today."

"Sweetheart, there's not a day that will go by without me seeing you."

She studied his face. From his steady gaze to the firm set of his jaw, everything about Logan was sure and confident. Trustworthy.

He placed another gentle kiss on her forehead. And as pitiful as it looked, a kiss from him made her feel safe. Protected.

"Did you eat your lunch?"

"No. I was waiting on Spencer when Randall ambushed me." An involuntary shudder racked her body when she said his name. "Maybe I should look for another job."

Logan's hands fisted at his side. If he ground his teeth any harder, he would need dentures.

"You are not quitting your job. You'll remain on staff, with me. I'll take care of this."

His voice was unwavering.

"Logan, what are you talking about? I don't want you to get tangled up in my drama. I found this job. I can find another." Unlike his kiss, her words did nothing to ease Logan's stiff posture. "He's gone Logan, relax."

"He wants you and I don't think he will stop without an incentive. He's dangerous."

Logan's jaw was clenched. He looked at her briefly before he darted another look behind and around her. Like he expected an enemy to attack at any moment.

Ava's eyes fell on the table to her right. It was empty. She raised her hand caressing the tension from his neck hoping to dispel his anger. When that didn't work she pressed her lips into his. At his surprise, she pushed into his mouth and slowly stroked his tongue. She quickly pulled away when he tugged at the bun pinned neatly at her nape. They both were panting.

"I love your hair loose and flowing."

"I'll remember that for Friday." She gestured to the abandoned food tray. "Now that I have your attention," she said, "eat with me. Spencer left food for two."

"You are a minx." Amusement hinted in his voice. "Sit," he commanded. "I'll stay while you eat."

"Spencer won't come back. I think he feels bad because he saw me cornered by Randall at the party. I'll reassure him when I return to the unit."

He raised an eyebrow. "Reassure him how?"

"Don't get cheeky, Logan. Spencer is my friend. Nothing more. Please don't give me a hard time."

"There's nothing hard about it. We all need our friends, but Spencer can get his own woman to reassure his pride. You are mine."

Glancing around the café, Ava noted more than a few eyes on them. Everyone on staff would know she was his by the end of the day.

Having escorted Ava back to the unit, Logan didn't second guess his next action. Exiting the medical center via the third floor breezeway he entered the administrative complex directly behind the facility. Ava had slowly caught and released her lower lip between her teeth again. She'd done the same worried mannerism twice before in his presence. He realized that wasn't a good thing. The urge to protect her burned with the intensity of a wild fire.

Logan crossed into a long hallway lined with glass office suites. Against the gleaming marble floors, his rubber clogs were silent. Several of the foundation board member names and titles lay under the etched SCMC logo. When he reached the large office at the end of the hallway, he identified himself at the security box discretely located to the left of the privacy etched glass door. He stepped into the well-appointed river view office, as familiar with these surroundings as he was with his own. He felt the weight of eyes watching him before the man spoke.

"What is this about Logan?"

The voice was refined and seasoned by age and experience.

"I need your help with something. I don't have all the details, but even if I did I would not disclose them."

Logan saw an eyebrow raise with concern.

"You know you only have to ask, but I don't understand the need for secrecy on the details."

Logan remained quiet calculating the best path to revealing his true intent. He would start with direct.

"A friend has been targeted by Randall Lester."

It only took a moment for Logan's meaning to register on the other man's face.

"Randall is a formidable adversary. At this juncture in your career, establishing and maintaining alliances are critical to your selection. You sure you want to cross paths with him? He is a shrewd businessman and an influential foundation board member. How invested is your friend with the medical center?"

Logan thought about that. He didn't know Ava's future plans at SCMC, but he knew he wasn't letting her go. And Randall would never have her.

"Whatever instrument of power he has over her I want it eliminated."

With that statement, the other man came to his feet.

"Her. Who is this woman to you?"

Logan's skin heated with the laser dissection aimed at him from across the large mahogany desk separating him from his soon to be accomplice.

"That business is my own," he said in an unquestioning tone.

The other man either missed the hint or didn't care because his next statement had the lines around Logan's mouth tightening.

"Not if you are asking me for help."

"Ava is a pediatric staff nurse. We are involved." Neither man spoke as the gravity of his confession compressed the vast space.

"Your mother will not be pleased."

That was an understatement. The truth was she would be furious, but his family would have to adjust. He was keeping Ava. He mentally spoke the words as much to himself as the universe conspiring against him.

"I know, but Ava stays with me." He ran his fingers through his hair, frustrated that he was trapped between his family responsibilities, the career he wanted, and the woman he needed more than all of them.

"What about Rebecca?"

He had all but forgotten about Rebecca Lynn Holbrook. Even now the mention of her name invoked little emotion.

"Rebecca is your choice, not mine. Ava is the woman I want."

His father released a sigh, then bent his long frame, so similar to Logan's, back to his top grain leather seat.

"Son, think about what you may be sacrificing. Sam Holbrook will not forgive a slight to his only daughter. The Masters and the Holbrook family have an established mutually beneficial business relationship. Your securing the board position is an integral part of that business agreement. You don't know this Ava."

Logan was getting pissed off.

"I know her well enough."

"A lot of unknown variables can hide behind the word *enough*. Maybe, she has some history with Randall. His oversight extends to staff hiring and promotion."

Logan's jaw clenched and unclenched at the insinuation that Ava had some shady involvement with Randall.

"My time is wasted here." Logan turned on his heel.

"Wait. Your decision to become involved with this Ava person has far-reaching negative implications to your career and the entire family."

Logan halted his departure, but he did not turn to face his father.

"Consider this before you lay claim to this woman and toss aside a perfectly acceptable match with Rebecca. There could be more to the story than you are privy to."

His father's would be wisdom echoed through his mind. Could all this be a deal gone wrong between Ava and Randall?

"No," he replied to his father and himself. "Ava is mine and no one else's."

"I'll look into it."

"This isn't about fact finding on Ava and her family tree, Dad. I want the problem fixed. No one threatens Ava."

Ava was numb. She robotically logged into the closest electronic documentation station, reviewing each patient's status updates during her absence. She should end this "thing" with Logan. Ava had no doubt that Randall would act on his threat. She knew Logan wanted the foundation board position though he rarely spoke of it with her.

"Ava."

The pediatric nurse manager approached from the nurse's station situated at the center of the unit. Each patient care pod consisted of three rooms and each suite held two single motorized beds. The pediatric unit had eight total pods.

"Hey, Kathryn. Thanks for covering my lunch break. I was just about finished up with my chart review. Can you give me a brief report on each patient before I resume care?" Ava offered a smile she didn't feel.

"No problem. Everything was quiet while you were away. Your favorite patient," the short, curvy, dark skinned woman pointed in the direction of the corner room Monique occupied. "She rang the call bell twice asking for you."

"Thanks, I'll check on her first."

A barely perceptible frown formed on Kathryn's face.

"What?" Ava asked curiously. Kathryn had never made a negative comment about how she interacted with her patients.

"Ava, she's getting attached to you. What is she going to do when you're selected for commissioning?"

Ava raised a stiff index finger to her lips looking directly at Kathryn as she mimicked a downward motion with her left hand. Kathryn was one of two people that knew she had completed the commissioning packet. The last thing Ava needed was for word to spread that she was pursuing a military career.

"I appreciate the vote of confidence but the election process is competitive. I really need to keep my submission packet under the radar. If I'm not selected this year there's no harm or foul to my employment at SCMC."

"Sorry Ava, I'll be more careful."

"About Monique, she's a sixteen-year-old girl with a multi-break arm fracture, pins and wires holding it together, compliments of her ex-boyfriend. She needs a friend on the inside, right now."

Ava identified with this girl more than she could ever tell anyone. She had trusted a man once. A man that asked for everything, and when she didn't give it he tried to destroy her. Physically and emotionally. She'd fought back, and yet she was the one left broken and bleeding on the floor. Stepped over with the disregarded trash. Her courage, self-esteem, and self-worth all left in shambles.

Maybe, Ava would have healed if she had more visible signs of the damage her relationship with Marcus Grant had wrought on her psyche. The scar to her right upper lip tingled at the thought of him. Her biggest fear was that Marcus had been right. That she was naive and worthless. A pretty burden that everyone had to make accommodations for because she was too weak to make her own decisions. She would never be of use to anyone for the long-term. Always measuring up short and never being enough.

"Hey?"

Ava broke loose from her dark memories at the touch to her elbow. Kathryn must have been trying to get her attention to no avail.

"You should probably go see what Monique wants. The next round of medications are due at two o'clock."

Ava smiled as she turned in the direction of Monique's room. No more thoughts of Randall or Marcus. Her patient needed her, trusted her judgment, and she wouldn't let her down. This she was good at.

Ava knocked twice on the door, and then entered the well lived-in room. Greeting cards, a 7-inch tablet in a hot pink case, nail polish bottles, teen girl magazines, and a homemade afghan littered the bed. Monique's room needed its own personal housekeeping staff.

"Ava!" The girl's eyes sparkled.

How did she manage to stay so cheerful after everything she had endured at the hands of someone she trusted?

"You rang?"

"I want to talk about boys."

"Don't know any." Ava laughed.

"It's one boy. His name is Jason. I met him during sophomore Science Technology Engineering and Math (STEM) orientation over twelve months ago. Anyway he's in my calculus class this year and he's been texting me every day since I got admitted. Today he hinted at wanting to come visit me here. He's cute and tall. And smart. He reads like five books a week. What do you think I should do?"

*Oh my Todd, she can't be serious.* Ava thought it was ten years too soon.

She couldn't wrap her head around Monique wanting a boy anywhere near her. It had been six years and Ava was still uncomfortable with most men. Fear and insecurity were constant companions. How had this sixteen-year-old girl found the strength to move past the trauma and reclaim her life? Monique was seeking the attention of a young man. Ava almost laughed at the irony. Monique had done what Ava had deemed impossible. Monique had found a way to stay anchored in her life, not allowing the hurt and pain of the past to push her off balance. The textbooks were right. Children were more resilient.

"How do you feel, considering recent events?" The delivery was awkward, but Ava thought it prudent to avoid the mention of specifics regarding the assault. She leaned forward, curious to hear Monique's answer. Monique positioned herself more upright, propping her injured limb on one bent knee.

"Nervous. Jason may not be into me the same way. Junior prom is in May. If I get to know him better, I'll ask him to be my date."

The inner workings of a teenaged girl's mind had Ava baffled.

"Are you afraid about Jason coming for a visit?"

To be alone with someone with the strength to overpower you. Hurt you. But, Ava didn't say those words aloud.

"The first time I was in the hospital, the day of my accident, I was afraid. I thought what did I do wrong that my friend would hurt me? I told my Dad how I felt. And you know what he said?"

"Tell me." Anxious to hear the pearl of wisdom from the mouth of babes, Ava sat on the edge of the bed. Eyes glued to Monique's.

"Dad said to choose not to be afraid. It was my decision. That bad things happen to us, but we choose how to deal with them."

"Really?"

"Yep and I'm not going to be afraid. So, is it okay to kiss a boy in a hospital?"

Ava laughed then. "This is a conversation for you and your mother."

"Come on Ava, my mom is deployed. I can't talk to my Dad about boys. We're friends and stuff. What did you do when Dr. Masters wanted to come see you? You know, outside of work?"

Ava was dumbfounded. How had she known about Logan? Was Monique fishing for information? Ava narrowed her eyes looking at the girl with suspicion wrapped in a smile.

"Why would you think Dr. Masters and I see each other outside of work?" Ava sincerely hoped the staff wasn't cognizant of her deliberate avoidance of Logan. Had she inadvertently revealed a detail of her personal life in the presence of a patient?

"If he's not your boyfriend, he wants to be."

"Monique Faulkner, Dr. Masters and I have a professional relationship." No way was she confirming the girl's suspicions.

"But … I can tell that he likes you. He watches you. I saw this episode on Animal Planet and the male lion watches before they claim the lioness by biting her on the neck. Or something like that."

Ava laughed. "I'm sure Dr. Masters would not appreciate that comparison."

"Okay. I guess I was wrong. But, his jaw twitches if another man comes within ten feet of you. He's such a guy."

Ava didn't know what to make of the observations of a sixteen-year-old girl. The very accurate observations that she would not discuss with her adolescent patient, thank you very much. After that display in the cafe, he *was* such a guy. Logan was protective, attentive, with a little cave man bravado thrown in for good measure. Perfect.

"You certainly see a lot from your bed," Ava said clearing her throat. It was probably best to end this conversation. "Listen, I have to check on the other patients before I come back with your medications."

"Okay," Monique replied without enthusiasm. "One more question, Ava?"

"Go ahead, I'm listening."

"I overheard Kathryn mention a commissioning packet. Are you leaving?"

"My goodness, you don't miss much, do you?"

"My dad retired from the US Navy. He was a commissioned officer. Are you joining the military?"

"It's a dream of mine to serve as a nurse corps officer in the US Navy. I am applying for commission, but it's a personal decision I decided not to share."

"Oh, I get it. You don't want Dr. Masters to know."

"Monique."

"Okay, okay. I won't mention anything about you and Dr. Masters being together again."

Ava offered a sideways glance before existing the room. Logan couldn't know. He would try and stop her. And she would consider it, for him.

# CHAPTER TEN

Logan didn't want to think about what he would do if Ava ever left him.

"Sweetheart, you are an amazing cook. If you continue cooking for me, my workouts will be extended by an hour."

Looking up from the sink full of dishes, she smiled up at him. He would never tire of seeing those full lips curved up in happiness. Happiness he had a hand in creating.

"Thank you for the compliment, but my cooking is nothing special."

In the three weeks they had been together the woman was still uncomfortable with compliments.

"I disagree. This chef's kitchen has seen more hot meals in three weeks, than in total of the previous five years. How did you learn to cook everything so well?"

She tilted her head before batting those mile-long lashes at him.

"Well ... I'm the direct descendant of an exceptional cook. It's relaxing to smell the combination of spices fill a room. Now, if you don't stop with all the accolades, your new career will be transporting my big head around the city."

She rinsed and stacked dinner plates as she spoke.

"I would carry said big head without complaint." He leaned forward across the counter top, placing a kiss on her forehead. And there was the blush spreading up her neck. It happened every time he touched her. So, he never passed on an opportunity to make contact with her.

Logan's kitchen was spacious with a center island. The double sinks were located in the island making it easy for her to set the kitchen right while he observed from one of the contoured swivel stools.

"I love to cook and you love to eat. We are a perfect pair."

Slack-jawed and momentarily paralyzed, Logan stared at her with open curiosity. Ava's smile slipped away and she stopped with the dishes.

"What is it? Did I say something wrong?"

Logan noticed her hands tighten on the sponge. The corner of her lip trapped between her teeth.

"Nothing is wrong." The sponge plopped in the water, punching a hole in the suds when she released it. Lip released, sponge gone, she was relaxed again.

"It's nice to hear you say we're perfect together. Do you believe it?" An unequivocal *yes* would be the best answer. He was analyzing, deciphering every nuance of her body language. Waiting for her response. A response that was slow in coming.

What did Ava believe about their relationship? She swallowed, not sure how much to divulge of her true feelings. Logan brows drew down low over his eyes at her silence. What could she say that would not leave her vulnerable?

"I believe … I like you, too much for my own sanity."

Work kept her busy, she canned and pickled her garden bounty, she talked with Lina, but she never felt sated until she saw Logan. She felt her resolve weaken every second around him. He was getting to her. Correction, he had gotten to her.

"What do you believe I feel for you?" Posture stiff and sporting a clenched jaw, he didn't look happy with her.

"Logan, you've told me how you feel." She glanced around, uneasy with the topic of discussion. No good deed goes unpunished.

"Answer my question, Ava. What do you believe?"

He would probably tire of her, leave her more of an emotional wreck than she already was.

"I know that you want me. I believe that you are committed to getting what you want."

A version of the truth was better than not answering.

"And after I get what I want. What happens next?"

He had both hands on the counter, boring into her with those piercing green eyes.

"You can't expect me to know that."

She didn't want to know. Thoughts of being tossed aside plagued her the longer they stayed together. And she couldn't bear to think of him with another woman. They operated in two very different worlds. She could be with him, but not forever.

He rose from his stool, leaving the last of his whiskey sour on the counter. He walked toward her never dropping his gaze. The brush of his knuckles against her cheek had her holding her breath.

"Remember what I'm about to tell you. I keep what I claim. No one takes it and I don't let it go." Heaven help them both if she claimed him back.

As he moved away she released the breath she had been holding. It was over. The fluttering in her chest would stop in a moment. The tumbler she was washing slipped through her fingers as his groin spooned her backside and his hand descended into the water. Her back stiffened.

"Logan what are you doing? You know I like to clean my own kitchen."

"I know what you like, but this is my kitchen. You asked me not to praise you. I'm helping you wash the dishes tonight. We'll finish faster with four hands."

He was stroking her wet forearms. Leaning back into his body heat, a tingle of pleasure skirted across her senses and her legs went weak.

"You can praise, but..." Her mind went blank as he pulled his hands from the warm water and placed them over her breasts. The water quickly seeped through the thin fabric of her spaghetti strapped tank top. Her skin heated. And yes, her pulse rate jumped like a cat on a hot tin roof. Nipples beaded and pushed against the lace cups of her bra, she instinctively moved closer to his heat.

"Logan?" Shaky voice, shaky legs, burning inside, this was not good.

"Yes, sweetheart."

He didn't waste any time pushing her bra aside to cup her breasts. He rolled taut buds between his fingers. Her breasts and her sex were on their own invisible pulley system. Each tug on her nipples delivered a corresponding pull, low and deep in her core. His fingers moved with firm, sure strokes over her peaks. Her breasts swelled to fill his hands. In a word, magic. Her body transported to another space in time.

"Oh, that feels good." Each time he moved, his manhood bumped against her bottom, sending electrified pulses through her veins.

"We both are going to have very large heads. Your response is great for my ego."

His voice just above a whisper, heated her more. Flushed and panting, with a human igniter wrapped around her body, there had to be steam rising from the sink because she was about to burn right out of her clothes.

"I can't think with your hands on me, you know." Her mind screamed for him to move away, while her traitorous body roared for him to keep working his magic.

"Don't think, feel."

He lifted her feet off the ground and placed her on the cool granite covering the kitchen island. His eyes, darkened with passion, caressed her skin as he pulled the straps of the tank down her arms. His handsome face, with that chiseled jaw was more breathtaking covered in a five o'clock shadow. His strong fingers adeptly released the front clasp of her bra. And she moaned as the constricting material fell away from her body revealing the mounds beneath.

"You are breathtaking."

His voice was low and silky. Swallowing, she met his gaze.

"And you are unbelievable. I struggle with the idea that you want me."

The kiss was deep, thorough, and promising. He pulled back, and she leaned forward seeking contact before he came into focus.

"Believe it, because it will never change."

His voice was unwavering, his eyes alert. Shoulders back as if challenging her to deny his declaration.

The warmth from his hands enveloped her breasts. She hissed at the heat of his touch and he captured every sound with his mouth. The feel of him kneading her breasts in a slow sensual pattern was pure intoxication. With each caress the pressure he applied intensified. She moaned. Her eyes drifted closed as she gave herself over to his ministrations. A soft pinch had her eyes opening, not in pain, but shear sexual excitement.

"I more than want you, Ava. I crave your scent, your touch, and your body. Everything."

He moved to capture her lips. Overwhelmed by his need for her, she turned her face away. She should stop, before she became a casualty of lust. Quickly followed by heartbreak.

"Stay put, Ava." Two strong hands on her hips brought her unbelievably close to his growing anatomy. If she could put a little distance between, maybe she could regain her equilibrium. Doubtful, but wishful thinking was free.

"The alcohol. You've nursed that drink all night." Okay it wasn't the best excuse. Redirecting Logan wasn't a skill she had mastered.

"First, a man does not nurse anything. Second, you will taste me. Nothing else."

Without further explanation he claimed her lips. This kiss was akin to opening the floodgate on the Hoover Dam. It was devastating. He'd ruined her. She couldn't kiss anyone over twelve months of age for as long as she lived.

The slow smile that spread across his gorgeous full lips said that had been his intention.

The tug on her nipples reignited his spell. Chasing each ragged breath, her eyes met his briefly before sliding to half-mast as the pressure gentled and intensified at a rhythmic pace. Then everything stopped. She opened her eyes to discover him watching. Noting her responses to everything he did. She wanted to demand he continue.

"Your verdict, madam?"

A gleam in his eyes and the relaxed posture spoke of his confidence in a positive report.

"You taste delicious." She could package his kind of passion to carry around her neck. Heck, she might hang a few vials on a charm bracelet in case of emergencies.

"You want to try one of the cute ladies' drinks the next time we are out?"

"With my history for mishaps, one drink of alcohol would probably result in me being a near drowning victim in Queens Bay." She hesitated sharing her complete thought. One bold gesture a day was her limit. "Besides … I like the way we drink." She felt the heat on her neck creep to her cheeks.

"You mean from my mouth, to yours?"

A nod was all she could give, because the smoldering look in his eyes threatened to topple her off the counter top.

"Taste." The only word he muttered before plunging back into her mouth. Breaching her defenses and going below the radar. She wanted to go as deep as he was willing to take her.

With him assaulting her mouth and those rhythmic pulls and strokes at her breasts again, she had to disengage from the kiss. She was making sounds no lady should be capable of producing. She was a hairline fracture away from melting into a puddle of chocolate, when a hot, wet mouth closed around her right breast. A throaty moan tore from her lips, and she pressed herself deeper into his mouth, grabbing his nape to hold him close.

"Oh my Todd."

He sucked hard on her nipple, the sensation bordering on pain.

"Logan," his name released on a hiss.

She groaned her protest when he released her. The warmth of his mouth lingered on her skin. Adding to her pleasure. His firm hand cupped her chin.

"Not Todd. Not God. My name."

She was learning what pleased him. And Logan was forthcoming in his demands. She nodded her head in understanding. How could she mess this up?

Seconds later, heat skirted up her belly as he licked and sucked at her taut peaks until she was mewling out of control. His talented, expertly skilled tongue had her bathing in sensual flames. She felt his teeth graze her nipple, and she arched her back desperately pushing more of her breast into his mouth.

"Logan, don't stop," she groaned.

He released the snap on her jeans, easing the zipper down while maintaining the hold on her breast. In sexual overdrive, she felt the silky material of her lace thong moisten in anticipation. She instinctively spread her legs wide wrapping them around the outside of his thighs. He was going to touch her, feel the dampness of her feminine curls just before he reached the heart of her wetness.

*Ring, Ring, Ring. Ring, Ring, Ring.*

Oh goodness, he had her head ringing in ecstasy. Her little nub throbbed; begging for a release she had no knowledge of.

*Ring, Ring, Ring.*

Her cellular ringtone brought her back to the earth's atmosphere.

"Logan, my phone is ringing."

He responded by applying more pressure to her already sensitive bundle of nerves, sending a zing of current through her veins.

She pressed at his shoulders. "Please." Her breath wispy and quick.

He released her breast and stepped back a fraction. "As you wish," he said, a barely audible whisper. His fingers made the slow ascent out of her panties.

He lifted her off the island countertop. "Answer your phone, we have all night to finish this."

A few more minutes and she would have been a crewmember of the Starship Enterprise. What he was doing to her was out of this world.

Discarding the bra and putting her pants right, she felt the spank to her backside the instant she turned away. The playful swat earned him a scowl of mock indignation. "Caveman," she teased, bounding off in search of the phone.

"Night nurse," he tossed back.

Ava dashed across the hardwood floors in the family room to grab her phone from his charger with a smile on her face.

"Hello?" The distraction would give her the opportunity to wrestle her X-rated urges into submission. Her grandmother's voice rang clear and true through the connection.

"Yes, I will stop by after work on Sunday." Ava listened then she stiffened.

She repeated Granny Lou's question, as though she hadn't heard it the first time. "Why do I sound out of breath? I sound out of breath because I ran from the kitchen to answer the phone before it stopped ringing."

Logan appeared in the doorway, his eyes were watchful again.

"You called my house." Something akin to panic gripped Ava's lungs. She couldn't lie to her grandmother.

"I'm at Logan's. I cooked the Puerto Rican chicken, black beans and rice with corn salsa." At the mention of Logan's name her grandmother hadn't asked any additional questions. Ava sagged in relief.

"Yes, ma'am. Have a good night." Hanging up, she let the phone drop to the couch. If Granny Lou hadn't called she would have done the "wild thing" with Logan.

"I should go home."

Logan walked up to her, taking her moist hands in his.

"You are not leaving me."

He kissed the top of her head. His scent mixed with the confusion stirring in her brain. She wanted him, but she didn't want to want him.

"Ava."

She looked at him.

"Stay the night. Nothing will happen until you are ready."

She looked down at the floor, not wanting him to see the uncertainty reflected in her eyes.

A heavy sigh filled the too quiet space. "You don't trust me."

She winced at the dead tone. She didn't trust herself. Not with a bedroom serving as her last line of defense before complete surrender. And, it would be surrender. Especially, if he offered an encore to what just happened in the kitchen.

"I do trust you or I wouldn't have let you touch me or do that stuff." She pointed at the kitchen island as heat rose to her cheeks. "Never mind." She replayed their culinary foreplay moments before and took in his unreadable expression. She should go home. For a woman with the sexual control of a bunny rabbit on fertility drugs, distance was the logical choice.

"I'll stay."

She squeezed his hands until he made eye contact.

Logan's smile wavered before it spread with satisfaction across his handsome features. His roguish smile never failed to warm her insides and make her feel sweet and sticky for him.

"Which bedroom is mine?"

His smile fell away.

"Ava, I hold the balance of life and death in my hands with a steady grip on a surgical blade day in and day out. I am capable of managing life altering decisions regarding complex medical conditions. But, I cannot have you under my roof sleeping in another bedroom. You will sleep with me."

"I can't sleep in your bed. Weird stuff happens when I get near you, when I smell you. Even the sound of your voice gets me panting and all kinds of other stuff. I might not be able to stop myself." She looked away embarrassed by her lack of control.

"Sweetheart, the same thing happens when you touch me. As long as I am the only man that makes you feel 'weird' stuff, we are great together. There are four other bedrooms in this house. You decide which bed we will christen tonight. I will gladly climb in any bed with you, even in a miniature doll house if you were by my side."

"You wouldn't fit in anything miniature."

"I'd figure out a way, if it made you happy."

They both laughed, but it didn't ease the tension.

"Logan, I'm scared."

She hated her weakness, her failure, and most of all her fear.

"I'm here and I'm not going anywhere. You are safe with me." He reached for her face, his thumb stroking her cheek. She started to heat up and warmth overflowed in her heart. He understood. Courage bolstered, she gave voice to her next fear.

"I don't know what to do." Her cheeks burned with the admission. Her battered self-esteem couldn't take it if she disappointed Logan. She hadn't been able to satisfy Marcus. She had tried, but the pain was unbearable. She hadn't "practiced" in a long time.

How could she please him with rusty lady parts?

"Ava, sweetheart, you are thinking too hard. We will share a bed, nothing more until you are ready."

"But you said we would finish what we started."

"And we will, when the time is right for both of us. For tonight, let's agree to a bedroom."

Her expression was nothing short of elation. Logan looked at her with a puzzled expression.

"You look a little too relieved. Care to share?"

"I was thinking my… that is, my 'lady parts' are a little rusty." She fidgeted and cleared her throat. She felt the heat rising to her cheeks.

"Sweetheart, I assure you, your lady parts are fine. When you give yourself to me, it will be my pleasure to teach you everything you want to know. I'll even let you demonstrate what you have learned."

The butterflies in her stomach lost some of their fluttering at his reassurance. He wasn't forcing her. It was her decision. Her choice.

"You are too good to be real. You always know what to do."

She closed her eyes, pushing against the fear threatening to engulf her.

*It's sleeping,* she reminded herself. *You sleep all the time.* The difference was her Kryptonite would be next to her. All six feet two inches, iron muscled, warm skinned male. She could do this. She wanted to do this for him. No, she wanted this for herself; to be close to him, intimately close.

"Everything to do with you and me is real. You're mine. I'll always take care of you. Come, tonight you will sleep in my arms."

She stared up at him, gripped by apprehension. She felt his hold on her hands loosen, she clutched at his fingers. "I'm ready."

Logan had grown accustomed to her scent, the way her chest rose and fell in sleep, how she draped her hair over the left shoulder so it brushed against his chest as he curled protectively around her. He still hadn't seen her fully unclothed, but he knew her body. It was getting harder, literally, for him to control his cravings for her.

Twice a week, three times if their schedules permitted, Ava would grace him with one of her home cooked meals. She would have it waiting for him after work. At night's end, she'd climb into one of the four guest beds and wrap that lithe, hot body around his and go to sleep. How she managed to sleep was beyond him. He spent half the night adjusting his erection. They had yet to share the master bedroom. He could be patient with her holding back her body, but she guarded something more precious. Trust. Her trust had not been given to him, not fully. What more could he offer her in reassurance? He knew he had a piece of her heart, but the essence of who she was remained under maximum security.

A familiar voice interrupted his imaginings.

"Logan, my friend why aren't you laced up?"

Logan placed the protein shake in his hand on the counter to glare at his best friend.

"I did tell you to stop walking into my house unexpectedly." He gestured for Graham to take a seat.

"And I told you to start locking your doors." Logan raised his brows. Graham had returned from a three-week visiting professor position in Washington, D.C. earlier in the week. His friend's usual good nature and pristine appearance was in short supply this morning. Already, dressed in his running gear, he looked haggard.

"I forgot about our run this morning. What's going on with you?" Logan studied his friend. Something was definitely up with him.

With a fixed stare, Graham released a noisy breath before he spoke.

"Why are you asking, Logan?"

"You look like crap. I don't usually have a pissed off grizzly in my house at eight o'clock in the morning."

Graham laughed at that. "Whatever. Are we running or not? You are not the man to advise me about a woman. I'd be better off talking to a Catholic priest."

Woman troubles. Logan could relate.

"A woman and secrets. Nothing good can come from the two of them together. What's her name?"

"This coming from the man shrouded in control with the emotional capacity of a clam shell. Take your own advice, Logan."

Graham had not disclosed the woman's name. Fascinating.

Ava picked that moment to call for him. Graham furrowed his brows.

"An overnight guest? What planet are you from and where have you taken Logan?" Graham was laughing at his own joke.

Logan was not amused. Graham was studying him now, all signs of amusement faded.

"Wasn't it you that mentioned secrecy? That's not Rebecca back there. What's mystery lady's name?"

Graham asked pointing toward the downstairs bedrooms.

"Mine." Maybe he should have chosen a less Neanderthal word, but truth was truth.

Graham laughed at him.

"Logan, you should change your name to universal remote, because you want to control everything."

"You are not my therapist, Hamilton the third."

Graham frowned at the use of his last name. The man hated being referred to as the third of anything. Logan resorted to name calling when Graham irritated him, like he was doing now.

"Her voice is sexy. Anyone I know?" Graham leaned on the counter.

"No. She doesn't mingle in our circle. And do not flirt with her."

"Me?"

Graham was irritating him.

"What's happening with the Holbrooks and the position on the board?"

"Nothing has changed with the Masters-Holbrook partnership." His friend looked at him with an against *medical advice* expression on his face.

"It will when Sam Holbrook sees you with a woman other than Rebecca. You're jeopardizing your future."

Another leash to keep him on the Masters' family path to success. He'd find a way to have both. Graham had the forethought to stop talking when Ava's voice drew closer. She emerged from the side hall. Rich milk chocolate eyes, backlit with happiness, and sun kissed chocolate locks flowing over her shoulders, all just for him. Any thoughts of family loyalty, partnerships and board positions faded from existence.

"Logan you didn't answer me." Ava's appealing voice was music to his ears. "Have you seen my noise-canceling earphones, they were here the last time."

Ava rounded the corner. Seeing Graham, she stopped mid-sentence. "Oh, I didn't realize you had a visitor. I'll be in the den."

"Come over, Ava. Meet Graham Hamilton III, my friend since undergraduate days."

"The Johns Hopkins class mate? Logan told me about you. It's nice to meet you Graham. I'm Ava Walters."

Graham closed his grip over Ava's slender fingers in a familiar hold. Logan waited two beats. Graham had not released her hand.

"Wow. You are gorgeous and the pleasure is all mine."

Graham raised Ava's hand to plant a kiss on her wrist. Logan had warned him.

At his snarl, Ava jumped and Graham stilled. Logan stood, snatching Ava's hand from his friend's grasp.

"If you put your lips on my woman, a ring of spinning stars will be the last thing you see before the EMTs wheel you to the ambulance."

"You did mention she was yours," Graham smiled. "My apologies, Ava."

Logan pulled her into his side. He saw Ava's jaw drop at his blatant threat. Not a threat, a promise.

Graham's laughter filled the room. "Hey, I was trying to understand the nature of your relationship with Ava."

"You're a pain in the..." At her glare Logan stopped short of his full comment.

Graham doubled over with laughter. "Nice move Ava. It's about time a woman curbed his proclivity for profanity. A terrible habit he picked up during residency."

"I can leave if we aren't running this morning," Graham said.

Logan was glad his friend had arrived at the correct answer without his input. He wouldn't leave Ava.

"Good idea to reschedule." If they didn't leave the house in the next ten minutes the sidewalks would be overrun with early morning java drinkers en route to any number of the Avondale coffee houses. Though he lived in a historic district, there was ample vehicular traffic, even this early on a Saturday morning. Running in the street was not safe. "No surgeries scheduled for Tuesday morning? I'll meet you at the river walk, say six thirty," he replied to Graham.

"Please don't change your plans for me, Logan." Ava released his hand to exit the kitchen. "I'll go."

He grabbed her around the waist, hauling her back to his side. "You are not leaving."

She cut her eyes at him. "I was saying before the interruption; I will go with you. A morning run would be nice."

Both men glanced at the other, unsure how to decline her request without offense.

"Sweetheart, we run ten miles on Saturdays." His comment earned him a tight face and a hard smile. Arms crossed over her chest she looked at him with narrowed eyes.

"A ten-mile run is no big deal."

Logan looked at her with incredulity. There was no need for Ava to try to impress him with her physical stamina. He had other ideas on how to test her endurance.

"If I slow you down I know how to find my way back home."

Was that a hint of sarcasm in her voice? He looked at her again. She rolled her eyes upward. He smiled to himself. She was getting more comfortable with their relationship.

Logan was still skeptical, as was Graham judging by his grim expression. Neither man wanted to deal with the fallout of telling any woman no.

"Alright," Logan said on a slow release. "You can go, but the side door will be unlocked."

She gave him a pointed look, moving toward the door. "Oh ye of little faith," came the snarky reply.

Definitely sarcasm. This was new. He loved it.

"I remember where I left my ear buds. Let me grab them and I will meet you at the door."

They exited the house turning in the direction of Bastian Point Park. The park was nestled at the far end of the neighborhood on the banks of the Saint Dasius River.

Ava ran alongside him in comfortable silence. He hadn't expected her to keep in step with their longer strides. She had established a steady pace. Looking at her form and even breathing he realized she was a trained runner.

Why hadn't she told him?

He and Graham were used to running without uttering one word in sixty minutes. Logan was about to break that unspoken rule.

"Why didn't you tell me you are a runner?"

She didn't answer.

At his touch, she glanced up.

"Sorry, I'm not used to sharing my run time with anyone. What did you say?"

So, she was a runner.

"You *are* a long distance runner."

Why was he irritated by the discovery? Because it was something about her he didn't know, a secret.

"Yes, I've been running since junior high. I ran track in high school. Running helps me decompress. It's my brand of escapism."

"You should have told me. We can run together after work."

"It's not a big deal. I run by myself. You know I like outdoor activities."

She was minimizing this breach of trust.

"When women say that it usually means shopping in open air malls or sitting on the beach."

"No thanks, I'd rather run."

Lengthening her stride she moved ahead, in line with Graham now. She could move fast. Logan sped up.

No woman would have the power to destroy him again. He would set the terms for their relationship. There would be no secrets and no half-truths. "What else don't I know about you?"

Ava's steps faltered at the accusation in Logan's tone. His obvious upset, at what he perceived as her withholding an insignificant detail, was irrational. She said the first thing that came to mind.

"Is it normal for you to talk this much on your runs?"

Her tongue brushed the scar on her lip. She controlled the fear. This was Logan. He wouldn't hurt her for speaking her mind.

Graham slowed his pace to observe the drama unfolding between her and Logan. Great.

A wave of laughter disrupted Ava's thoughts and caused Logan to glare.

"She's got you there."

Mirth danced in Graham's eyes. Logan didn't look pleased with his friend's comment.

"Stay out of this Hamilton the third," Logan ribbed back.

Graham frowned. She guessed being called that was a point of contention between the men.

Ava trapped her lower left lip to stop the burn.

"Let's talk at home Logan. It's a beautiful day and I *want* to finish my run."

Her concentration was shot to pieces. Finish the run, get keys, and go home. That was the plan.

"Yeah, Logan. Your nagging is blowing my runners high."

Graham, similar to Lina, tried to lighten the mood.

She could feel Logan's eyes at her back. His anger was palpable, even in an open space. She knew better than to get too close. The habit of staying the night with Logan was officially a step in the wrong direction.

This unpleasant conversation was evidence of her poor decision making ability. She would grab her overnight bag the second they returned. Goodbye, nice to meet you song and dance for Graham's benefit, then she would be on her way home.

Logan's deep timber interrupted her escape planning. "I know how your mind works Ava. Do not try to leave when we return home."

She sighed, put on a placating smile and lied. "I was thinking about my plans for tomorrow."

She did need to see Lina. Her friend had dropped off the radar and Ava was worried. She knew it had something to do with Jace. Whatever he'd done extended way beyond the break-up. Jace couldn't meet her eyes during the general staff meeting last week.

"You mean our plans, sweetheart."

Not this time, buddy. His smooth talking was a wasted effort.

"Are you *planning* to attend church with me in the morning?" She tossed the invitation out there, knowing he had a seven thirty-five tee time with his father and Darwin. Good. They needed some time apart.

"Logan, when did you start going to church?" Graham asked.

Logan narrowed his eyes, flattened his lip and glared at his friend. "Stop interrupting Graham, or I'll clip you in the knee."

He turned back to Ava. "I was there for two and a half hours last Sunday that should count as a double shift."

"So you're not coming," she offered in a singsong voice. "I'll see you at work on Monday."

Logan looked at her. She shrugged.

"Granny Lou is cooking since my parents are on vacation. She has one rule for Sunday dinners. Commune with Jehovah or no brunch when it's over. If you don't go to church, you don't eat anything she's prepared. There's leftover salmon in the fridge."

"Ava, you can cook and you make sure he's fed before you leave. You are an angel. Are you sure you want this guy? I'm a domesticated house cat compared to Logan."

She peered around Logan's sweat glistened body to look at Graham.

"I've noticed." Of course, she had to be infatuated with, probably falling head over stupid heels for the most controlling man in the southeastern corridor.

"Stop flirting with her and what do you mean you've noticed?"

Ava shifted her eyes to look at Logan. "It's not anything bad. Graham seems to be more temperate. That's all I meant."

"Don't compare me to another man." Slowing her pace, Ava shook her head in disbelief. He had morphed into a madman.

She glanced in Logan's direction, felt the flames of his anger directed at her. This was a disaster. Whatever he was truly mad about, she couldn't fix. Time stopped, she backed away from both men.

"I'm going home." Her lips began to quiver. She stumbled back on her heel, turned and sprinted in the opposite direction. Fighting back a tear, a haze of emotion obscuring her vision.

Logan had messed up. There was still a breeze coming off the river, even with the warmth of the sun, but all he felt was the icy cold of regret.

"Masters, you are dipped in stupid."

He turned to find his best friend's brows knitted together in anger.

"I know," he barked. His chest felt tight with anguish.

"Take some advice for once in your life. When handling a butterfly, take care not to crush it." He stared at Graham for a moment.

"I have no idea why I did that to her. The thought of not knowing everything about her is grating. She amazes me, but I keep screwing up." He ran his fingers threw his hair, mentally kicking himself again, because he fully understood the ramifications of his actions. Ava would pull away.

"I want her, Graham. My need for Ava borders on fanaticism. I don't understand the intensity of what I feel. But, I will not tolerate secrets between us."

"The fact that she likes to run and you didn't know, doesn't strike me as a major stumbling block to a healthy relationship," Graham said. "Your response, on the other hand, is a game stopper."

Logan blew out a breath.

"You verbally attacked her. A lesser woman probably would have broken down into tears. Are you sure you're ready for this relationship?"

"Careful, Graham." Logan's spine went ramrod straight, jaw clenching, and fists tight.

"I'm a friend that is not threatened by your roar. I get why you despise secrets, but Ava is not Brooke."

Logan raised both hands, halting the conversation. "I am well aware of who Ava is without you stating the obvious. My relationship with Ava has nothing to do with my past."

The doubtful look on Graham's face had his nostrils flaring.

"Be sure that what happened with Brooke isn't driving you to control every aspect of your relationship with Ava. You're very possessive of her."

"I am protective of her. Ava is mine." His posture remained rigid, bracing for the next blow.

"That's what I'm talking about. How long have you been with her?"

"Four weeks, but time is irrelevant. I would still feel possessive and protective of her."

"She might be the one for you. She's cute as a pin-up model, but keep a cork in that testosterone factory of yours. She makes you happy, I can see that, but stop trying to control her."

With the conversation shifted away from Brooke, Logan's shoulders relaxed.

"She is the one and I will not lose her. Nothing good comes from having secrets."

"I get it. Your fiancée and your friend sleeping together is a load of crap by anyone's definition. But, dial back on the demands and get rid of the accusatory tone. You obviously have not told her anything about what happened during your residency."

And Logan never would. Sleeping with his friend wasn't the worst of what Brooke Tyler had done.

"Brooke is my past. I will not talk with you or anyone else about what happened."

"Okay, let's talk about something more pressing. Has Ava met your family?"

Logan served an icy glare in Graham's direction. "Not yet. She will."

"If she hasn't met your family, then she doesn't know about Rebecca. Who's really keeping secrets here, Logan?"

"She never asks me anything. I met her family less than twenty-four hours after our first date. Her family doesn't care about my money or political connections, neither does she. She asks for nothing in return. I've never been with a woman like Ava. I know she's with me, we are doing the relationship song and dance, but I can feel a barrier between us. She regards what we have together like a placeholder in her life. I don't understand." He rubbed the back of his neck as he took in a deep breath, releasing it with a heavy sigh of frustration.

"Have you asked her?" Graham inquired.

Logan shook his head in denial.

"You know the saying don't ask the question if you really don't want the answer. Ava keeps our relationship in a vacuum-sealed jar; separate from everything." Blowing out a breath, he ran his fingers through his hair. A blaring horn had him flinching. The city was awake now. The Saturday morning cruisers littered the streets looking for parking places or were already double-parked.

"I need to know she is connected to me. She is pulling against our bond. Ava wants what's happening between us, but I can't shake the feeling I'm going to lose her."

Graham offered him a skeptical look.

"What? You think I'm making this up?"

"Are you? I mean you just met her. Is she that into you?"

Logan's head pounded. Why wasn't he enough? He needed her to want him, need *him*. Not because he was a surgeon, not because of the money, and definitely not because of a business alliance.

"It's not a figment of my imagination, Graham. I know when a woman wants me." Logan's voice was rough with indignation. Yes, Brooke's betrayal had done a number on him, but what he had with Ava was real.

"You have some serious repair work to do when you get home." Pity crossed Graham's face before he shook his head and lengthened his stride.

"You finish the run. I'm going to catch up to Ava. I'll see you back at the house." What was he going to say when he caught up to her?

The sidewalk that ran the length of historic Avondale was filled with morning shoppers and browsers. Couples in coordinated athletic gear sat at outdoor bistro tables drinking signature coffees. Every blue haired, southern lady within a three-mile radius was on the sidewalk with a teacup dog. The run back to the house would be slower.

"I'm not about to miss you groveling at Ava's feet." They turned in unison, their steps double timed in the direction Ava had gone.

Logan scanned the early morning shoppers dotting the sidewalk. "She's fast. Do you see her?"

"No, she's not on this block. She's jackrabbit fast if she can turn on this type of speed after running four miles. How young is she?"

"You too?"

"Me too what? What you are talking about?"

"Ava and her family are kind of sensitive about our age difference. They haven't said anything since our first meeting, but I get the sense that they are on high alert in case the old geezer goes crazy on their daughter. The first direct question Ava asked of me was my age."

"What's her story?"

"I wish I knew. She's doesn't share much about her past, but I have my suspicions."

They sped up in hopes of catching Ava.

Logan was the first to spot her cinnamon colored locks swaying in the wind.

"There she is on the far side of The Coffee House." Logan lengthened his stride. "I'll see you back at the house."

It seemed as if the wind itself propelled her forward. She was running away, rather than towards his home. She was running from him.

Just as Logan was extending a hand to touch her shoulder, Ava darted between two parked cars and started across the street. He saw the car like a director clipping a film reel for effect just as Ava ran into the direct path of the oncoming vehicle.

Logan bellowed her name just as she screamed. He could hear the screech of the tires, smell the burnt rubber on the asphalt.

"No." Heartbeat thrashing in his ears, a primal roar in his head, his legs burned as he charged every muscle fiber in his body to move faster.

*Dear God, let me reach her in time.*

He pushed off with all his strength forcing his body through the air.

She stood frozen in the intersection as Logan came down at her back, throwing them both into the grass covered median at the last second. Rotating, he took the brunt of the impact from the fall. Her tremors, increasing in seismic intensity, ricocheted through him. Tears streamed unbridled down her face.

"I have you, sweetheart. You are safe." She shook uncontrollably. He needed to get her home.

"Ava." Her head fell back; her sports top was drenched in tears. "Ava talk to me."

She would not open her eyes. He tried to soothe her, but nothing worked. Terrified and feeling useless, he squeezed her tighter.

Just then, Graham ran to his side. "I saw what happened. Is she okay?"

Logan didn't answer. His focus was on the frightened woman in his arms. "Sweetheart, I am going to pick you up." She offered no words, just squeezed her eyes tighter, refusing to open them.

"Ava, please. Say something."

"I think she's in shock and you're shaking." Graham fashioned a cradle with his arms. "Give her to me."

"I can carry her."

"Logan you are in no condition."

Logan rose to his feet. He stood with Ava lifted high on his chest. His biceps pillowed her head as she cried. Her body was so rigid he felt she might shatter if he jostled her.

This was his fault. His actions forced her to leave his side. She wanted to escape. He had almost killed the woman he wanted more than his next breath.

What would she see when she looked at him? Ava's hand gripped and released the material of his shirt. Her hand moved again, this time it didn't halt. Rather she slowly moved back and forth against his chest. He realized she was trying to comfort him. He briefly closed his eyes placing a delicate kiss on her head.

"You are more than precious to me Ava. I am so sorry."

She still sobbed, but they were quieter now. Her hand continued to rub his chest. Logan kept his face expressionless, afraid he would crumble if he looked anywhere but straight ahead. She hadn't said a single word to him.

The somber trio walked the length of Logan's driveway entering the house through the side door. He placed her on the couch in the den, pulling the afghan from the headrest to cover her. Seeing Ava sobbing because of his actions nearly brought him to his knees. Instead of protecting her, he had shoved her in harm's way. When Ava needed him most, he had failed her.

Giving one long look at Ava, Logan exited the den. She lay on the leather sectional curled in a ball. Though her sobs were silent, he could see the tremors of her body when she inhaled a breath. Ashamed of his behavior, he joined Graham by the side entry door. What had he done?

"Masters, you are too quiet. What's going on in that head of yours?"

"She was running from me."

"I just met her, but that's not how she will see what happened."

"You and I both know the truth. She was trying to get away from me. I am the reason she was almost killed."

"If she felt that way, she would not have been in your arms."

Logan heard her soft sniffle from the den. Something akin to relief washed over him.

Graham was hesitant as he spoke. "I can drive the both of you to an urgent care? A mild sedative will help her relax."

"No. I will take care of Ava. You can go."

Graham gave his shoulder a brief hold in support before moving in the direction of the door.

"Go back in there and take care of your woman. Call me if you need anything."

How had the morning turned into such a mess?

From the doorway, Logan took in the fragile woman curled protectively in a ball on his couch and his heart constricted. He would not lose her. He crossed the room and scooped her up into his arms. Logan never took his eyes from Ava as he cradled her back in his embrace. He held her in silence as long as he could. He needed to know she was okay.

"Sweetheart, please say something. I am coming unglued. You can rail at me. Punch me. I do not care. I just want to hear your voice. Know that you are okay. Please."

She sniffled. "I don't want to run with you anymore."

Once again, she took him by surprise with the unexpected.

"You are a terrible running buddy. You talk too much."

"That is all you have to say? That I am a lousy running partner, after I almost got you killed?"

"I almost got myself killed, not you."

"No way. This is my fault, you were trying to put distance between us. You ran away because I was being a jerk." She was trying to defend him. There was no way he would allow her to shoulder the responsibility for what almost happened.

"You were being *that*, but it's not your fault I almost got pancaked by a car."

"Yes, it was."

"Logan, I can't argue with you about why we both almost got hit and killed. You shouldn't have jumped in front of a speeding car to save me. You could have been hurt."

"You can't be serious. I would jump in front of a thousand bullet trains to save you. Don't you understand your worth to me?"

She didn't respond to his question. He was sure of his feelings for her. His confession caused a warm sensation to form in his chest. He couldn't deny what he felt for Ava any longer. She was a part of his soul. She had captured him in her spell, made him vulnerable, but when he looked at her none of that mattered.

"The truth is my inattention put us both in harm's way, Logan."

He looked at her in disbelief. She spared his feelings. "Do not try to spare me a guilty conscience. Let's not talk about this anymore. I think I should put you to bed."

"I'm not sleepy."

"I can fix that." He picked her up, pulled in a deep breath, pushing her honeyed scent to the four corners of his soul, quieting the fear and the helplessness he felt at almost losing her. He knew in that moment he could never be without her. He loved Ava.

It had been a week since the near death experience. Logan was struggling to contain his yearning and frustration. Though he had not made love to Ava, he'd become accustomed to her sleeping beside him. Something she had avoided since the running incident. The events of that day had changed them. Not them, her. She still cooked, but always made an excuse to get back to her house.

Logan felt uncertain and exposed. He didn't care for the feeling. Ava's workday generally ended three hours before his. But today he had left the hospital an hour early. She'd be in his arms in a matter of minutes. They would have dinner together and he would talk her into staying with him. He smiled to himself at the thought of Ava gracing his sheets tonight

# CHAPTER ELEVEN

Logan maneuvered the Lexus sedan into the garage of his Avondale address and his mood immediately darkened. Ava's Jeep was not in the second parking space. Not bothering to exit the car, he dialed her cell phone number, before engaging the hands free communication link on the steering wheel controls.

"Hello" was all she said before the line went silent.

"Is everything okay?" Don't crush the butterfly. Graham's words replayed in his head. Don't jump to conclusions. Don't jump period. Keep a chain around the testosterone.

"Yes Logan, everything is fine."

If everything was fine she should have been at home waiting for him. Hands gripping the braided leather wheel, blanched knuckles, he struggled to keep his voice level.

"Where are you?" he said through clenched teeth. Errands, shopping, or any number of innocuous activities could have delayed her commute home.

She could be en route at this very minute, back to him.

"I'm at home."

He heard her take a breath. Silence again.

"I am at home Ava and you are not here." A lie. The first link in the chain snapped, he felt his control slip.

"Logan I have my own house."

Second chain link snapped, igniting the matchstick that lit the flame. Remember she's the butterfly. *I am in control.* He continued with caution, unsure what to expect.

"How long before you're back here?" A reasonable relationship question he thought.

She didn't respond. "Ava?"

It hit him with the force of a steel beam to the gut. She was widening the distance. The plan was not to come back. She'd left his bed, now she'd left his house. If he didn't put a stop to this, she would leave his life. *Control gone.*

In a low, steely voice Logan said, "I am coming for you. Be there Ava." Or crap was going to hit the proverbial fan. But he did not say that aloud. "Do not make me chase you."

Logan peeled out of the garage. Hearing the screech of the tires as he left his driveway, he pressed the gas pedal delivering more power than necessary. An unfamiliar tightness filled his chest as he navigated the back streets to where Ava lived.

Even though Logan's home was farther away from the hospital they usually stayed at his house. His remodeled 19th century colonial had a larger kitchen, which Ava loved and an indoor gym complete with mirrored walls and mounted flat screen televisions on each wall. Ten minutes later Logan turned off the ignition in front of Ava's bungalow style home. He was prepared to use his key to the front door when the side door by the carport opened.

Ava stood in the doorway looking adorable in orange boy shorts and a green t-shirt with the Florida A&M University Rattler in the center. Her dainty feet with red polished toes, set off with a delicate yellow gold anklet sparkled in the sunlight.

He let out a breath he didn't know he was holding until he reached her and locked in on her intoxicating scent, vanilla, honey and something uniquely her.

She reached for him and he bent his six foot two inch frame to meet her five foot four inches, he angled her face upward capturing her mouth and pushing deep between her lips.

He plundered her mouth, holding the kiss until he had to take a breath. He pulled back, guiding her into the small kitchen and stepping fully through the door closing it behind him.

She turned to walk away and he snaked his arm around her waist hauling her back to his body.

"Ava, what are you doing here?"

She looked down at the floor and did not answer his question.

"Please look at me," he said lifting her chin. "Give me an answer."

It was a demand. When it came to them staying together he wouldn't give her an option to leave.

"This is my home," she said, "I wanted to come home, that's all."

"We have a home, together. What has changed between us that you need to distance yourself from me?" This was not how he saw their night together unfolding.

"We shouldn't be together."

He rocked back on his heels. Her words were a physical blow that threatened to topple him.

"Why are you saying this, now? We are together. That is not changing. What's the reason that has you trying to end our relationship?" There had to be more than the incident last week fueling her actions. She wasn't telling him something important.

"This," he felt her slender fingers curl against his dress shirt, "should never have happened."

He didn't think she was aware of how tight she was holding onto him. She'd narrowed the distance between them, stroking his skin as she spoke. The comfort offered by the action was contrary to her words. The action spoke louder.

Encouraged by her fierce grip, he proceeded cautiously with his next question.

"You are trying to keep us apart. Why?"

When her lips moved to answer he stroked his thumb across her lips. Her eyes slid to half-mast. "If it's because of the job, or the board position, or what happened with Randall, I won't accept it." He took her chin and tilted her face up. Their eyes met.

"Now, tell me why you don't want me."

Ava was unable to utter the words that would send them in separate directions. Logan had pressed his advantage and she had surrendered. Considering she hadn't mounted a fight, surrender was probably a poor word choice. The addiction to him was stronger than her self-preservation skills. But her foolish heart was too busy falling for him to care. And he recognized her dilemma. When she couldn't voice the words, he took that to mean their relationship was full steam ahead. Powerless when it came to him, she'd unabashedly stumbled on two achy feet back into his open arms.

Weeks had passed since the, *we shouldn't be together* fiasco, but Logan was more vigilant now that ever. His mini mansion served as relationship headquarters. His territory. His terms. He stood as sentry determined to keep her from escape. The state of their relationship chafed, because truth was, she didn't want to leave Logan. Trust seemed to be an elusive target for both of them. In some ways, Logan was just as wounded as she was. Not that she knew why.

Ava soon discovered Logan was on a mission. He'd orchestrated events to meet every person of remote significance in her contact list. Run dates today, buying lunch for all the nurses tomorrow. Charm, attentiveness, and free food had every nurse giggling the moment he walked on the pediatric unit. He'd even talked her mother into planting a garden in his backyard. Logan had given her mother a key to his house so she could map the garden at her leisure. He was intrusive, overprotective, and loyal, and she was crazy for him.

When Janna came home on a one week leave for her birthday, Logan took the day off work to help her shop for the party. The two of them were instant best buds. The woman actually enjoyed watching ESPN, while most women Ava knew only feigned interest. Playing pool and hitting the gym five days a week were a part of Janna's routine. She was the perfect man's man, except she was a woman. Thanks to Janna, two weeks after her departure, Ava was sprawled across Logan's chest watching Sports Center on a Friday night. The light from the eighty-five inch LCD screen illuminated the darkened room casting a sensual shadow over Logan's features.

Ava tried not to think about Logan naked. But the physical contact with all those flexing muscles and the present fullness in his jeans had her licking her lips. Logan, his usual attentive self, lifted her face up to meet his and took her mouth. As his tongue glided over her bottom lip, she opened to his invasion giving him full access to take as he pleased. Her skin was hot and stretched tight. She instinctively ground her hips into him, wanting more. When he pulled back she mourned the loss.

If kissing were a measure of things to come, sex with Logan would be recorded as an orgasm of atomic proportion. She barely had control of herself without them having sex. Images of her riding him untamed with the skill of a seasoned bareback cowgirl had her drenched in sweat and shaking with need on the nights she spent without him. She buried her face in the angle of his neck at the memory.

"Are my kisses shameful?"

She flicked her eyes in his direction to find him watching her intently. Heat infused her face. His voice was a hot water spring seeping into all the dry, neglected places in her life.

"No," she offered in a husky voice she barely recognized. He sat up then, positioning her higher on his chest. They were face to face now, her hands pressed against his shoulders.

"Ava, are you really with me?"

Logan and his world tilting questions were forever a stumbling block for her. How to answer his question had her head swimming. She gave what she could, without losing herself. Something that was harder to maintain with each passing day. Could she truthfully reply yes knowing she kept a part of herself hidden?

"I'm with you as much as I know how to be." That much was true. Cautiously she searched his face, not sure what she would find there. What she saw reflected on his handsome features unleashed a sudden heated rush under her skin. Acceptance, desire, and something deeper than both combined. And that something more had her turning inside out.

Logan cupped her face with both hands and gave Ava a long, lingering kiss. This kiss felt different. The sensation unlocked the door to an experience they hadn't shared before tonight. Wanting him closer, Ava dug her nails into his shoulders, and returned the kiss with a fervor that matched his own. The threads of doubt and insecurity loosened their hold. She took every ounce of what he promised with that kiss because she wanted him more than anything. Logan released the kiss and she waited. Eyes shrouded in passion, she watched as he placed large hands over her breasts. Eager for more contact, Ava pressed her now aching mounds into his warm palms. She didn't move when he released the first three buttons on her blouse and unfastened her bra. Pure male appreciation shone in his eyes at the sight of her bare breasts. Ava moaned when the heat from his hands soaked into her skin. His caress was liquid heat, raising her temperature to a fever pitch that left her craving for more.

"Tell me to stop Ava. Anything less, I will have all of you before the sun rises tomorrow."

His voice a deep rumble. Filled with the same hunger stirring in her. Why did he have to talk now? She wanted to feel, not think.

That little reserve of doubt and insecurity started to expand. Her body cooled. She felt the tautness in her muscles. What if she couldn't satisfy him? Pulling back a fraction, she let her head fall forward. As if reading her mind, Logan spoke the words that broke through her doubts.

"You don't have to do anything. I'm in charge."

Ava tilted her head back to meet his eyes. She didn't see a demanding male. She saw his sincerity and care, and immediately her body reignited.

He would satisfy both of them. Would he take responsibility for their pleasure? Not blame her if he was left wanting. Could sex be this simple between them? She reached up, ran her fingers through his ruddy colored locks, more for herself than him. He groaned at the contact.

"Don't stop." She had said the words out loud, for them and where tonight would lead. His chest expanded as he took a deep breath. The smoldering look in his eyes said she was about to get the answers to her questions.

*Don't stop.* Two of the sweetest words in the English language Ava had spoken to him. Logan wanted her to enjoy what he did, but he could feel the tension in her body. He needed her relaxed. Let him introduce her to a world of new pleasures. Stroking the length of her arm, he caressed her back, sweeping lower to cup her bottom until she began to soften in his arms. Logan watched the play of emotion flicker across her face. Nervous, but desire lit her eyes, the rising color of her skin outweighed the anxiety about the next step they were taking.

"Taste," he said pulling her down to press their lips together. Savoring her exquisite blend of vanilla and honey. She was the only thing that existed in his world. Kissing her and feeling her warm body atop his was more than a want. It was a basic need. Breaking their kiss, he bent his head and took her breast into his mouth, lavishing them with attention in equal measure. Feeling a tug at his belt buckle he reluctantly released his bounty. Their first time together would be in his bed, not on the couch. He heard her whimper and his erection pulsed in response.

"Logan?"

Confusion at why he'd stopped was in her voice. Lips swollen and wet from his kisses, breasts taut and full, she looked beautiful.

"Sweetheart, I'm not going anywhere without you. Our first time making love will be in the bed we will share from this night forward." He sat up with Ava still pressed against him from chest to hip. He swung both feet onto the carpeted floor.

"Wrap your legs around me."

With a sure hold around his neck, she followed his instruction. Gripping her bottom in his hands, he lifted Ava higher and stood to his feet. He took purposeful steps, moving them up the stairs to his bedroom, breathing fast in eager anticipation of claiming Ava as his own.

Logan's bed was spacious enough for six people. The room, bathed in moonlight, was classically rugged with warm shades and squared patterns. No rounded edges in sight, all clean, sharp angles so indicative of the man. The hardwood floor was bare, except for a gingham rug near the bed that complemented the luxurious bed covers. The tufted leather headboard reached a quarter of the way to the ceiling. Metal artwork hung on the wall overlooking the bed draped in an alternating pattern of warm and neutral shades. A fireplace surrounded by a media console and built-in bookcases occupied one wall. The only window in the room would rival a department store display, and overlooked the side yard leading to the detached garage. Her mouth felt dry at the thought of what was about to happen between them.

"I'm not on birth control." At her statement Logan looked momentarily stunned. "I haven't had a reason to," she stumbled on.

"I'll protect you." He crossed the room to the bed carrying her as if she weighed nothing at all. Ava released the hold around his neck when he lowered her to the bed.

"You look beautiful in my bed."

She gave him a shaky smile as she continued to scan the room. This man had changed her. No, she was changing for him. The thought came to her unbidden. She was going to have sex with Logan.

"Undress for me Ava. Let me see."

His voice was a low, sexy grumble. She felt her body quicken as it flushed with heat all over again. She hesitated. What was his expectation? Should she take everything off fast or slow? Did he want her to lie back or stand up? Her head started to pound.

"Logan, I don't want to mess everything up. I don't know what you want and …. "

He cut her off mid-sentence. He bent his long muscled frame to her and trailed a single thumb down her cheek. Gently, he kissed her lips, before looking into her eyes.

"What I want is to be with you. Your scent, your hands, your mouth, I want them on me."

He laved wet kisses the length of her exposed neck as he spoke. "I want to love you. I want to wake up to you in my arms. We can go as slow as you need. I won't rush what's happening between us."

She released a breath of relief. Logan stood tall now, looking down at her.

"Take off your blouse and your bra, then lie back on the bed."

She did as she was told. The room air was cool against her skin.

Turning her head to the side, she looked up expectantly and her breath caught as Logan dropped to his knees. His face now even with her parted legs. She felt the skin on skin heat trail as he slid his hands up her inner thigh under her skirt.

She held her breath when his thick fingers gripped her thong and pressed into her hips, before retracing their original path. Burning with need, she trembled, when wide shoulders filled the space between her spread thighs. Pulling air back into her lungs, heart drumming in her chest, Ava felt primal pleasure wash over her when a warm breath touched her moist folds. Then delicious suction had her digging her nails into the bed covers for purchase as his mouth drove her past the shore of unknown passion into the cresting waves of ecstasy.

"What are you doing to me?" She barely got the words out before another onslaught of unrestrained pleasure assailed her body. Bolts of sexual energy shot through her, and her legs began to quake. Her body bowed off the bed and she screamed Logan's name as she shattered into a million pieces when passion so raw and deep exploded in her center. Each particle imprinted with Logan's name.

Ava screamed his name with her orgasm and he nearly came undone. Logan stood, discarded his clothing, and retrieved the condoms from the bedside stand. Sheathing himself, he dropped the foil roll of discs onto the bed by Ava's right hip. He stood between her legs, watching as she glowed with sexual satisfaction from the release he'd given her. Hair loose, wild curls framing her face.

"You are gorgeous when you come for me." Her orgasm was explosive.

"Seeing you naked makes me want to do it again."

Her skirt had ridden up to her waist.

"Lift up, sweetheart. I'm going to give you what you want."

Eyes open, still drawing in short breaths, she repositioned herself higher on the mattress, raising her hips. He made quick work of removing her last article of clothing before climbing on the bed with her. He spread her legs farther apart and positioned himself at her entrance.

"That was the most powerful orgasm I have ever witnessed. You are so responsive I almost came with you. Has it been awhile since your last time?"

"No," she responded still trying to breathe. "I have never had that happen before."

"You mean the force of the orgasm," Logan flashed what he knew was a slow, cocky smile.

"That's not what I meant. I've never had an orgasm," Ava said into the air, still chasing her breathe.

His hands stilled on her thighs, he shifted back onto his knees trying to see her expression in the shadows of the room.

"Ava. Tell me you have done what we are about to do before tonight." He wasn't in the business of deflowering virgins, but he knew he wasn't capable of walking away from her at this point.

"I have been with a man, but I have never had sex. I mean I've never experienced an orgasm. Is it always this awesome with sex? I never came with Mar...." He interrupted her next word, firmness in his tone.

"Don't say another man's name while you're in bed with me. I don't want to hear 'Oh my Todd' either. To answer your question, no, it's not this way for most couples. It will be for us."

Ava rose onto her elbows, studying him. When her eyes landed on the condom roll near her right hip they widened in what looked to be disbelief. She moved her arm to reach for them.

"Stay where I put you Ava."

"That's a lot of condoms. Should I be concerned that you keep a stock?"

"I am not a player, too possessive of what I consider to be mine. I bought them the night of our first dance."

"That confident in your abilities to woo me?"

"Confidence has its merit. I find unrelenting determination more beneficial. No more talk." He bent forward to claim her mouth, rubbing against her body, exploring her curves. He captured her very sweet sigh and responded with a growl of his own.

Positioned over her, he pressed his erection against her womanhood and she made a throaty sound that had him straining not to drive into her and bury himself to the hilt.

He pushed forward and she tensed. He repositioned himself and started slowly moving into her, her body resisted his invasion.

"Sweetheart, relax and open for me."

"I'm trying," she said in a small voice.

Logan started with a light kiss on her lips, then her neck and up to her eyelids. He felt her body relax. He angled to enter her, he looked down, sought her face wanting to see her passion as he claimed her. When he looked down at her face, he didn't see shared passion. Ava's eyelids were squeezed tight. Tension lines bracketed her mouth.

He leaned forward and cupped her face in both hands. Her eyes opened then and he recognized the emotion reflected in their chocolate depth. It was shame.

Ava looked away from him. "I'm so sorry."

She wiggled underneath him, in an attempt to push her slender frame backward on the bed.

"Sorry for what? Where are you going?"

He grabbed her hip and pulled her moist center flush with his lengthening erection.

"I think it would be best if I went home."

He rolled on his back so quickly pulling her with him she looked disoriented straddling his body. He had released her hip, wrapped an arm around her waist, dropped one elbow to the mattress and pulled her on top.

"There's nothing to be sorry about," he said with both hands at her waist now. "We are not done. We'll go slowly. I don't care if it takes until

Monday."

"It's Friday night, Logan."

"Duly noted, neither of us is leaving this bed, until you are mine. Would you be more relaxed if you were in control?"

"You'd let me do that?"

"You can do anything you want with my body. Ride me Ava, you set the pace. Just put your hands on me." He relinquished control to her, something that should've had him running for the high ground. But, this was Ava, the one woman made for him.

Ava's light touches down his chest and abdomen drove him crazy. He kept his hands pinned behind his head, afraid that if he touched her she would stop her exploration.

"That's it sweetheart. Touch me. I'm all yours." His hardness pulsed between them with each heated caress and he moved closer to the edge of his control. He'd never let her go after tonight.

Logan's response to her touch spurred Ava to continue her methodical exploration of his body. She felt the power of his muscled body underneath her, knew he could hurt her, and she would be defenseless against him. As she caressed the bronzed skin of his torso, she saw that he fought his need to touch her. Honoring his word to go as slow as she needed. She leaned over his sculpted abs and lowered her body, pressing her breasts to the heated skin of his chest.

"Your body is magnificent, Logan." The delicious contact had her nipples tingling and she sucked in a breath to his corresponding groan. Comfortable now, she rocked her hips against his erection, letting him feel her feminine heat.

"Easy sweetheart, when I come I want to be deep inside of you."

At that, she raised her hips and positioned him at her center. He had barely entered her and already she felt the stretch, the impossibly tight fit. He was too large.

"How long?"

She knew what he was asking.

"Six years," she said in a strained voice.

"Hold onto me," he said.

Strong arms curled around her bottom. She looked at him, those gorgeous emerald eyes that she could swim in. As soon as she placed her hands on his shoulders he surged up into her snug channel. Her eyes flew open and she screamed at the delicious burn of being stretched by him. She steadied herself by digging her nails into his shoulders as he rocked into her. He pushed deeper and her body sparked, caught fire, and pure sexual flames consumed her.

"Logan," she moaned his name, reveling in the perfection of feeling his body connected to hers.

"I've got you."

With each push inside her, Ava clung to him, eager and urgent, demanding everything he had to give. Closing her eyes, she gave herself over to his demands.

"Open your eyes sweetheart, see and feel as I make you mine," he growled.

His strong hands dug into her hips holding her in place, giving her what her body demanded. She didn't want him to ever stop. Her brain was in overdrive.

The energy racing through her body curled her toes. She felt the damp sheets, his sweat covered body, the flexing muscles as he drove into her. His hands curled around her nape drawing her down to meet his lips in a sizzling kiss. A kiss she returned with a ferocity to match his own.

She felt his fingers glide into her hair before her brain registered what was happening. *Oh God.* Her body tensed. Closing her eyes she readied herself. The pain would be next. Don't scream she told herself. That only made the pain last longer.

This wasn't right. The feeling of connection with Ava had been severed. Logan's eyes flew to Ava's face. What he saw was terrifying. Ava's brows were bunched together, her lower lip was trapped between her teeth, and her chin trembled.

"Ava?" She didn't respond. Logan went still. "Open your eyes. Look at me."

She squeezed them tighter. He could feel a cool sweat forming on her body. What was happening to her? He needed her to come back to him for both their sanity.

"Open. Your. Eyes. Ava. Look at me now," he snapped." His voice was firm, too firm, but her eyes opened at his command.

She was unfocused, unseeing before sad cappuccino eyes found his face.

"See me, sweetheart please." He applied gentle hands, caressing her back, touching her with care. God she looked to be in pain. He didn't want his contact to make it worse. She looked vulnerable. Wounded.

"I see you." A deep breathe left her body. "Safe," he heard her whisper before she sagged atop him.

"Keep your eyes on me." Something, no someone else had claimed her. Worried and concerned for Ava, Logan gripped her hips and lifted, to pull free of her body. He wanted to cradle her in his arms, slay all her demons.

Her hand at his chest stayed him. She was looking at him now. The sadness was still there, but there was another emotion her saw in her firmed lip and alert eyes.

"No, Logan, I don't want us to stop." He studied her. He was wary to grant her request so soon after her obvious distress. He was thinking of a way to change her mind when she frowned. A subtle fortitude reflected in her eyes.

"I know what I'm asking. Help me."

Logan nodded in understanding. Ava needed new memories. He would give them to her tonight. "Don't take your eyes off me and say my name."

She stared at him in confusion. Not understanding his request.

"Logan." With that he hardened inside of her, but didn't move. Her soft groan of pleasure spurred him.

"Say it again, tell me you see me. Only me."

"Logan, I see you."

"Again."

"I see you, Logan." The tension started to leave her body. Slick heat welcomed him. A slow burn licked through his veins as she moved on him. He began to drive inside of her.

"Yes." Her eyes drifted closed.

A surge of power filled him as he drove them both toward the brink between lost and found. He pushed deep knowing he was stretching her to the limit.

"Open your eyes sweetheart. Stay with me." She did as he commanded.

"I see you, Logan."

He watched as her head fell backwards, exposing her slender neck, her cries echoing off the ceiling. He claimed her with every powerful thrust. She was his. No one else would ever have her. Possession resonated in every thrust into her satiny heat. "Yes … Logan."

"You're mine Ava," he groaned. Logan was pressed so deep inside of her, the confines of his body blurred and fused with her.

"Yes, Logan" He thrust into her again and again with an urgency that sent their passion blazing out of control. Her body squeezed, and clenched around him. And when the end came for both of them it was carnal, consuming, and explosive. She collapsed beside him and he tucked her close into his side.

"There will be many nights spent in pleasure for us Ava," he said as fatigue slowly claimed them both.

Ava snuggled closer in his arms and he heard her sigh of contentment. He looked at the beautiful woman lying in his arms, head pillowed on his chest, eyes closed, with a soft curl to her lips. She looked satiated even in sleep. There was a unique scar on the back of her right shoulder he hadn't seen before tonight. This angle allowed him to study it more closely. He ran his fingers over the evenly spaced indentations and immediately he recognized what they were. Anger, raw and bloodthirsty, rushed through him. A human bite. He pulled her closer wanting to shield her from every hurt. She meant everything to him.

Ava awoke naked with an equally naked Logan grinning down at her. Smiling back at him, her body quickened at the sight of his messy bed hair and a night's growth of stubble covering that chiseled jaw. Stretching her frame over his body, she lifted her head, curls in every direction and grinned at him. She took in her surroundings with the wide eyes of new discovery. The reality that she'd had sex with Logan last night and they both liked it had her mind reeling. He grinned back at her.

"Good morning." She placed a light kiss on his chin. Kissing him like this, waking up in Logan's bed, made her feel like a normal woman. Before she had only known pain and fear.

He captured her chin, lifted her face and drove into her mouth claiming his prize.

"Good morning beautiful. You look well satisfied."

"I probably look tired." Because good sex made you tired, she thought with glee.

"If you expected to look the same as when you entered my bedroom you should not have picked me."

She moved to fully extricate herself from his arms and he gripped her wrist.

"Stay." That arrogant, wide grin of his said that she wouldn't be going back to sleep anytime soon.

"I'm just going to the bathroom, Logan."

He released his grip. "Don't be gone long."

His eyes closed on the last word. He looked exhausted. Somehow that pleased her to know she might be the death of him too. She certainly didn't want to be the only one behaving as a sex crazed lunatic. Her body was singing in all the right places. Her thighs were tight and sore, similar to the aftermath of a Brazilian dance class, but better. Logan had worked her in the most delicious ways imaginable. She still couldn't believe that sex could be so out of this world amazing. The tingle between her legs made her smile. Logan had turned her into a sex addict in one night.

Ava stood in the bathroom door mouth gaped open at the expansive luxury of Logan's master bath. It was bigger than both her bedrooms combined. Sunlight poured into the room from triple skylights in the exposed wood beam ceiling. The monochromatic natural stone floors with coordinating dual sink tops on the far wall were a striking contrast to the dark cabinets and iron hardware. The wall length beveled mirror reflected a multicolored river rock wall with an embedded fireplace behind the footed spa tub. There was even a sheepskin rug with perfectly placed slippers by the rainfall shower.

"OMG, you have a fireplace in your bathroom?" Whoa. If she had known this sumptuous space was available to her weeks ago, she would've jumped at the chance to share his master suite.

"Hot and naked is preferred."

Behind her Logan's powerful, bare arms circled her waist. He brushed his lips over her curls. She let her body soften, molded herself to him and waited. Her thoughts were racing as she felt his burgeoning hardness press into her bottom. *She wanted him again too* and that scared her a little.

"Go back to bed. I'll be back in a minute." Covering his hands with hers, she marveled at the indulgence of touching him, of feeling all the power and strength of him made gentle for her sake. Last night he had given her a gift she never dreamt to receive. She felt her feminine power with him. She loved very physical, toe curling, hoarse crying, multi-orgasmic sex with Logan. And, that admission scared her a lot.

"I asked you not to be gone a long time, this is officially too long."

He gathered her in his muscled arms and placed a soft kiss on her cheek.

"Get all your sweetness back in our bed," he teased.

"It's almost eleven in the morning Logan, I should go home."

His expression hardened. "Why are you trying to go home?"

His grip firmed around her shoulders. He pulled her closer, as if he were afraid she would vanish.

"I don't live here with you." He took a deep inhale, his expanded chest pressed against her back.

"You could." Looking straight ahead into the mirror, she saw the crease between his brows. The thinning of his full lips in displeasure. He'd used those lips to taste every inch of her skin. The strain of her reluctance clearly reflected on his face. Line in the sand, this was a boundary she wouldn't cross.

"My things are at my house," she pushed the words out with a resolve that didn't quite echo her feelings. "I need to get cleaned up. Start my day. I still have a life outside of you Logan."

"You can start your day from here. Being with me should not exist in some far off realm. I am a permanent part of your life, whether you realize it or not. Your life includes me, the same holds true where I'm concerned. I explained this to you already and you acted as if you understood. I want us together in every sense of the word. My definition of together includes physically together. Ava, I have never asked this of another woman. What exists between us is a new experience for me, but I know I don't want it to end."

"My going home doesn't translate as the end. Why do you need to see me, touch me, to know I'm with you?"

His body stiffened behind her, she took in his blank stare. His normally verdant eyes were the muted green of jade stone. She didn't think he would answer the question.

He spoke, but his voice was cold, flat, and minus emotion.

"Women don't always do what they say," he stated, matter-of-factly. "I want to know where you are. Know that you are mine."

She was speechless. No man had ever felt this level of intensity for her. Logan's words were everything a woman wanted to hear from her man, but his words terrified her. One night of sex with Logan and she couldn't go home, literally and figuratively speaking.

"Logan, we had sex. It doesn't mean we have to move in together and our previous lives cease to exist."

"I didn't just have sex last night. I made love with you. I want you here with me. Our lives are not connected, they were blended together, and were forever changed the second you gave yourself to me. You are mine, my woman. I would give you the world if you asked for it, but don't ask me to let go. I am not letting you go."

Beyond speechless. It was official. The line from the *Wizard of Oz* came to mind, *"You're not in Kansas anymore Dorothy."* What the heck had she gotten herself into?

"Logan, we need to talk."

"I don't need to talk. You should have talked before you gave yourself to me. Willingly Ava. You gave yourself willingly." He was clenching his jaw now at the continued conversation. "I never misled you. You knew what I wanted from day one. For some unknown reason you have been afraid of a relationship with me from the moment we met. Last night you tamed your fear and gave me one of the most precious gifts a woman can honor a man with, her body. You chose me and I in turn will honor you. We will take it slower. You have all the time you need to process everything that has happened between us, but I refuse to back down, back off, step back, or any other nonsense." He kissed her with a slow, thorough passion, liquefying her resolve. "I am keeping you." His roguish smile causing somersaults in her belly. He kissed the top of her head. "Everything you need is here with me." Logan pulled her in close, squeezing her waist.

"I'm going to get us some breakfast. Be here when I get back Ava."

He dressed quickly, leaving the bedroom without another word in her direction. She heard the door leading to the garage close. Finally, she was alone with her thoughts. She needed to busy herself to calm the onslaught of emotion flooding her brain. Images of her joined with Logan permeated her thoughts. His body was muscles of steel wrapped in the finest linen. His touch, his voice, his breath on her skin was a long lost caress; a heated wave overtaking her, cleansing away the fingerprints of everything that came before him. Could she do what he asked?

Logan was demanding everything. Her foolish heart was ready to surrender, but what would he do if he discovered her secret? It was a risk she wasn't willing to take, not yet. Absentmindedly she stepped into the deluxe shower enclosure, complete with heated tiles and a rainfall shower control in the ceiling and washed away the evidence of the previous night's passion. Donning her wrinkled blouse and a pair of Logan's boxers, her bra nowhere in sight, she finger combed her damp curls into a messy cascade. She would change clothes once she reached her room downstairs.

She never imagined how good sharing her body with Logan could be. She felt connected to him in a way she didn't know was possible. This was the first time in her life that she had participated in sex. More than just a hapless bystander in the act, allowing a man to use her body for his pleasure. Her eyes settled on her bra tangled in the bed sheets, all but forgotten after Logan stripped her bare. She was the only one in the house, no need for the chest binder at this point. A shiver ran through her body as she recalled the moist heat of his mouth on her skin. The fabric of her blouse chafed against her budding nipples. *Get yourself under control Ava.* She smiled to herself. Even the thought of him commanded a response from her body.

# CHAPTER TWELVE

The faint verbal chime of Ava's phone signaled a new text message. She crossed the room searching through the two piles of discarded clothes looking for her phone. It wasn't there. She dropped to her knees to inspect under the bed before climbing onto the bed lifting all the bedcovers.

*Check the sofa*, she thought to herself with a snap of her fingers.

With bare feet she bounced down the stairs as she delighted in the joy of having Logan love her last night.

"Let's go to breakfast," Lina's text message read. Ava texted back, "Busy."

Seconds later her phone rang.

"Busy doing what?" Lina asked. Straight to the point.

"I'm having breakfast with Logan." At Lina's squeal, Ava pulled the phone away from her ear. She wandered around the family room touching and mock arranging the plaques and trophies on the mantel.

"What time did he pick you up this morning?"

Ava positioned the phone back to her ear. She remained quiet, cursing her routine life. Nervousness crept up her spine, trying to permeate her voice, she managed to steel her tone before answering the expected question.

"He didn't." Ava closed her eyes bracing for Lina's reply.

Ava pulled the receiver away again, but not before the scream and laughter resounded off her ringing eardrum.

"You stayed the night with the love doctor didn't you?" Lina said, in a sensual mock tone, full of breathy endings and giggles.

"Don't call him that."

"You're defending him? O-M-Goosebumps, he got you good." Ava heard the sharp intake of breath before Lina dropped the verbal bomb.

"Logan met Cricket!" her friend screamed.

You would think someone had won the lottery listening to Lina holler in the background.

"Don't hold out on me girlfriend. How much action did Cricket get?"

Ava could not respond. She was embarrassed that her best friend knew all the details of her previously non-existent sex life. She didn't realize there was a post-sex celebration requirement between best friends.

"Yes, yes, yes!" Lina chanted into the phone. "Ladies and gentlemen, Cricket has left the stall, she's burning up the track, she's rounded the bend, hurdle in her sight and she nails it."

They both burst into laughter.

"Are you supposed to be this happy for me? I don't think it's customary for women to rejoice over each other's sex life."

"I'm celebrating your sex life. There is no ship pulling into my harbor. Besides, we're best friends, we can celebrate anything we want." Ava heard Lina clear her throat. "So was he all that and a bowl of steaming hot, buttery, slow cooked grits?"

"I'm not kissing and telling. My mortification at you celebrating my love life should be enough to fuel your one woman party."

"So, what all did you kiss?" Lina asked low and playfully. "Does he have skills in the bedroom or not?"

Maybe, a little sharing was okay. No details.

"Lina," Ava said, in a singsong voice, "The man had me climbing the octave scale higher than vintage Mariah at the MTV awards. Cricket was doing back flips, swinging from the high bar, and flash dancing all at the same time."

"Dang, girl. You got a show under the big top and all the stuffed animals."

"It was all that Lina." Giddy at retelling the story, Ava couldn't contain her happy feeling. "Oh my goose bumps is right. I want to break off a little piece of him, then hide the rest away because I'm afraid I might run out if I eat it too fast."

Lina screamed into the phone. "Girl, I'm jumping up and down in this condo. My neighbors are going to call the cops. Yeah, you found yourself a Master Cricket Tamer." Lina was giggling now. "I am so happy for you Ava."

A sound coming from the kitchen caught Ava's attention. "I'll call you back, I hear Logan in the kitchen." Not wanting to be caught sharing details about their night together, Ava was anxious to end the call.

"You got him cooking?"

"Yeah, right. He left to go get us breakfast." This was the opening to ask about what had happened between her and Jace. "How are things between you and Jace?" Logan could wait a few minutes, especially since the conversation had shifted from talk about last night.

"Don't blow my secondary high by mentioning *his* name."

"What's happening, Lina?"

"It doesn't matter. Jace is officially a part of black history."

"Black history?"

"As in, my big, black butt is history. In more ways than I care to discuss." Lina sounded more than sad. Ava recognized the hurt.

"I'm so sorry. Are you really okay? You haven't been available in the last few weeks. And why aren't you working on the psychiatric unit?"

"You know me. When love calls, I answer. When love hangs up, I find myself another number to call."

Ava wasn't convinced Lina was coping as well as she claimed.

"No more talk about me and another sad love song. Kudos to you Ava, you've got that man out of bed on a Saturday morning to do your bidding. Logan is a keeper."

That's what she was afraid of.

Ava ended the call with Lina. She hummed as she glided across the carpeted floor to the cool kitchen tiles. She was happy. Her elation had everything to do with Logan especially after her love summit with Lina. Logan was a keeper. And she would be doing the keeping.

She halted in her tracks. There was a man in the kitchen. A young, broad shouldered, chiseled jawline, ruggedly handsome man. He wore faded denim jeans that fit with the custom cut of being tailored and a black tee shirt that clung in all the right places. Ava glanced down at his well-worn, expensive boots before drawing her eyes back to his face. In Ava's opinion, he was underdressed compared to the other people in Logan's social circle. When he smiled, recognition dawned.

"You must be Logan's younger brother, Darwin."

He was tall like Logan, but where Logan looked roguishly polished,

Darwin looked casual with a glint of danger behind his easy smile. He stood extending his hand towards her. She accepted, offering a firm handshake.

"I am his brother. You can drop the 'young' modifier. It makes Logan feel old and me infantile."

"You're not what I expected," he said still holding Ava's hand.

She wasn't sure how to take his comment. She tugged her hand from his grip, curling her fingers into the cotton fabric covering her leg.

"I apologize. I left my southern charm in the truck. It's nice to meet you Ava."

"How do you know my name?" His blue eyes looked troubled.

"Graham told me about you, but I still find myself dumb struck by your loveliness."

Ava felt herself blush. She wondered what Graham had told Darwin about her. He had witnessed how destructive she could be not only to herself, but to others. Barely escaping with her life out on a Saturday stroll. Had Logan shared about their relationship? Apart from Lina who was an investigative journalist when it came to matters of the heart, she had avoided conversations about Logan with her friends. Her family was a separate matter. They never failed to insert a question about Logan into the conversation. But at least, they employed some stealth to disguise their inquiries. She'd kept her most intimate thoughts about Logan private. Perhaps Logan hadn't done the same. Not knowing how to respond to Darwin's confession, an unnatural silence settled over the room.

Darwin was taking in her appearance. The wet hair, men's boxers, and no bra probably told most of the story. The *morning after costume*, following a rough tumble in the sheets based on her state of undress. A broad smile crossed his face reflecting that he had just reached the same embarrassing conclusion.

"Logan should return any moment. Saturday errands are calling, so I'm going to go. It was nice meeting you."

His sly smile was telling. Not as casual as he appeared. He analyzed and calculated with the same finesse as Logan, definitely a Masters descendant.

"Don't leave on my account. You just got here, right?"

Why was everyone teasing her this morning? First Lina about Cricket, now Darwin with his disarming wit about her presence. Another confession would not be heard from her lips.

"I know my brother. He will be pissed at me if you leave before he returns." He was no longer joking. "We don't want any trouble with Logan."

He offered her another one of those knowing smiles.

"Have a seat Ava. I interrupted your conversation, sorry about that."

His smile brightened, definitely mischievous.

"I heard you talking on the phone when I came in. Logan really should lock his doors. A person can't be held responsible for what they overhear." He raised one eyebrow at her.

"How much did you hear?" Was it her fate to be uncomfortable meeting anyone associated with Logan?

"Barely anything."

"Oh my To …" She needed to stop the habit, especially now that Logan had objected to the saying. "This is worse than my dance with Logan. Let's talk about something else. Logan told me you are former Navy. Tell me about your experience." Gone was the easy smile. Tightness covered his face, his eyes narrowed, his expression darkened. She wouldn't mention the Navy to him again.

"Earth to Darwin." Looking her in the eye he laughed at the jest, but it sounded forced.

"You got Logan on a dance floor."

It was her turn to raise a brow. Logan was a skilled dance partner. He didn't have a problem keeping her occupied.

"It was his suggestion."

"I'll tell my mother those dance lessons were not in vain. She will be happy."

He motioned for her to join him.

"Relax. Brothers do not divulge details of one another's private life. Besides, if Logan comes home to find you gone, you may never see me again."

The door that should have been locked, but never was, clicked with the twist of the knob.

"Ava?"

That was her man's voice. Her foolish heart skipped a beat. Logan was back.

"In the kitchen," she called in answer.

Both she and Darwin were seated at the countertop bar when Logan rounded the corner. Those green eyes sought her first, and then glanced in Darwin's direction.

"Ah, the prodigal brother returns. It has been weeks since I heard from you. How long have you been here?"

"Long enough to get acquainted with the beautiful Miss Ava Walters."

Darwin's smile was just as breathtaking as his older brother's, but it did not have the same effect as Logan's on her insides. Nothing compared to Logan, especially after the way he loved her body last night.

"Logan, I was about to leave so you can spend some time with your brother."

The crumpled brown bag he was holding made a distinct sound as it dropped to the countertop, then he lowered the compressed paper tray holding their coffee next to the bag. Logan looked at her through narrowed eyes, and inclined his head. She knew that look never bode well for her.

"Goodbye Darwin. I'll meet you upstairs sweetheart."

Logan's eyes never strayed from hers. His words rang with authority. This was no request; it was a dictate to all within hearing range.

At her hesitation, Logan crossed the room, his voice low so only she could hear, and said, "We both need to eat."

He placed a barely there kiss on her forehead. Thank the heavens it wasn't more. She knew Darwin watched and her body was responding with the attentiveness of a prodigy obeying its master. His breath on her neck sent tingles zinging through her body, her knees went weak. Barely able to support her own weight, his hand at the small of her back guided her towards the staircase.

Not wanting to be rude, Ava turned in Darwin's direction, "It was nice meeting you."

"It was my pleasure. Look me up on Facebook if you really want to know more about my experience, sweetheart." He was grinning at her.

"Don't call her that. You call her Ava." Logan glared at his brother.

"What?" Darwin shrugged with a devilish smile covering his face. "You just called her sweetheart."

"I know what I can do Darwin," Logan growled.

Logan was being unnecessarily gruff.

"Logan," she snapped, trying to control the annoyance she felt at his treatment of Darwin. The conversation with his brother came to an abrupt halt. Logan looked at her.

"Enough. Stop giving Darwin a hard time. You've been impossible all morning."

"I apologize. It's been a morning of unforeseen circumstance."

Darwin raised his eyebrows at their exchange. Ava quickly exited the room, before another shame-faced moment could present itself.

Logan was anxious to get back to Ava. Darwin, who was watching him with an assessing stare, needed to go home.

"So big brother, it's that good between the two of you?"

He knew what Darwin was asking, but it was not any of his business. Darwin had formed a habit of probing Logan about the women in his life. Logan tolerated the questions about Rebecca the night of the fundraiser, but what happened between him and Ava was off limits.

"What are you talking about?" Logan waited, interested to hear what his brother would say next.

He wasn't offering any information about his Ava.

"You have a woman in your house. A woman you are eager to get back to."

Logan remained silent.

"You're out buying breakfast. Not the other way around."

Darwin threw up his hands in a 'that's all that needs to be said gesture'.

"What is your point?"

"You all but commanded Ava to go back to the cave and wait. You haven't seen me, your only brother, in almost three weeks yet I have the impression you want to physically remove me from your new love den."

Logan moved toward the door. Time was up.

"Go home, Darwin."

"We need to talk about Rebecca. Soon."

Darwin's brow furrowed, but Logan was not in the mood to discuss business deals or Rebecca.

"I will call you when I am available."

"Take a break from your woman and call me before Monday."

"Jealous much, brother?"

"Never jealous. Pleasantly surprised that you put yourself above the family's plan for you."

Darwin never understood Logan's ambitious drive. As the firstborn, Logan had the responsibility of elevating the Masters' family name drummed into him from birth. He was to follow in his father's footsteps, then surpass them. And he would do that and more, but on his own terms. Having Ava changed everything.

"Goodbye, Darwin."

"Enjoy your weekend, but call me. We both have important decisions to make."

"I'm going to enjoy every second of it."

With that, he closed and locked the door.

Logan climbed the stairs with two steaming cups of coffee, two bagels, a fruit bowl and one yogurt parfait. As he ascended the stairs leading to his bedroom Ava materialized on the landing fully dressed.

"Why are you dressed?"

"The naked sacrifice thing didn't feel right with your brother still in the house."

"I should have hidden your clothes while you were in the bathroom."

"I don't know much about South Carolina where your folks are from, but in Florida it would be considered highly improper to walk around someone's house naked."

She teased him again, a tantalizing smile on her face. *Mine* echoed through his head.

He'd institute a reward if she lost the layers. Though she wasn't wearing much, it was more than he ever wanted to see her wearing at home.

"I give you permission to relinquish all clothing upon crossing the threshold into my domain."

He reached the landing and locked onto her lips, slowly nibbling at the lower lip. Fire immediately swept through his veins, swift and ferocious, barreling to his pelvis, and her moans fuel to the rising flames. Her breath came in pants.

Logan pulled back transfixed on what was before him. Lust was pulsating between them, a beacon bringing both to a single location. He spoke first.

"Turn around, go into the bedroom and take off your clothes."

She stiffened, eyes wide with fear and breathing at a halt. A look of being dunked in a frigid bath marred her face.

"Ava?" He placed the contents in his hands on the landing table carefully gripping her upper arms pulling her to him. She resisted initially.

"Sweetheart, tell me what's happening?" His heart was beating against his chest, but he maintained his outward calm.

Whatever it was, she was reliving it, again. He gentled his voice. Concern for her escalating when she did not answer. Wanting to squeeze her closer to him, he held back, knowing that it could make the memory more vivid for her. Last night, his voice had broken the nightmare's pull, maybe it would work this time.

"Ava, look at me." Nothing. He roughened his voice. "Ava," he repeated her name once more. "Tell me you see me, Logan."

And just like that, sad eyes looked up at him. She was back. His Ava. Her breathing was ragged, but she was looking at him. Unable to stop himself, he pulled her into his arms. God, some man had hurt her badly. Rage at knowing she'd been hurt had him tightening his hold on her.

"Tell me what happened, sweetheart. Who hurt you?"

"No."

Tears swam in her fearful eyes as she held her lower lip between her teeth.

Logan could see her pain. He felt the heat from the emotional blade slicing through him.

"What we have is real," he said stroking her hair. "I'll always be here for you. I would never hurt you, Ava." Knowing some poor excuse for a man in her past had hurt her so deeply that retelling the story brought both pain and fear to her eyes angered him. After witnessing the horror of what she must have experienced for the second time, Logan's urge to protect intensified.

She pushed at his chest. "It's nothing."

The words incongruent with the tremors he felt holding her this close. He looked down at her then, remnants of pain still visible on her face.

"You look ready to collapse."

She turned away, but he captured her chin, turning her to face him. He placed a tender kiss on her lips.

"Talk to me. You can tell me anything." The way her face remained fixed, he knew she didn't believe him. At her silence, he continued on hoping something he said would cut through her doubts.

"I triggered something last night and it happened again. I can't help but touch you. I want it to feel good for both of us. Tell me how to stop causing you pain."

"I wish I knew. I had a bad relationship in college. I don't want to talk about it."

He took her face in his hands, cradled her as gently as he knew how. Those tear filled eyes squeezed his heart. "I don't need your submission, Ava. I need your trust."

Logan pressed his lips to hers and breathed in her vanilla and honey fragrance. The caress along the length of his jawline had him lingering in her taste, relishing her touch on his skin. As the seconds passed his pulse rate normalized and he ended the kiss. He pulled her into his arms, pressed her head to his chest.

"Your heart is safe with me, Ava. Give it to me." He felt her body tremble, before her arms came around his middle.

"I am going to put you in bed and feed you from my hand. You like that idea?"

She nodded her head without lifting it from his chest.

"Then we are going to make new memories together. Maybe, do a few things to make you scream my name. Keep the faint at heart from dropping by uninvited. Huh?" He felt her smile against his chest. The fist squeezing his heart released its grip.

"Okay," she replied.

He was proud of her. His Ava had pushed her pain and fears away for him, for them.

He reluctantly released her. She gave him a half smile before turning in the direction of the bedroom. Logan grabbed the bags from the table, followed her into the bedroom and closed the door. *Mine.*

# CHAPTER THIRTEEN

Ava was on day two of her emotional high. For the first time in her adult life, she felt complete. A patient occupied every bed in her pod when she started her shift at six forty-five this morning. Late breakfast trays nearly triggered an international incident and the pharmacy hadn't supplied her the medications for the day. But not one of those things dampened the melody in Ava's heart. Thoughts of falling asleep in Logan's arms tonight had her humming love songs in between comforting parents and calming babies.

Kathryn had left a message for Ava to stop by her office. She could hear the beep of the telemetry monitor located at the central nurse's station from her patient care area. Being able to hear the monitoring equipment over the unit activity was as good as any indication that the morning rush had come to an end.

Ava motioned to Patty, the round faced, gray haired woman who worked as the nursing assistant on her team.

"Patty, I'm going to meet with Kathryn before her day ends. Please update each patient's intake and output record before lunch arrives. Our patients are stable, but I'll ask Spencer to cover while I'm away."

The woman nodded her head in agreement and went back to reading the computer screen.

The physician teams wouldn't return until the end of the day. The procession of gurneys that formed a make shift human train leading to the radiology suite had dwindled to one.

It was best to use the reprieve wisely. Ava locked her computer terminal then headed in the direction of Kathryn's office. She exited her work station, covered the short distance to where Spencer sat in a swivel chair that strained at the rivets under the weight of his muscled physique. Spencer looked up from his computer terminal and smiled with pure devilment in his eyes.

Ava didn't want to know what had put that smile on his sculpted face. "Cover for me while I meet with Kathryn?"

"Sure thing. How long?"

"Maybe fifteen minutes."

"Done and done."

She wouldn't linger in the nurse manager's office. Kathryn was one of the few administrative nurses who still could provide direct patient care with ease. Though she'd worked in the position for two years, Ava knew Kathryn took great pride in being a floor nurse first and an administrator second.

Ava knocked on the door, announced herself, and then waited for the invitation to enter.

"Come on in," Ava heard the woman say.

Kathryn's face looked solemn. Ava wondered what could make this usually jovial woman look so glum.

"Hi, you wanted to see me?"

The small, windowless center hall office was located off the inner corridor of the pediatric unit. The desk was uncluttered and color coordinated photo frames of Kathryn and her husband, Cannon, occupied both front desk corners.

"Please have a seat." She gestured to the two aluminum and cloth office chairs positioned in front of the desk.

Kathryn's impersonal tone had the hairs at Ava's nape standing on end.

"Has something happened?"

Kathryn was having trouble maintaining eye contact with her. The hairs on the back of her neck had little arcs of electricity flowing through them at that.

"Ava. There's been a complaint filed against you."

Ava's throat constricted, her stomach roiled at the words. She felt nauseous.

"A patient complained about me?" Oh no, not now, a complaint could jeopardize her receiving the endorsement for her commissioning package.

"No."

No? Ava furrowed her brows in confusion.

"But, you said …"

Kathryn interrupted her by holding up one hand. "It's not a patient complaint. One of the foundation's donors filed a complaint against you."

At the mention of the foundation, Ava instantly knew the source of her trouble and anger coursed through Ava's veins. She had a white knuckled grip on the arms of the chair, willing the sudden surge of rage back into a box. It had to be Commando Barbie.

"What are the allegations in the complaint?" Ava inquired.

"That's the concerning part." At Ava's obvious confusion Kathryn continued.

"Randall Lester paid a visit to my office this morning. Apparently, he was personally made aware of the complaint. Mentioned that he didn't consider you a qualified candidate for a professional endorsement and returned your commissioning packet."

The breath froze in Ava's chest. A fissure opened in her heart, a sharp burn filled her chest.

"However," Kathryn continued while Ava sat paralyzed, the feeling of doom threatening to pull her to her knees, "he did not provide me with a written statement detailing the allegations against you."

If Randall knew about the complaint, Ava knew the rest of what Kathryn had to say would only be worse for her. She couldn't let him do this to her. But what power did she have to stop him?

"Kathryn, what's going to happen now?" Ava could hear the quake in her voice, the desperation as she forced the words past trembling lips.

"I can't be sure, but I thought it unusual that the Director of Operations personally delivered the message, rather than informing the nursing director."

Ava offered a cautious nod, leery of trusting Kathryn with the details of Randall's increasing advances and threats. She had no doubt he would use this new information to his advantage. Would she ever be the master of her own life, again? So lost in her own misery, she barely heard the words Kathryn spoke.

"I took the liberty of asking Mr. Lester's secretary if any correspondence pertaining to you had been received by his office. Nothing beyond your commissioning packet and endorsement request has been routed through his office. It would appear that your package was being held in his inbox for signature. Sheila, his secretary, and I were in the same military spouse support group a few years back when our husbands were on deployment."

Ava released a shaky breath. Closing her eyes, she fought to hold back the tears threatening to fall. Her dreams were sifting through her fingers.

Dear God, she didn't think she could stand. Her whole body started to shake.

"Ava you're going to be okay. Why has Randall Lester taken a personal interest in you?"

Ava shook her head in denial. Nothing was going to be okay. Randall knew she was vulnerable now. He would move in for the kill and she would be a casualty in the game he played. Her job, her reputation, her dream would crumble with the force of a mortar round striking concrete because she would never give herself to a man like Randall.

A single tear slid down her cheek. "It's never going to be okay again."

Kathryn stood and came around her desk to sit at Ava's side. Taking Ava's trembling hand.

"You can trust me. I won't do or say anything to make the situation more difficult for you. Tell me what's going on and I'll do what I can to help."

Ava respected Kathryn. She had seen her be an advocate for nurses with the medical staff and administrators. There was no reason not to trust Kathryn's offer to help. Could she trust her own judgment when her dream was at risk? The protective circle that shielded her heart broke open and she told Kathryn everything.

Ava had been distracted for days, Logan noticed. When he'd questioned her, she denied that there was a problem. But she seemed more fragile and solitary. Even with him in the room, she withdrew inside herself, seemingly afraid to maintain the connection between them. The Shell Cove Medical Foundation social was fast approaching. He wanted her at his side when he made the final push for the board position.

"Ava."

She looked up from the novel she was reading. Her feet curled protectively under her on the other end of the couch. She had tried to leave him, but it was like she wasn't expecting him to stay.

"Hmm?"

"I want you to come with me on Tuesday to the foundation's social at the Tower Club. It is a business meeting masquerading as a social because they provide refreshments."

"Logan, I think we should keep your career and our relationship in separate corners. I don't know those people and they probably don't want to know me."

Her tone was apologetic and laced with regret. Was his world as shallow as she believed it to be?

Why didn't she want to be a part of every aspect of his life? Something she refused to share with him was holding her back from truly being with him. What more could he do to reassure her he was not going anywhere? They would be together. The tingle in the back of his cranium reinforced that something was wrong. Her reluctance to share his life did not make sense.

"Are you seeing someone else?" As the color drained from her face, Logan mentally berated himself for uttering the hurtful words. She closed the novel, both hands lay still in her lap then she raised her chin and leveled him with disbelief etched on her face.

"How can you ask me that question?" The desolate stare she settled on him made him feel like the worst kind of jerk. The tightness in his chest didn't keep him from going to her, in two powerful strides he was at her side taking her in his arms.

"I'm sorry, sweetheart." She was rigid as a steel blade in his arms. He had hurt her again. He wanted to do the right thing where Ava was concerned, but he continued to fall short.

"How could you think that about me?" Delivered in a whisper, the hurt in her voice rang out a resounding clang in his chest.

"I don't know what to think. I want you to want to be with me."

Ava had yet to meet any of his friends, besides Graham. To give him credit she had met Gideon Rice, but she already knew him as one of the psychiatrists on staff. Logan thought having Ava attend a Shell Cove Medical Foundation social with him would serve as an introduction to his circle of acquaintances.

"I want you, Logan. Don't ever doubt that." She looked up into his eyes, honesty shone bright in the depths.

"Then come with me on Tuesday. I'm not above bribery to get what I want. Say yes," he nibbled her earlobe earning him a playful swat to the abdomen.

"No one knows me and I'd just be in the way. What's the bribe?"

"You know me. That's enough." He reached into his trouser pocket and pulled out a square, signature blue jewelry box. At the sight of the box, Ava narrowed her eyes. She watched him as he lifted her left hand to his lips, kissed each finger before turning her palm up and lowering the box to the center.

Gently he sucked her lower lip between his teeth before he kissed her. He deepened the kiss. Laying her back on the couch, covering her body with his broad frame. He used his tongue to tease and tantalize until she was panting and reaching for him. Passion, raw and wild, straining for release thrummed through her body. He had done that to her.

"What's in the box?" She regarded him with uncertainty.

"Open it and see." Slowly, as if expecting a fatal bite, she removed the lid from the outer box and lifted the velvet-covered case from its confines. When the two-carat diamond heart necklace came into view she drew in a sharp breath.

"It's a beautiful necklace Logan, but you can't give this to me," she said extending the case back to him.

She hadn't bothered to touch it. He frowned a little before it occurred to him what she needed to hear to accept what he was offering. She had to know why.

"It's my heart, Ava." He saw the small tremble to her lower lip, first. He continued needing her to understand what she meant to him. "I'm giving you my heart, because you are mine and I am yours." Tears filled her eyes as she pulled the box closer to her own heart and lightly touched her fingers to the pendant. She smiled up at him and laughed. With tears of happiness flowing down her beautiful face, she laughed and he could breathe again.

"Logan."

At the husky sound of his name coming from her lips, he reached for the pendant and pulled it free of its anchor. Unhooking the clasp, he placed it around her neck and secured it at her nape. "Don't take it off," he said as he claimed her mouth once more.

"I won't."

Did she understand the significance of those two words? He loved her. Neither of them had said the words aloud, but this had to mean she shared the same feelings. He wanted to believe she loved him.

"Say yes to everything and I will finish what I started." He felt her hands close around his neck as she pulled him flush with her body.

"Yes, Logan."

Yes had never sounded so good. He smiled as he slid her tank top over her head and reclaimed her lips.

Tonight was Ava's introduction into the Masters' world. A step she had been avoiding until now. His friends and business acquaintances appeared welcoming, at least on the surface. Ava received more second glances instead of conversations, from both men and women. It was important that this meeting go well for Logan. Ava knew the support of tonight's attendees was critical to him securing the majority of the foundation's current board of director's votes. She observed his skillful navigation from one group of local influencers to another. His conversation transitioned from politics to the stock market onto sport statistics with seamless ease. The venue was small, elegant of course. The men were in business suits, the women in dark blue, black or grey dress suits with a single strand of pearls adorning their collars. A sea of homogeneity and her.

Ava excused herself from the circle to order another club soda from the bar when she was stopped by an impeccably dressed, medium height, mousy haired man.

"Hello beautiful lady. I haven't had the pleasure of making your acquaintance." Ava blushed and released a tentative smile at the compliment. This man was the first person to initiate a dialogue with her. Maybe she could fit into Logan's world, one person at a time.

"Holton Faraday, one of the foundation board members." He introduced himself.

"Thank you, Holton." He rubbed his jaw on one side as he studied her with an odd expression. She fingered the heart pendant on her neckline to camouflage her nervous movements.

Holton was not a classically handsome man. His nose was hawkish, his lips too thin and tight. His brown hair looked disheveled with inattention.

"Your pendant is quite lovely," he said with an amused tone.

"It was a gift." She blushed in remembrance of what Logan had done to her after placing the pendant around her neck.

"You'd be radiant in the matching earrings or bracelet." Ava thought his comment odd. She gave a tentative smile, unsure where to take the conversation.

"Are you from The House?"

Ava's mouth fell open at the question. The bottom fell out of her stomach as bile rose in her throat. *Oh my God.*

'The House' was on the southwest side of Shell Cove. The women in residence there engaged in the oldest profession in the world. That part of the city lived by another set of rules. It was the proverbial 'other side of the tracks'. Ava knew intimate details about the House because of her best friend Janna.

That Holton would think such a thing was bad enough, but to hear the words aimed at her, left Ava reeling.

"No. If you'll excuse me." Ava took a shaky step back when she recognized the unnatural interest in the man's eyes. Him approaching her spoke louder than any of his words. The implication of his bold proposition was profound. The message screamed the only way a black woman would be present in this elite circle was as a paid escort.

*Where was Logan?*

"Another establishment then. I've never known Logan to dabble on the dark side, but you are stunning. I'll take your contact information now. When are you available?"

Ava was about to push past the man, when Logan finally arrived.

"Holton," Logan inclined his head in the other man's direction. "Ava, come with me, there's someone I'd like you to meet." He proffered his elbow.

"Don't rush her off. I was just about to get her details before you arrived."

Logan dropped his elbow, turned to face Holton, spine straight, as waves of menace pulsed from his eyes.

"What details were you getting?" Logan's voice was deep and animalistic.

Holton took a step backward at Logan's tone. "Why all the bravado? I can wait till you're done with her."

At that, Logan took a threatening step toward Holton, who hadn't realized he was in mortal danger until that moment. The business meeting drummed on oblivious to the impending death match near the bar. Ava threw both her arms around Logan's bicep, planting her feet to anchor him in place.

"If you touched her they will find pieces of you scattered on the lawn in the morning."

The man's eyes stretched wide in dawning comprehension. "Wait. You can't be serious about this." Holton gestured his hands from Ava back to Logan. "Staying with this woman will ruin your chances at the board position. Not even your family name could save you from the scandal. You'll never recover."

"We're leaving before I have to kill this son of a..." It was Ava's turn to interrupt.

"Don't say it. Enough damage has been done for one night." She felt hollow inside.

"Get away from us, Holton."

He didn't need to be told twice. Ava watched as Holton joined a large group of prominent businessmen and women. None of them she would have personally met without being on Logan's arm. In his world, she was little more than a possession to be passed from one master to the next.

"Ava, look at me."

She didn't want to look at anyone. More importantly, she didn't want anyone to look at her. Did all these people think she was a whore? Hired entertainment to fulfill Logan's exotic taste of forbidden pleasures.

She couldn't look at him. He had done nothing wrong, but she didn't want to look into his mesmerizing green eyes and forget what had happened tonight. She needed to remember. She needed to find her place in the world. *You can't keep him.*

"I'm fine Logan." It was a lie.

Logan walked into his office on Wednesday morning, shaking the precipitation from his jacket, to find Samuel Holbrook sitting in his chair behind his desk. Evidently the incident with Holton had circulated beyond the gossip mill because Holbrook didn't leave his estate throne unless his kingdom was under attack.

The other man was the first to speak.

"Just the man I was looking for." His voice boomed with enough bass to vibrate the glass panes at his back. "Seems we've missed one another at the club."

Logan got the message loud and clear. The gentlemanly Mister Holbrook was not pleased that he had to come to him.

"Sam. I was not expecting you this morning." That earned Logan a narrowed glance.

"You should have, after that stunt you pulled last night."

Logan held his position by the door. He wasn't in the mood to have anyone chastising him for defending Ava.

"Not inviting my daughter to the foundation social was a mistake."

Lines creased around Holbrook's mouth. He had a white knuckled grip on the leather armrests of the high back desk chair.

Logan didn't engage the man in conversation, not trusting himself to remain calm if the subject of Ava was raised. He didn't care what business alliances existed between Holbrook and the Masters families. All bets were off when it came to his woman. And Ava, not Rebecca, was his woman.

"The alliance between our two families is conditional. It's based on your relationship with Rebecca. It appears to me that my daughter is the only one holding up her end of the bargain."

Logan's jaw tightened and his fists clenched. "Rebecca has not said anything to me about our arrangement."

Logan had not seen or heard from her since the night of the gala. He needed to make that phone call to Darwin and get some answers.

"I'll take care of the mess you created last night by bringing your flavor of the month to the social."

"Do not go there, Sam."

"Don't even think about reneging on your part of the bargain. My daughter will have the Masters' last name and you'll be the foundation's newest board member. Keep your eye on the prize, Logan."

Holbrook rose from the chair and moved towards him. Placing a firm hand on Logan's shoulder he came to a stop.

"I was a young man very similar to you. But, I never let lust get in the way of business."

Logan shook the other man's grip off his shoulder. What he felt for Ava went beyond lust.

"What are the words you used? *The cameras are flashing.* Remember that, Logan. The cameras are flashing and your pictures have the wrong woman in them." Sam met his eye now.

"Get rid of the girl Logan, or I'll bury the both of you."

He met Sam's glare with one of his own. "Don't threaten me Sam."

Logan seethed with anger. No business deal was going to dictate the woman in his bed. Had he towed the family's predetermined path for so long that Sam thought he wasn't his own man? That he was some extension of the Masters' family product line?

"No threat involved, think of it as a campaign promise."

A threat was aimed at Ava because of her association with him. Sam had influence on the foundation's board of directors and the research grant funding. He'd fix this. His priority was to protect Ava. He needed the support of another powerful ally. He needed his family.

# CHAPTER FOURTEEN

Ava had changed. They were physically closer, but a new emotional distance hung between them. She surrendered her body to Logan's demands, but the wall around her heart was reinforced. And it was getting harder to breach. Her body melted under his ministrations, and then the wall would expand.

Logan lay with his back against the arm of the couch. Ava lay on her stomach, head resting on his chest. Looking down, her eyes were fixed on the floor. The weight of the world reflected in their sadness.

"Dr. Masters paging RN Walters." He laughed at his attempt to lighten the mood. "Sweetheart, come back to me."

Logan had to address this divide forming between them. He recognized the signs of Ava's withdrawal. What he didn't know was why.

She looked up briefly then looked away. Pain and loss flashed in her eyes, then it was gone.

"Ava, what is going on with you?" Logan could feel Ava closing herself off to him. And it pissed him off.

"Logan, don't push."

Don't push. Was she crazy? He would push the world off its axis to reach her, to keep her.

"Sweetheart, I can feel your thoughts, and they are not good. Whatever scenario is going through your head right now, stop it. We are stronger than all the forces that want to tear us apart. Including the ones in your head." He nuzzled her hair, gently kissing her forehead. "Talk to me. I'm right here. We can work through whatever is making you feel you have to pull away from me."

"I'm not pushing you away Logan." The rise and fall of her chest had increased. He could feel her anxiety rising, the emotional walls descended to lock firmly into place.

"You are not pushing me away, but you are putting barriers up to keep me from reaching you." He released a breath laden with frustration. "Do you honestly believe I can't feel you shutting me out?"

"Sorry, I'm not doing it on purpose. Will you let me get up?"

He didn't move. Encapsulating her between his expansive chest, his arms around her waist.

"Something has changed between us. I don't like it."

"Logan please, let me move." Her eyes focused on the television straight ahead, but the muscles along her back tensed.

He released his hold. "I don't want to let you go." Not ever.

She gently pushed against his body and he felt the loss as she moved away.

"I know, but we both have a lot going on and this conversation will only make it worse." She wouldn't meet his eyes.

"What is going on in your life? Specifically." She wouldn't look at him.

He could let her walk away or push her to talk. Either option wasn't good for him, but maybe he would gain insight.

"Ava look at me. I realize I can be a Neanderthal, but I have this need to remind you that you belong with me. The unanswered question is why it feels as if I am losing you?"

Ave remained silent her eyes glued to a single spot on his chest.

"Did I do something for you to doubt that I want you?"

"It's nothing you've done."

So, someone else caused the change.

"If there is anything that needs to be handled, so that you feel secure, tell me." He hated secrets. Especially when it was attached to his woman. "Commitment to us is my first priority."

"But it shouldn't be." He sat up then, brow furrowed. He reached for her, connecting them once again. He lifted her chin to meet his eyes.

"You come first. Why should it be different?"

There was no bright light at the end of the tunnel without Ava. The pot of gold was just a pot if she left. Logan wouldn't accept it.

"I know your grant funding is temporarily suspended. Not to mention the board position."

How could she know about the funding? He had just been informed last week. Sam Holbrook was playing hardball.

"Who told you?"

"It's not important who told me. What is important is that I know."

Realization dawned. She thought the problems with the grant stemmed from them being together. She must believe that the funding cut was her fault, but Logan had a plan. In three weeks, he would present his research at the International Pediatric Medicine conference in Australia. His goal was to secure funding outside of the foundation's control.

"Ava, I will get the funding to continue my research. What I can't get is another you." He kissed her. She sank into his body and he tightened his hold. "I won't let us fail. Do you hear me?"

He pulled her arms around his waist securing her wrists in one of his large hands, effectively trapping her against his body. "Look at me."

She hesitated before meeting his gaze. He glimpsed something new behind her façade. Longing. But as quickly as it appeared it vanished.

"I am your man. You are the woman whom I adore with everything I am. Why can't you trust me?" Logan asked while cradling her face in his gentle caress. "I am willing to do whatever it takes for us to stay together. I'm not ever giving up what we have."

"We're not failing Logan. I never said those words."

"You have not said let's move forward. Am I the Titanic in an ocean of submerged icebergs?"

"Moving forward in relationships is overrated. Moving forward in my experience means you're that much closer to hitting the guardrail."

"Don't give up on us. On me. We have a life together. You are more important to me than a board position or grant funding. Say you will stay with me." She looked defeated. Lost.

"I'm with you. Know that I am giving everything that I have to offer."

He felt consumed by possessiveness, an animalistic need to tie her to him.

He also felt cornered. Sam Holbrook's threat, the suspended funding, family loyalty and the patients depending on him weighed heavy on his mind. Without funding the research protocols and medications were unavailable to patients.

He'd talked with his father about Ava. Robert Masters would support his son, alliances notwithstanding. He would introduce Ava to his father, and then she would see everything was under control. There was no threat to their being together. After that asshole Holton propositioned her, Ava refused to attend any events with him. The plan for Ava to meet his family was not the best, but it would suffice.

"It's our six week anniversary. How should we celebrate?"

She looked puzzled. "It's too soon. There's no back of the calendar gift guide for six week anniversaries."

It was not too soon for him. At the rate they were going, he should probably celebrate daily.

"We can do whatever we want. There's no guidelines, sweetheart."

"I don't have anything in mind. Since you brought it up, what's the first thing that comes to mind?"

"I want you to have brunch with me and my father this Sunday. Darwin will meet us at the club."

"What about your mother?"

"Uh. It will only be the four of us." The showdown with his mother could wait another week. "Can you convince Granny Lou to share you with the Masters family this Sunday? I promise to return you well-fed and unharmed."

"I'll tell her tomorrow."

"Call your parents, too. When Granny Lou tells them you missed church, the fallout could be detrimental to my health. My father is looking forward to meeting my woman."

She looked away, uncomfortable with the reference. When would she be comfortable being connected to him? They ate and worked together. They slept in each other's arms and pleasured one another, but he couldn't escape the feeling of a limited connectivity. Like she could disappear from his life in the blink of an eye.

"Look at me, sweetheart."

She wouldn't meet his eyes. "Ava, please."

"You. Are. Mine. Get used to it. It will not change." He would prove his words to be true.

The opulence of the Reserves Country Club rendered Ava speechless. She stood in the most lavish dining area she had ever seen. Panoramic views of the dense greens of the golf course, rippling waves and vivid blue sky was visible from every table. Waiters in black tie and jackets strategically placed at the ready to take orders. Soft notes from the pianist drifted across her ears and she sighed. This was Logan's childhood home. She was not acquainted with one person that lived in the exclusive community. Here she was at The Reserves, a private country club, with the Masters. Definitely moving forward by her standards even if Logan felt they were at an impasse. Logan's father stood beside their table to greet her.

"I'm Robert Masters," he said extending his hand.

Ava looked up into welcoming green eyes, they were Logan's eyes. He was tall, in great shape by anyone's standards, with gray at his temples. He looked distinguished and powerful. "It's nice to meet you, Mr. Masters. I'm Ava Walters."

"Call me Robert Lee. I feel like I know you. Logan talks of little else."

Ava blushed under the knowing attention of the older man. Darwin stepped around his father pulling Ava into a sisterly embrace.

"Hey Ava, it's good to see you again."

Logan pulled a heavy mahogany wood upholstered chair from the table for her to sit. Together, the men of the Masters family were ruggedly handsome and charming. Secretly, she tooted her own horn for resisting

Logan's masculine appeal for all of seven days.

The view of the manicured golf course overlooking Queens Bay to the north was spectacular. Ava choose an entree of roasted quail, braised carrots and asparagus, rather than a breakfast fare. The blend of flavors had her taste buds taking notes. She had a new recipe for the next family dinner. Everything was perfect. Logan's business associates may not accept her, but his family did. Family connections meant more to her.

"Logan honey, I thought that was you."

At the sound of that voice, the blood slowed in Ava's veins. Commando Barbie was approaching the table draped in a pastel colored St. Johns outfit, with enough diamonds glittering to imitate a star filled night. Her blonde hair was meticulously coiffed, complementing her flawless make-up.

"I didn't know you were joining us for brunch at the club. What a pleasant surprise."

The woman settled into one of the two empty seats at the table and fixed her narrowed gaze on Ava.

"Hello Mother."

Commando Barbie was Logan's mother. Bile rose in Ava's throat. The quail took flight in Ava's stomach. Closing her eyes, she willed her stomach to stop pitching high and low. She was going to be sick.

"If I didn't know any better I would think you intentionally didn't invite me." She looked pointedly at Logan. "Logan, who is this with you?"

"This is my girlfriend, Ava Walters." Logan's voice was tight. Ava looked up from her half eaten meal and came eye to eye with Logan's mother. This was worse than bad. Horrible. And the increasing waves of nausea in her stomach said it was about to get much worse.

"We are finished with brunch," Logan said. Ava darted a look, Logan's face was unreadable. Half eaten meals were visible on the plate. Something wasn't right.

"Leaving so soon? I've just arrived." Disapproval registered in his mother's tone. "What mother wouldn't want to spend time with her sons? My husband failed to mention that both my boys would be at brunch."

"Maribelle, it's not what you're making it out to be," Robert Lee commented.

From the woman's comment Ava knew this was going to be a challenging encounter for all.

"Girlfriend? Is this the reason you are single handedly ruining your chances of securing the board position?" The woman had the audacity to point a finger at Ava.

"My personal relationship with Ava has no bearing on the board selection process."

Ava didn't look up, but she heard Logan's anger.

"Does Rebecca know of your connection to this woman?" She did look up at the mention of another woman. Who was Rebecca? Maribelle's lips curled in distaste as she dissected Ava. "Tell me girlie, how is it that you met my son?" Another blow delivered.

*Girlie! She just referred to me as a girl! I don't like your mother* she wanted to scream. And she was sure her expression was as fierce as the one aimed at her. Logan's mother wanted a scene, but Ava had been raised to respect her elders, so she mustered her inner chi and responded to the wicked witch of the south.

"Logan and I met at work."

"Are you a surgeon?" Ava knew where this was going. The haves and the have-nots.

"No, I'm not."

"A nurse then, or some sort of technician," she said on a bitter laugh.

"I am a pediatric nurse." She was proud of what she had accomplished.

"Mother, leave Ava alone. Whatever you have to say, say it to me." Logan's voice was tight and brusque.

"Maribelle, that's enough," Robert Lee said. The words were short and choppy. His face drawn, deep furrows marred his brow as he looked on at his sons and Ava.

"I'm making small talk with a nurse." Her tone dripped with venom. "You must be proud of yourself gaining the attention of a surgeon, but you have overextended your reach. The Masters family has a certain standard."

And so did Ava as she detected a faint scent of alcohol on Maribelle. She wasn't so perfect after all.

"Ah crap," Darwin bellowed aloud. "Mom let me drive you home."

A gamut of emotions assailed Ava as she sat at the table with the Masters family flanking her; shock, disbelief, anger, hurt and betrayal. She was ready to leave, to be away from this place and this disdainful woman. This was his family. His world. In the natural order of life, they weren't meant to be together. As much as it hurt to admit, she couldn't stay here.

"I won't let you get your hooks in my son. The pediatric nurse that was too good to bring me a bottle of water. I almost didn't recognize you out of your service clothes."

So she did remember their one encounter. Lucky Ava.

"What are you talking about, Mother?" The men at the table sported deep furrows between their brows at Maribelle's comment.

"I filed a complaint against her weeks ago." Maribelle responded with a tone of superiority. "This is a dangerous game of retribution. Targeting my son was a mistake."

"Why did you file a complaint against Ava?" Logan had leaned his body protectively in front of Ava. Too bad, all the bombs were verbal.

"I know the damage tainted women can cause. You lure them in for your own personal gain." Another blow delivered.

"Darwin, get her out of here. Get her away from Ava. I don't care if you have to drag her out."

Logan was visibly shaking, his fingers clenching and unclenching. Ava could hear the "pop" each time he curled and straightened his fingers.

That's when the full arsenal was unleashed.

"No child of mine, will place a lesser before me. Don't you dare touch me on account of her," Maribelle hissed. "You will not send me away to keep company with another tramp, Logan Masters. This one is probably worse than Brooke. You are my son. I will never allow this to happen."

Nearby club patrons tossed disapproving glares in their direction. This was the family he'd pressed her to meet. Thinking how she had summoned her mom to spare him Granny Lou's interrogation, she felt foolish. She tried to protect him from Granny Lou. She could not protect herself from his family. What would Lina do in her situation? Maybe if she kept chanting to herself she would arrive at the right answer, because Ava Elaine Walters was a millisecond away from sucker punching a well-to-do hag in the side of her head. She laughed at the violent thought.

"He deserves better. You will never be enough for him."

Maribelle's words cut with surgical precision. There you have it. What Ava already knew to be true, spoken for the universe to hear. Knockout blow, delivered.

Ava was numb. The words pierced her soul. She felt the blood seeping through the wound, stealing the warmth from her body, leaving icy darkness in its place. Her second emotional hemorrhage. The first time she felt this soul wrenching pain a man she thought loved her had inflicted it. This time was far worse, because Logan was the man she knew she could love. She refused to allow these people to see how they had injured her.

It was time to go home. She was stupid to believe the outcome would be better with Logan. Men were bad medicine. Logan was a different class of drug compared to Marcus, but the side effect was the same. Pain and humiliation. She needed her safe haven. The home she'd neglected since her relationship with Logan began. Home was where she felt safe and protected.

*Get up. Home is waiting.*

Ava reached for her clutch. It was Prada, a loaner from Lina because she wanted to look her best for Logan's family. The joke was on her. These people would never accept her. Ava stood, stretching her spine tall with every ounce of grace she could muster. Taking a deep breath, she raised her head, stiffened her chin, and settled her eyes on the occupants at the table. The numbness was taking hold, but this had to be done first.

"Words cannot express how grateful I am to have met the entire Masters family." She emphasized entire, because not inviting his mother was a purposeful act of deception. With a deliberate slow motion her focus shifted to Maribelle Masters. Ava narrowed her eyes focusing on the cold glare just for her.

"You have nothing to worry about regarding your son and I," Ava stated flatly, the numbness in her eyes mirrored in her voice. She looked at Logan, there was only one thing left to say. "You broke your promise." Without another glance at the Masters family, Ava walked away.

Logan had said no harm would come to her. He was wrong.

A thousand bee stings would hurt less. Oh God, he had hurt her. Ava walked away from him. Her glare could have splintered steel. His body didn't want to work. The agony he felt looking into her eyes nearly crippled him. He forced his body to move.

"Ava wait!" Logan jumped to his feet, his chair nearly falling over. A waiter, with water pitcher in hand, took one look at Logan's face and scurried out of his path.

"Son," Robert Lee said in a strained voice.

"I am ashamed to be your son. How did you let that happen? You know what's at stake. That's my woman," he said pointing in the direction Ava had gone. "Not Rebecca. I'm not a Masters family stock holding. I can't give any more to this family, than I already have."

Ava needed him. And, he needed her. Logan walked away from his family unconcerned with the damage his words may have caused, his only thought was he had to get to Ava.

She was under the portico of the country club by the time Logan reached her. She was looking straight ahead. He came to stand in front of her, it was then he saw the tears threatening to spill from her eyes.

"Sweetheart," he said cautiously. "Come here."

He opened his arms needing to feel her goodness and warmth around him.

"Don't tell me what to do. I hate it when you try to control me." He jerked as her words slammed into him.

"This is not about control. You are hurting. I am here for you." She looked at him then. And what he saw in her eyes chilled his blood. Her lower lip was trapped between her teeth, that was never a good sign.

"I don't want your hands on me. You think I want to see your face, hear your words after what happened back there." His heart was hammering in his ears. She was rejecting his comfort. His everything. *Think, Logan.* But, the words were all wrong.

"Sweetheart please, I want to hold you."

"Go *hold* Rebecca. Take me home. To my house," Ava said, with a growl.

"I have no interest in Rebecca Holbrook. My mother wants me to be with her, but I only want you. We can talk about some of the things she said to you." If he took her home, she may never open the door to him again. His only hope was to speak reason to her.

"There is nothing that was said that requires clarification. I'm a worthless tramp who will never be good enough for you or your family." She was looking at him, but she held her purse like she wanted to hit him with it. He took a cautionary step toward her. This was getting out of hand. Ava was eyeing him with disgust.

"Get away. Do not put your hands on me." She was snarling at him, but he would risk her bite. *Talk, don't touch.* He could do that for her. Anything to be able to hold her, comfort her.

"I didn't know she would say those things to you." She had to know he would never subject her to a known threat. He had no idea Ava had met his mother.

"You must think I'm a stupid girl too," she said, with contempt.

"Why are you saying this to me? Of course you are not stupid." His mind was a mass of confusion.

"You may not have known the exact words she would say, but you knew she would say something about 'the nurse'. What happened in there is your fault." She was right. "You didn't want us to meet. When you shoved this brunch down my throat I asked about your mother. She didn't have plans like you led me to believe. You didn't invite her. Where I grew up we have a saying, *the apple doesn't fall far from the tree.* As your mother pointedly stated, you are her son; from her tree, her fruit. I trusted you. You lied to me. I don't want you to hold me. I don't want anything from you." Ava's breath sawed in and out, audible and sharp, cutting out the crack of metal clubs striking balls and the grind of electric carts around them.

"Wait a minute," he said with rising panic. "How can you say that to me? I am not like my mother. You know me."

"I don't know you, but you are teaching me a valuable lesson about cavorting with strangers. You can't be trusted."

Logan's head felt like it would explode. Ava said she didn't trust him. Everything was unraveling. Cold sweat covered his body, his chest ached, and his heart was beating too fast. His brain wasn't processing fast enough.

"And this is a promise you can bet I'll keep. I will never forget what happened today." Mind reeling, Logan didn't know what to do.

"Are you going to drive me home or should 'the help' start walking back to town?"

"Don't, sweetheart, this isn't us," his voice almost pleading. "I'm sorry baby, sorry for everything, more than you could ever know."

She cut him off before he could say another word.

"I'll walk." Ava backed away from him, and started the walk down the brick laid circular drive.

He ran after her and gripped her elbow.

Ava spun on him. "Get your hands off of me," she said, with fire in her eyes.

He let his hand fall in defeat. "I'll drive you home. Wait here, I will drive the car around."

Every few miles, Logan would glance at the passenger seat Ava occupied hoping she would look at him. She didn't. He watched as she fingered the heart necklace he had given her as the miles slipped by. When she closed her fingers around the pendant and tugged, he thought he'd careen off the road.

They rode the forty-six miles to Shell Cove in silence. When they arrived at Ava's house, she leapt from the car like piranhas were at her heels. Logan attempted to walk her to the door. She stopped him in his tracks.

"Go home Dr. Masters."

"Let me come inside. We can stay here tonight." Keeping her by his side was his priority. *Do not let her run*, he told himself.

"No," she said with finality in her tone. "I haven't changed my mind." She unlocked her door, went inside, and shut the door never looking back.

Logan was still in Ava's driveway thirty minutes later. He could not bring himself to leave her with his mother's poisonous words hanging between them. How could he fix this? Ava wouldn't look at him, she wouldn't let him touch her. An emotion Logan had no experience with surfaced, fear; raw, guttural, and unrelenting.

The ringtone from his phone interrupted his thoughts.

"Is Ava okay?" Darwin asked with concern in his voice.

"She is as far from okay as east is from west. Darwin she won't even look at me. I will probably be arrested for parking in her driveway overnight."

"Brother, this is beyond messed up."

"She won't let me in the house," he said in a frustrated tone. "Told me to go home, but I can't leave her." He ran his fingers through his hair repeatedly in an attempt to calm down.

"The stuff mom said was crazy. I almost can't believe it happened. I knew she had some extreme views on status, but I never imagined she would have said those things to anyone."

"I am pissed at her. Money does not give you the right to trample on other people." Logan knew his mother was a snob, but her behavior bordered on hatred.

"When I left Dad looked like a two by four had split his head open and

Mom was crying about some stuff that happened after you were born."

"I can't lose Ava," Logan broke in on his brother's update.

"You won't lose her. Ava cares about you, she needs time to deal with her own feelings without having to worry about yours. Maybe you should go home."

"You are insane." Logan was pissed that Darwin would suggest such an asinine idea. "I am not leaving my woman alone after what just happened to her. You don't have a woman. What you use your women for doesn't constitute a relationship. You've never had a woman you wanted to keep." Logan's voice was low and desolate.

"Stop trying to piss me off and listen. Ava might need some space and time to clear her head. Respect her wishes on this. She just found out her boyfriend's mother is an elitist and a drunk," Darwin said, bluntly. "That is a significant bit of information to process for most mortal minds."

"Stop being a smart ass, Darwin."

"I'll ignore that because you're upset. But think about Ava's feelings after being in our mother's company for three minutes, knowing our mother does not respect her, may never like her. Mom believes your relationship is against the natural order." Darwin sighed. "I recommend you give her space. Use the time to get your rage under control."

"Ava is mine. I will not let her leave me."

"Listen to yourself. Ava is hurting. This isn't about what you want. You can't drive her to your desired conclusion. All she asked was that you go home. She didn't end the relationship according to what you told me. Give her some breathing room in the relationship."

"Giving a woman breathing room is an opportunity for them to mess everything up," Logan said through a clinched jaw.

"Not giving your woman breathing room, leads to you messing

everything up, big brother. Ava is sweet, but she's not a weak willed woman you can control. And, she's not Brooke."

Logan growled into the phone. He did not need another reminder of the differences between Ava and Brooke. Brooke could not be trusted. Ava had his trust. But, having her close insured an impenetrable bond. That's what he told himself.

"Goodbye Darwin," he pushed the end button on his cell and threw it in the passenger seat.

Taking a deep breath, he opened the car door, and stepped outside. One thought in mind.

*Go get your woman.*

Hearing the jingle of keys at her front door had Ava bounding off the couch.

"Logan Masters, if you open that door you will live to regret this day." She saw the door handle move from her position by the door. When she didn't open it, he rang the doorbell.

"Please, let me in. I already regret this day, more than words can convey."

She couldn't see him, but from the sound of his voice he was running finger tracks through his hair. God, she wanted him.

"Ava," his tone pleading, "don't leave me out here."

Either he pushed the door, or laid his head to rest against it. "I want to be with you." She heard the muted words.

"I know." The tears fell staining the front of her dress. "But, you can't fix this." Ava pressed her forehead against the cool wood of the door, a connection to him, as the pain of today's events eroded the fantasy of a life with Logan. She fought to steady her breathing as tears flooded her eyes. He couldn't be the one to comfort her through this.

"Logan." Her heart was breaking for both of him.

"I'm here sweetheart."

"Go home." Tears flowed with the intensity of a swift moving stream.

"I am not leaving you." The steel in his voice said he'd bind their wrists together until his demands were met.

"You aren't leaving me. I'm asking you to go. Do this for me, okay."

"I want us." A soft thud sounded against the door. She knew he hurt, too. There was no camouflage for the pain she'd seen in his eyes, heard in his voice...but she couldn't be the one to soothe him.

"I know what you want, but this is what I need." Ava backed away, inhaling a measure of courage. Would he respect her request? She wouldn't trick herself into believing she knew what would happen next.

"For you, I'll go." She released a breath of relief at his acquiescence.

"Ava."

"I'm here," she said reaching a trembling hand to her neckline. His heart is with me.

"I will be back for you." Her breath hitched at the resolve in his voice. She heard his footsteps become more distant, then the slow rumble of the car engine as he pulled out of her driveway.

*I'll be back for you.*

Stupid heart. Trying to hold on to a man that could never be hers. Stumbling to her bedroom, she tripped over a bag. Her toiletries, and flat iron spilled from the bag, caught under her foot and sent her barreling toward the floor. Catching her balance by grabbing the corner of the bed, Ava let her body slide to the floor. This is where she stayed, drowning in her tears of sorrow.

Her head on the carpeted floor, she spied her tablet amongst the contents scattered around her feet. She needed to talk. Lina had her own relationship troubles. She would call Janna in Okinawa, Japan. With the change in time zones it was Sunday evening in Japan.

Ava wiped her face with the bed coverlet, logged in to Skype and dialed Janna's number. Relief washed over her when Janna's face appeared on the screen.

"To what do I owe this pleasure?" Ava looked into the camera and Janna's smile fell away. Janna and Ava were roommates after everything went wrong with Marcus. Ava hadn't felt safe living alone, back then.

"Hello Lieutenant." Ava felt a pang of loss referring to her rank. As young women, they had plans to join the military on the buddy system. But, all that changed after the assault.

"I wanted to talk to a friend." Ava offered a weak smile.

"You wanting to talk is unlikely," Janna said, in a low concerned tone. "What's wrong?"

"I wanted to talk with you about joining the Navy."

"Are you thinking about joining after all these years?"

She had never stopped thinking about the decision to come back home to lick her wounds. Wounds that still drove her decisions. Wounds that served as an endless well for her insecurities and doubts.

"I completed my commissioning packet," she said between sniffles. "I don't think anything will come of it, because my employer endorsement wasn't approved."

"I'm proud of you. Why was your endorsement denied?"

"It's a tale I don't have the energy to repeat tonight, but can you do anything to help me?"

"What about Logan?" At his name, the tears started flowing again.

"Let's not talk about Logan. I want to talk about me, my future. Why are my friends so concerned about Logan's plans for me?" she cried. "Does anyone consider that I have plans for my life and I don't need Logan?" She could feel her lips starting to quiver. Her shoulders shook with anger and grief ...oh yes, and heartbreak. She didn't need Logan, but she wanted him.

"Ava what happened?" Janna paused. Waiting for her to regain some composure.

"I can't get away from us." Ava said with a torturous cry. "I eat, sleep and breathe Logan. I'm drowning in him. And I don't fit into his world." She was struggling to take a breath. The sobs racking her body, she dropped the tablet. Collapsing onto her back Ava sobbed. Gripping the material of her dress, praying for the pain to stop.

"Ava!" Janna's voice was high pitched, startling.

"I'm here."

"Come to the camera. I can't see you."

Ava did as she was told. Her thin fingers trembled when she picked up the tablet. Janna's wide eyes filled the display.

"I'm worried about you."

"I'm a wreck and I should not have called. But, I feel so alone." She had asked him to leave. But she was inexplicably fused to Logan, to a man and a life he couldn't share with her.

"Has Logan hurt you?"

No, but she was hurting because of him. Because he couldn't stay without losing everything. And she couldn't go without losing everything.

"He's not physically hurting me. He could do whatever he wanted to me and I would probably let him. What if it gets like before?" Ava was almost in a panic thinking of her past. She had allowed Marcus to keep her bent on hands and knees to please him. A man she didn't love. "Logan could hurt me worse than Marcus. I don't think I would recover, Janna."

"Logan is crazy for you. Talk to him about your feelings. Don't do this to yourself. You are afraid because of Marcus. You don't have to be afraid anymore. You are a different woman. You're stronger and it's going to be okay."

"Nothing is okay," she screamed. "I think we make each other crazy. Everything centers on what Logan wants. It's like a force I can't resist is slowly absorbing me. The yearning I have for him is beyond understanding. I feel caged, waiting for the gate to rise when I'm away from him. That can't be healthy to want someone so badly."

*And now he's gone.*

"I am not the best person for relationship advice. You know I am a 'boy toy' kind of woman. I steer clear of complicated relationship stuff, but I am going to step out on a limb."

"This better be good." The first smile Ava felt since she'd crossed paths with Maribelle 'Commando Barbie' Masters.

"If being with Logan helps to relieve the pressure perhaps your relationship with him isn't the cause of the problem. Maybe you are fighting your feelings for him. The past is just that."

"If the answer lies there then I may never reach a solution," Ava interrupted.

"Maybe, you should explore your own feelings. Separate them from what you feel for Logan."

"You aren't going to help. Everything is feelings and Logan."

"Ava, just think about what it is you really want. What would you be risking?"

Ava's hope dimmed. Logan had ram-shackled her world. Hijacked her two friends she trusted more than anyone in the world. She had no one.

"I don't need your help. I can do this on my own."

"That's not true. I'll do what I can to help you. My friend, Morgan, was a navy recruiter. Give me twenty-four hours to make contact and follow-up."

A genuine smile stretched across Ava's face. "Thank you so much. You have no idea how much your help means to me," Ava sniffed. "Now that you're my friend again, how are you and Dawson?"

"He's committed to the Marine Corps, me the Navy. Neither one of us has the time for a relationship. We scratch one another's itch."

"A lot of itching taking place these four months. I don't want to spring any surprises on you, with you being trained in self-defense, but you've been in a relationship for months."

"We have fun relieving some pressure. It's nothing serious, not what you and Logan have together."

"You are too stubborn for your own good, but I love you just the way you are."

"I love you too, but be sure you are ready for what comes your way."

"Thanks for answering my call. And don't think I missed you changing the subject from you and Dawson, to me."

"Goodnight, Ava." Her tears had all but stopped.

Ava was excited when she ended the call. She had taken the first steps in securing her own future. She had made a decision for herself, a smile shone through her tears. She could move forward without Logan.

# CHAPTER FIFTEEN

Two weeks without Ava. She had arranged her schedule to avoid working with him. Logan refused to talk with anyone in his family. Sunday golf outings with his father and Darwin were a thing of the past. When he heard their voices, images of Ava's face looking at him with unshed tears in her eyes replayed the personal horror movie in his head.

When he heard the distinct hum of his father's engine in his driveway. Logan did not budge from his office chair when Robert Lee all but tore the front door off the hinges trying to get inside. He had finally taken Graham's advice to lock all the doors. Logan didn't answer his front door or let his father inside. He didn't want to hear what his father had to say. He did not want to hear what any of them had to say, not even Darwin. Darwin suggested giving Ava space. Now Logan could not find her. He had exhausted every possible avenue available to him save one. Not wanting to pull Ava's best friend in the middle of their rift, he had no other choice. Lina was his only link to Ava. He was angry with himself for not being able to protect her. He was angry at his family for jeopardizing what he had with Ava. And he was angry with Ava, for not caring enough about him to resist running away.

As Logan walked through the door of the psychiatric unit he reassured himself the opportunity to reclaim her would come. If he had to seize the opportunity by the throat and drag it punching and clawing he would do it. He had to believe he would get her back. Unlike the other inpatient units, the psychiatric floor had a glass to floor nurse station that housed all the IT equipment, communications, and medications. Located in the center of the unit, with a three hundred and sixty degree view of the patient rooms and lounges, the care hub could be locked from the inside if ever there was a threat to the staff. He saw the nurse he was searching for directing a patient into a group therapy room.

"Lina." She turned in his direction and flames ignited in her dark eyes.

"Yes, Dr. Masters."

It took a moment for him to comprehend her words. He directed her to step into a private therapy suite. "Lina?"

"What is it that you want?" she snapped.

Logan closed his eyes in frustration. The weight of her censure, the size of a boulder, dropped onto his back. "You've talked to Ava. Lina please let me explain. I never meant to hurt her."

"Of course you didn't. Especially when taking an unmistakably black woman to brunch with a family full of elitist and possibly closet racists is considered protective by anyone's standards."

He ground his teeth, clenching his fingers into fists. "Lina, my family is not racist. My mother is a snob and a drunk, but she is not what you said."

"In my experience the -isms stick together." Anger reflected on her face. He looked at her in bewilderment.

"Classism, racism, sexism; you get the picture. You meet one, scratch their surface, low and behold, there's another -ism reinforcing the one you see. Save your song and dance for some other sucker, because I'm not buying it. The most generous, kind hearted woman in the world isn't good enough for the Masters family."

"My family is none of those things. It was my mother, no one else in my family. We are friends. What happened between my mother, Ava and I has no bearing on our friendship."

"You know the old adage, *mama's baby*. Most of us are a byproduct of our mother's beliefs and values."

"I am not a hen pecked boy nor am I an ignorant man. I have my own beliefs and values. None of them include treating people differently because of money, status, and definitely not because of their skin color."

"Logan, I thought you were different. Ava trusted me. You don't understand the significance of having her trust. I foolishly entrusted my best friend to you. That night at the party, you made me hopeful for both of us. But she was right to be leery. Women like us don't belong with men like you. You had both of us whitewashed. We never saw the curveball coming."

"What are you talking about a man like me?" Accustomed to a fun-loving Lina, Logan realized he needed to proceed with caution now that she believed he'd betrayed her trust by hurting Ava. "Lina explain to me what is really happening. Tell me what Ava said to you," he pleaded. "This is not adding up. Explain everything that you said. I want specifics because I need your help to get her back."

With wide eyes, livid with anger, and one hand on her hip, Lina stepped into his personal space. "You want me to help you hurt her again? I helped when I saw her look at you with hope in her eyes." She jabbed an index finger in his direction. "I helped when she called me the morning following the party asking about you. I helped you destroy her," she said on a whisper. The light behind her eyes dimmed. "I won't do it again."

Tension and anger rose in equal measure inside him. Ava was hurting and he didn't know where to find her.

"What do you mean destroyed her?" His pulse raced, wild and untamed. "Please Lina, I am begging you. Tell me where she is. Let me go to her. I will not lose her over some antiquated belief system that I don't practice. Ava is mine. I would never intentionally hurt her."

"Leave her alone," she hissed.

"It will never happen. I will tear this city apart until I find her. I told her and I am telling you, I am coming for her. Nothing or no one will stop me from finding her." Logan felt a presence at his back. He turned to see his friend, Gideon Rice, a former Marine now adult psychiatrist approach them.

"Lina, is everything alright in here?"

"Lina is fine. We are talking." Logan could not afford Gideon's interruption. Lina was a romantic at heart. If she refused, it would take that much longer to find Ava.

"I didn't ask you Logan. I am asking Lina."

"I'm fine Dr. Rice. Thank you."

"I have additional information regarding my patient. Finish your conversation with her, Logan. Lina is essential to daily operations in this unit."

Logan peered over his right shoulder staring at the other man. Wondering what this scene was about. Lina had a similar expression on her face. Logan turned a slow curious gaze down at Lina. *Something was not right.* Gideon looked ready to snatch Lina away from him. He hated not knowing.

Something had happened that he was not privy to.

"Lina what's going on with you and Jace?"

Her body stiffened, the tiny veins of redness crawled across the white of her eyes. She narrowed them, but not before he saw the tears threatening to fall. The pain he saw in her eyes made Logan want to find Jace and pummel him into the ground. What had he done to Lina?

That was it. Ava and Lina were both hurting. Feeding from one another's pain.

"How does it relate to Ava avoiding me?"

"I will not sacrifice Ava's friendship for any man." The rise and fall of her chest came faster, more panting than actual breathing.

"You are like a sister to Ava, but I am not just any man. I am your friend. I practically cried with you watching that Steel Magnolias movie." A hint of a smile from Lina was a good sign. "I don't know what Jace has done, but I am not him. Ava is my life. This is my promise to you, tell me where I can find her and I will make things right between us. I will make her happy again. Believe me Lina. I am telling you the truth."

"Logan," she hesitated.

He released a shaky breath. Lina addressed him with familiarity. She trusted him. If they were anywhere other than the hospital he would be on his knees.

"Point me in the right direction. I know she's not sleeping at home or her parent's house. Before I can even turn off the car ignition, Granny Lou is on the front porch shaking her head no."

"I can't tell you where Ava's holing up. I believe you care about Ava and more importantly you know her. You'll figure it out. After weeks sitting at the Walters' dinner table I am sure you know where Ava is spending her nights."

"What kind of clue is that? She's not at home with me where she belongs. The places she frequented are the church, the track, and the farmer's market. You have got to give me more than that to go on?"

"No, I don't." Lina was not divulging useful information.

Logan could've howled in frustration. He didn't know what Lina was trying to tell him. Cymbals clanged against his temples only to collide with the bells ringing in his ears.

"I have seen everyone from Sunday dinner except Ava."

"Interesting. I helped Ava lug eight chairs and a dining table into her house. In fact, last Thanksgiving we had to add two chairs to the table for my mom and Shaylah." Comprehension dawned, a slow smile spread across Logan's face and the vice grip around his heart loosened its hold.

"Lina James, I could kiss you." He leaned forward to do just that when a harsh voice stopped him.

"Lina come with me, now please."

They both turned to see Gideon Rice's broad frame filling the doorway to the individual therapy room. He looked ready to attack.

"Gideon, what is your issue? Find another nurse to help you." Lina interrupted Logan before he could say more. She stepped around him as she spoke.

"Ah, Logan, I should go back to work. Remember, you made me a promise. I expect you to deliver. Thanks Dr. Rice for being patient."

"I'll wait for you. No one else." He looked pointedly at Logan.

Logan replayed Gideon's behavior, the muscles in the man's jaw was twitching, his arms had been loose at his sides on a fully erect spine. He had been readying himself to launch at him.

That was a question for later after he acquired the address for one Mr. and Mrs. Aron Walters. "I am coming for you Ava mine."

Why had Ava agreed to go to that country club? She and Logan were good together, before business meetings, blackmail and Maribelle. Most nights she stayed at Aron and Zari's townhouse. But she didn't sleep, occupying a bed was more accurate. Logan had never visited their home, so she was safe from unwanted visits. She couldn't be with him, but it was difficult to be without him.

The emptiness had returned. It was worse, because she knew how it felt to be cared for, maybe, even loved. She needed Logan more than ever. He would love her hurt away; help her get over the heartbreak. *Tragic.* She was pining for Logan.

A car Ava didn't recognize blocked her driveway. She slowed the Jeep to a stop and cut the engine at the curb. Robert Lee Masters stood beside a classic blue and white 1967 Ford Mustang Shelby GT 500 wearing chinos and a Caribbean blue golf shirt. As she approached him, he extended his hand.

"Good to see you again Ava."

"The feeling is not mutual I assure you," Ava said, not offering her hand.

There was no hesitancy in his voice, rather a beseeching tone.

"I apologize for what you endured at the hands of my family. Words cannot express the remorse I feel for how we treated you."

Ava took in the dark circles under his eyes, and the tension lines at the corners of his mouth. He looked unnaturally aged, where she had considered him handsome at their first meeting.

"You didn't have to show up at my house to tell me that. You don't owe me anything."

"That's not true. I owe you a great deal. You make my son happy. His happiness is important to me; therefore, you are important to me."

The sincerity and weight of his words surprised Ava.

"Mr. Masters, Logan and I are no longer together. You are wasting both of our time. I have nothing to say to Logan."

"I know that, but I also know the two of you would still be together if it wasn't for us. My son cares a great deal about you. I believe you feel the same way towards him. Logan is a stubborn man. He's gone to extraordinary lengths to show his family how important you are to him."

"I don't think you should be sharing this with me."

"My own son won't accept my calls. Logan won't let me in his house because of what we did to you."

Ava was speechless.

"I've been playing golf with my boys since they were knee high to me. They've stopped visiting me. I am married to a power hungry woman that drinks too much." Robert Lee's face looked stony.

Ava's lips tightened at the mention of Maribelle.

"My sons are all I have." His voice pitched low. At the mention of his sons, emotion filled his voice. "Logan believes he's lost you and if he's lost you, I've lost them both." He cleared his throat.

"Ava please, talk to Logan. Take one of his telephone calls. I'd be indebted to you if you would just have one conversation with him. Logan deserves to be happy. You do that for him."

Ava didn't have a response for Robert Lee. She knew Logan was upset with his mother after what happened. Shunning his entire family was an unforeseen consequence. The strained relationship with his mother made sense after meeting the woman. But he treasured his time with Darwin and his father. This separation had to be difficult for him.

"Thank you for listening. And I want you to know, I've done everything in my power to help you and Logan."

She was unsure what to make of the comment. The derailment was in progress for her and Logan.

He offered his hand in farewell, and this time she accepted. He held it a few seconds before releasing her hand and returning to his car. He gave a slight smile in her direction, backed out of the drive, and revved the engine. She heard the deep rumble of the car as he turned the corner, and disappeared from sight.

Robert Lee's heartfelt request tossed her back into emotional turmoil. For such a powerful man to humble himself, admit his wife was obsessed with power and status, and that he was a father that loved his sons. Logan had alienated his family because of her. Before her courage failed, she went into the house and dialed his number.

Logan strained to complete another pull-up, forcing his body past the point of physical exhaustion. He needed the physical pain, a momentary escape from the emotional wasteland that plagued him. Arm and chest muscles burning from overuse, he dropped to the floor. His breath coming in short gasps, he began the third set of crunches. He needed to pack and review his presentation one last time. The conference was in two days and failure to secure funding was not an option.

When the phone rang, Logan continued his rhythmic contract release sequence. Having deleted Darwin's and his parents' previous messages, the voice mailbox was ready to hold another round of unsolicited calls until he deleted those, too. Expecting another of his mother's rants, he dug deeper. Wanting the scream of pain to drown out her dictates.

"We need to talk." Logan's breath stopped in his throat. He froze in the upright position.

Recognizing Ava's voice, Logan, with his heart pounding, took to his feet, noting her home number displayed on the television LCD. He wiped his face, exited the gym, and grabbed his keys from the countertop. He made double strides in the direction of the garage. Whatever she had to say, she would tell him in person. He would not be discarded via phone message.

In record time he pulled in her driveway. He banged on her front door, prepared to battle Heaven and Hell to get her back.

"Ava." Not caring if he roused the neighborhood, his baritone boomed in the still night. "Open up."

She opened the door. His eyes fixed on Ava, her familiar sundress and bare feet had his pulse racing. Internally uncertainty kept his hands at fisted at his side, but then she looked at him and he saw the slight flare of her nostrils. Decision made, he would take the risk.

He scooped her off her feet and into his arms. He missed her. Burying his face in her soft ringlets, her vanilla scent unleashed havoc in his body. The muscle pain he felt was now a dull ache. Blood rushed to his lower half. She was back in his arms.

Ava was his and Maribelle's tirade would not be their undoing. Their relationship had unique challenges, but he and Ava would overcome this hurdle.

"You never have to see them again," he mumbled into her hair. He held her tight against his body, fusing them together. He stroked up and down her back, reassuring himself this moment was real.

"Logan let me go." She leveraged her weight on his shoulders, pressing up to meet his stare.

"Never," he responded and tightened his bear hug hold on her waist.

"Just to close the door. Anyone driving by can see us."

He stepped into the living room, kicking the door closed behind them, never loosening his grip on her. With one arm around her waist, he used the other hand to tunnel into her loose tresses, bringing her head to rest on his shoulder. Nothing had ever felt so right as having Ava pressed against him.

"I missed you, sweetheart. Nothing is right without you." He kissed her, slow and thorough, with a new reverence. His heart leapt in his chest when she opened wider, welcoming his oral invasion. She returned his kiss signaling an end of this purgatory they found themselves in. Her heat, her scent, her presence filled his body with electricity. A fire spread through his veins, nothing in his life could match what Ava did to him. What he needed only she possessed.

"My family messed us up. I am sorry about everything. We hurt you. It will never happen again. I will protect you better." He said every thought aloud. Praying she heard the sincerity in his words.

He crossed the entryway and lowered them to the couch, setting her astride his legs. When she attempted to rise, he gripped her waist, anchoring them together.

"Stay with me."

Slowly, her muscles relaxed and she settled into place.

"Just let me hold you. Feel your body close to mine." He took a slow deep breath pulling her scent down into his lungs. The tension of two weeks of separation started a steady retreat. He was back where he belonged, with her. Forever this time.

Her arms circled his neck, and then she pulled him in close. Her warm breath teased his ear when she spoke.

"I missed you, too."

They remained locked in each other's arms. He was grateful she wasn't fighting him. He pulled at her forearms, breaking the hold around his neck.

Maintaining possession of her arms, he positioned her so their eyes met.

"Do not ask me to leave you ever again. You are the only woman for me."

She nodded.

"I don't care what anyone thinks about me being with you. It is you and me against the world." And he meant every word. It did not matter if his friends and family accepted Ava. Their opinion held no merit.

"Please, say something. Tell me we are back together." For once, he could not read her expression.

"My legs are going numb, Logan. My calves are tight from running up and down the stairwells last night."

He stood with her in tow, gently placing her bare feet on the area rug. Ava had not said one word to allay his concerns about their relationship. As usual, he was doing all the talking, but he couldn't stop himself. He'd talk all night trying to find the right words to make her understand what she meant to him.

"Ava I'm in misery. Tell me something about where we stand as a couple."

"Is that all?" She snorted at his comment. "I moved past misery and plummeted into despair one week ago." She scrambled backward, standing apart from him.

"You invited me to brunch with your family and I get blindsided by an old south sympathizer. Forgive me if I need more than flowery words and a weekend to get over your betrayal."

Ava was breathing hard, with that lower lip trapped between her teeth.

"I don't know where to go from here Logan." A sad expression marred her beautiful face. That's when he noticed his heart pendant wasn't around her neck.

His internal alarm signaled in warning. The look on her face was not good. His stomach dropped to his feet.

"What do you mean you don't know where to go from here? My family and I are separate and distinct. Not a package deal. You have to be willing to separate my mother's actions from the man you are in a relationship with. How can you justify throwing away what we have, because of someone else's actions?"

"I'm not throwing us away."

"You gave yourself to me. We share a life together. I am not walking away from you."

She was quiet and watchful. And, she was doing the lip thing again. Did she think he would hurt her? True, she was trying to end their relationship, but he'd never hit a woman in his life. He could see it in her eyes. Fear. Say the right words Logan. Don't mess this up.

"This isn't about my mother. This is about you, me, and trust." Logan ran his fingers through his hair trying to calm his racing pulse. His words got her attention. She focused on him again.

"I trust you more than anyone else. I'm not throwing us away."

"What's your term for what's happening? You have a wall around me and another around your heart. I have been chasing after you for weeks. Do you care about me at all, Ava?"

"I called you, remember? You know how I feel about you. I didn't start this."

"I didn't start this either. I'm trying to hold onto you while you're backpedaling away from me. I thought I knew your feelings towards me, but right now I'm not certain of much. This one-sided conversation is not very reassuring."

"I liked being with you. If I hadn't cared about you, what happened wouldn't have hurt so much," she said, when their gazes locked.

"Everything you said is past tense, Ava."

"I know." They could be mistaken for statues since neither moved.

"If you don't want me anymore, just say it. Don't use my mother as an excuse." Fear of losing her made his voice hard and dry.

"I want you Logan, but..." He interrupted her. Whatever else she said would not help his cause.

"Good enough." Standing, he swept her into his arms and headed for the bedroom. She opened her mouth. "Do not say one word to undo what you just said. I am miserable and so are you. We make one another happy, that's our fresh start."

"I can't forget everything that happened, with a snap." She snapped her fingers. "I'm not wired that way."

"I could never forget anything I did that caused you pain. You offered us a new beginning, I'll take it." He entered the bedroom and he placed her bare feet on the carpet. She looked nervous and unsure of herself.

"Will you please climb into this bed with me?"

"I am not having sex with you. Don't try anything to tempt me." Her voice was less than confident, and Logan smiled. She definitely wanted him. He sent a silent thank you to heaven above.

"Define tempt?"

Her grin was sexy and playful. Logan felt himself thickening. His heart beat double time. He could not force her hand. She had to do this on her own. If any part of her body touched the mattress she was his.

When he saw, those red, polished toes flex, foot off the ground, knee bent, body leaning forward moving toward the bed; his entire body tensed with anticipation.

The moment her knee made a slight indentation in the quilt Logan pulled her to him, partially covering her body with his larger frame.

"This is our second chance. I won't fail you, again."

Ava wiggled in his arms until she rested across his chest.

"I've been going out of my mind without you." He placed a kiss to her forehead. "Will you put my heart back where it belongs?" He was speaking of more than the necklace, but that was a start.

"Yes, I'll put your heart where it belongs." She planted a firm kiss to his jaw.

"Don't take it off again, sweetheart." God help him, he was lost without her. He loved Ava.

"I won't, Logan. I promise you."

He wanted to tell her that he loved her, but it was too soon. They had been back together for all of five minutes and his confession would have her running for the hills.

For the first time in two weeks, he felt peaceful. His was in control of his life once more.

"Logan, I have something to tell you."

She sounded hesitant. He noticed the pinched shoulders and the tension lines in her face. One giant slaying per day should be enough.

"Will it make either of us unhappy?" Not wanting to ruin the mood, it could wait until they had a chance to heal from what had been done. Logan had no illusions that the path ahead would be easier for them.

"Possibly."

She absently stroked his chest. He remembered she did that to comfort him. Always concerned about others. That was his Ava. It was high time someone took care of her.

"Can it wait until I return from the conference?"

"I think so."

Good. She was back in his arms. He'd be gone four weeks at the most, including prep time, negotiations, and travel days. They'd miss the holidays together, but he'd make it up to her ten-fold when he returned home.

"Rest, then." Logan slept soundly with Ava in his arms. They had a lifetime to work out their issues. Neither of them was going anywhere.

# CHAPTER SIXTEEN

Ava sat in the break room eating her lunch with thoughts of Logan to keep her company. Kathryn and Spencer were on Randall patrol with Logan away, but their vigilance was unnecessary. She hadn't seen Randall in weeks. Thank all the heavens something kept him occupied. With Logan gone she could not risk another encounter.

She shifted in the seat and the letter she'd carried with her every day for four weeks, poked out of her pocket. The United States Navy official seal called to her like a honey bun to a fat kid. To see the letter in her mailbox was beyond a shock. Kathryn promised to do what she could in getting the endorsement, but Ava had little hope when she'd walked out of the manager's office. The night she and Logan reconciled, she wanted to tell him, but everything felt right after being messed up for weeks. She didn't want to ruin the moment, either.

How fitting that fate would give her a way out, when she wanted nothing more than to stay. This was her dream. It was hers for the taking, but now she wasn't so sure she wanted it with the same intensity.

Logan had taken up a space in her heart. She had waged a valiant fight. Her defense system was woefully inadequate against his magnetic pull. She would tell him about the direct appointment to the Navy Nurse corps when he returned. He wouldn't be pleased, but they would find an option to keep them together. There had to be a way, even if she couldn't see it.

She heard the doorknob turn. The break room door blew open and slammed into the wall. Ava's attention flew in that direction.

"You will destroy everything he's worked for."

Maribelle Masters stood in the open door way, an air of superiority swirled around her. Her distaste for Ava created a physical vortex that sucked the oxygen out of the room.

"My son has been groomed from birth for power and influence over others," her voice infused with steely superiority as she entered the room.

"He needs the right kind of woman by his side. A well-bred woman, not like you." Disdain dripped from every word.

Ava rallied her courage. "Logan chose me. The decision was his." There she had said it. She was Logan's choice. She was the woman he wanted.

"Do you think he would have chosen you if he knew how weak and pathetic you are?"

This woman was vicious.

"What kind of woman let's a man tie her up for kicks."

Ava's eyes widened and a thin layer of sweat broke on her skin. She could feel the icy breath enter and exit her body. Maribelle knew.

"I know all about your pitiful existence. It's not surprising you ended up bloody, and discarded on the floor."

Ava rose to her feet. She would not remain seated for another verbal lashing from this woman.

"Get out of here, Maribelle. Logan doesn't care about my past."

Maribelle looked at her in smug satisfaction. "That's because he doesn't know."

There was a promise in those words. He doesn't know for now.

"How can he enter a room with his head held high, with another man's whipping toy on his arm?"

"That's not who I am."

"Oh, really. Then why haven't you told him? Afraid he will see who you really are? After discovering your secret, it occurred to me that Holton propositioned you because he saw that darkness you try to hide."

"You can deny what you are, but I know."

Oh God, Ava's head was spinning. She had to get away from here. She could feel her heart being ripped from her body. She couldn't tell Logan. She couldn't bear to have her past exposed. What could she say? The truth.

"Logan will never leave me." That she knew to be true.

"You're right. He's loyal to a fault, but he'll never be happy with a woman like you. You can't meet Logan's need for power and control. Even now, his board position hangs in the balance."

Ava wouldn't believe anything this woman said.

"Logan is the best candidate for the position. The board wouldn't overlook his qualifications because of me."

Maribelle looked at her like she was the biggest idiot. "The board considers the complete package. His future was secure until he met you. His life's work is hanging by a thread. He left to go beg strangers for money because the foundation pulled his funding. That little girl with the broken arm is not getting better because of you." Maribelle's words dripped with contempt.

Logan would lose everything if she stayed, and Monique would suffer.

Ava's heart sank. Logan wanted everything, and therein lied the problem. She knew it. But with her by his side, he would forfeit everything he wanted. They're being together saved and doomed them both, all at once.

"Let him go. He needs a woman that can navigate his world without being labeled a whore. Alliances make or break a career. Logan aligning himself with you leaves him with nothing. He can't see it, but you will never be accepted in his world."

Ava knew what she had to do.

Not seeing Ava for four weeks had Logan sprinting out of business class down the jet way to baggage claim. Her phone calls had been scarce and when he called her it went to voicemail. He talked with her more than twenty-four hours ago prior to boarding the flight for home. She sounded tired, but there was something else in her voice that he did not recognize.

He powered on his phone and dialed her number. The sweet soprano of her voicemail greeting had his brow tweaking in surprise. Why wasn't she answering his call? His plane landed thirty minutes ago.

"Where are you, sweetheart? I am on my way to you." He ended the call.

He drove by her house first. What he saw made him want to leap from behind the wheel, fall to his knees and thank the heavens. The *For Rent Sign* mounted to an aluminum post displayed in the front yard had him smiling bigger than a third grader on picture day. She had taken the next step. Ava had moved into his home while he was away. He had everything he ever wanted; the grant was secure, his career was back on track, and the woman he loved by his side. He violated at least a dozen traffic laws to get to her. After placing the third call to her and not receiving an answer he drove in subdued jubilation. It could be she had gone for a run.

Unease had him gripping and releasing the wheel pushing the blood out of his fingertips. White knuckles tightened on the steering wheel as he maneuvered the sedan into the garage. He pulled the car to a stop in the empty garage. His mouth thinned into a flat line. The Jeep wasn't where it was supposed to be. She wasn't waiting for him. He needed to see her.

He swung open the side door entrance to his house. The fragrance of cinnamon and nutmeg assailed him. On the countertop sat Zari's signature spiced pound cake. A smile spread across his face, Ava knew it was his favorite. Where was the woman that made his house a home?

The house smelled warm and inviting. But at the same time, it felt different to Logan. Everything appeared to be the same, but something was missing. He walked into the kitchen scanning the center island. Heat infused his groin remembering Ava offering herself to him on that very counter, his feast of choice.

The counter resembled a slumber party prep station. The spice cake took up center stage, but the counter brimmed with raw almonds packets, trail mix bags, and all his favorite snacks. Ava power shopped during his absence.

He opened the reefer to find the freezer stuffed to capacity with storage containers. She had cooked enough for a small army. His smiled slipped, a little.

"I guess she's taking a break from cooking." Intrigued. What had she been doing? He pulled out his phone dialing her cell.

"Sweetheart, where are you? Come home soon or I'll have eaten all the sugar on the counter and have enough stamina to keep Cricket hopping into next week." He frowned as he ended the call.

He climbed the stairs to the master suite eager to shed his travel attire, shower and dress in something comfortable. He had taken the first flight available from Australia to home. The Melbourne conference and follow-on negotiations were worth the forty hours in flight.

Tyson Advantis, a professional wound care company, based in Ireland had agreed to fund his research for an additional two years. With the final agreement in the drafting stages Logan had donned his suit coat, bid farewell to the legal team and hailed a taxi to the airport.

Pulling his head free of the shirt, the glint of metal on the bedside stand caught his eye. A key. A single sheet of monogramed paper rested underneath. He read the words:

Logan,

I accepted a commission in the Navy Nurse Corps. I will miss you while I'm in Newport, Rhode Island. Please don't be upset. I'll explain everything.

Always yours, Ava

His breath froze. His heart stopped, then fractured into a thousand pieces. "No." Rage bellowed through the depths of his soul. She had chosen a career that took her from him. Love doesn't do that. But Ava had never said she loved him.

"She left me." The words struck with the force of a brick against his head.

"Gone." The weight of reality crushed him. The phone case creaked as he ripped it from the waist holster. The ache in his chest intensified as he dialed her number again. *Betrayed. Just like Brooke.*

Betrayed at the hands of another woman. The control he fought to maintain in their relationship hadn't prevented Ava from leaving. It had only served to blind him to her leaving. He dialed her number. This time, she answered. He did not give her the opportunity to speak. Pain consumed him and he unleashed it on her.

"Go get in the Jeep and come home right now. Better yet, go to the airport, there will be a ticket waiting for you. I'll buy you another car." He shook with anger and fury.

"I left class to answer your call. You know I can't leave. But, I left for you. For us."

"How did you arrive at that conclusion? Leaving me is good for us," he hissed. "Are you delusional?"

"No, and stop being cruel." Her voice shook when she spoke.

"I will tell you what's cruel. Coming home, expecting to find your woman waiting for you only to be confronted with a kitchen full of conciliatory gifts, a key, and a for rent sign."

"Logan listen to me, please. I didn't want to stress you while..." His roar halted her words.

"The only thing I want to hear is that you are on your way back to me. I don't need to hear your excuse. I understand you perfectly. You would rather traipse all over God's green earth uprooting your life every three years for the Navy than be with me. You chose a job over me!" The truth nearly crumbled him.

"Calm down. Let me explain."

He could hear her sobs. But he would not allow himself to care.

"Your leaving me is explanation enough. I don't have to tolerate this from another woman. You are a heartless, selfish coward. I don't know who you are."

"You don't get to call me selfish. I sacrificed myself for you. I may be a coward, but not for the reason you think. You are so busy dictating your wants you can't hear me. You are the sole decision maker in our relationship. You're not committed to me, Logan. You're committed to keeping me. There's a difference."

Then the line went dead.

Logan's cell phone buzzed signaling Darwin's ringtone. Darwin's face came into view as he pressed the release on his belt loop. Logan touched the talk icon.

"I know your plane only landed an hour ago, but how are you doing without Ava?"

"How did you know she was gone? I just discovered it."

"What are you talking about? Ava's been updating her Facebook page since she left two weeks ago."

"Two weeks!" That explained the scarce phone calls. She had played him for a fool. "You knew she left me and you didn't tell me."

"When did that happen?"

Logan growled into the phone. Frustrated with Darwin tranquil disposition at Ava's blatant abandonment.

"You tell me, Darwin."

"I didn't know she left you. Ava had to report for officer development school in Newport, Rhode Island. I knew she wanted to join the Navy, her entire Facebook page is a tribute to naval history and the Nurse Corps."

"She left me."

"You got a Dear John letter. Man that's ballsy considering everything Dad did."

Logan could not hear anything beyond the resounding gong of anger and betrayal playing in his head.

"I didn't get anything."

"How do you know she left you?"

"Are you listening to me? I came back and she's not here."

"Wait. I didn't get the impression that Ava was leaving you. She updates her Facebook page to stay connected with everyone in Shell Cove."

"She packed her clothes and left town without telling me. The keys to our house, I am looking at them."

"I never saw that one coming."

"That goes for the both of us," Logan lamented. "I'll call you back." Disconnecting the call, Logan punched the Facebook icon on his smartphone. There was the answer to his question on social media for all to see.

The post read:

*Hello all my Facebook family and friends!*

*Great news everybody, I survived the 1,000+ mile road trip from Shell Cove to Newport, RI with my car and sanity intact. It was the longest road trip in memory and one I wish not to repeat. I am so glad to be out of the car and into my rack. Yeah, I am already using military lingo. Beds are for civilians. I arrived last night and checked in at King Hall. Woke this morning to a frigid, but beautiful winter day. Snow flurries are expected later today. Go figure, this Florida girl marching in the snow.*

*Met my company division officer yesterday who informed me the days start at 0430. Early mornings are nothing new to a unit nurse.*

*I have an amazing view of the ocean from four decks up (no floors in the Navy). Love the location.*

*Everything is within walking distance, which is a plus because we are not allowed to operate our cars during the first two weeks of officer training. The only bad thing is the fire station is located directly across the street from my quarters. I had to evacuate at least twice in the past three days for fire drills. That gets annoying, but that is the only downside so far.*

*All kidding aside, I'm really excited (and nervous) to start my Navy career. If I fall off the radar over the next five weeks I'll resurface again after my graduation.*

*Love you and GO Navy,*
*Ensign Ava Walters*
*United States Navy*

# CHAPTER SEVENTEEN

Logan sat across from Graham at the bar staring into his Seven and Seven drink. They were at O'Brien's Pub, a dim drinking hole, with scuffed tables, scarred wood floors and limited conversation. Darwin had introduced them both to this mostly male sanctuary. The only women in sight were serving the drinks.

"You are the only doctor I know who cannot keep a woman," Graham said jokingly.

Logan glared at his closest friend with a scowl in place. "You are the only doctor I know that is surrounded by women all day, and can't get one to stick around long enough to meet your friends." Graham, unlike Logan was able to keep his private life just that. Outside of the mystery woman from weeks back, Graham never mentioned his love life to him.

"I have a woman." His thoughts refused to release Ava. He didn't question whether it was stupidity or stubbornness that kept him holding on.

"Tell me more about this wonderful woman that's earned your devotion, in absentia," he drawled.

Logan heard Graham's contempt, but chose to ignore it.

"I have not lost Ava. This commission is a dream come true for her. The career she always wanted." Logan repeated what he'd read on her Facebook page. He refused to call. His only connection to her were the images on social media and the ones etched in his memories. Idiot. Wanting a woman that had run out on him. How many times would he chase her? Let go, his brain told him. But his heart would not accept the logical choice.

"Pull your head out of the Florida sand. Every woman gets her career started," Graham gestured invisible quotation marks, "by quitting her job, packing up her entire house, and joining the military." Graham offered a grunt in disbelief. "Let's not leave out the best part, she tells you after she's been gone for two weeks."

"She needs to come home."

Graham looked at him with pity. And Logan downed the rest of his drink, drowning his feelings of inadequacy. He had not been enough for either of the women in his life. Ava left, and Brooke would have left.

"Logan, before you pursue this relationship to any end. What exactly do you want from her?"

"The next words I am about to say go no further than this space. I feel foolish saying this, especially to you. I am undone without her. Nothing else matters."

"You look the same."

"My life was fine before her. But now that I have had a taste of what it can be like, I will not be without her."

Graham stared at him in dawning horror. His friend thought him the worst kind of limp noodle because of a woman.

"Stop gawking at me."

"Sorry, I didn't realize until now that you're in love with her. This is worse than I imagined one man could get tangled up in. What can you do? Ava is gone."

"It's obvious I don't know what love looks like, but I will not stop until I have her." But he wasn't ready to talk to her. Afraid he would say something stupid like *I love you.*

"Don't look to my life, but you're not denying you love her."

"I need a plan. First, I have to get Rebecca off my scent. Recently, she's been calling more than the auto warranty telemarketers. I think my mother or Sam got to her." What else could he do? Graham's brows were knit together. His 'Logan's a pathetic moron face' was on again.

"But Ava has to take the first step. Show some sign of wanting me back. I could wring her beautiful neck until she comes to her senses. If that doesn't work, I could handcuff her to my bed, and convince her she belongs to me."

"Sounds more on par with wishful thinking. If that's your best plan you'd better ask Darwin to flesh out the details. He's the strategist."

"On the other hand, true love finds a way. You can't stop love unless..." Graham stopped short, taking a deep draw to empty his bottle.

"Unless what, Hamilton the third?"

"There's a restraining order."

Graham laughed at his own joke, signaled the bartender for another round. The anguish that Logan had tethered on a short leash was reaching for an outlet as he took in his friend's sullen expression. Graham hid it well, but some woman had him twisted by the hairs.

"I am angry with Ava, but I can't stop what I feel. She is the one woman for me, but she can't see it."

"She had me fooled. I was already updating my schedule with the delivery of your firstborn." Logan scowled then.

"You will not be delivering our babies." He would be the only one to see Ava's body. Graham was smiling at him over a now full bottle of beer. No doubt, following Logan's train of thought.

"You are not helping."

"I'm getting drunk with you and paying the bill. I'll put you in a cab to ensure you get home safely." Graham threw his hands in the air in mock frustration. "What more do you want from your best friend?"

Logan raised his glass in acknowledgment. "Point taken."

"Have you considered the challenges you both will face if you do make a go of it? Florida's a vacation paradise for people from around the globe, but it's still the south."

"Ava and I don't have color issues."

"True. Your problem is far more insidious; you and Ava can't communicate because neither one of you is willing to trust the other." Graham downed half of his drink.

"Not this again." Memories of Brooke sparked in his mind. He pushed them back into the abyss where they belonged. "I trusted Ava." He wanted to scream. He had committed to her, asked her to move into his home. He had plans for their life together.

"Does Ava know you were engaged to be married? That your fiancée slept with one of your best friends, including the morning she died? You both brought big ass elephants into the relationship."

"It did not make a difference. Ava left regardless of my past."

"Your past controlled how you treated her. You tried to rule over her. You could not listen to her without superimposing your demands. It's been more than ten years Logan and you haven't dealt with your feelings about Brooke's betrayal." Brooke's betrayal paled in comparison to the pain Ava had awoken in him.

"Do yourself a favor and pick someone else," Graham said bluntly.

"I want Ava," Logan grounded out.

"Look," Graham ground out, "I'm trying to help you. You don't trust her enough to be honest. Not a good foundation for a lasting relationship. Your past is directing your destiny. If you're not going to learn from it, to change your future, then take my advice and find yourself a status crazed socialite that's easy on the eyes and freaky like a porn star. Take her to five-star restaurants and buy a few baubles every couple of months. You can keep your secrets and control the relationship. If she leaves you, nothing's lost."

Ava's food rivaled a five-star restaurant. And she didn't want anything money could buy.

"I'm going to get her back," Logan said with determination in his voice.

"The woman quit her job, sold her house, and left town under the cover of night. Talk about an exit strategy. Heck, she's perfect for the military."

"She did not sell her house. It's for rent."

"Either way, it sends the same message. She's not coming back any time soon. If that doesn't say it's over, what else do you need?"

"She's running from herself, not me."

"She could have fooled me. She could have told you something about her plans. I get that she made you happy for a time. After the stuff that went down all those years ago with Brooke, you deserve it. But, Ava is gone and it's probably for the best."

Had Logan pushed Ava too hard to give everything, while he remained emotionally safe? He, like Ava, had brought another person into their relationship. His failure with Brooke, the fear of not being enough drove him to not trust Ava with his love for her. *I want you back sweetheart. Give me a sign you want me, too.* He prayed as the last of his drink slid down his throat.

Ava experienced the five stages of grief simultaneously. She sat in a hidden window seat, in one of the closed barracks wings. Looking at the waves crashing against the rocks. Her longing for Logan came from the deepest place in her soul. Crippled by the ache in her heart, food held no appeal. She could barely part her lips without a sob escaping. Officer training thus far had been a failure of epic proportions.

A military march was near impossible when you didn't have the strength to put one foot in front of the other. All she really wanted was to be back in Shell Cove with Logan. If it weren't for all the direct orders, she'd be in her rack huddled under her favorite quilt crying her eyes out.

The urge to call Logan grew stronger with each passing day, but she couldn't muster up the courage after the argument when he returned to find her gone. He had called her a selfish coward and she had foolishly ended the call. That had been the last call from him. An unsettling sense of panic had entered her thoughts and she could not rid herself of the feeling.

Had Logan moved on to Rebecca Holbrook? According to Ava's research, Rebecca was related to the Chairman of the Shell Cove Medical Foundation. He risked his career for their relationship. Logan wouldn't jeopardize his career if he didn't love her, right? Brooke was the other name Maribelle mentioned. Brooke didn't have a connection to the foundation that Ava could find. Logan hadn't offered any information on Brooke, only Rebecca. Brooke had to be the woman he'd referred to during their argument. Brooke was the other woman that had left him.

Ava needed to talk to someone. Phone in hand she dialed the one person that had never led her astray in the advice department. She answered on the first ring.

"Granny Lou, it's Ava."

"I'm not so old that I don't know my own grandchild's voice," her grandmother chuckled. "How are you, baby?" True concern laced her grandmother's words.

How should she answer the question? I'm just as much of a failure in the Navy as I was at home." Ava blinked her lids in succession to staunch the tears from flowing.

"I'm on probation." Ava sniffled. "Tell Dad not to buy those plane tickets. Not yet anyway, I don't want the family to waste the money on me." Granny Lou was silent on the other end.

"You are not going to flunk out of training," her grandmother said matter of factly. "I can hear that something is troubling you beyond what you just told me. Granny's listening."

Ava started to cry in earnest. She couldn't fool Granny Lou. Talking with her grandmother about her man troubles seemed wrong.

"Ava Elaine, you can talk to me about anything. Go on now."

"I messed up everything with Logan. I was trying to save him," she sobbed. "They were going to destroy everything he'd worked for because of me." Her soul opened and all the darkness started rushing out.

"Slow down, baby."

Ava was breathing fast between her sobs. Now that she was talking, the purge had a life of its own. Months of dealing with the secrets had siphoned her joy away. She went back to the beginning with Randall and the endorsement. Offering as much detail as she could about the Holbrook family and the foundation.

"Then, Logan left for the conference and his mother threatened to tell him everything." Ava sobbed openly, losing her composure.

"His mother threatened you? And Sam Holbrook is involved?"

Ava shook her head, forgetting Granny Lou couldn't see her. "She was going to tell Logan about what Marcus did. I couldn't bear it, Granny."

"Hush, now. You have nothing to be ashamed of. It wasn't your fault. You trusted Marcus. He abused and manipulated that trust."

Ava didn't feel better. She cried harder. Gut wrenching wales for the stupid girl she had been. No one in their right mind should have gotten themselves in that position.

"You don't understand. Marcus had been hurting me for a while, but I was too stupid to stop him, until it was too late. I let him do and say awful things to me because I thought he loved me. He said I was worthless with poor judgment. I wasn't enough, a pretty burden he called me. I started to believe him."

"Listen to Granny Lou." Her grandmother's voice was soft, but firm. "Stop telling yourself you were stupid to care for a man. You are an intelligent and wonderfully made woman who was ensnarled by a predator. Marcus had us all fooled. He was a liar. A snake, manipulating you into believing your actions triggered his abuse. It was all lies baby, forgive yourself."

"But, I keep making bad decisions. Logan … Logan stopped calling." She'd made the wrong decision. "My insides feel as if they are being shredded with dull, jagged pieces of glass. Something inside of me is dying. What if he doesn't call anymore?"

"Have you called him?"

"No. I'm afraid he will reject me."

"You've expended too much energy being afraid. Logan has never rejected you. I still remember the look on his face, standing in your dining room, telling your whole family that he would be sticking around. I never doubted he meant every word." She could hear the smile in Granny Lou's voice.

"This could be a first."

"You should know, Logan came to visit us the day he discovered you were gone. He told me how he feels about you. How much he misses you. Logan doesn't understand why you ran. He believes you truly don't care about him."

"Did he say anything about us?"

Ava's question was ignored.

"I want to protect you from ever experiencing heartbreak, but I can't save you any more than I can spare myself. But I'll tell you this. When you find the man you love, that love strengthens you. It builds you up. Tell me what you feel when you think about your relationship with Logan."

"He's the best thing that has ever happened to me and the worst. I love everything about him. It scares me so much that I want to run as far away from him as I can, but I feel the safest when I'm in his arms. My feelings don't make sense to me."

"Ask yourself, why you keep running away."

"I didn't run away. I accepted my commission." Ava heard the weighted sigh across the miles.

"You never lied to your Granny before, no sense in starting today. You have to be comfortable with the decisions you make, even when they hurt the people you love. I understand the need to isolate yourself in order to think about a major decision. Joining the Navy and moving thousands of miles away is a bit extreme, but I am very proud of you for making your dream a reality."

"It's the truth." Her grandmother ignored her, again. It was part truth. Being selected for commission was a dream come true. But, she could have delayed her departure and waited for Logan to come home. It was just that she was so scared, one look in his eyes and she would have chosen him. The truth about her would eventually come to light and she would lose him in the end. Looking back, it seemed she'd made the wrong choice and would lose everything she ever wanted. Her performance as a Navy Officer was lackluster to date and Logan didn't want to talk to her.

"Logan loves you, baby. His mother's threat held no sting, and I think you know that. This wall between you and Logan is built on fear and insecurities from the past. And it's a wall you both had a hand in constructing. Fear and love can't coexist in equal parts. Whatever Marcus did to you all those years ago was wrong. Don't be afraid to trust your own judgment."

"Did Logan say that he loves me?"

"What more do you want him to say, when he's shown you how much he loves you. Remember what I told you when I left your house?"

"To be myself."

"That's it! Show Logan that you love him and he's worth fighting for. Logan struggles with the same self-doubt that you do. He needs you to claim him, as much as you need him to do the same. I told you Logan came to visit. He and Andrew talked. Actually the two of them and Robert Lee played golf together last Sunday."

"Dad played golf?"

"Your father described it more like skipping rocks across land, but he had a nice time."

"Logan wants so much from me."

"Like what, baby?"

"He wants all of me. No secrets, no hiding places, no sanctuary outside of him."

"Do you want the same from him?"

"I have him. Or I had him." Before she had ruined everything by leaving.

"He wants from you what he is willing to give."

It sounded so reasonable when Granny Lou said it. She'd been a fool to leave.

"Yeah, I guess. I'm scared I may have lost him."

"You and Logan are both broken without each other. You have the power to fix this if you want to be with Logan. The man loves you."

"Logan loves me." She repeated it. He loves me.

"You know how fear and brokenness feel, allow yourself to experience love. None of us can change the past, but we all have some control over our future. Not every man will take your heart and abuse it. Accepting love is one of the hardest things you will ever do, but it is the most rewarding. I think you left so you could think clearly. You know where your happiness is, where you feel the beautiful warmth of love. Learning to love yourself and others is a lifelong endeavor. It's okay to start the journey Ava."

Logan pushed through his day, praying for some relief from the soul deep pain coursing through every fiber of his being. Ava had not called. She wasn't coming back. The thought of living life without her sent pain so sharp through his gut that he felt the serrated edge of the blade severing his vital organs.

"Logan."

It was Spencer calling his name. He looked up and recognized the apprehension in the other man's eyes. His gut tightened in anger. He didn't want pity. He wanted Ava. The irony that he still wanted a woman that had run out on him, after vowing he would never get emotionally involved again, was not lost on him. Yes, he was pitiful. The numbness he felt at Brooke's betrayal was nothing compared to the soul shredding devastation of losing

Ava.

"What can I do for you, Spencer?" By the look in the other man's eye he knew better than to mention her name.

"It's about Monique Faulkner." Logan immediately tabled his despair at the mention of his patient. Spencer's pensive stance had Logan's concern for the young girl moving up a notch.

"Fever?" he asked, anxious to know Monique's condition.

"No." Logan released a shaky breath. Having a patient develop a fever, weeks after an invasive surgery was a surgeon's worst nightmare. Thank heavens. So, what was wrong with her? At his heavy sigh, Spencer ended his torment.

"She misses Ava, I think. I know you and Ava had a medical Rat Pack thing going with her. Maybe, she'll open up to you. She's refused to participate in any of the Child Life activities for weeks." Hell, he could fix that. His expression must have mirrored his thoughts.

"She's been asking for you. A lot."

The aftermath of hurricane Ava, her absence was doing a number on both their lives.

"I'll talk with her."

Logan didn't make any promises. He did not know how to help Monique. He didn't know how to help himself.

Giving Spencer a single nod, he headed in the direction of the girl's room. Knocking, he opened the door to find the lights turned off and Monique buried to her neck in blankets. This was a first. The bed was usually cluttered with magazines, something or other, and girly stuff. Not even her iPod was playing that all boy group on repeat.

"I thought I heard your voice. Did Spencer call the surgeon patrol on me?" Her petulant tone reminded him of the girl he knew before Ava left them.

"Spencer's no snitch. I am making my rounds. How are you feeling today?"

"I feel terrible."

"What's hurting?"

"Not because of this," she said, pointing to her suspended arm. "Because I knew Ava was trying to join the Navy before she left. I know why she had to leave, but I miss her. I want her to come back."

There were tears in Monique's eyes. Oh my Todd, where was one of the nurses? Even Spencer, had to be better at addressing the tears of a sixteen-year-old girl, than him.

"Ava left because she was selected to serve in the Navy Nurse Corps. It's what she always dreamed of." He understood that now, but it didn't soften the blow that she had chosen a career over a life with him.

"That's not why she left." The confidence in Monique's voice piqued his interest.

"Tell me why Ava left." He moved closer to the bed, studying Monique as she became more animated.

"She left because some super rich lady threatened her because of you. She said I was getting worse because of Ava."

Logan stumbled back a step. "Are you sure?"

"Yeah. I overheard Kathryn and Spencer talking about a butt wipe named Randall too," she said waving one hand through the air. "Ava left because of you and me."

He felt hope swell in his heart, then it plummeted to his feet. Ava had not told him any of this. She hadn't trusted him to take care of her.

"Can you get her back, Dr. Masters?" The innocence in her request had him nodding his head in the affirmative.

"I knew you would. You like her, just as much as she likes you." Monique was grinning now. The bedcovers hung near the floor because she sat up to turn on the light over the bed.

Monique's smile was filled with the innocence of youth and simple solutions. "I recognize that glimmer in your eyes. I don't have a red cape under this lab coat. She's in the armed forces, Monique. Ava can't leave and come back home. It doesn't work that way." He wished it did.

"I know. My dad retired from the Navy."

"So you understand, Ava can't come home because you want it to happen." He wanted her back, too. More than anything in his whole life he needed Ava by his side.

"I'll call my Dad, he can help us get Ava back."

The likelihood of a military retiree being able to impact the assignment process was slim, but Monique was enthused and happy.

"You do that." He didn't want to be the cause of that smile turning upside down. The super-rich lady was his mother. What did she know to make Ava run? He'd let his father handle Maribelle. Randall Lester had a bull's eye center mass, and Logan had his missile locked and loaded.

# CHAPTER EIGHTEEN

Ava loved Logan. There, she had said it. Her watch read ten twenty at night. Tucked away in her usual stairwell at lights out, she dialed his number. Ocean waves crashing on the rocks outside sounded mute compared to the hammering in her chest. The familiar click of a connection filled her ear. Logan answered on the first ring.

"Ava?" He sounded surprised, rather than the elated she'd hoped for.

"I miss you." Straight to the point Logan would appreciate directness.

"Is everything alright, sweetheart?"

He had called her sweetheart. Her eyes started dripping water. God help her. She couldn't be crying again. Something had to be wrong with her tear ducts. She needed to schedule an appointment at medical for further evaluation. She didn't think she cried this much as a baby.

"No."

"What's wrong?"

The rehearsed profession of love escaped her. Where should she start when she'd done so many things wrong in their relationship? Admit it, own up to your role.

"It isn't considered a conversation if you don't talk Ava."

After a few long seconds, she found her voice. "I'm sorry for leaving the way I did. I miss you." The line fell silent. "Are you still there?"

"I'm here, but I can hardly believe my ears. You shared your feelings with me without being prodded. Say it again."

She smiled. "I know you're still on the line, you are talking to me." It felt good to tease with him, again.

"Repeat the part about missing me."

"Oh that. I miss you, terribly. If I were there I would be in your arms, cuddled up close. I can't wait to see you." A relieved sigh, it felt so good to hear his voice. She should've called sooner.

"Why do you want to see me?"

His question was a slap to the face. She hadn't expected him to question her motives. Inherently she understood the importance of her response.

"You're mine, and I am yours. I was wrong to leave while you were away; it won't ever happen again. I made a mistake. I left Shell Cove. I didn't leave you. What I did was immature and I should have tried harder. I will never do that to us again. I promise. Logan say something."

"How is training?"

"I've had some challenges. But things are looking up."

"Is it everything you wanted?"

Logan hadn't acknowledged what she'd said about missing him. He was everything she wanted, yet it had been her choice to walk away.

"It's not as fulfilling as I had imagined," she admitted.

"Similar to your experience with me."

She gasped at his comment, obviously meant to be a dig on her.

"You are more than I deserve. I would undo how I left if I had the power. Hurting you was never a part of my plan."

He grunted at her confession.

"When are you coming home?"

The line was eerily still and Ava knew he would not appreciate her answer.

"I have a permanent change of station orders to Virginia. The Navy has a large medical center there," she said quietly. "It's a wonderful area I understand."

"That is good news for you, Ensign Walters."

His tone was troubling. Ava started to get nervous. "Logan we can make this work between us. Virginia is not very far from Florida. We can see each other at least twice a month."

"You finally tell me how you feel about me. Now you make promises to me, knowing you won't be coming back."

"No," she said in a rush. "It's not what you are thinking Logan. I mean every word."

"I'm sure you do. Will you feel the same when you are standing face to face with me? Or will you run, push me away at the first sign of trouble? I know you Ava. You've been running away from the beginning."

"I didn't run from you. I was running from myself. The depth of my feelings for you terrified me. Being apart from you is harder than I ever imagined. I want you in my life." Yes. We are communicating.

"Are you sure you aren't using me as a crutch? Your parents told me you are failing officer training. Toying with me, have me run to your rescue, only to have you sail away after training. I don't know if you were ever committed to me."

The flat tone in his voice broke her heart. "I accept full responsibility for the damage I caused by leaving, but I will not allow you to second guess everything I've done in our relationship because of one error in judgment. I am committed to you. You are still the only man under heaven above that I want to hold me, to make love to me. I was afraid and the only way I knew how to deal with the fear was to guard my heart."

"You don't trust me Ava. What kind of relationship can we possibly sustain without trust? God knows that I want you. You say you want me, but how can I know I won't come home from work to find you gone again."

It killed her to hear his doubts about her feelings for him, her commitment to their relationship. But she didn't have a counter argument other than what she had already said.

"It's me I don't trust. Not you. If I didn't trust you this entire conversation would be pointless."

The hope that she had at the beginning of the conversation was slowly capsizing. "Do you want to be with me after everything that has happened between us?"

"You know the answer to the question, Ava."

Then why was he acting as if he'd had a change of heart? "I've learned since joining the military to trust, but verify. Humor me. I want to hear you say the words." She took a move from his playbook.

"You are the one that left, the real question is do you want me?"

"You're stalling, Logan. I asked first, good manners dictate that you be the first to respond." She hoped she sounded confident because that was not how she felt. Logan never beat around the bush. He always plowed head on into confrontation. Oh God, the shaking started in her hands, he was going to reject her.

She had ruined everything they had together when she fled. She should not have left Shell Cove, she should have waited for Logan to return, and told him about her past. She was being honest, talking about her feelings. There had to be a better way to broach the subject. She had gotten nowhere.

What good did it do to share your feelings with a man, when he beat them out of you like Marcus had? Or threw them back in your face? She was glad to be in Rhode Island right now. This would be the fresh start she talked about. No more reaching back for things you couldn't have. Dang, her eyes were dripping again.

"I understand if you can't be with me. I should let you go. Thanks for hearing me out."

"Don't put down the phone Ava. You are about to do it again."

"Do what?"

"There is nothing okay about the way you left me. You couldn't possibly understand how I feel. I was honest with you that first night. I don't play games," he growled.

She could hear his anger at what she had done to him.

"I told you our lives were forever changed after we made love. You walked out on me like it meant nothing. So how could you possibly understand how I feel when you never really were honest with me? You didn't give yourself to me. I gave you everything I am, but it wasn't enough."

"You are more than enough for me."

"How can you ask me to believe you? It is so easy for you to walk away from me. To leave without an explanation, then hang up on me. I can hear it in your voice. You are getting ready to leave me again. To discard me." She was crying in earnest.

"I can barely breathe without you. I feel like a fool for wanting you back Ava."

"Nothing about you has been easy for me Logan. I wasn't honest with myself, so it wasn't possible to be fully honest with you. What you saw when we were together was an expression of my feelings for you. I can't fake my response for you, my desire for you." She took a breath and plowed through her confession. "Logan I am trying to fix my mistake. I'm setting myself up to be crushed by the man that holds my happiness in his hands. First..."

Logan's call waiting indicator interrupted her plea. "I was saying ..."

"Ava I have to take this call, hold the line. I will only be a moment."

Dumbfounded was the only way to express what she felt. She poured her heart out to the man she loved and he put her on hold. Who was so important Logan had to take another call while they were repairing their relationship?

Logan would squash this business alliance once and for all. Sam Holbrook was calling. And he was not in the mood to keep rehashing the failed partnership. Ava waited for him on the other line. The sign he'd been praying for had come. Knowing that she left in a misguided attempt to protect him and Monique made everything better. She had not left him behind. But, he still had a lot of resentment to deal with. Resentment that had come through in their phone conversation.

"Sam, say what you have to say, and let's be done with this business."

"Hi, Logan." Rebecca knew he had blocked all calls from her phone numbers.

"I told you not to call anymore. I know you're not hearing impaired."

"That's rude Logan. First, I apologize for all the phone calls. I was trying to cheer you up. Besides, my father really wants this alliance and I have a favor to ask."

"The answer is no." Rebecca, like him had been reared to do her father's bidding. Since Ava left she had redoubled her efforts to continue their illusion of a relationship.

"The foundation is having a Ladies' Day fundraiser at the Reserves Saturday after next. The guy manning the booth with me backed out at the last minute."

"Find someone else and don't call again." Logan blew out a breath in frustration.

"The monies benefit the pediatric surgical unit. Two hours in my company, then you are free to go. I'll even swing by your place and drop off your research review proposal. The paperwork from Tyson Advantis came through legal affairs this week."

"I am with Ava, and nothing is going to change that. I will not have you jeopardizing my relationship." He didn't want her getting any ideas about them being together.

"You can't be with someone who isn't here. We can come to an arrangement. Our partnership can still work."

He was done with pretenses. Ava was his woman and the rest of the world would have to adjust.

"Good bye Rebecca Lynn." He ended the connection, then transferred the line back over to Ava.

"Sorry I took so long, some business I had to finish up."

"You sound upset. Who was on the other line?"

"One of my mother's friends." He wanted to talk about their relationship.

"Which one?" Ava's tone was curt though she tried to camouflage it.

"Rebecca Hol..." Before he could finish his sentence, Ava was speaking.

"Why is Rebecca Holbrook calling you at this time of night?"

"My mother keeps orchestrating events to push us together. It's not going to happen."

"I remember your mother mentioning her. Have you been seeing her while we've been together?"

"I just told you. Nothing happened between us. We have a difference of opinion regarding a business arrangement. I handled it. She's coming over to deliver some paperwork regarding the research grant. That is it," he said, tracking fingers through his hair.

"You invited her to our house! Have you been dating other women?"

"You left me. I will not have you grilling me about what's happened in my life since your departure." She was jealous. She was angry at the thought of him with another woman. This was a first, but he would not have her accusing him of wrongdoing.

"I left, but I never left you. You are mine. You will always be mine. So, you had better get rid of that woman Logan Masters. I'm not the pre-game show, either."

Ava's voice was so loud he could probably hear her from the garage.

"I don't trust your mother. In all the time that I've known you, no woman has ever called you in the middle of the night. Did you sleep with her?"

"Sweetheart, calm down."

"Don't tell me to calm down. Answer the freaking question."

The sound coming through the receiver resembled a bull getting ready to charge out of the pen.

Whoa, this conversation had disintegrated fast. Leave it to Rebecca Lynn and his stupidity for answering the call to make matters worse. Hindsight is a cruel teacher.

"I haven't been with anyone else Ava. Put the lioness back in the cage. It's still just you and me. No added drama."

"I want you to come up to Newport for the ceremony. Mom and dad will be here as well."

"I will be with you in spirit, but I can't come."

"What do you mean you can't? Why not?"

Because I have plans for us to be together he wanted to say. I have to be here to follow through on securing our new life. He didn't say that either. He remained silent.

"Not that week, but I will see you soon." And that was a promise.

"Only two days are allotted for travel between Rhode Island and my duty station. I want to see you."

He wanted to tell her everything, but it was too soon. When he had confirmation he would tell her. "Don't worry, sweetheart. We will work something out."

"When? I can't come there, and you won't come here. Logan, you gave me your heart." The sorrow in her voice squeezed his heart.

"I did, but you never gave me yours. I have a busy surgery schedule tomorrow. We can talk again tomorrow." He needed to get off the phone, before he was on a flight straight into her arms.

"You're dismissing me," her tone incredulous.

"No sweetheart, I am saying good night."

She would be back in his arms, soon.

# CHAPTER NINETEEN

Graduation day had finally arrived. It was so nice for Ava to look out into the audience and see her parent's proud smiles. Aron and Zari had surprised her by accompanying her parents to Newport. When she saw them she had hoped Logan would be amongst the familiar faces. She was a little sad that he didn't change his plans for her. The old Logan would have been there for her, but the new Ava wasn't waiting to be rescued. After her conversation with Logan she knew she wouldn't move forward without him. She had two days to convince Logan she loved him.

Ava was grateful Janna had introduced her to Morgan. He had enlisted in the Navy prior to becoming an officer. During the first few weeks of officer development school, it was his encouragement that kept her from quitting the program. He was a dear friend and a mentor. Her family loved him. They had a great time getting to know one another over lunch following the ceremony.

"Ava, you both look so sharp in your uniforms," her father beamed.

"The entire Walters family stands proud this day because you are the first commissioned officer in our family."

"Everyone sends their love, especially Granny Lou. Your father and I tried for weeks to convince her airline travel was safe. She said if she couldn't see the driver she wasn't going."

Her mom could not stop talking. She was so excited to tour the training base and meet Ava's instructors. "We took a picture with anyone who was stopped including the housekeeping staff." Her mother giggled, flashing her smartphone screen at Morgan.

Her father and brother helped her load the car with her luggage. Her military uniforms had added another thirty pounds to her garment bag. Thank goodness she had a Jeep, since Morgan's things would be making the return trip.

She followed her family's rental car to the airport. They all looked puzzled when she boarded the rental car shuttle with a carry-on bag.

"Where are you going?" her father asked.

"I'm going back to Shell Cove. I love Logan and he needs to see it." Logan needed the words, but she needed to show him how much she loved him. She needed to show him that he was worth fighting for.

The direct flight from Newport to Shell Cove was quick. Ava could use an additional hour or two to harness her courage. To face Logan, she needed every ounce of mettle she possessed.

She buckled into the passenger seat of Aron's SUV. Monkeys flipped in her stomach. "You can drop me off at Logan's house. I want to be there when he returns from his evening run."

"Ava are you sure you don't want me to come back to pick you up in an hour?"

She cut her eyes at Aron, allowing her annoyance to show. "No Aron.

What's between Logan and I will take more than an hour to fix. If it makes you feel better, you can wait in the driveway until Logan arrives. Seriously little brother, don't worry about me. I can handle Logan." At least, she hoped so.

"I'm not convinced Ava. I don't want to interfere with your relationship, but ..."

"Then don't. I can manage my own life without a junior chaperone." *God, I shouldn't have said that. He wants to help.*

"Maybe I deserved that sharp jab, but I doubt it. Just hear me out. Not two months ago, you were sleeping in my spare bedroom because of Logan and his family. You left him for a reason. Do yourself a favor and remember it. I have to believe your reasons for abandoning your life in Shell Cove were substantial, considering you didn't tell him in advance."

Ava winced, jab returned.

"That was a mistake. I should have trusted Logan with the truth." She inhaled a deep breath. She would not be deterred. She loved Logan.

"Ava you didn't tell anyone you were leaving. You joined an organization that is designed to take you away. It's counterintuitive to establishing a home life. The real kicker is I never realized you were unhappy."

The pain lacing his words pierced jagged splinters into her heart.

"I never meant to hurt anyone, but everyone treated me like a porcelain doll. I was being buried in everyone's concern for me. I'm bruised up a bit, but I'm not broken. And, I won't break." Aron smiled at her then.

"Since you met Logan you have acted out of character."

"I disagree. With Logan I can be the woman I am, flaws included."

"You value the safety of a routine life. In five months, you have morphed into a woman I don't recognize. Your behavior is not the Ava I know."

"I am glad I have a brother that loves me enough to care about what is happening in my life. Truth is I've been hiding in plain view. I feel good about most of my decisions. My relationship with Logan should've been handled differently. The opportunity to leave presented itself, and at the time I believed that was the best way for all involved."

Aron briefly slid his eyes from the road to glare at Ava. "You have to be joking."

"Okay, it was better for me to keep everyone in the dark. I was afraid the family would convince me to stay in Shell Cove. Without a doubt, Logan would have sequestered me at home, chained me to the …"

At Aron's sharp intake of breath, Ava quickly rephrased her sentence. "He would have kept me under lock and key."

"I would have helped him. Thanks for not completing the sentence, the visual that was forming in my head was causing stomach pains." He shuddered for effect.

"That attitude is why I didn't say anything. You are my younger brother. Somehow I had allowed myself to become everyone's charity case. I'm the big sister. It's my responsibility to mentor you. I don't regret joining the Navy, it's a dream come true."

"So, the Navy is good?" He glanced in her direction.

She nodded her head in the affirmative. "In some ways, I have to thank Logan for pushing me to leave my comfort zone in several areas of my life. Something terrible happened to me in college. I got involved with the wrong type of man and he hurt me." Aron's expression darkened.

"Before you ask for more information, I don't want to go into details. It was years ago; I will not channel anymore energy into that period in my life." She was focused on her future with Logan, the man she loved.

A smile near to bursting spread across her face at the sight of their house. Aron had been driving slower during their conversation, so she didn't have much time before Logan would be home. Fingers curled around the door handle before the vehicle came to a stop in the driveway.

"How are you going to get in the house?"

"Logan always forgets to lock the side entry door." At Aron's disapproving glare, Ava grinned. "Ava?" Disapproval reflected in his eyes.

"I have a key, Mr. Overly Cautious."

"Any man that enters another man's house uninvited has a reason to be cautious. When you left, Logan made a point of sharing with Mom and Dad you had left the keys to his house."

"I returned the extra set from my house when the movers packed my household goods. I kept my personal set." A sadness crossed Aron's face. "What?"

"Nothing. I am grateful you weren't here to see Logan after you left."

"What happened with Logan after I left? I've asked him, but he won't tell me."

"It wasn't pretty. You go on inside, we'll talk more when I bring the luggage."

Ava grabbed her purse from the center console, opened the passenger door, and walked past the front porch toward the side door.

The image that greeted her anchored her feet just inches shy of the door threshold.

A pair of long, tanned legs were in her kitchen, rummaging through her refrigerator. The legs were attached to a shapely young woman with warm sun kissed blonde hair cut to perfection at her mid back. Instinctively, she knew this was Rebecca Lynn Holbrook, Ava's replacement. Logan had taken the bait; the beautiful, blonde haired, blue eyed, perfect bait.

Ava took in the gray pumps by the entryway. A designer handbag, a key ring and what looked to be the mail was strewn across the kitchen counter. The same things she did when she had lived here. She had lost him. Tears swelled in her eyes as if tsunami force rains fueled the current. "No." That single word resonated in her mind, heart, body and soul.

The tanned legs must have heard her because she turned in the direction of the side door.

"Ah, hello I'm Rebecca Lynn. Logan's not home yet. I'm about to get a cold drink, do you want something?" She wore a short gray business skirt with a sheer white blouse with a delicate lace border at the cuffs and collar. Flesh colored nylons and French manicured toes, not the red Ava wore on her toes. It was the perfect combination for a woman in corporate America. Classic colors, feminine cut with a hint of sexy. The right kind of woman. *Rebecca was her rival. Not anymore. She was Ava's successor.*

Ava stepped away from the door, slowly backing herself onto the brick paver driveway. *She had lost everything. Her heart, her home, her hero.*

The human brain is a remarkable organ. It works even when you are incapable of functioning. In fact, she was malfunctioning.

The raised trunk concealed Ava from view. Aron couldn't see her walk of shame. She was a poor excuse for a big sister.

Then, as if on cue, Logan rounded the tall green shrubs of the neighboring property. The bare muscles of his chest ripped and coated in sweat. He looked leaner, stronger, and meaner than when she had left. Arms pumping, pecks flexing, abdominal muscles rippling. Her stomach did a triple dip with a backwards somersault into a split. Seeing him after all these weeks shot her internal temperature gauge to fever pitch. Would he feel the same? Ava coming back to Shell Cove probably ruined his plans with Rebecca.

"Ava. What are you doing here?"

The tears couldn't be contained. They flowed like river rapids. Each tear seeming to pull a more forceful surge than the one before. They left a heated trail down her cheeks. Logan was moving toward her now. He looked good. He had a full shadow. He never had a beard before. Rebecca must like her man with a beard.

She walked past him. She couldn't stop. If she stopped she would crumple to his feet in heartbreak.

"Why are you crying?"

She looked at him incredulously. "How dare you ask me that question? I know you think I'm a selfish coward, but I would never do what you've done. I can cry if I want. I may never stop crying. But you'll never know." She walked away from the man she loved. Aron's truck was now her getaway vehicle.

"Where are you going? " Logan baritone blasted through the air like gunfire. "Ava, what's happened?"

She ignored him. Logan was moving toward her, but before he could reach her, Aron planted himself in front of her.

"Leave her alone."

"I will not. Why is she crying?" he pressed.

"She was smiling before she came back to your house."

Ava could see the challenge in Aron's eye. Logan's face took on a questioning expression.

"Ava please, this doesn't make any sense. Talk to me sweetheart."

She shook her head no. She knew if she opened her mouth no force on this earth could contain the sobs of anguish that would be unleashed.

"Aron, we need to leave," she sobbed. There was no use in trying to contain her sorrow.

"Ava, do not leave."

"Logan, is everything alright out here?"

Ava's replacement peeked around the doorframe, her French manicured toenails barely visible.

"What are you doing in my house?" Logan's bellow had her jumping, the birds taking flight from nearby trees.

Ava couldn't watch anymore. Logan had lied to her. He had something going on with Rebecca. Why else would she be dressed that way?

She walked to the vehicle she'd exited only minutes before, opened the door and collapsed in the seat. She pulled her knees to her chest, let her head fall onto the glass window, then she let what remained of her emotional dam crack wide open. She wailed, and she didn't want to stop. She may never stop crying.

"Sis, what can I do?"

Ava turned to face Aron in the driver's seat then closed her eyes, but not before she recognized the pity in Aron's eyes. Humiliating. Here she was spouting off about what she needed from Logan. When he didn't need anything from her.

"Just drive."

"I can do that," he said, a grim expression on his face.

Ava felt the hum of the engine, before the backward slide of the tires took her away from Logan.

"Ava! No!"

She lifted her head to see Logan's eyes locked on her. It caused too much pain to look at him. She lowered her head back to the warmth of the glass closing her eyes. "Get me out of here," she said between sobs.

She wanted to lie down and not wake up. Her face was wet with tears. Her body was damp, fine hairs stuck to her forehead where it rested against the window. Aron hadn't said a word. She didn't know how much time had passed. She didn't care. That wasn't true. She felt guilty for dragging Aron into her melodrama. *I'm such a mess.*

"Logan is with another woman. He said he wanted me. I believed him. How stupid am I?" Raw, guttural sobs broke from her lips.

"You're not stupid. Please stop crying, Ava. I don't know what else to do. I want to turn this car around and knock Logan on his ass. Let me take you home. It's been a long day. You need to eat and get some rest."

She had the best brother in the world. He was trying to comfort her even though he was uncomfortable with her tears. She was mad at herself for putting that helpless look on his face.

"I don't want to go home. I can't face anyone." She curled her fingers in the material of her dress to keep from screaming. She wanted to scream, wail, and hit something. She wanted to grab Rebecca by her long glossy blonde strands and drag her out of their house. But it wasn't her house anymore. Ava had been replaced.

"We are your family. You haven't been gone so long that you've forgotten that our love is unconditional. You know Mom and Granny Lou will worry and rip out my tail feathers if I come home without you."

"I need to be by myself."

"It's not happening. You can stay with Zari and me or at Mom's house. Those are your options. I will not leave my sister standing on the street, crying and alone."

"I've lost the only man I will ever love because I was too afraid to be honest with him. I think I have earned the privilege of wallowing in self-pity without the audience of my family." Trembles racked her body with that admission. She had sabotaged her happiness.

"I knew you loved him. Trust me, all relationships have rough patches. Remember when I arrived in Zari's classroom to find her whispering with some man. I almost ripped little Nathan Carter father's head off. Now she tells me well in advance about parent teacher conferences. Our family never chooses the easy road."

"No we don't. I am a saboteur. I should get an award for the best intentions with the worse outcomes. It seems to be my trademark. But, I love him Aron. I can admit I love him, only he's with another woman. I can't believe it."

"Then don't."

"Are you serious? How can I ignore what I saw?"

He stared at her briefly before turning his eyes back to the road. "What did you see Ava?"

"I saw the same thing you did."

"I saw Logan pleading with you to stay and talk to him."

Ava was stunned. "Did you forget Miss Legs for Days that came sauntering out of his house?"

"No, I didn't forget the woman. Logan is possessive, thick skulled, a borderline control freak, but he doesn't strike me as a cheater."

"You're taking his side over your own sister's?"

"I'm your brother. I'm not taking his side, don't insinuate anything different." His voice was stern. "I didn't see Logan with another woman. I saw a woman come out of his house while he was begging you to stay."

"How do you explain the blonde pin-up girl in his kitchen?" Ava sobbed. "She was throwing away the food I cooked for him." Tears filled her eyes. "She said Logan didn't want my food anymore."

"Stopping cry, it's killing me. I don't have all the answers, but Logan does. You need to talk with him."

"I can't face him knowing he's with her. I messed up and he's moved on."

"Logan's mom basically called you a gold digging tramp, and he didn't move on. He couldn't find you for two weeks and he tore this town apart looking for you. His research funding was suspended and he didn't move on. You just walked away from him and he roared loud enough to rip the veil open between heaven and earth. I think it's a reasonable assumption that he has not moved on."

Ava caught his side-glance and smiled. She sniffled and turned to Aron. "When did you become relationship savvy?"

"When I got a wife. I discovered quickly, it's a lot of work to keep my wife." They both laughed, but Ava knew he was serious. "Ava relationships, marriages, whatever the term is when two people decide to share a life, they don't last if you can't talk to each other. If you aren't willing to talk to Logan then, you should move on."

They rode in silence to nowhere in particular. Ava closed her eyes and considered all that they had discussed. Weariness had settled over her when the car came to a complete stop and cut the engine. She tensed expecting to see her parent's house come into view.

Aron had parked the car in front of the high school track and field they ran on as children. Where could she run to now?

# CHAPTER TWENTY

Two hours later, Aron parked behind their mother's candy red, four-door sedan. Her family's two-story Victorian home sat on a corner lot surrounded by a white painted fence. The rose shrub garden complete with an ivy trellis entryway gave the neighborhood an enchanted feel. The familiar sight of Granny Lou, on the porch, occupying her padded rocking chair greeted them. Ava waved to her beloved Granny Lou from the car. Tilting her face away from the windshield, she wiped away the remnants of heartbreak.

"Be more convincing," Aron stated without moving his lips. "One look at you and they will know something is wrong."

"I'm not ready to get out of the car." Ava sniffled, wiping at her nose.

"See what I mean," he pointed toward the porch. "She's already slowed the rocking speed."

Ava made the mistake of looking up. Granny Lou moved forward on the rocker's edge, peered into the car, only to push to her feet seconds later. Snow cone blue sequined sneakers peeked through the railing. She called out for both of them to exit the vehicle post haste. When that didn't produce the desired results, Granny went formal.

"Ava Elaine, get out of that car so your Granny can see you."

Make-up ruined, puffy eyes brimmed with tears and blotchy cheeks didn't say homecoming. Her feet were rooted to the floorboards. Her legs wouldn't move. There would be questions about Logan. Questions she didn't want to answer.

"If you don't get out of the car, she's going to think we're conspiring to hide something." Aron had his hand on the door handle.

"We are." At that, Ava took a deep breath, mustering her tattered courage. She hopped out of the car and bounded up the steps. Hopefully, she moved fast enough that Granny Lou didn't see her red eyes. She wrapped her arms around her grandmother's soft middle and squeezed. Taking in the powdery, lavender scent that accompanied her brought a smile to Ava's face. It was good to be home, even if Logan was lost to her.

"I missed you, Granny Lou." A single tear rolled down her cheek.

"Step back and let me take a look at my naval officer."

Granny Lou held her at arm's length assessing Ava from head to toe. The sparkle in her grandmother's eyes shone bright with love and pride. More tears spilled down Ava's face. A sense of loss cinched her chest so tight, she couldn't share in that pride. All she felt was the sting of failure. Neighbors in nearby yards waved in greeting. Ava smiled and returned the gesture.

"Let's go inside. I want to hear about the antics at the senior's center."

The other woman didn't budge. Hands on her hips now, narrowed eyes trained on Ava.

"Your Granny wears glasses, but I'm not blind. Those are not tears of joy streaming down your face."

"Tears are normal at homecomings." *Good comeback.* Neither Aron nor her grandmother took the bait.

"Logan called for you."

That had her spine stiffening. Ava plastered a smile in place. Even though she saw Aron making the cut sign at his throat in her peripheral vision.

"He's involved with another woman, Granny Lou. Probably, best that I leave him alone and get on with my life."

"Your momma told me you came home to talk with Logan. Did you tell him that you loved him?"

"No ma'am. Rebecca was at his house when I arrived." The smiled slipped. A new wave of pain crested and broke over her heart. The tears swelled, her lip quivered, and her body shook with absolute devastation. Empty again.

"We've had the fear-love talk already. That woman has nothing to do with you telling Logan how you feel."

Her stomach knotted. Her plan had been to tell Logan. But, seeing Rebecca in Logan's house shattered her dream of sharing a love with Logan and her confidence all at once.

"Granny Lou?" Those feelings of inadequacy, of not being enough, bombarded her system.

"Do what you came home to do, Ensign Walters."

With that, Granny Lou, pivoted on her snow cone sneakers, opened the screened door, and walked into the house. With Granny Lou out of hearing range, Aron offered his commentary.

"When she put her hands on her hips, I thought she'd drive you back to Logan's herself."

Ava threw a riotous glare in his direction.

"What? Be thankful you're in the eye of the storm. Get some rest big sister. Tomorrow is hurricane force winds for you and Logan."

Would she weather the storm or be thrown overboard?

Saturday morning, Ava was up and at 'em with Logan's heart around her neck and Lina in tow. They walked the Reserves Country Club grounds, eyes peeled for a six foot two, blond haired surgeon. Aron offered to drive her, but this was a job for a best friend. The vivid blue sky served as the perfect backdrop for a Ladies Day event. A slight breeze blowing off the bay brought the fragrance of fresh cut grass and salt in the air. There were several white tents spaced equal distance apart, each with themed decorations representing a different division at the medical center.

The quiet loomed with the presence of a tusked elephant between her and Lina. Her friend struggled to maintain eye contact. It had been that way since Lina arrived at the Walters family home to pick her up in a brand new car. A metallic purple Camaro bouncing on twenty-four inch rims. Lina raved about the new wheels. The car offered as a gift from her mother, to cheer her up. Lina took great pride in the fact that her mother was a self-sufficient woman, even though her father deserted the family more than a decade ago.

"Spit it out, Lina. What's wrong with you?"

"You didn't tell me about your plans. I'm your best friend."

Ava could hear the hitch in Lina's voice. The way she left caused more sadness and heartache than she'd ever imagined. "I didn't tell, because either you or my family would have tried to change my mind."

"Is that the truth?" Lina's eyes stretched wide, a hopeful wisp to her voice.

"Of course, what else could be the reason?"

"Maybe you don't..." Lina's words trailed off. Sadness shadowed Lina's features.

"It's not like to you hold your tongue. Maybe, I don't what?" Ava's voice was firmer than she intended.

"Maybe, you don't trust me anymore to have your back."

That made Ava pause. Turning, Ava hugged the only best friend she had in the world. "That's ridiculous and it isn't true. We are sisters and I love you. But it's time for me live my life without fear crowding my every decision. Being a Navy nurse is my dream come true. I can't keep running home for rescue every time my life takes a wrong turn. I have to figure out some things by myself. My life was a recurring episode of 'Saving Ava'. I needed to learn how to trust on my own judgment. I know I won't get it right every time, but it's okay to forgive yourself. I understand that now."

"Okay, that's all I needed to hear, because I can't ruin this make-up." Always the diva. "Logan is ahead, one hundred yards to the left of us."

Lina's low-pitched voice had Ava swinging her gaze over the sea of couture-draped attendees. She scanned the assembly of people quickly, not seeing Logan from her height challenged vantage point.

Ava moved in slow motion in the direction Lina pointed. There was Logan, in the arms of Rebecca "legs for days" Holbrook. Her world stopped spinning on its axis. That vamp had invaded her kitchen and had her arms around her man. Blinding fury flooded her senses. Shards of red flashed in her vision. There was a reason to smash a woman in the pelvic girdle with a bedpan, and his name was Logan.

"Drop the murderous look girlfriend. Your stare is attracting attention," Lina said at her ear.

"She had better get away from my man."

"Repeat what you just said, because the body snatchers must have abducted my best friend." Lina fist pumped the air.

"You heard me. She needs to step away from Logan."

"Logan," she infused every ounce of possession she held for him into her voice.

He couldn't see her, now that she had entered the crowd. Ava moved at a fast pace through the crowd of leisurely, well-coiffed charity event attendees. Her pace garnered the curious gazes of nearby onlookers. The throng of people hampered her ability to reach Logan. She had entered a human labyrinth. If she couldn't get to Mohammed, she would bring Mohammed to her.

"Come to me, Logan." At the repeat of his name, she could see him scanning each face in the crowd. She pressed harder to reach him. Then he looked directly at her. With his eyes fixed on her, Ava watched as he disentangled himself from Rebecca. In motion, she moved toward her man with every primitive instinct on high alert. But now his longer strides ate up the distance.

For the first time, Ava reveled in the predatory gleam in Logan's eyes. Something new and wondrous happened between them. She responded to the fire of possessiveness in his eyes unabashedly. And smiled lovingly up at him, the feeling of shared possession new and welcomed. Her body ignited clear through to her soul.

They reached each other at the same moment, but Ava's gaze locked with the other woman's.

"Taste." The only word she said before gripping the nape of his neck, threading her fingers through his hair, and pulling his mouth down to hers. The kiss was slow, deliberately thorough, and penetrating. An erotic dance enacted for all to see. This was her moment to stand her ground. She knew Logan needed the outward display of her commitment to him. Never again would he have to fight alone for their love. This was the proof she knew

Logan needed. She reveled in the triumph.

She heard a shout of "hallelujah" in the distance, immediately proceeded by a panicky "oh my heavens, no." The male voice was Robert Lee offering his blessing. Followed by Maribelle's companion curse. Rebecca wasn't in sight when Ava released Logan from her very public claiming.

He looked down at her, in study. Okay, maybe she had been a little over the top.

"I came home for you," she said in a rush. "I'm not leaving without you. I know there's nothing between you and Rebecca, but I thought you might need me." She wiped at his lip, removing the traces of lip color from his mouth as she searched his face gauging a reaction. Finally, he broke into a body quickening, panty soaking, classic Logan smile.

"I missed you, sweetheart. Thank you for rescuing me."

Ava sighed in relief when he wrapped a steely arm around her waist, pulling her intimately close. She breathed in his woodsy scent heating her core temperature another ten degrees. *Thank you God for bringing him back to me.*

"I missed you too." It felt like heaven on earth to be in his arms again. They stayed locked together silent and content. He smoothed his hands over her toned back.

"Praise the United States Navy," she heard his sexy rumble at her ear. "I've got my very own wonder woman. You look amazing."

She giggled at his obvious pleasure in her tightened physique. "I'm glad you like what you see." She wanted to please him. Not out of some misguided obligation, but because he worked to please her.

"I more than like it. I love what I see."

The adoration in his eyes set her blood to boil. She diverted her gaze, sure that her cheeks flamed crimson.

"We need to talk now," he said gesturing his head away from the crowd.

She nodded her head in agreement.

Logan took her hand and led them to a back patio of the clubhouse, overlooking the greens. He took a seat on a bench, and then pulled her down beside him. She settled back into his arms. Content to stay there forever.

"What does my mother know about you that I don't? Tell me what happened to you. Why you had trouble trusting me, and yourself?"

This was a conversation she didn't want to have, but they both needed her to talk about it. It was time to release the hurts of the past. Marcus's abuse no longer held any power over her. Turning in his arms, so that they were face to face, Ava stared at the man she loved. Knowing she could tell him everything, even if it had been painful once upon a time.

"Before we talk about that. I wanted to tell you about my commission the night we reconciled, but everything was so perfect. I didn't want to spoil it."

"But something happened while I was in Australia to make you believe you had to leave."

It was a statement. Had Maribelle already provided him with some details? She nodded her head in agreement. Voice too tight to speak.

"You can tell me everything, Ava."

"I know that now." Giving him a genuine smile. "Your mother knows what happened with Marcus, my college boyfriend. He would hurt me when he got upset. If I disagreed with him or was too vocal in my opinions." She felt his arm tighten around her. He stroked up and down her arm.

"That's nothing to be ashamed of. You were a victim."

"That's not everything. When we had sex he would restrain me."

His hand stilled on her arm.

She swallowed and continued. "It didn't start that way. He said we were experimenting, but each time he would do something more painful than the last time. He would braid my hair, then wrap it around his fist so I couldn't get away." She dropped her head in shame. "So, when you touched my hair that first time in bed, everything came flooding back. Not being able to get free or get away from the pain."

"Look at me Ava." She did as he asked. "Sexual experimentation is not consent for abuse. You were manipulated. There is no burden of shame for you to bear."

He wasn't repulsed. He wasn't blaming her for what happened, nor telling her how stupid she was.

"There's more. I got so wrapped up in doing what he wanted that I lost myself. Whatever he said, I believed him. He told me I was worthless and when the abuse started I felt stupid for allowing it to continue for months. I didn't want anyone to know that I had allowed him to do horrible things to me. So I didn't press charges. Stupid, I know ..."

Logan placed a finger over her lips. "Ava, you got out of the relationship. You completed your education; you help children heal and you made your dreams come. Your courage astounds me."

He lowered his mouth to hers and she kissed him. Her heart overflowed with joy. He lingered his tongue over the scar on her lip, but it didn't burn or register as pain. He pulled back and looked at her face - support, acceptance, and what she recognized now as love on his face.

"Tell me about the scar on your lip." She swallowed her fear, knowing with Logan she could be herself. She didn't have to hide.

"The night I got away from Marcus. He came to my apartment with ropes. He had never used them before with me. I refused and he hit me. Only this time he didn't stop until I was on the floor."

Logan caressed her arms with such gentleness as she talked, all she felt was the safety of his love.

"I managed to call Janna before he came back. She called the police and my parents. They wanted me to come home, but instead I moved in with Janna."

"You thought I would hurt you if you told me how you felt? Ava I would never lay a hand on you to cause you pain."

"I know that. My heart knows you would never hurt me, but a basic instinct would kick in, and I would lose my reasoning abilities. You would get frustrated when I tried to put space between us. The scar was a constant reminder of what could happen with the wrong man. And the right words never came to tell you how I felt. The words failed."

"And now?"

She didn't feel any pain or anxiety when she touched her lip now. "And now I choose not to be afraid. I am healed, like the scar." Her spirit soared at the revelation. She had the power to heal, to control her own destiny.

"Are those marks on your shoulder from him, too?"

She nodded her head in agreement.

"You are incredible." His voice had gone low.

She pushed at his chest. "Don't unleash that sexy voice on me. I haven't finished answering your questions."

"I'm listening, sweetheart."

"When I realized I was attracted to you, the depth of my feelings terrified me. I ran because I didn't want to be vulnerable again. I didn't want to risk losing myself in another man. Once we were together and I knew you were different, I was so ashamed of my past I kept the barriers in place to guard my secrets. Believing that if you ever discovered the truth about me, you would leave. You give me more happiness than I thought possible between a man and a woman."

"I am sorry for making you feel you couldn't talk to me. You sharing your ideas, thoughts, and opinions only make us better. I'll be a better listener and you don't allow the words to fail. There is no threat on this earth that holds the power to separate me from you. You will always be mine." Cradling her face in his hands Logan kissed her until she was dizzy.

"I'm crazy for you, and I can't wait to get you home, but I still have to spend one hour at the smooch booth. It historically has been our most lucrative fundraiser. I doubt Rebecca will be eager to share in the duty with me after our very satisfying public display of affection."

She grabbed his forearm, staying his retreat. "It's more than affection. I love you, Logan." The look in his eyes at her confession washed every doubt out of existence but them.

"You love me?" She nodded her head. "The words, Ava."

"I love you. I've been in love with you, from the beginning." Her feet left the ground as he picked her up and swung her around. She was still laughing like a loon when her feet sank into the grass.

"Aren't you forgetting something?" She smiled up at him, waiting for his declaration of love. He offered nothing.

"I need the words, too."

"Oh, that. It feels good to have you chasing me. I thought I would have you sweat it out for another hour or two." She gave him a faux belly blow. "You are mine, Ava. Of course, I love you."

With that he took hold of her hand and led them to the smooch booth.

Thirty minutes into Logan's shift, not one person approached the booth. Logan knew Maribelle was behind the sabotage. No matter, he and Ava were in love, and would spend their lives together. Ava's stiff posture told him she realized the abrupt loss of patrons was no coincidence. She smiled, but he seethed at the sadness in her eyes. Knowing his own mother may never accept her caused a tick in his jaw. He squeezed her shoulder.

"Don't let it get to you. It's their loss." Ava hugged him tight around the waist. He wished he could shield her from any disappointment.

"You are the best thing to ever happen to me, Logan Masters. I love you so much."

A very, loud throat clearing had them looking at the counter.

His father stood there; tall, broad shouldered, with a navy blazer, white cotton shirt and khaki trousers. In his hand, stacks of crisp bills were on display.

"I want a sample of what I saw Logan getting, young lady."

His father offered a devilish smile before winking at him. He could always count of his father.

"Gladly," she beamed.

Then his Ava rounded the counter, threw her arms around Robert Lee's neck and planted a kiss on his cheek.

"Thank you for saving the day, again." Logan heard her whisper.

That was an interesting choice of words.

"There's no need to thank me. Seeing my son happy again has made this one of the best days of my life. Thank you Ava for coming home to him."

His father clapped him on the back. "You are a very lucky man. Don't let her get away, son."

Ava chimed in before Logan could respond, "I'm not going anywhere."

"I know I am a lucky man, but I appreciate hearing it from you."

"Little lady, that was the sweetest kiss I've had in a long time." Robert Lee pulled his wallet from his back pant pocket and deposited at least thirty one hundred dollar bills in the donation jar.

"Oh my goodness, are you for real," Ava cheered.

Logan laughed aloud as Ava stared at the jar.

"You are awesome, Mr. Masters."

To see Ava's face alight with joy, Logan could not be more proud of his dad in that moment.

"Did my father do something I don't know about?" Ava offered him a puzzled look.

"Logan, your Dad signed my employer endorsement. He's the reason I'm in the Navy."

Logan was floored. "You signed the packet, so she could leave?" He'd had no idea.

"You're the one that asked me to eliminate whatever Randall was holding over her head. He denied her endorsement. Kathryn gave it to me once I started making inquiries about Ava, at your request."

Ava looked to him. "You had your father take care of Randall for me?"

"Of course I did. If you had confided in me the continued threats, he would have been taken care of sooner. Your career, my research was never in any real danger from Randall. An investigation revealed Randall had a long history of abusing his power. No one on SCMC staff will have to suffer his attentions ever again."

"Oh my goodness, all these weeks apart. You were protecting me while I was protecting you." The tears forming in her eyes made his heart pang in his chest.

"It's over, sweetheart. You have your commission, I have my research funding, and we have each other."

"Who did the foundation elect for the new board position?"

"Because of your knowledge and expertise, you are kissing the newest board member of the SCMC Foundation. I'll meet the entire board during the annual meeting next month. With Randall gone, there's another open seat."

"Because of me? I don't understand."

Logan went on to explain. "I recently discovered Deacon Hill has been the caretaker for Susan Holbrook's estate for over twenty-five years. Samuel's sister was one of the members in the tour you conducted on the pediatric unit. She's a petite blonde, in her fifties with expressive eyes."

Ava look confused and said she did not get the connection.

"She was impressed with your clinical knowledge and professionalism. You did such a thorough job of explaining my research and how it impacted the patients, you earned me her vote of confidence. I think Granny Lou had a hand in the Deacon speaking to Susan on our behalf." Logan kissed her again, tasting her love for him.

"Oh my God, when I told Granny Lou about Samuel Holbrook and the threats, I had no idea. This is a miracle." Tears spilled down her cheeks.

Logan pulled her into his embrace, feeling her tears through his shirt. Hearing his name called for the third time in under one hour, he looked up to see Lina's runway stride moving towards them.

"Logan, if you have hurt Ava again, I'm going to bury you in one of these sand traps."

Ava moved away for him, wiping her eyes. His father picked that moment to exit stage left.

"I'm fine, Lina. I'm great."

Gideon picked that moment to approach with his checkbook in hand. "Lina you working the booth with Ava?"

Neither woman paid attention to him. Ava retold Lina about his father's generosity. Both women were busy celebrating the contribution.

"No Gideon, Ava doesn't need me to be a backup anymore," Lina said, finally acknowledging his question.

"Well sweetness, you're standing at a smooch booth. And I want my kiss, from you."

"You can't be serious Gideon. I'm not on the menu."

"Okay," Gideon said.

Logan watched as Gideon slid the checkbook into his breast pocket preparing to walk away. How was this going to play out?

"Come on Lina, it's for charity," Ava chimed in.

Gideon halted his retreat.

"All right, all right Ava, but only with him."

No sooner had Lina spoken, Gideon cupped the back of her head, sealed his mouth on hers and kissed her. Hungry and insatiable, all mixed together.

When he released her, Lina's eye remained closed. Gideon was smiling and Logan was holding Ava tighter at the waist.

"Don't ever put your lips on Ava," Logan said with a scowl on his face.

"Ava's yours. Lina's fair game," was Gideon's reply. Gideon retrieved his checkbook, ripped out the check and deposited it in the collection and walked away.

Lina's eyes were open now. "I think I'm pregnant with his baby," she said on a breathy sigh.

Logan's laugh vibrated through the tent poles, until Ava commented.

"Me, too," Ava grinned.

Logan offered a fierce scowl at her comment.

"I think I need a sandwich and a cigarette after that kiss. How much was his donation?"

Ava's nimble fingers fished out the check from the narrow deposit slit. Her eyes resembled silver dollar pancakes, mouth open and closed, without making a sound. Logan reached for the check and read the amount.

Ava did a twirl while holding the check overhead. "Five thousand dollars."

Logan smiled to himself. Lina was in trouble, whether she knew it or not.

Lina shook her head from side to side, fingers pressing her temple on either side. "This booth is going to have me stumbling back into serious like with another doctor. Take care of Ava. I'm punching out, girl. Call me tomorrow."

Good that she realized Gideon had her scent trail.

"Where do you think she's going?" Ava asked him.

"Not my concern. But your babies will be mine, no vicarious impregnations allowed."

Ava looked up at him, head angled over her shoulder. "You want to have babies with me?"

He laughed at the shocked expression on her face. "Yes, Ava I do. As soon as you marry me and let the world know that you are mine."

"I am yours, Logan." Her unrepentant affirmation brought him to his knees. At last she was his. "Marriage? We are going to get married and have babies?" she repeated.

"You have to know that husbands and wives grow up to be mommies and daddies." Her eyes widened. "Do you want to be married to me, Ava?" He would give her the sun and moon if it made her happy.

"I asked first, and I'm the senior officer." His laughter rang out then.

"I'd be honored to be your husband. And make beautiful babies that look just like their mother." The kiss between them was deep, raw, and breathtaking. Logan pulled away first, smiling at Ava's kiss swollen lips.

"Our time is up. I need to swing by the office, then I'm taking you home."

# CHAPTER TWENTY-ONE

Darwin stood back and watched the sparks ignite between Logan and Ava. He was happy for his brother. He hoped his mother would see that they belonged together and stop her plotting and scheming.

Rebecca Lynn was gorgeous, yet she would never hold Logan's attention. He, however, was thoroughly entangled in her web. He took off in the direction he had last seen her. She sat on a wrought iron bench underneath a magnolia tree. Her garden hat rested in her lap while her blonde waves slightly lifted away from her face on the breeze. She looked serene until he approached. Venom and something else he didn't care to investigate reflected back in her soft blue eyes as she raked him over from head to foot.

"How long you plan on hiding out from these people?"

"I do not hide," she chided in that syrupy drawl he loved. "I was relaxing until you came over." She rolled her eyes heavenward, before perching that silly hat back on her head.

"You ready to leave?"

"Darwin, please. I am not leaving with you. Your brother has done enough to embarrass me. I'm not going to put another nail in my coffin by walking out of here with you. You don't have to entertain me."

"I like entertaining you. And you've known from the beginning your pursuit of Logan was a futile effort."

"I do not believe I asked your opinion on the subject."

He ignored her clipped tone and extended his hand. "Take my hand, Rebecca Lynn. Walk out with me."

Her eyes were partially hidden by the hat brim, but he saw her decision before she spoke the words. "I can't."

His jaw tightened. "You gonna let me in tonight?"

"Don't I always?" came her cool reply.

Gosh, this woman drove him crazy. "See you tonight, darling." He turned and walked away. Smiling to himself, he headed for the exit. "You're mine, Rebecca Lynn."

# CHAPTER TWENTY-TWO

Ava and Logan entered SCMC at the outpatient clinic entrance. Saturday afternoon offered a reprieve from the heavy influx of patients during the weekdays. As the doors slid closed behind them, the familiar scent of orange oil reminded her that she hadn't touched a patient in five weeks. She'd been focused on learning the Navy's customs and traditions. The expectations of a commissioned officer and command structure were her priorities now.

As they navigated the hallway, Ava took in the skeleton crews manning the check-in desks through the glass fronts. A few patients were scattered throughout in the lobbies of their respective clinics waiting for appointments.

"Why did we come this way? The main entrance is closer to your office."

"Let's stop in the physical therapy suite, first."

He was probably concerned about one of the patients enrolled in the wound research project. They stopped in front of the PT suite, and Logan opened the door for her. Ava entered with him close behind.

"Come with me. The session started ten minutes ago." Ava followed as

Logan led her through a series of corridors and deserted office space. Finally, they reached an oak paneled door with a slim glass insert. Ava could see exercise equipment through the door, but the room appeared to be empty. Logan pushed open the door and ushered her through.

"Ava!"

Monique Faulkner was perched on what looked to be a stationary bike, but pedals occupied the place handle bars would normally be. The girl came to a quick stop, pulling her hands off the pedals. Hopping off the bike Monique ran across the room and threw her arms around Ava's waist. Ava hugged her back, having missed their unique friendship.

"Monique you look great. I'm so happy to see you."

Big, innocent eyes locked on Logan. Tears swelled in her eyes as Monique held onto Ava.

"You did it Dr. Masters. You brought Ava back."

"I told you that I would."

Ava looked over at him. Logan had made plans to come for her in Virginia. His eyes told her he intended to remind her why it was good to be back home. Her heart raced knowing the truth, she loved this man.

"Dad."

Having ignored everyone in the room except Monique, Ava took in the therapy suite. A lanky, teenaged boy sat in the chair closet to the window with his head buried in a book. Ava looked over his bent frame to see a familiar face. He was seated in an armless chair against the back wall, his intelligent eyes regarded with professional pride. During the donor tour all those months ago he'd worn his hair in the same military buzz cut.

"You're Monique's father?"

Monique had released the bear hug, so Ava could shake hands.

"Nice to meet you, Ava. I'm Matthew Keaton, and I'm Monique's stepfather. Monique was an infant when her mother and I got married. I retired from the Navy one year ago. Her mom is currently deployed to Qatar."

Monique called to the bookworm in the corner. "Jason, say hello to my friend Ava." The lanky boy glanced up for a second, tossing a non-descript gesture in Ava's general direction. Ava remembered Monique mentioning Jason wanting to visit during her hospital stay. Things had worked themselves out.

"My goodness, Monique. Jason is handsome," Ava whispered.

Monique giggled. "He's taking me to the prom," Monique whispered conspiratorially. "Dad. Tell Ava how you can help. He can make it so you get to stay here, in Shell Cove."

Ava thought she saw Logan's ears perk up.

"I'm listening," Logan said. Ava was too, but she didn't want to get her hopes up.

"Monique's been giving me an earful for weeks about getting you back to Shell Cove. I explained to her that you had to complete ODS first, before we could negotiate with the assignment officers. You had me concerned for the first few weeks, Ensign Walters."

Ava's eyes bugged out of her head in surprise. "You followed my progression through officer training?"

He nodded his head in affirmation. "Queens Bay Naval Clinic has a position for a nurse, if you are interested?"

Ava's heart started beating at a rapid pace. Was it possible to have Logan, be close to her family and serve her country? This man was offering her a dream.

She swallowed the knot in her throat. "May I ask your rank at retirement?"

He didn't answer right away. Instead, he directed Monique back to the exercise machine and waited until she started arm pedaling. Ava's heart plummeted. It was just a dream. Returning, he focused those dark, intelligent eyes on her.

"I retired as an Vice Admiral, three stars."

Monique's dad was a three-star Admiral. At that rank, you're speaking on Capitol Hill and talking on CNN. Wow, talk about life coming full circle. Ava immediately stiffened her spine, stealthily coming to attention. Logan eyes seemed to glow, keeping steady eye contact with the Admiral.

Logan came forward. "You have the connections to do what you say? She'll take it."

"Logan," she chastised, "don't answer for me." She grinned up at him. Her lip biting days were over.

"Ava. Don't play. I told the department I was taking a sabbatical before your call from officer training. I was coming for you."

"You what!" Logan was putting his career on hold for her. The fountains connected to her eyes sprang to the "on" position.

"Admiral, I would welcome the opportunity to serve as the clinic nurse at Queens Bay. Thank you, sir."

"Please call me Matthew. It took almost three months for me to respond to my first name. After, thirty-three years in uniform, it's taking more than twelve months to adjust to civilian life."

"Thank you, Matthew." Ava excused herself. "I'm going to the ladies room," she responded before Logan could ask.

Face refreshed, Ava entered the outpatient hallway and slammed into a mountain of soft flesh. She tried to push away only to discover her wrists were manacled in a man's large grip. Her head shot up, and her eyes landed on the distorted features of Randall Lester.

"Hello little doll, it must be my lucky day finding you all alone."

Her heart was beating fast, but not erratic. Ava maintained control of her emotions. Her first instinct was to recoil, but then she thought of her new life. The life she'd always wanted. A life filled with love, free from insecurity and doubt. Her love for life and Logan fueled her. It was hers now and no one was taking anything from her ever again.

"Get your hands off of me." Ava pulled against his hold. There was no leeway.

"They fired me because of you and that surgeon of yours."

*She was Logan's. And she didn't share.* "I was about to leave a departing gift in the research lab, but I think I'll leave my mark on you." A newfound instinct took over.

"This is not your lucky day. It's my homecoming," Ava roared. She curled her body, pulled her knee up and drove as much power as possible through her calf, her knee, and her thigh. She plowed straight into dangling parts like a pile driver during road construction.

Randall released her to cup between his legs, but she held on trying to relocate his reproductive anatomy to his throat. His cry was that of a wounded animal. The sound rebounded through the empty hallway. He would pay for his torment, and his planned sabotage. She was positioned to deliver another blow when Logan and Matthew rounded the corner at a run.

"Ava!" She heard Logan and more than one other person running to her location.

"I'm okay," she called back. Ava felt herself being pulled into warmth. Logan had her now, secured in his arms. Her eyes stayed trained on the enemy. Randall was doubled over, but his breathing was less labored.

A vicious war cry tore from Randall's lips, as he got to his feet and charged them.

Everything happened at once. Logan pushed her away from him, spun on his heel and hit Randall square in the nose. Blood seemed to pour from a faucet down Randall's face onto his starched, white dress shirt. Randall was crumpled on the floor swearing up a red, white and blue streak. Oh God, Logan moved towards him muscles strained, teeth bared, and nostrils flared.

Ava moved toward Logan. Not looking back at her, he extended his hand, palm up, fingers splayed wide. She froze. Logan stood over the other man.

"Don't ever come near Ava again. I'll punch a hole in your chest, rip your heart out, and feed it to you if you do."

Ava was glad she was a safe distance away. Logan's voice was bordering on animalistic. At the sound of a commotion in the hallway, Ava looked up to see Matthew Keaton and two men wearing dark blue security uniforms.

"You okay, ma'am?" The shorter of the two men asked the question.

"I'm fine, thank you."

Logan remained at her side, standing guard. Ava felt light, as if a weight had been lifted off her shoulders. "Logan, let's wait over by the door." They both moved to stand by the sliding doors leading to the parking lot. Matthew approached then, spine straight, fists loose at his side; the look of a warrior, ever ready when needed.

"The Shell Cove authorities are on the way," Matthew said. "I'll stay with the medical center security team and guard the perpetrator until they arrive. After Ava makes her statement, you two should be able to go."

"Okay, and thank you Matthew." Ava offered her thanks as he walked away.

"Do you want to make a statement?" Logan asked. "I can talk to the authorities on your behalf."

She laughed and kissed him. She'd never tire of his need to protect her.

"Try and stop me." Ava blinked back tears of joy as she threw herself into Logan's arms. Randall's threat that night in the ballroom had brought her and Logan together. Though she fought the attraction, he'd chased her until his love caught her in an embrace she never wanted to be without. Today, confronting Randall helped her finally heal all the wounds of the past. She was worthy of love. She was courageous enough to stand and fight for herself and those she loved. She was no longer chasing Ava.

"I love you, Ensign Ava Walters, Navy Nurse Corps officer."

Ava nodded, tears in her eyes. "I love you, Logan. Now and forever."

"Don't say anything you don't mean, Ava. I'll hold you to it." Logan grinned at her.

"For you, I can deliver." As Logan held her close, Ava felt all the joy of having all her dreams come true. Logan was her hero, the man that would always fight for their love. And she would do the same for him, both now and forever

.

# EPILOGUE

Ava pulled the pot roast from the oven and placed the roaster on the stovetop. Removing her oven mitts, she watched as Logan placed the finishing touches on the dining room table. Since her house was rented, the Walters-Masters family dinners happened at Logan's house. Ava had temporarily moved her things in the apartment over Logan's garage. A decision he grumbled about daily. She could continue the forty-minute commute to the Queens Bay Naval clinic from Logan's, but she was actively looking for a place closer to work.

Logan grimaced as he set the serving tray on the countertop. "Why did you invite everyone we know to Sunday dinner?"

Ava dropped a kiss on his lips and Logan smiled like a loon. *He was so easy.* "You're the one that volunteered to help me in the kitchen."

"I know, but twelve people, Ava? I have never had more than four people in this house at once."

"I'll be sure to tell any children we have that their daddy has a four maximum rule for their birthday parties." Grabbing the carving knife off the block, Ava sliced the meat, layering it on the serving tray.

"Speaking of children. When are you going to set a wedding date?"

*As soon as you tell me everything about Brooke, we can set a date.* Just then, the side door, that Logan still periodically forgot to lock, opened and the room filled with people.

"We can talk after dinner," he said, moving to the door to greet their houseguests. The Walters families plus one were the first to arrive; her parents, Aron and Zari, and Granny Lou with Deacon Hill in tow.

"What's up, sis?"

"You, little brother."

Aron smirked at her. "You've got jokes."

"Hi Ava, I made a sour cream pound cake for dessert," Zari, the resident baker, never let Ava down.

Lina decided to join the fun now that the threat of laxatives in her food was no longer warranted.

"Ava! I'm so glad you get to stay here in Shell Cove with me," Lina said from the doorway.

"The food smells delicious," Ava's mother said, placing a kiss on her cheek. Granny Lou entered the kitchen.

"How is grandma's naval officer?"

"I'm great, Granny Lou. Never better."

"I can see that with my own two eyes." Granny Lou stretched out a weathered hand over Ava's and squeezed. "I can see."

"Ava, my girl, make sure I eat light today, no more than two plates. Since you've been gone I've gained ten pounds."

"Oh no, Deacon."

"It's true. All those ladies down at the church feeding me those processed foods. They messed up my well-oiled machinery." He was shaking his head in dismay.

"Come on in, the food is on the table. The roast is still piping hot and there are plenty of vegetables to help with the machinery," she laughed over the rising voices.

At the table covered in serving dishes, everyone moved to take their seats, when Robert Lee, Darwin and Gideon entered the house.

"Robert Lee," her father called, "when are we hitting the links again?"

Her father had found a new hobby in retirement and a new golfing partner in Robert Lee.

"Tomorrow works for me, Andrew. We can be on the course with the other Dew Sweepers at first light."

Her father gave a thumbs up.

Gideon shook hands with Logan, before turning his attention to her. "Thanks for the invitation, Ava."

"I'm glad you decided to come." Though he nodded in her general direction, his eyes were fixed on Lina. Darwin entered the kitchen and wrapped Ava in a sisterly embrace.

"Get your hands off my woman," Logan bellowed. *Some things would never change.*

Be sure to look for Siera's next novel in the BACHELORS OF SHELL COVE series CONVINCING LINA. It's available in print and ebook at your favorite retailer.

Here's a sneak peek at Siera London's CONVINCING LINA.

Gideon and Lina's story is book two in the Bachelors of Shell Cove series.

For the second time in a week Lina James contemplated assault and battery as a viable option. Each word complemented the other, like cheese and crackers. Or peanut butter and jelly. The sun heated her exposed arm and she sank further under her lounge chair's protective awning. Sipping her Arnold Palmer though a peppermint striped straw, she sighed as cool rivulets of condensation trailed between the glass and her skin. A gust of warm air blew from across the water, lifting her thick tresses off her neck, blowing tendrils forward dancing before her eyes. Cool mornings with a light breeze should be mandatory in January. Even in Florida.

Eyes closed, she took another deep breath. Her abdomen expanded to maximum capacity, she relaxed into the breath as a sense of resolve settled over her.

"Yes, that's it." Assault and battery was the better choice because killing was a sin. Experienced psychiatric nurses de-escalated stressful situations with practiced control. That skill set would not be utilized this morning. Killing would be considered escalation. And Lina refused to add to her long list of recent missteps.

The rattling and musical chime of her doorbell for the twelfth time in ten minutes dampened the peaceful quiet of Sunday morning in Shell Cove. The man having the physical altercation with her front door was a bargain basement remnant item she'd tried to turn into a showroom spotlight. Slow inhale in, exhale out. The breathing exercises prepared her for the impending showdown.

"Jace Harper, if you remain at my door there's going to be bloodshed," she yelled over her shoulder.

Her new and improved self didn't have emotional floor space for anymore male shenanigans. She wanted a life filled with a husband and children. Unfortunately, the universe had a penchant for hurling cosmic crap in her direction at lightning speed. Fool me once, no opportunity to fool me twice. And today marked three months plus one day since Jace Harper made a fool of her. Couple that with six weeks of dates with bad breath, bad manners and bad math. The last guy stuck her with the dinner bill, where he ordered a bottle of wine, an appetizer, a main entree and dessert to go. She was done with dating.

"Lee-na, please open the door."

Hearing the singsong quality he added to the first syllable of her name had her breathing in a hiss.

No man would have the opportunity to abandon her, because she was on a thirty-day man fast. No new relationship baggage allowed. The purge would be complete on her twenty-seventh birthday. The next man that professed to love her would have to write his declaration on a stone tablet-in blood. Bishop was the only exception. The man at her door was a one hundred and eighty-five pound human splinter. Old baggage. Excising him from her life was the first item on the sacrificial table. Failure was not an option. Unlike the men in her life, Lina never let herself down.

Swinging her feet to the ground, she leaned forward in her seat placing the petal pink vinyl bag she held on the matching Adirondack table. The wide, dark pink shoulder strap snagged on the arm chair pinning her in place. With care she dislodged the strap, gently folding the length over the bag's zipper.

Inhaling the salt filled air, Lina pushed to her feet. The cool ocean breeze kissed her dark skin. She raised her face to the sun with a smile.

Sundays spent with the sun and sea was her favorite activity. Ignoring the cacophony of fist pounding intermixed with cascading chimes, she spread her arms wide, allowing the seagulls' serene to usher in calm. The noise at the front door climbed another octave squashing her tranquil state.

"I know you can hear me. Open the door."

She let her arms fall to her side. Time to discard the baggage. Turning around, she stalked through the open balcony door, crossing the glass and steel dining kitchen combo room en route to the front entrance. At the incessant knocking and unrelenting buzzing she reached for BETAS, the smooth hardwood stick she kept by the door. Jace would be the first person to experience the power of her woodland deterrent.

A leather tie long enough to slip over her wrist held it suspended by a j-hook on the adjacent wall. She was thankful the beveled glass inlay door separated her from the intended target. Standing in her foyer, she offered him a final opportunity to walk away from her welcome mat.

"I have BETAS with me and we both agree it's in your best interest to get away from my door." Grateful it was Sunday morning, her neighbor usually slept until noon. The thought of Estrella witnessing a live breaking news event, she could do without.

"Betas. Who is Betas?"

Steam that could rival a teakettle rolled off her at his tone and inflection. Abandoned me and he had questions? Not in this lifetime, buddy.

"Lina." The singsong quality was gone. His voice was sharp with disapproval.

Lina grabbed the door handle, turned the lever, and pulled the door open a fraction. Jace's lean frame darkened a sliver of her doorway. For a moment, they both regarded each other, without exchanging a word. He stood in his white, long-sleeved button-down collared shirt paired with a navy sweater vest. The dark blue and green pinstriped tie she purchased for his birthday knotted to perfection at his thin neck. Khaki dockers and black oxfords completed the ensemble. She felt her brows bunch and her lips purse. The unwelcome intrusion had her fist tightening on BETAS.

The morning breeze carried the floral amber scent of his cologne through the partially open door. It was seventy-seven degrees in the shade. Most native Floridians would consider that hot for an Atlantic coast January. Coupled with the mid-morning humidity, the smell was about as welcoming as a park trash can. Bile rose up in her throat and she swallowed in succession. Gastric disaster averted.

"It's about time. I'm melting out here."

Beads of sweat dotted his forehead and the bridge of his nose. His dark brown mess of curls plastered to his forehead where a sharp contrast to his pale blue eyes and reddening skin.

"Then go home." He moved to step inside her condominium, but her full-figure blocked his path. Considering she was two inches taller in her bare feet, he was the one to halt. He regarded her, irritation clear on his boyish face.

"Does he know I'm at the door?"

He had the audacity to be territorial after the crap he'd done to her. "Who Jace?" An image of her curling her fingers around his tie, pulling him close flashed in her mind. Feeling the warmth of his breath on her chin, while she inched the knot higher up his neck. Watching as he turned a kaleidoscope of colors before losing consciousness brought a smile to her face. To kill was sinful, but to choke was divine payback. Right?

"Do I know Betas?"

"No, but he wants to meet you," she gave a saccharine smile. The stick resting at her side seemed to pulse against her palm. The leather lariat around her left wrist felt tighter. She glanced downward, and he tracked her movement. His eyes came to rest on the stick in her hand. Eyes wide in alarm, he took a cautionary step back. Yep, caution warranted. She'd had enough of his drop by visits.

"Meet BETAS, my beat-that-ass-stick." Jace took a step back. "If I raise this stick above my kneecap, he doesn't go back on the wall until somebody gets their ass beat."

"Lina, be reasonable."

Was he reasonable the night he ended their relationship? When he told her they were too different. From her wide nose to her, full lips, and even fuller hips, Lina was unmistakably an African American woman. According to Jace, being seen with her garnered too much attention. Negative attention.

"You at my door, gives me a reason to club you across the head and shoulders for every second of my life wasted." Looking him square in the eye, BETAS had his name in queue.

"It doesn't have to be like this between us."

"How would you like it to be?"

"I want to see you, sometimes. What will it take to convince you I'm the man..."

She interrupted his futile effort at this point in their non-relationship. "Convince me you're a man by leaving, never to return." It was his decision that created this reality TV episode at her door.

"We can come to an agreement that suits both our interests."

"I have zero interest in a man that dumps me on our anniversary."

"Technically, I suggested we explore other dating options, but continue caring for one another's needs."

"You are going to need critical care if you continue," she hissed. "You could have told me it was over before you lured me to my favorite beach hide-a-way."

"I wanted you to be relaxed."

This was her punishment for dating a clinical psychologist. Listen to the sound of crashing ocean waves, take deep breaths in and out while he ripped the beating heart from her chest. BETAS started inching upward.

"You are considerate," she offered with a smirk.

"I think I am." His shoulders dropped away from his ears as his hands relaxed at his side. Sarcasm wasted.

"You thought of everything, except that I wouldn't welcome you to my bed while you explored other options." The vanilla icing minus the chocolate topping on Jace's surprise after six months together—she was too curvy, too pigmented, and too ethnic for them to have a long-term commitment. All the attributes he claimed to love about her when they'd met. Of course, that was before the second glances and off-color remarks from his family. So why was he at her door? Ah yes. He wanted on-call booty privileges.

"It was never my intention for us to end. What is it going to take for you to forgive me?"

"Forgiveness was an option before you had me removed from my nursing unit."

Scarlet crept from under his collar and spread to his face.

"You upset me by not taking my calls. I don't want things to end between us. We were good together."

Now it was her fault that he sabotaged her career. With damp palms, she squeezed BETAS, focusing her rising anger into the tense muscles in her arm.

"It's obvious Jace, good was not good enough." She stepped back to close the door and he reached for her.

"It's not like I had you fired."

The hand gripping BETAS moved faster than her conscious thought, the horizontal plane of the wood made contact with his open palm. "You don't get to touch me ever again," she hissed.

"You were fine with me touching you, before I said I didn't want to date you anymore," he drawled.

There was a look of smug satisfaction on his face. Seriously? He challenged her because she refused to give up her goodies. She'd had her fill of this conversation. "Insightful, but it will never happen."

"I miss you." Harsh laughter gushed out of her, spilling over them both.

"Did you miss me before or after your hand got tired?" She saw him drinking her in from head to toe. Blessed with Jill Scott curves that men craved, and then cursed to suffer the fallout once the novelty disappeared. She was fifteen the first time a man compared her figure to the Rhythm & Blues songstress.

Regret shone on his face. "Lina give me a break."

She was disappointed when their relationship dissipated, but to say she missed him would be a lie. Six months with Jace, paled in comparison to the single kiss she'd shared with the just-her-size psychiatrist on staff at Shell Cove Medical Center. She still wanted to drop her panties faster than the Falcon's Fury Free Fall ride at the Busch Gardens theme park just thinking about Gideon. It was in her best interest to steer a wide berth away from any man that remotely held her interest. The men in her life never stayed.

"You're right. I'm being snarky."

He beamed at her comment. No doubt thinking he'd won her over. She hadn't seen Jace's abandonment coming, but she should have.

"Finally, we are speaking the same language."

What conversation was he a part of? For the first time, she had the opportunity to give a man his walking papers.

"Good, then I only need to farewell once." She should have an online certificate mounted on her wall for a four point grade average in mending a broken heart.

"What?" Jace questioned, his voice high pitched.

Never one to leave a loose end, Lina looked him in the eye, as she launched the second strategic deterrent in her male detoxification plan. "One more thing before you leave. Stop sending those awful white roses." His perplexed look made her ire rise. "White roses symbolize innocence, chastity, everlasting love, and sympathy. The first three are inapplicable, and I don't need your sympathy, so stop sending them."

"But, I'm making an effort to..."

She leveled him with a vicious stare, he stopped talking. She thought about the effort he put into planning their break-up. It was ingenious really—dinner, dancing, and remote corner of the beach on a starlit night. Perfect. "I have a new mantra thanks to you," she let a peaceful expression cover her face.

"What is it?"

Using the singsong voice he favored, she said, "No effort, no entry, and definitely no more jackassery." His mouth gaped out in silent outrage.

As if cued by some offsite director, Estrella's South American accent reached her ear before she heard foot steps.

"Lina?" Her new food buddy's warm olive face, bare of makeup and framed by shiny ebony locks came into view. She stood shoulder to shoulder with Jace, whose scowl resembled a petulant two-year-old.

"Is everything okay?" Eyes rolling heavenward, Lina exhaled a large breath willing herself not to push Jace over the stone railing. Embarrassed, she turned to address her friend.

"I'm fine, Estrella. Dr. Harper was just leaving."

"I was not. We still need to talk."

"I should call the police." Though offered as a sign of support, Lina could hear the hesitancy in the other woman's voice.

"No, you should not," Jace said in a raised voice. No doubt offended that she would suggest such an action.

"No worries, I have a friend here with me that's itching to make contact with Dr. Harper."

Taking in the added pallor to Jace's complexion he recalled that BETA was ready for action.

"I know what would happen if..." Jace interrupted before she could finish her sentence.

"This is the way you want it to be between us?"

She nodded. "I'm done with you, boo boo."

"Colorful, Lina." "You might change your mind."

"Too colorful for you, remember. Get off my doorstep before you have a leading role in the live adaptation of Misery."

Jace smiled, but his teeth were clenched tight and his face had reddened tenfold in the past five minutes. Unsure if the burgeoning redness to his face was from the heat or heightened emotion she was tempted to offer him a bottle of water before she sent him on his way.

"I'll see you at work in the morning," he said.

Now why did that sound like a threat?

Buy Now: CONVINCING LINA

<<<<>>>>

# About the Author

Siera London, a former naval officer, is a writer of contemporary romance and women's fiction. A native Floridian, her love of coastal towns and bustling cities shines through in her sassy and sexy storytelling. Currently she resides in the Washington, D.C. area with her husband and a color patch tabby that has free reign of the house.

She loves to hear from her readers. To learn more about Siera and her books,

please visit www.sieralondon.com and www.facebook.com/siera.london.

*Connect with Siera London*

E-mail me at: sieralondonwrites@gmail.com

Like me on Facebook: http://facebook.com/authorsieralondon Follow me on Twitter: http://twitter.com/siera_london

Follow me of Pinterest: http://pinterest.com/sieralondon Visit my website: www.sieralondon.com

Made in the USA
Lexington, KY
22 April 2018